BARON

The Knickerbocker Club

JOANNA SHUPE

ZEBRA BOOKS
KENSINGTON PUBLISHING CORP.

http://www.kensingtonbooks.com

ZEBRA BOOKS are published by

Kensington Publishing Corp.
119 West 40th Street
New York, NY 10018

All Kensington titles, imprints, and distributed lines are available at special quantity discounts for bulk purchases for sales promotion, premiums, fund-raising, educational, or institutional use.

Special book excerpts or customized printings can also be created to fit specific needs. For details, write or phone the office of the Kensington Sales Manager: Attn.: Sales Department. Kensington Publishing Corp., 119 West 40th Street, New York, NY 10018. Phone: 1-800-221-2647.

Zebra and the Z logo Reg. U.S. Pat. & TM Off.

First Printing: November 2016
ISBN-13: 978-1-4201-3986-0
ISBN-10: 1-4201-3986-X

eISBN-13: 978-1-4201-3987-7
eISBN-10: 1-4201-3987-8

10 9 8 7 6 5 4 3 2 1

Printed in the United States of America

Joanna Shupe's Wicked Deceptions Series Is the Talk of the *Ton*!

The Lady Hellion

"A beautiful and complex love story featuring a hero who suffers from post-traumatic stress disorder and a heroine with a penchant for saving the day. Shupe is very talented, walking a fine line between Quint's demons and Sophie's charming, almost madcap character. These two sparkle in this wildly entertaining story."
—Sarah MacLean, the *Washington Post*

"Shupe invites readers to sit back and enjoy the terrific chemistry between the unconventional Lord Quint and the exasperating Lady Sophie in the conclusion to the Wicked Deceptions trilogy. With emotional intensity, poignancy, passion, and murder, they won't be disappointed."
—*RT Book Reviews*, 4.5 stars

"Sophie's independent nature makes her a delightful protagonist . . . The romance is delectable as sensual love scenes balance the well-woven mystery subplot."
—*Publishers Weekly*

"I enjoyed this series quite a lot, and am looking forward to seeing what Shupe writes in the future."
—*Smart Bitches, Trashy Books*

"*The Lady Hellion* is a fabulous, wonderful book! Sophie is a superb heroine, the kind little girls dream of being. It is also refreshing that Quint is neither a rake nor a rogue, but he is most definitely a brooding hero, and it is totally relevant to the story arc. *The Lady Hellion* is built upon a very clever premise, and Ms. Shupe crafts an exciting and meticulously researched story fraught with suspense and startling plot twists combined with frissons of sexual tension and a beautiful, tender love story. And what an ending! Absolutely terrific!"
—*Fresh Fiction*

The Harlot Countess

"With her knowledge of the modes and morals of the Regency era, Shupe delivers a well-crafted novel in this second installment of her Wicked Deceptions series. Steady pacing, delightful characters, and an ability to build steamy sexual tension make for a lively love story."
—*RT Book Reviews*, 4.5 stars

"A good story well told. This is a fun series."
—*Romance Reviews Today*

"An intriguing tale, *The Harlot Countess*, the second book in author Joanna Shupe's Wicked Deceptions series, is an emotion-packed, sexy historical romance that will keep readers captivated right up to the very end. Angst, heartache, vengeance, blackmail, secrets, miscommunication, passion, forgiveness, romance, and love all intertwine in a story that readers will not soon forget."
—*Romance Junkies*

The Courtesan Duchess

"The powerful passion in this riveting tale of betrayal and forgiveness will knock your socks off!"
—*Sabrina Jeffries*

"Joanna Shupe's compelling story of an estranged couple brims with emotion and sensuality."
—*Miranda Neville*

"Heartfelt . . . This original and alluring novel is a very promising beginning to Shupe's career."
—*Publishers Weekly*

Books by Joanna Shupe

Wicked Deceptions

The Courtesan Duchess

The Harlot Countess

The Lady Hellion

The Knickerbocker Club

Tycoon
(novella)

Magnate

Baron

Mogul
(coming February 2017)

Published by Kensington Publishing Corporation

*For Lin, one of the kindest and
most generous people on the planet.
Thanks for keeping me on my toes.*

ACKNOWLEDGMENTS

This book was so much fun to write. Some of you may remember Will, the heroine's stuffy older brother from *Magnate*. After I finished that first book, I couldn't wait to give this handsome railroad baron his *own* happily ever after.

One of the reasons I enjoyed writing *Baron* was because its leading lady is a medium. At the end of the Civil War, there was a sharp rise in the interest in spiritualism in America. (Mary Todd Lincoln even hosted a séance in the White House.) Few career options were available to women at the time, so spiritualism became a popular way for ladies to earn a living. And with so many young sons and husbands having died during the war, you can imagine how lucrative this career was for some.

I owe a huge thank-you to my pal Todd Robbins, co-creator of the Off-Broadway show *Play Dead* and author of *The Modern Con-Man: How to Get Something for Nothing*. Todd is a walking, talking encyclopedia of spiritualism facts and trivia, and I picked his brain for hours when writing this book. All of Ava's tricks resulted from these conversations.

A Gilded Age series set in New York would not be complete without touching on politics and Tammany Hall. As a political organization that played a major role in New York elections and government for almost two hundred years, Tammany is most famous for its unparalleled corruption. Thanks to Jon Grinspan for his talks about the tactics used by political parties in the late nineteenth century, which helped me immensely in writing the campaign details for *Baron*.

My books are always made better with the help of others. Michele Mannon spent a lovely lunch with me atop a Pennsylvania mountain where we worked out the details on Will. JB Schroeder poked holes in my plot over pizza. Lin Gavin dished up her awesome homemade pancakes while we discussed character arcs. Diana Quincy offered suggestions for improvements over brunch. (I guess I think best when food is involved?) Thanks to all these ladies. I love you all!

Thank you to Peter Senftleben for tweets that always make me laugh and for being a kick-ass editor; the fabulous Jane Nutter and the rest of the team at Kensington for their tremendous efforts on my stories; Laura Bradford for her all-around awesomeness; Sonali Dev for generously sharing her wisdom and wit; and all my writer pals—the Dashing Duchesses, the Lucky 13s, NJRW, and the Violet Femmes—for the wine, laughs, and support.

A huge thank-you to my husband and daughters, who are more patient and understanding than any writer deserves. Love always to my mother, who adores romance just as much as I do, and the rest of my crazy family for their unwavering support.

Lastly, but most importantly, thank you to the readers and fans of historical romance. I am so grateful for each and every one of you!

Chapter One

*There's an honest graft, and I'm an example of how it works. I might sum up the whole thing by sayin':
"I seen my opportunities and I took 'em."*

—George Washington Plunkitt,
Gilded Age New York state senator,
member of the Tammany Hall political machine

Atlantic Theater, New York City
May 1888

William Sloane did not believe in the ability to commune with the spirit world. Hell, he didn't even believe there *was* a spirit world.

Yet here he sat, inside a ramshackle theater in the Tenderloin district, watching this audacious spectacle. Madam Zolikoff, she called herself. The mystifying medium who could commune with spirits and perform extraordinary feats. The woman was the worst actress he'd ever seen—and Will had seen plenty.

Eyes closed, she swayed and waved her hands, all while chanting. The man across from her, one she'd pulled up onstage, stared, enthralled, as Madam attempted to speak to his dead mother. The electric lights overhead flickered, and the audience tittered.

"Ah! I think we are close!" she announced loudly in an appalling Russian accent.

Will nearly rolled his eyes. Was anyone really buying this charade?

Shifting in his uncomfortable seat, he took in the meager audience. About twenty men and women, all average-looking, a far cry from the extravagant crowd he usually associated with. No diamond tiaras or ostrich feathers here, just derby hats and plain bonnets. But every pair of eyes was trained on the young woman working the stage.

She was attractive, he supposed, if one preferred liars and cheats, which he most definitely did not. Still, her pale blond hair showed off her striking light brown eyes. Straight, delicate nose. High cheekbones. Arching brows. Full lips painted a scandalous red.

He liked those lips. Quite a lot, in fact. If he were dead, those lips alone might bring him back.

"I hear her!" A steady rapping reverberated around the room. An accomplice, no doubt, yet the audience gasped.

"Mr. Fox, your mother is here with us now. What would you like to ask her?"

The man onstage asked simple questions for the next fifteen minutes, with Madam Zolikoff "interpreting" the dead mother's answers. Will absently rubbed his stomach, anger burning over this performance, that she would take advantage of someone's grief in such a profoundly fraudulent way. When Will's own mother had died, he'd fervently wished for something—anything—to bring her back. Nothing had, however, and he'd been left in a cold house with an even colder man.

Madam Zolikoff prattled on, regaining his attention. Had this woman no shame? No empathy for the heartbreak that went along with losing a loved one? For the first time since he sat down, he looked forward to the confrontation with her.

He planned to shut the medium down. Run her out of Manhattan, if necessary, because she was standing in the way of something greater, a different sort of power than he possessed now, but one of greater import. A power he would not fall short of achieving.

John Bennett, a former New York State senator and current gubernatorial candidate, had asked Will to partner on the ticket as lieutenant governor. It was something Will's father had always wanted, to wield political influence, yet he'd died before his political career could take wing. Now Will would be the Sloane achieving that goal—and dancing on his father's grave after he and Bennett won.

But John Bennett had a weakness, one by the name of Madam Zolikoff. Seemed the madam had dug her hooks into Bennett, and the candidate would not listen to reason regarding the dangers this presented. But Will wasn't about to allow her to jeopardize Bennett's political career—or his own. They could not afford a scandal six months before the election.

When the performance finally ended, Will didn't bother clapping or stamping his feet like the other patrons. He rose, turned on his heel, and headed straight for the door he'd learned would take him backstage.

No one stopped him. More than a few curious glances were thrown his way and he tugged his derby lower to obscure his face. He'd run Northeast Railroad for the last thirteen years and came from one of the most prominent families in New York. The name Sloane was as well known as Astor, Stuyvesant, and Van Rensselaer. Consequently, Will had never shied from public attention, but he'd rather not be recognized here.

For several minutes, he cut through the long hallways in

the bowels of the theater. Now at the door to her dressing room, he knocked. A slide of a lock and then the door opened to reveal a brunette woman in a black shirtwaist and skirt, the same costume she'd worn on stage. Her lips were still painted a deep red. He inclined his head ever so slightly. "Madam Zolikoff."

"Come in, please." Her voice was deep and husky, a sultry tone more suited to a bedroom than a stage. Thankfully, there was no trace of that ludicrous Russian accent she'd used in front of the crowd. Perhaps this conversation would not be as difficult as he'd feared.

She stepped aside. "I've been expecting you, Mr. Sloane."

No surprise she knew his face, but had she noticed him in the audience? Three steps brought him inside her dressing room, if one could call a space no bigger than a cupboard a "room." Not enough square footage existed here to allow for more than the small table and chair already in place. A mirror hung on the wall above the table, and a blond wig rested on a stand atop said table. With nowhere to go, he folded his hands behind his back.

She glided around him and lowered into the sole chair, facing away from him, and reached for a cloth. He watched in the mirror as she slowly swiped the cloth over her mouth to remove the lip color. She didn't rush and Will had plenty of time to study her mouth. He highly suspected the display another type of performance, one designed to throw him off balance.

"Is there another name I may call you, other than your stage name?"

"No."

"I feel ridiculous calling you Madam Zolikoff."

"That is your problem, not mine." Finished with her cloth, she dropped the scrap to the table and caught his gaze in the mirror. "We are not friends, Mr. Sloane, so let's not pretend otherwise. I know why you are here."

"Is that so?" He hadn't expected her to be so forthright. In his mind, she'd been meek and frightened, concerned over the unpleasantness a man in his position could bring down on a woman in her position. But this woman seemed neither meek nor frightened. "And why am I here?"

"You want to scare me away from John. Get him away from my evil clutches." She wriggled her fingers menacingly on this last sentence. "How's that?"

"Good. This saves us both time. Now you may agree to never see Bennett again, stop bilking him out of hundreds of dollars, and stay out of his life forever."

"Bilking him?" Her lip curled, drawing Will's attention back to her mouth, damn it. "I've got news for you, mugwump, I've earned every dollar providing services to your friend—and not those kind of services, either. John and I are strictly business."

Will smirked. He'd never met an unmarried man and woman who spent hours together with money exchanged who were "strictly business." "Miss whomever you are, I don't care what kind of lies you're shoveling out there to audiences, but I'm not some rube fresh off the farm. I know what you're about, and all of it stinks."

"Oh, indeed? So what am I about, then?"

"Blackmail. And if he doesn't pay, you'll take whatever personal details you've learned about him to the papers and turn him into a laughingstock. I will not let that happen."

She rose, and, because of the tight space, this put her close enough to where he could see the hazel flecks in her brown eyes. Were those freckles on her nose? "I don't care who you are or what you think of me. If you think I'm going to let some stuffed, pompous railroad man scare me away from my best client, you are dead wrong."

* * *

Ava Jones struggled to contain her smile while the handsome man across from her worked to understand her last sentence.

Yeah, you're catching on, railroad man. I'm not afraid of you.

Everyone in New York knew William Sloane. Obscenely wealthy and from one of the snobbish, high-society families, he was mentioned frequently in the papers, both in the financial and the social pages. No doubt men and women bowed to his demands all day, every day. Not Ava. She owed him nothing and did not care about his demands. If not for her desire to get rid of him for good, she would've completely ignored him.

At least she would have *tried* to ignore him. Unfortunately, Mr. Sloane was a man one noticed. She'd spotted him in the audience immediately. Strong, angular jaw. Pronounced cheekbones that highlighted an aristocratic nose. Sandy blond hair, oiled with precision, was swept off his forehead, and a sharp, unsmiling mouth that challenged a woman to see what it would take to loosen him up.

Up close, the view improved markedly. Piercing eyes that had seemed blue in the theater but were actually gunmetal gray. He was tall, with an air of confidence suitable for a prince and a near-palpable energy radiating from his frame. Wide shoulders filled out the cut of his fancy coat quite nicely. She'd always been drawn to sturdy, capable shoulders. Something about Atlas bearing the weight of the world . . .

But she'd learned long ago there was no one to bear the weight of her burdens. Those were hers alone.

"Client?" he scoffed. "Wouldn't 'mark' be a more accurate term?"

Goodness, she was growing to dislike this man. "You assume I am swindling him when I am providing a service."

"By communing with John's dead relatives? Come now, Madam Zolikoff. We both know that's impossible."

She tapped her foot in annoyance. Did he have any idea how lonely John Bennett was? Whether her clients believed in her powers or not, most needed someone to care about them. A friend with whom to talk. A person to give them hope that there was something beyond this drudgery called life. That was what Madam Zolikoff provided—for a nominal fee, of course.

These performances were another matter. People wanted a spectacle. A unique experience to share with their friends and neighbors. A bit of the fantastic to distract from the fatigue. Not everyone came from a wealthy family and ran a big company as a lark; most people needed a break from their daily trials.

"You speak of things you do not understand," she told him. "When I hear from John that he no longer requires my gift, then I will respectfully back off. But you act as if he is an opium eater and I am providing him with the drug. I am not forcing him to see me."

"What I understand is that you are preying on a wealthy and soon-to-be influential man."

Her muscles tightened, anger building in every inch of her body. "I would never blackmail him—I'm not trying to make trouble. The governor as my client would only *help* me." Bigger-named clients meant more clients, which equated to more income. All she needed to do was save up enough money to get her two brothers and sister out of the factories. By her calculations, she had only four more months to go if all held steady. Four more months, after adopting the Madam Zolikoff likeness two years ago, and she'd have enough to keep her family safe.

Out of the city. Away from the filth and toils of life in

this city. Away from bitter memories. Instead, they'd have clean air and open spaces on a farm upstate. *Freedom.*

Mr. Sloane shook his head and pinched the bridge of his nose with two fingers, which caused Ava to roll her eyes. How could someone so wealthy appear this aggrieved? Did this man not know real problems? The tip of her tongue burned with an offer to take him to the match factory to show him cases of phossy jaw. Had he seen the young girls with their rotting faces, jawbones glowing in the dark, all because they'd needed to put food on their table?

Those were hardships. Not the fact that his friend and political partner paid her five dollars a week to read tea leaves and pass on bits of "news" from the great beyond.

"How much will it take?" Sloane asked her. "How much do you need to walk away?"

Oh, so tempting. Ava could throw out a high number and see if railroad man would bite. If he did, her siblings could quit their factory jobs. She would have enough to buy that piece of property and they could all be together. Finally.

But she couldn't. First, pride would not allow her. Taking Sloane's money would be akin to admitting she was robbing people, which she was not. Second, she knew better than most that accepting money never came without strings. If you took what was offered, they felt as if they owned you.

And no one owned Ava Jones. Not any longer.

"You don't have enough money to make me disappear. But if it makes you feel better, I'll give you a discount on a séance."

He made a sound in his throat. "That is the *last* thing I need."

A knock sounded on the door before Robbie, one of the assistants, called, "Ava, hurry up. I need the room."

Mr. Sloane's brows jumped and Ava cursed inwardly, irritated at the small revelation. "Ava," he drawled, as if testing the sound on his tongue. "Pretty. Also, I like your hair better this way, without the wig."

She turned and began shoving her things into her carpetbag, trying to ignore the fluttering in her belly. The compliments were as unexpected as they were unwelcome. "Save the poetry for your Fifth Avenue debutantes, railroad man. You're wasting your time with me." She carefully lowered her wig and wig stand into the bag. Found her bonnet. Then she began shrugging into her coat.

A large hand caught the coat and held it up. She easily slipped her arms through. "Thank you," she mumbled.

Without waiting for him, she pushed into the hall and strode toward the exit. The heels of her high boots ticked on the hard floor, and she could hear Sloane's fancy evening shoes keeping pace. No doubt he was headed somewhere glamorous, like the opera or a high society ball. Not to a cramped three-room apartment in a West Side boarding-house that she shared with her siblings.

She opened the door to the lobby. "Everything all right, Ava?" Robbie eyed her carefully, gaze bouncing to the silent man behind her.

"Fine, Robbie. Tell your sister I'll be by tomorrow. See you next week."

He nodded and she continued out the main doors. An early evening rain had fallen during her performance, cooling the air a bit more than one would expect in mid-spring. Gaslight from the street lamps cast a yellow glow over the dark, wet cobblestones. Ava loved the rain. It washed the city clean and provided the residents with a reprieve from the usual odors, those of sweat, trash, rotting food, and horse excrement.

"You've acquired quite a following for these shows."

"You're still here?" She started walking, not caring whether he followed. Unfortunately, his long legs had no problem keeping pace with her. "I'm very good at what I do, Mr. Sloane. Admit it, you were entertained."

His mouth twisted as if he'd sucked a lemon. "I was offended, if you must know."

Now at the corner, she crossed over Twenty-Seventh Street, heading south, and tried to contain her annoyance. "We don't serve champagne and caviar, so I can imagine what a hardship the evening was for you."

"I was referring to the flimflam you performed on those poor unsuspecting people."

"Flimflam? Those 'poor unsuspecting people' wanted a show, and that's what I gave them. There's a reason I perform in a theater, and I'm damn good at what I do."

"You take their money and pretend their dead relatives are speaking to you."

He spoke to her as if she were a criminal, his tone condescending and cutting, and blood rushed in her ears. "First of all, how are you so certain my talents are not real?" He started to open his mouth, so she stopped on the sidewalk and pointed a finger in his face. "You don't have any idea, Mr. Sloane, so save your judgment. Second, I wasn't aware that your own business practices were always so scrupulous." His eyes dimmed, and she knew she'd landed a blow. "I'm sure while running a big railroad you never skirt the law or buy political favor. So save me your sanctimonious attitude."

"Fine," he snarled, leaning closer. "Run your con anywhere you want, sweetheart, but leave John Bennett alone."

Will Sloane was tall, much larger than she, yet she

didn't back down, not for one second. She'd already let one overprivileged, handsome man try to wreck her life. No way would she repeat the mistake.

She glared up at him. "Not in your wildest dreams do I take orders from the likes of you. Go bully someone else."

Goddamn this woman.

Will could not believe her. He'd offered her any amount of money to back off, and she'd laughed in his face. Him, William Sloane. The sheer gall was staggering.

Now she was walking away, so he hurried after her, his long strides eating up the narrow sidewalk. A particularly rough part of town, the Tenderloin was no place for a young woman after dark. Yet she held her head high, unconcerned over her safety.

He took a moment to study her—Ava, not Madam Zolikoff. The simple, military-style cut of her coat hugged her small shoulders and upper body, revealing generous curves and accenting a small waist. A small straw bonnet with fake flowers covered sable-brown hair. Her boots were worn, but clean. No jewelry. He hadn't noticed a wedding ring before she donned her gloves, yet he had noted how she generously filled out the bodice of her shirtwaist.

Men loitered in a doorway near the corner, and their gazes tracked Ava as she went by. One of the toughs pushed off the stoop, as if to follow her, and Will pointed a finger at the man. *Don't,* he mouthed, and the man stopped in his tracks, raising his hands in surrender.

Two more steps brought Will alongside her. "You should have an escort. This is not an area of town safe for a woman out alone."

She snorted. "There isn't any area of town safe for a woman out alone. Not even in your fancy neighborhood."

She shoved her hands into the pockets of her coat. "And you don't need to protect me. I can take care of myself."

He didn't doubt that. The image of a lioness came to mind, one that would chew a man up and spit him out. "Are you always so difficult?"

She threw her head back and laughed—a genuine, sultry sound that hit him square in the gut. He pushed down the reaction, put it in a place with all the other things he ignored.

"Only with men who try to boss me around."

"A lot of those in your life?"

"Just one, apparently. Any ideas on how to get rid of him?"

Will's lips twitched from suppressing a smile. "No, unless you're ready to give in. I won't disappear until you leave John alone."

She stopped in her tracks and put her hands on her hips. Her brown gaze lit up with fire and brimstone, her generous bosom heaving in a distractingly enticing manner. "Why do you care so much? Your money could buy whatever election you wanted, cover up any hint of scandal that might occur. Therefore, you don't really care about what I'm doing to John. Tell me, why are you following me? 'Cause I need to tell you, I'm not buying it."

What the hell was she implying? That he was after *her*? His muscles clenched as he stepped closer, hoping to intimidate her with their difference in height. Surprisingly, she held her ground, merely lifted a brow as if to say, *Get on with it*. He tried not to be impressed.

"First, I would never use my money to buy an election. I want to *win*, and I mean to do that fairly. Second, I can cover up just about any scandal I want, but all it takes is one whiff, one *hint* of impropriety, and my political career will be over before it begins. I'll be a laughingstock. And there's no way I'll allow that to happen."

"No, John will be a laughingstock. John's political career will be over. And"—she made a disbelieving sound—"you act as if New York politics are clean and fair. We both know politicians are dirtier than chimney sweeps, and that's saying something."

"I wouldn't throw stones at the legitimacy of other vocations, were I you."

"Oh!" She threw up her hands and stomped away. "Leave me alone, William Sloane."

He trailed after her, catching up in a few steps. "You're wrong. In my world, you're judged not only on your own actions, but the actions of those around you. The company you keep. If John goes down, I go down as well."

"Then I can only imagine what *your world* would think of you keeping company with me in the Tenderloin."

"They'd think I'd lost my ever-loving mind," he muttered.

"Then scurry back home to Fifth Avenue. I'm sure your butler has brandy and cigars waiting. No one here is stopping you."

"Washington Square."

Her head swung toward him. "Pardon?"

"I live on Washington Square." It had been a long time since he'd had to tell anyone that. The Sloanes had been in that location since the city covered up the graves and converted the space to a public park.

"Oh, excuse me," she said with mock sincerity. "Scurry back home to *Washington Square*."

"After you promise to stop your shenanigans with John."

"Sloane!"

The voice came from behind them, so he spun to see who was there. A few people were out, but no one close enough. No one came forward or even met his eye. Who had called his name?

Strange.

Facing forward, he instantly noticed something else. He was now alone.

"Ava?" Feet planted, his gaze swept the sidewalk and the street, searching. He peered across to the other side, thinking maybe she had crossed the street.

There was no sign of her. Nothing. She had disappeared into thin air.

Chapter Two

Ava trudged up the few steps outside the boarding-house. She'd walked all the way from the theater, not bothing to jump on a late streetcar. The night air and exercise had helped to clear her head. Not to mention, she'd rather save the fare.

Had there ever been a man more aggravating than Will Sloane?

In my world . . . I won't disappear until you leave John alone . . . I live on Washington Square. Ava shoved her key in the lock, turned it roughly. Sakes alive, he'd been everything she had assumed: pompous, overbearing, privileged.

That's not all you thought of him.

Yes, fine. He was more handsome than any man in his position had a right to be. But those sorts of thoughts would only get her into trouble.

After pushing her way inside, she began the climb to the third floor. The stairs creaked beneath her tired feet. Rent was due in less than a week. She needed to see how much her siblings could contribute this month. The amount always varied, depending on work at the factories, whether one had been sick, holidays, and so forth. Ava had almost all of the rent herself, and she could take the rest out of their savings, but she'd prefer not to. If necessary, she could skip meals for the next few days to make up a bit of money. *Saving money means not spending it.*

Madam Zolikoff afforded them a decent living. Certainly better than most they'd grown up with downtown. She could buy her brothers and sister new clothes, shoes, food. They were clean and had a respectable roof over their heads. Fourteen months ago, she'd been able to move them out of the leaky old tenement on the Lower East Side—a feat her parents hadn't managed while they'd been alive.

Furthermore, she was saving money for their future. Soon, she'd uproot her family out of this godforsaken hell-hole and into a nice, wide-open space. The kids could grow up as . . . kids, not overworked and underpaid workers, no better treated than the stray dogs wandering the alleys. Where they wouldn't make the same mistakes she had once upon a time.

Therefore, no, William Sloane. She wouldn't be giving up. Not now, not when she was so close.

She unlocked the door to their rooms, stepped inside, and set her carpetbag down. The rich smell of potato soup hit her nose, and she found Tom and Mary eating at the table. "Good evening." She bolted the door and unbuttoned her coat. "I see you started on the soup I made earlier."

Her sister nodded, her thirteen-year-old shoulders slumped in exhaustion. "It's delicious. Thank you, Ava." Mary worked as a finisher in a clothing factory on Ludlow. Her job was to sew the final touches on a garment by hand. While the work was tedious and exhausting, thank God it wasn't dangerous.

Tom said nothing, merely shoved more soup in his mouth. Ava knew this was likely the fifteen-year-old's first morsel since breakfast. He worked in a cigar factory on Rivington, not far from Mary's shop.

"Where's Sam?"

Mary swallowed and said, "He's lying down. Says he feels sick."

An all-too-familiar knot of apprehension tightened in Ava's chest. Sam had not been a well child. Weak blood, their mother had often said, though Ava knew that to be poppycock. For whatever reason, twelve-year-old Sam tended to become ill more than the rest of them. Ava was certain he would improve once they left New York, once he could rest and breathe fresh air.

She went to Sam and Tom's bedroom and knocked on the closed door. "Sam, honey, it's Ava. May I come in?"

A muffled cough, then Sam's voice said, "Yes."

Dark shadows cloaked the room. Leaving the door open to filter in light, she lit the gas lamp by his bed. A thin figure was buried under the covers, shivering though the room was adequately heated. "Sam, what's wrong?"

"I had to leave my corner. Thought I was going to faint."

She brushed back his shaggy brown hair and felt his forehead. "You're burning with fever. How long have you felt this way?"

"Since yesterday," he admitted. "I'm sorry, Ava. I had to leave before I had a chance to sell all my papers. . . ." She could hear the waver in his voice. As a newsie, any papers Sam didn't sell were taken out of his pay. Newspaper companies would not accept returned copies.

"Oh, don't worry about that. It's important that you get better."

"I'll be better tomorrow. I have to be. Someone'll take my corner if I'm not out there."

A newsie's corner meant everything to him, as a busy stretch could mean the difference between selling a hundred copies instead of ten. Sam had fought hard to maintain his corner near Broadway and Vesey. "Fine, if you're well enough. I wouldn't risk it, though. Did you eat dinner?"

"No, I'm not hungry. I just want to sleep."

"I'm getting you a cool cloth, and you're going to eat. Then sleep."

"Ava—"

"No whining." She went to the cupboard and found a clean rag. They shared the water closet in the hall with the other family on the floor. Ava hurried there and soaked the cloth with cool water before returning to fix Sam a bowl of soup. Once she had him settled, she sat heavily in a chair at the kitchen table.

"Rough day?" Tom had finished his dinner and sat nursing a glass of ale. Mary appeared, a bowl of hot soup in her hand, which she placed in front of Ava.

"Thank you. Sit, Mary. You look exhausted."

"I'm fine. Sitting and sewing's not so hard. Not compared to what you do."

Ava would beg to differ, of course. She knew Mary's hands were constantly sore from holding a needle, a perpetual backache from hunching over. "The show went well tonight. There was an even bigger crowd than last week."

"Mary, I've got to talk to Ava," Tom said. "Alone."

Their sister's brow furrowed, and Ava sought to reassure her even as her own insides twisted. Tom's anger and frustration had been apparent in the last few months. It seemed the older he grew, the more he disagreed with Ava. "It's all right, Mary. Go to bed."

Mary glanced between the two of them then rested her gaze on Tom. "Fine. But this had better not be about those boys I saw you talking to after work."

"I told you to mind your own business," their brother snapped.

"Ava, he wants to join a gang." Mary folded her bony arms. "Those boys steal things, I've seen them."

"Shut up, Mary!" Tom bellowed, and he looked so much like their father in that instant that Ava's heart hurt.

"Mary, please. Let me talk with him."

Biting her lip, Mary nodded and left them alone. No one spoke for a long moment. Finally Ava pushed her bowl away, soup untouched. "Is this true? Are you hoping to join a gang?"

"They aren't a gang." He drained the rest of his ale and sat back. "They're just a bunch of friends."

"Who steal. A bunch of friends who steal things and then sell them for money."

"You act like that's a terrible thing when you're nearly doin' the same. Meeting with those rich folks and convincin' them you hear their dead parents. Come on, Ava."

That stung, especially since Will Sloane had accused her of the same not even two hours ago. "But what I do doesn't hurt anyone. They willingly give me money for entertainment. It's completely different than outright stealing from people."

The shadows haunting his eyes deepened. "I hate that goddamn factory. You asked me to stick it out another year, but I can't stand it any longer. I'm exhausted. This job is going to kill me or take my sanity. Either way, I can't do it no more."

"I know, Tom. But I only need four more months, if things continue. Four more months and then we'll all be able to leave this godforsaken—"

"Maybe I don't want to leave. Maybe Mary and Sam don't want to leave either. Have you thought of that?"

Her mind stumbled over that information. Why would they want to stay here when they could have a house of their own and a piece of property? "We can have a better life outside the city."

"Where we work on a farm from sunup to sundown? How the hell is that any different than what we do now? I'm tired of working all the time, Ava. There are people who have money—real money—and they don't work fourteen hours a day, six days a week."

"Because they steal it, you mean."

He shrugged. "Beg, borrow, steal . . . what's the difference?"

"A lot, Tom. There's a big difference. And I do not want you turning to a life of petty thievery. You're better than that."

"No, I'm not. And the sooner we all realize it, the better off we'll be." He stood. "You've done so much for us. Never think I'm not grateful. But I'm almost sixteen, and it's time for me to do my share for the family."

"Please, give me four more months. That's all we need."

He crossed his arms and stared at the window, lines of unhappiness bracketing his mouth. "I'll try. That's all I can promise."

New York City had many faces, and Will loved each one. From the crowded, dirty tenements of the Lower East Side, the bohemians and immigrants just north of his beloved Washington Square, and the giant stores and growing commerce of Union Square, to the amusements near Longacre Square, he appreciated them all. Every corner, building, and house in this city was rooted deep in the marrow of his bones.

This was his city. The Sloanes had helped Manhattan grow, their money reinvested in the infrastructure to provide the necessary foundation. His great-grandfather had been instrumental in piping water in from a reservoir to supply the city, while Will had invested in elevated trains as well as the telephone and telegraph lines crisscrossing the sky like a fisherman's net.

He'd started running Northeast Railroad when he was

sixteen years old, working without a break since he turned nineteen. Years of long hours, little sleep, worrying and plotting, the fate of his family's enormous legacy in his hands. There had been quite a lot to learn in a short period of time.

Hatred had fueled him for many of those years. Loathing for a cruel, cold dead man had driven Will to succeed. *You're weak, just like your mother.* How often had Will been called a disappointment, an embarrassment to the Sloane name? All because he'd contracted scarlet fever as a child and, he was later told, could not bear to be parted from his mother, even after he recovered. How could Will have known that his parents hated each other, or that his father would view Will's love for his mother as a betrayal? The years dragged on, yet his father had largely ignored his only son.

And when the bastard died, Will had sworn to build on and far exceed everything Archibald Sloane accomplished.

All had nearly been destroyed, however, when Will's investment firm had embezzled money—a *lot* of money—from the company. Everything he'd worked for, all the blood and sweat, almost taken from him, and the shame of his failure caused his stomach to burn constantly. *You'll run it all into the ground,* his father's voice sneered.

With undue haste, the situation had been remedied, and the company was once again thriving. Yet even now, he couldn't step into the office without a sharp pain erupting under his sternum, as if the guilt made him physically sick.

"You mustn't work so hard, William," his physician, Dr. van Kirkland, had told him. "You ought to visit a sanatorium. Get some rest, otherwise your body will never restore itself."

"Of course," Will had snapped in response. "Because

the stock won't tumble when it's discovered the Northeast Railroad president is ill."

He couldn't step away, give up the company and everything his ancestors had built up, in order to recuperate. As much as he needed a respite, he would not jeopardize the empire he'd forged—especially not when the political office his father had once dreamed of was within reach. In fact, lieutenant governor seemed a leisurely stroll in the park compared to what Will dealt with each day. Therefore, he would perform both duties upon election to office. Hell, he *wanted* to do both. Even if he only slept four hours a night instead of five.

Madam Zolikoff was the unforeseen wrinkle. She threatened his plan with her undoubtedly nefarious presence in Bennett's life. Will would not allow the venerable Sloane name to become a public joke. Chuckled and guffawed about in taverns and clubs from the Battery to the Bronx. No, not while he still breathed. He would win this election cleanly and without scandal.

Such was the reason for a mad dash up Fifth Avenue on a Thursday afternoon, deep into the land of vulgar, over-sized mansions. The hubris of these mini-palaces staggered him. Each one bigger and more garish than the last, including his new brother-in-law's monstrosity. Did these people have no sense of taste? The point of money was not to show it off, but to wield it into the one thing that mattered: power.

He recognized the house from down the block. Will threw open the brougham's door before the wheels even stopped rolling. He hoped he wasn't too late.

The butler appeared and immediately pulled the panel wide. "Mr. Sloane, please come in. Mr. Bennett is currently engaged in his study with a guest, but you are welcome to wait in the blue salon until he is—"

Will strode by the butler. He knew the guest as well as what they were doing. Hadn't he told that woman three days ago to stay the hell away from John Bennett?

When he pushed into the study, he found the two of them cozied up on the long velvet sofa, Ava's head bent close to Bennett's as she stared at the bottom of a china teacup.

They both glanced up at the door, Bennett's face awash in surprise. Ava's generous, full top lip slowly curled in distaste, and Will felt his own sneer emerge in response. *The gorgeous charlatan.*

"Sloane." Bennett rose and walked over to shake Will's hand. "Had we an appointment?"

Will removed his derby with his free hand. "No, but I heard Madam Zolikoff was visiting and could not stay away." He turned toward Ava. "You don't mind, do you? I am quite curious about your renowned talents."

Her look communicated she knew precisely what he was about, but she said in her terrible Russian accent, "Of course. You must sit. Sit, Mr. Sloane."

"Thank you." Without giving Bennett the opportunity to say otherwise, Will lowered into a chair. "Please, don't mind me. Continue on."

Bennett retook his seat and addressed the woman earnestly. "Will his presence throw off the reading?"

"No." She waved a hand. "I can easily pretend he does not exist." Will bit back a smile, remaining silent as she returned to her tea leaves. "Now here I see an insect." She pointed somewhere at the bottom of the cup. "That means you are suffering distractions. Or complications. Is there someone in your life preventing you from your purpose?"

"Yes," Bennett agreed easily. "How did you know?"

Perhaps because everyone suffers distractions and

complications. Will sighed heavily, but they ignored him as Ava went on.

"The tea leaves, they never lie. You need to cast aside this person who is not entirely on your side. He will only attempt to bring you down."

Will gripped the armrest of the chair. Was she speaking of him? Before he could comment, she continued with her inane predictions.

"This appears to be a foot, which is a sign that you need to move forward. Move on. That you will have a change in your location or career."

Bennett straightened, his face brightening considerably. "The election. Hear that, Sloane? We're about to move into the governor's house."

Will made a noncommittal sound, and the reading commenced, Ava's head bent over the china piece. "Now, over here I see a barking dog. This means someone close to you has been saying things he should not. He is untrustworthy. Do you know who this could be?"

Bennett shifted in his seat, his brows pinched, as if considering this ridiculousness, and Will felt the tips of his ears grow hot. *How dare she.* This bogus reading had turned into an assault on *him*, and he didn't care for it one bit.

As revenge, she was trying to make trouble between him and Bennett. An egregious error on her part. Bennett knew Will to be a loyal friend—one who would never try to sabotage their future. Unlike a certain little brown-haired minx who dealt in lies and swindles, creating havoc everywhere she went.

Two could play this game.

"Do you see anything specific there for Mr. Bennett?" he called out. "Perhaps the tea leaves could tell him the name of a horse to bet on at Saratoga Springs tomorrow?"

Madam Zolikoff wrinkled her nose in distaste. "The tea

leaves do not work for horse racing, Mr. Sloane. The spirits are not for insignificant things, like gambling."

"Insignificant? Tell that to the losers," Will muttered.

Her brown eyes narrowed dangerously, and Will lifted a brow in challenge. "John," she said to her client, "perhaps I should come back tomorrow. There is negative energy in this room."

"That's quite all right, Madam Zolikoff. We are nearly to our allotted time anyway." He stood and held out his hand, helping her to her feet as if she were a blushing debutante and not a hardened fraud. God Almighty, was Will the only rational man left in this city?

Bennett stared at him expectantly, and Will realized he was still seated. Not that he'd shown the disrespect on purpose, but she was not an easy woman to respect. He slowly rose. "May I drop you somewhere, Madam Zolikoff?"

Her right eye twitched slightly. No doubt she wanted to blister his backside with her sharp tongue, but Bennett's presence meant restraint. "That is not necessary, Mr. Sloane," she managed. "I am quite capable—"

"Oh, undoubtedly you are, but it would be my pleasure."

"Now, Madam, don't fight Sloane here." Bennett patted her hand. "He's a gentleman through and through. There's no better man to ride alone with. You shouldn't be scared at all."

"I'm not scared." Anger stripped her voice of the fake Russian accent, leaving the warm, raspy tone Will preferred. But she quickly caught herself, resumed her persona. "That is, I am sure Mr. Sloane has much better things to do with his time. After all, he came here to meet with you, John."

With exaggerated flair, Will snapped his fingers, tilted his head back. "Yes, but now I've completely forgotten what I needed to speak with Bennett about. No mind. I'll cable you if I remember, Bennett."

"Excellent, it's settled," Bennett said. "Take care with her, Sloane. This one is a gift from the heavens."

"'A gift from the heavens,'" the man next to her sneered. "Christ, how do you sleep at night?"

Ava kept her stare firmly fixed on the window of the brougham. Difficult enough to concentrate when Sloane's thigh and hip were pressed tight to her body, and his large shoulder bumped into hers every time they hit a divot in the street. She wished she weren't so aware of him, but the man was impossible to ignore. Larger than life, he exuded fortitude and determination in spades, a nearly palpable confidence. Power had always attracted her; however, this man had a nasty disposition to match. He was hard and spoiled, a bully in a swallowtail.

She must remain strong.

Ava's grin dripped with false sincerity. "I sleep the same way you do, railroad man. Like a baby. On top of a pile of money."

"I don't believe you. If you had money, you'd possess better footwear. And your own carriage."

He was right, but she wouldn't admit it. Ava saved every penny she could, and that meant wearing out her shoes as she traveled about the city. No use paying for the elevated or a hack if she could use her own two legs getting there. "Did you accomplish what you'd hoped, rescuing John from my undue influence?"

"Hardly. You have that man so deep in your clutches he may never see daylight. Where am I taking you? All you told my driver was south."

"As if I'd give you my address. No, you drive to your house, and I'll walk from there."

"Afraid of letting me see your gingerbread house where you roast small children?"

"Not small children, no. Everyone knows obnoxious, self-indulgent rich men taste so much better. Best to stay clear—I might not be able to resist the temptation."

He snorted but remained silent, for once. She'd rather he kept talking, distracting her from noting his arrogance and self-possession, the qualities he exuded merely by breathing. No idea why she found them so appealing, but some women never learned, she supposed.

His leg bounced, a habit she'd noted before. Did she unnerve him? She purposely averted her eyes, determined to stop noticing anything about him. "Why did you insist on driving me, anyway?"

"Because we never finished our conversation the other night. Damnedest thing, I thought I heard someone calling my name. But when I turned around, no one was about."

"Strange." She fought a smile. Learning how to throw her voice had been one of the first tricks she'd perfected. "Still, we've said all that needed to be said to each other, don't you think?"

"No, it is obvious we have not." He clasped her chin gently and brought her around to face him. Tingles swept over Ava's skin, womanly tingles that signaled very unfortunate, inappropriate things. He dropped his arm, releasing her. "You don't seem to grasp the gravity of the situation. My job is to make you understand. By whatever means necessary."

"Whatever means necessary? Goodness, you are determined. What if I said I'd leave John alone if you agreed to play a part in my act next Monday?"

"A-a part . . in your act?" He threw his head back and

laughed, the strong cords of his throat popping and shifting under rough skin. She suddenly experienced a sharp urge to drag her tongue over those ridges, to taste his laugh on her lips.

Sakes alive, she had to stop this. She jerked her gaze to the street, mortification burning through her veins. There could be no thoughts of that nature, especially around William Sloane. For pity's sake, he probably demanded proof of a woman's pedigree before he agreed to kiss her. Besides, she'd flirted with her baser nature years ago, as a young girl, and where had that gotten her? A lump formed in her throat, and the heavy weight of regret stole her breath.

You played with fire, girl. Now you've gone and gotten yourself burned.

Her mother's shrill voice rang in Ava's head. Yes, she had been stupid. Not a day went by when she didn't remind herself never to be stupid again.

He finally stopped laughing, the cad. "I wouldn't lower myself to a part in your act if it would secure me the presidency."

"Are you certain? Because I can easily convince John he needs to see me twice a week."

That drove the amusement from his expression. "You wouldn't dare. I swear, if you do—"

"Calm down, railroad man. I do have other clients. Even for John, I'm not certain I have the time." She shot him a glare. "But I could *make* the time if you don't leave me alone."

"I cannot leave you alone until you promise to leave *John* alone. I have too much to lose if this gets out. Or if you decide to sell his secrets."

"You have my word I won't," she snapped. "Why can't you accept it and go back to passing out campaign buttons?"

"Forgive me if I have a problem accepting the word

of a woman donning a blond wig and adopting a Russian accent—which is abysmal, by the way. Have you ever met a real Russian?"

Mercy, she was tired of insults from this man. As if he had to remind everyone he met how inferior they were to his sublime greatness. "Don't you have an empire to run? How is it that a man in charge of so much has this much free time to gad about the city?"

"I do not possess any free time," he said. "Absolutely none. In fact, I left a very important meeting when I learned you were at Bennett's. Which means my nine o'clock dinner reservations will be forfeit for supper at my desk instead."

She slid her bottom lip out in a pout. "Oh, you poor, poor millionaire. I'm sure whichever half-witted innocent you were escorting tonight will understand."

Funny, his eyes stayed on her lips. Did railroad man have an affinity for plump lips? Hers were on the large side, along with her bosom. He'd stared at that a time or two as well, she'd noticed. No doubt he was used to the thin, graceful women of the upper Fifth Avenue set, pale women who remained indoors. Who never had a hair out of place. Who could afford a decent corset to flatten their breasts. Ava's curves and olive skin probably fascinated him, like one of Barnum's oddities.

Well, he could stare all he liked. Perhaps she could even use his fascination to her advantage. Men like Will Sloane would not care for an aggressive, modern woman. Undoubtedly, he'd prefer a docile creature who stayed at home, sipping tea, until he returned from his club. Wasn't that what every spoiled, rich man desired?

If such was the case, a little boldness on her part should scare him off for good.

"Do you ever back down?" he asked her.

She leaned in, pleased to see his gray eyes flash and darken. He smelled faintly of expensive soap, like sandalwood and lemons, and she looked at him through her lashes. "Never," she whispered. "I never back down, and you would do well to remember it, Mr. Sloane."

Raising a fist, she pounded on the side of the carriage. "Here, if you please!" The driver pulled to the side of the street and slowed the horse. When they came to a stop, she opened the door. "Thank you for the ride." Jumping down to the sidewalk, she disappeared into the crowd.

Chapter Three

Will tapped his fingers on the railing and surveyed the well-dressed Saturday evening crowd from his second-tier box. Though opera season had ended prior to Lent, the summer season in Newport hadn't yet begun, which meant tonight's benefit performance of *Much Ado About Nothing* had attracted a large number of society's elite to the Metropolitan Opera House.

While Will supported the cause—improving the lives of the city's poor—he'd attended for a very specific reason. He'd recently decided to take a bride.

The time had come. Even his baby sister, the girl he'd raised since the death of their parents when he was sixteen, had married. Why shouldn't he marry as well? He was almost thirty, after all. He'd sorted some financial troubles a few months back—firing his thieving investment firm and hiring his sister instead—and the Sloane coffers were overflowing once again. He'd even cut loose his mistress, Mrs. Osborne, last week.

The publicity surrounding his nuptials certainly wouldn't hurt in the campaign, either. Soon, he'd be lieutenant governor, married, and free from the nagging stomach pain plaguing him.

Currently there were four candidates for the honor of becoming the next Mrs. Sloane. Each carefully researched, the families above reproach. All were beautiful and innocent, exactly as his mother had been when she married his father, before Archibald had weighted her down with cruel, biting words.

Will's marriage would be nothing like his parents' union. He would respect his bride. He would not cut her down before their son, bringing tears to her eyes over the breakfast table. Ignore her year after year in favor of singers and actresses. No, whomever he chose would be treated carefully, with honor and consideration above all things, until he died.

The image of a tiny brunette with round eyes and an even rounder figure popped into his head. His jaw clenched, remembering how Ava had leaned in and stared up at him in the carriage. Mere inches had separated them, and he easily could've closed the distance and kissed her. And for half a beat, he'd been certain she wanted him to. The woman was trouble.

Worse, nothing had been resolved between them. He wanted Ava to stay the hell away from Bennett. Why was that so difficult? Now he'd need to attend her show on Monday just to talk some sense into her. God Almighty, he was getting tired of chasing that charlatan all over New York.

"Will!"

He spun at the sound of his sister's voice. Lizzie, wearing a stunning white opera gown adorned with ostrich feathers, came toward him. A large figure followed behind her, and Will ground his teeth to smother a sound of annoyance.

Smiling fondly, he went to greet her, kissing her cheek. "Hello, Lizzie. Thank you for joining me. You look beautiful."

"And you look quite dashing yourself. You remember Emmett."

A heavy silence descended, and Will forced out, "Cavanaugh."

His sister's hulking husband inclined his head. "Sloane."

"Oh, you two." Lizzie sighed dramatically, a familiar sound to Will's ears. He'd taken care of her since she was eight, after all. "Please stop already. I expect you both to be civil."

Not likely, considering Cavanaugh had seduced Lizzie and nearly ruined her reputation. "Of course," he said smoothly. "Why would we be anything else?"

"Because you're the two most stubborn men in New York. But I'm happy tonight so do not spoil the evening for me. That goes for you, too," she told Cavanaugh over her shoulder.

Her husband took her hand and kissed the gloved knuckles, a besotted look on his face that had Will's dinner threatening to reappear. "Of course, Elizabeth."

Will shook his head. Never thought he'd see the mighty Emmett Cavanaugh—former Five Points b'hoy and now the owner of East Coast Steel—tamed by a woman. But it made sense, since Lizzie was unlike any woman on earth, and as long as Cavanaugh remembered that, Will would remain civil.

"Now," Lizzie said, turning back to Will. "You said it was important that we join you tonight. Why is that, exactly?"

"I need your help. I've decided to marry."

Cavanaugh barked a laugh, a loud, booming sound that

Joanna Shupe

attracted the attention of several of their neighbors. He tried to cover it with a cough, but Will and Lizzie both shot daggers at him.

"Emmett, why don't you fetch a glass of whatever Will has stocked in the salon? And I'd love some lemonade."

Wearing a smirk that had Will's fist clenching, Cavanaugh kissed his wife's cheek. "I'll leave you and your brother"—he snickered—"alone for a moment." Shoulders shaking with amusement, the oaf lumbered away.

"There are so many worthy young men in New York." Will crossed his arms over his chest. "You could have chosen any man other than *him*."

"You forced the marriage, so you only have yourself to blame. But it's too late because I'm keeping him. I happen to love him madly—and he's the father of your forthcoming niece or nephew, so be nice."

"A child whom I categorically believe to have originated through immaculate conception—and do not dare dissuade me of that notion."

"Of course, dear brother," she said, patting his lapel. "Just as I pretend not to know about your Mrs. Osborne."

"You . . ." His mouth fell open. "Lizzie! You should not know of . . ."

"Your mistress?" Lizzie finished blithely, as if hearing that word out of his younger sister's mouth didn't mortify the hell out of him. "Yes, I know. Everyone who meets her knows. She brags about you quite openly—not that I've lingered to hear details."

Shooting pain erupted under Will's sternum, causing him to wince. He'd gone to great lengths to shelter Lizzie, even before their parents died, from any impropriety. Obviously, he'd failed with regard to his mistress. "I no longer have an association with her. I'm serious about this marriage business."

Lizzie's gray eyes, so like his own, widened. "My, you must be serious." She clapped her gloved hands once and then rubbed them together. "Well, then, let's see . . . There's my friend, Edith. A bit spirited, but she's good fun. Then there's the Chester girl. She's related to the Roosevelts by marriage."

He held up a hand. "I've already narrowed the choices to four girls: Misses Iselin, Cameron, Baldwin, and Rives."

Lizzie's face fell, her brows drawing together. "I hope you're joking."

"Of course I'm not joking. Marriage is not something I would joke about. And Miss Cameron has just arrived. I need you to come with me. You know her family better than I do." He made a move to start up the aisle, but Lizzie put a hand out to stop him.

"Will, those four girls are completely wrong for you. I should like to see you married, but to someone you care about. Someone worthy of you, not some foolish girl who can't carry a conversation. The Rives girl can hardly remember her own name. Don't you want the sort of marriage our mother and father had?"

Will nearly winced. Lizzie had no idea of the true nature of their parents' marriage—and he meant to see it stayed that way.

He gazed out over the sea of black tailcoats and glittering jewels, thinking on the type of marriage he preferred. What he wanted was a peaceful union with measured expectations and traditional duties. An honorable business arrangement with respect and serenity. Lizzie had found love, but Will had no intention of the same for himself. "Come, let's visit the Cameron box."

"Why are you in such a hurry? Why not wait until the next round of parties in the fall?"

Stood to reason Lizzie would get the heart of it, and

he knew better than to lie to her. In a flash, she'd sense the untruth and dig until he confessed the real reason. "The wedding publicity will help with the election."

"You want to get married to . . . win votes? *Are you insane?*"

"Keep your voice down." He nodded at Mrs. McVickar in the adjoining box, gave the older woman a practiced smile. She blushed and began fanning her face. Satisfied, he murmured to Lizzie, "The public likes a happily married man in office, and I need a hostess. I think it's a sound plan."

"Of course you do. You're the groom, not a girl who will someday discover she's a pawn in your political career. Damnation, Will."

"I'm not certain I favor the curse words peppering your vocabulary since you married Cavanaugh."

"Do not try to make this about me. I will not allow you to ruin your life—and someone else's—just to win."

"Lizzie, it'll ruin my life if I *don't* win. This is a huge opportunity, and I'm not going to let anything stop me." Certainly not his sister's disapproval.

And certainly not some swindler medium out to make a quick buck—even if he did have distracting fantasies about her mouth.

"Will, you already have nearly everything a man could want. You don't need a political career as well. You drive yourself so hard, and I've never understood why. What more do you need to accomplish?"

Logically a part of him knew she was right. He'd never been satisfied with what he had; he always wanted *more*. Perhaps he'd never have enough. But that was a worry for several years down the road. "A career in politics, that's what. I wish you'd stop trying to talk me out of my entirely sound ideas, too."

"Fine, but I am not in approval of said ideas."

"So noted. Come along to the Cameron box." He placed her hand on his sleeve and led her toward the back of the box. "You need to leave your husband behind, however. He'll only scare the others."

By the time Lizzie and Will arrived at the Cameron box, the family was talking quietly amongst themselves. Mrs. Cameron noticed them first and came to her feet, dragging Miss Cameron along with her. "Good evening, Elizabeth." The two women greeted each other while Will shook Mr. Cameron's hand, and then Mrs. Cameron lifted her hand to Will. "Good evening, Mr. Sloane. How lovely for you to stop by."

"Good evening, Mrs. Cameron." Will bowed over her extended hand.

"You both remember my daughter?" She gripped the elbow of the younger woman and pulled her forward a bit.

"Of course," Lizzie said smoothly. "How beautiful you look tonight, Miss Cameron."

And the girl did look beautiful, with her light brown hair carefully styled close to her head, highlighting large-yet-tasteful pearl-drop earrings. A matching pearl necklace wrapped her throat in the modest neckline of her fashionable cream gown. Her face was pleasing, pale and unblemished. While she did not set off sparks inside him, neither did she repulse him.

And then she giggled, a girlish, uneven tittering that scraped across the back of his neck like phantom finger-nails. "Good evening, Mrs. Cavanaugh," Miss Cameron said politely before turning to Will and presenting her hand. "Mr. Sloane."

He performed the obligatory bow. "Miss Cameron."

That sound—a high-pitched, jagged giggle—emerged again and Will repressed a shudder. Perhaps the girl was nervous. Everyone present knew why the call had been paid, that Miss Cameron was the lure with which to draw a single gentleman into the box. The ritual was no surprise, yet he could imagine it a daunting experience for the lure.

"Are you looking forward to the play?" he asked her.

"Very much," she replied, another giggle succeeding her words.

Would she titter at everything he said? He turned to his sister, polite smile in place but eyes pleading. Lizzie, being the smartest woman on earth, read him perfectly. She leaned toward Miss Cameron. "Have you seen this particular Shakespeare play performed before?"

"No, I've only read it."

"Lillian is very well read," her mother said proudly.

Will loved books as well. Perhaps they could start there. "And who is your favorite author, then?"

"Oh, I don't have a favorite." A giggle. "Besides, I'd much rather hear *your* favorite author, Mr. Sloane."

His mood plummeted. Even without the giggle, a woman unable to voice an opinion would bore him to tears. Too many years with Lizzie, no doubt. His sister never shied from speaking her mind . . . and neither did Ava Jones. He stiffened. Why in God's name had she popped into his head?

He forced his attention back to the conversation. "I have many," he answered smoothly. "But I mostly read newspapers and business reports these days."

Lizzie patted his arm. "My brother is not a good deal of fun, I'm afraid. He works entirely too hard." Before he could open his mouth to protest, his sister asked, "What do you like to do for fun, Miss Cameron?"

The young woman blinked. "Fun? As in . . ."

"As in fun," Lizzie said amicably in what Will recognized as a desperate attempt to draw the girl out. "You know, hobbies. Do you have any hobbies or interests besides"—she swept her hand to indicate the opera house—"all this?"

Miss Cameron opened her mouth, but nothing came out. She glanced at her mother, helpless, and Mrs. Cameron said sharply, "My daughter is an accomplished musician. She speaks three languages and will make an excellent hostess one day. Not all women aspire to work in business, Mrs. Cavanaugh." The older woman's lips pursed together in clear disapproval over his sister's decision to open an investment firm.

Lizzie went rigid beside him, and Will acted swiftly, putting an end to the visit before the night took a disastrous turn. "And those are noble endeavors, indeed. I see the performance is about to start. Perhaps we should all be seated. Good evening, ladies."

As quickly as he could without seeming rude, he escorted his obviously angry sister to the corridor.

"How dare that woman," Lizzie hissed on the way to Will's box. "Did you hear her? Did you hear her insult me? The gall of her to—"

"Calm down, Lizzie. Do not waste your anger on such unworthy targets."

"You are not marrying her. I forbid it."

He gave a soft chuckle and nodded at a passing acquaintance in the corridor. "I recall saying something similar to you about your husband not too long ago."

"It's not funny, Will. She is perfectly wrong for you, and the mother is a monster."

"Don't worry. That giggle was enough to put me off marriage, let alone her mother's poor treatment of you." The giggle sounded akin to a goose choking on a handful of pebbles. He couldn't imagine hearing that noise every day for the rest of his life.

His sister relaxed somewhat. "Thank goodness. You need a woman who will challenge you—and shake you loose when you become too concerned with propriety and society's silly rules. Not to mention when you stay at your desk all hours of the night."

"You make me sound unbearable."

"Well . . ."

He tried not to be offended. "Keep it up and I shall not spoil my niece or nephew."

"As if I'd believe that," Lizzie scoffed. "You've already sent over enough gifts for six children. Speaking of that, Emmett said the giant rocking horse must go if it's a girl."

"That is ridiculous. He has met you, hasn't he? Hard to imagine any daughter of yours being afraid of anything."

Lizzie stopped abruptly, just outside the curtain to their box, and put her free hand to her mouth. Will glanced down, his brow drawn tight. Dear God, there were tears swimming in her eyes. "Are you . . . crying?"

"That is the nicest thing you've ever said to me." Rising on her toes, she pressed a kiss to his cheek. "You're a good brother."

Emotion swelled and stuck in his throat. She told him that often, and he considered himself lucky that she'd never discovered the truth about their parents. The shame and fear their mother had lived with. The coldness of the Sloane household before Father died. The countless lies spun by an older brother to reassure a small girl who'd lost both her parents.

Lizzie had grown up believing their parents had been in love, utterly devoted to each other, and Will never had any intention of letting her learn otherwise. He'd cut off his own arm before disabusing her of an idyllic childhood.

They entered the salon at the back of the Sloane box, Lizzie gliding in first, and Cavanaugh shot to his feet, his thunderous gaze bouncing from his wife's face over to Will. "What did you say to her?"

Lizzie wiped her eyes. "Calm down. He said something sweet, I swear—and you of all people should know how I cry at everything these days."

Cavanaugh relaxed and reached for her. With his free hand, he brushed a thumb over Lizzie's cheek, murmuring to her.

Will had no desire to witness the tender moment, so he continued to his seat inside the box. The performance had started, and he tried not to feel disappointed in the evening thus far. After all, there were three more girls on his list. He'd have a betrothal in place before the end of the summer.

The show was an unmitigated disaster.

Some Mondays, Ava had trouble connecting with her audience. They weren't as ready to believe in her talents, seemed more reluctant to participate than other crowds. Using her abundant charm, however, she always found her way, coaxing them into expressing shock and wonder during her performance.

Tonight's audience, however, could not be coaxed. They could not be charmed. She felt sweat beading on her forehead, her upper lip, as she struggled. Only unsmiling faces verging on scowls glared back at her, unwilling participants in the give-and-take she normally found so easy.

She refused to believe her failure had to do with the fact

that *he* was once again in attendance. Just as the show started, Will Sloane had taken a seat in the front row, arms crossed over his impeccably dressed chest, and commenced frowning at her.

God, she hated that man.

He made her . . . jumpy. Nervous. *Unsettled.* And she didn't understand why. She'd seen plenty of handsome men before—New York was practically dripping with them— so it couldn't be merely that. But there was something different about Will Sloane, something powerful that caused a reaction inside her. A spell he cast to turn her into a quivering mass of female foolishness.

Time for drastic measures.

She signaled behind her chair where the audience couldn't see. Matthew, the boy who worked the curtain, slid two heavy wires beneath the fabric at her back. Pretending to be in a trance, Ava flailed about in the near darkness. While moving her arms and legs, she slipped the looped ends of the wires under two opposite legs of the small table. When the dark wires were secure, she gave Matthew another hand motion.

The wires tightened, Matthew hoisting them up over the rigging, and the table began to lift, rocking back and forth over the stage. The crowd tittered, and she thought she might have them—until Matthew dropped the wires prematurely. One of the table legs landed on her toe, the pain causing tears to spring to her eyes, and she wanted to cut the show short right there.

In the end, her theatrics fizzled. Will Sloane's expression turned positively smug, as if he were feeding off her misery. Ava ended the show abruptly, barely waiting for the meager applause to die down before dashing behind the stage to her dressing room.

She ripped off her wig, shoved it in her bag, and threw

on her coat. Not even bothering to remove her heavy cosmetics, she hurried to the service door of the theater. This exit proved a longer walk home, but at least she wouldn't have William Sloane waiting for her out front. Pushing into the alley, she clutched her carpetbag tighter and strode toward the street.

A slow clapping erupted out of the darkness before she even took five steps. *Oh, dash it.* Sloane slid out from the gloom, applauding, his derby pulled low and an ebony cane tucked under an arm. A wide smile transformed his face into something breathtaking, and her dress felt too tight all of a sudden. Yet she struggled to remain stoic. She did not want him sensing her discomfort. God knew he'd gloat about that as well. *You're an actress, a performer. So perform, Ava.*

"Thank you, Mr. Sloane. Did you enjoy the show?"

"Oh, yes. Quite entertaining. I was trying to decide if they would throw the bruised tomatoes or rotten lettuce first."

She clenched her teeth. He was a plague. An impossible, spoiled man with too much free time. "Why are you here? You are worse than typhoid to get rid of." She started for the street. Eventually she could lose him in a crowd.

"I came to strike a bargain with you."

She dodged a few drunken men stumbling down Twenty-Sixth Street, waving away the stench of whiskey with her hand. Sometimes she loathed this city. "I am not interested in bargaining with you, not when I haven't done anything wrong."

"We keep dancing around this issue, and I'm losing patience, Ava."

Her head whipped over her shoulder. "I did not give you permission to use that name."

"I have no other name by which to call you, other than Madam Zolikoff. Remember?"

"Then I'll address you as Will, I suppose." He stiffened, disapproval etched on his handsome face, and she nearly grinned. So proper and condescending. Hearing his given name on her lips must grate against every bit of his fancy upbringing. "Because to refuse reveals you as a top-rate hypocrite."

"I'd rather you gave me your last name."

"No chance, Wiiiiiiill." She drew out his name for good measure, satisfied when he scowled.

He was impeccably dressed once again, his black wool coat fitted to his tall, poised frame. No frays or stains. No stitch marks from mending. His high-gloss cane had a polished silver handle. What was it like to come from so much privilege and wealth? To never have to worry about how you were going to feed or clothe yourself, let alone three siblings? That sort of security had never been within Ava's reach; she'd lived with the stress over their future every day since her parents died—and probably even before.

William Sloane, on the other hand, was the king of New York City. Or a grand prince, at least. He ran one of the biggest companies in the country. Hobnobbed with important politicians and society's elite. Wealthy and handsome, he undoubtedly had armies of employees and servants who rushed to accommodate him at every turn. Ava had seen his name in the papers no fewer than thirty-two times in the last week alone.

But she would not accommodate him. The endgame for her and her siblings was in sight. Because if she failed . . . A vision of Tom behind bars flickered in her mind and turned her blood to ice. She shivered.

"Cold?"

"No," she snapped. The concern in his voice annoyed her. If she dropped dead of an illness, his problems would be solved. So why fake the interest in her well-being?

She cut right to cross Twenty-Fifth Street, hurrying to beat an oncoming carriage. Sloane kept pace, taking her elbow to assist her across, his body placed between her and the impending traffic. The chivalrous gesture caused her chest to flutter, even as she knew the reaction to be ridiculous. Undoubtedly the behavior was executed by rote, not a purposeful courtesy to her. Another way the two of them were completely different.

"Are you planning to walk the length of the city with me? Because I wish you'd say whatever it is you want and disappear."

He made a sound. "If you would stop and listen to me, I wouldn't need to chase you everywhere." Now on the other side of the street, he took her elbow and pulled her over to the buildings. "I want you to hear me out."

He did not release her arm, and the two of them stood close, much closer than any etiquette book in his fancy library would have allowed for. She looked up at him, struck by their difference in height. He towered over her—most men did, after all—and Ava expected to hate it. Strangely, the opposite was true.

The smooth skin of his throat above his collar stretched up to a pronounced jawline. No hint of stubble there, no facial hair to hide behind. He was supreme confidence in a derby hat, all male swagger and keen intelligence. And while part of her was repelled by him, an inexplicable attraction simmered as well. A coil of heat unfurled in her belly, the urge to fold herself into his big frame vibrating under her skin.

"I would love to know what you are thinking right now,"

he said in a quiet, intimate tone she hadn't heard him use before.

"Laundry," she lied. "I'm thinking about the wash awaiting me tomorrow. I really do not have time to waste, so spit out whatever it is you need to say so that I may get home."

Chapter Four

While she was a practiced liar, Will did not believe her for a moment. Laundry would not be responsible for that spark in her honey brown eyes, a spark that strongly resembled prurient interest. Not that she'd leered at him, but there had definitely been heat. A flash. Something unexpected—and his body leapt to attention.

Do not glance at her lips or the fall and rise of her generous bosom. Too late. Damn it.

She still wore the lip paint from her performance—a bright red color visible from Brooklyn, no doubt—and the sight of the plump flesh so tantalizingly on display had his skin growing tight and itchy. The reaction bothered him, but he was only a man, for God's sake. Any woman's mouth this lush and tempting would arouse him. Wouldn't it? Pity the mouth was attached to a woman he couldn't tolerate.

She stepped back, jerking her arm out of his grasp. "Now you don't feel like talking? I don't have time for this, Will." She spun on her heel and hurried down the walk at a brisk and determined pace. *Hell.*

He forced his legs to move. When he caught up to her,

he blurted, "Bennett and I have a political rally in Albany next week. I want you to attend."

She stopped and gaped at him. "What? Why on earth would I go to your rally? Besides, I cannot travel to Albany next week. I have *responsibilities*," she said, drawing out the last word, as if he did not understand the meaning.

"I realize that, which is why I'm inviting you to next week's rally instead of this Saturday's event in Yonkers. I want you to see what your presence is risking. Bennett and I have an opportunity to do quite a lot of good for the people of New York. Once you see that, you'll better understand why I am so keen to keep you away from Bennett."

One thing he'd learned during his years in business: Arguing was sometimes not enough. Some opponents had to be shown they were wrong. Those who picketed Northeast in '83 with claims of unfair compensation for the rail workers? He'd personally escorted the leaders to a town in Pennsylvania and let them observe the better-than-average living conditions for Northeast employees. Or when reporters claimed the railroad companies were not paying for worker injuries out in West Virginia? Will had organized a trip to visit several families there who continued to receive Northeast benefits after being hurt on the job.

Often, people had to see it in order to believe it. Not Ava's clients, of course; they were happy to believe without any proof whatsoever. But Will didn't believe in blind faith. He believed in facts, and the sooner she understood what he and Bennett hoped to accomplish, that they planned to destroy Tammany's destructive grip on the state, she would be reasonable regarding her association with the future governor.

"God, your arrogance!" she said. "If you want to keep me away from him, then why invite me? Isn't that counter-productive?"

"You're going as Ava, not Madam Zolikoff. And you won't speak to Bennett. You're there merely to observe."

Her eyes narrowed, her brain undoubtedly planning to fight him every step of the way. But he was prepared to fight unfairly, as unfairly as necessary to prove his point.

"I have no desire to see any political rally in Albany, no matter who is speaking."

"That may be true," he said, "but I think you should consider coming—especially when you hear what might happen if you *don't*." He jabbed his polished ebony cane into the walk for emphasis.

She pressed her lips together, probably to hold back from shouting at him. "You're threatening me."

"I once told you that a man in my position can make things uncomfortable for a woman in your line of work. Have you heard of the Society for Mediumship Research?"

Even in the dim gaslight of Twenty-Third Street, he could see her face pale. "No."

"A group out of England. Studies the validity of psychic phenomenon. A strange thing happens to every medium they investigate. Would you care to guess what?"

She shook her head, obviously bright enough to follow the implication. Will continued, just to be certain. "Each medium this organization looks into is exposed as a fraud. Run out of town. Forced to move and start over somewhere else." He paused to let it sink in. "Is that what you want, Ava? Because I can send them a telegram and book their passage. They can be here before the summer season starts in Newport."

"You are a bastard, Will Sloane."

"True. Now, are you still going to turn me down for the rally?"

She shifted to face the street. If he needed to play an unpopular card to win the hand against an opponent, he could do so without blinking. He hadn't built Northeast Railroad into one of the most powerful companies in the country by coddling anyone. *Better to collect enemies than friends.*

He let the silence drag. Ava was stubborn but not stupid. Certainly she could see that refusing his simple request— traveling to Albany, not the ends of the earth—would be detrimental to her livelihood. Unless she didn't believe he'd actually do it . . . which would be a colossal mistake on her part.

She appeared tired tonight, with her brown hair a bit mussed and dark circles forming under her eyes. The show had not gone off well, and he did feel a pang of guilt for further complicating her day. Still, he would not let her ruin any political career of his before it started.

She dragged in a breath and locked gazes with him. Anger sparked bright in the brown depths, her cheeks flushed, and a feeling of foreboding settled into his stomach.

"Go to hell, Will."

Damn it. Disappointment caused him to snap, "You'll regret this."

"No, I won't. Regret is letting some man I hardly know dictate how I live my life. Do your worst, railroad man." Spinning, she stepped toward the street. Her arm went up to wave at a passing hack, and the driver jerked the horses to a halt. Before Will could assist her up, she disappeared inside and rolled off into the night.

Ava let the driver take her three blocks, then she asked him to stop. She didn't want to waste the fare home but

had needed to get away from Will Sloane. After passing the
driver a few of her hard-earned coins, Ava jumped to the
sidewalk and kept walking south.

Dratted arrogant man.

Just when she thought he couldn't make her any angrier.
Let him bring whatever group he wanted to investigate her.
What she was doing wasn't a crime. They had to prove she
was knowingly swindling people, which was nearly impossible to do. Mediums never claimed their powers infallible—
there had to be room for error. Therefore, no group, British
or American, would be able to throw her in jail or run her
out of town. She might need to find other work, but Ava
had performed many jobs over the years. Finding one more
would not be a hardship.

*And you'd earn a fraction of what Madam Zolikoff
gains you.*

True. Before she'd transformed into one of New York's
most popular mediums, she had clerked in an office for
two dollars a week. Before that, a hatcheck girl in a restaurant. She'd swept floors, washed laundry, served food . . .
anything to keep her siblings fed and safe. But Madam
Zolikoff had been a stroke of genius.

The idea came from a friend who had seen a medium
perform. She gave Ava all the details on the experience.
Ava had then researched psychic abilities and even went to
see a few performances. The act had seemed easy, especially when one considered the money involved.

People paid handsomely for entertainment in New York.
In one night as Madam Zolikoff, Ava earned more than
three times what she'd taken home in a month from her
last job. Not to mention better hours and more freedom . . .
and no handsome young men, determined to take advantage
of her.

Ava's chest compressed with regret and shame over the
memory. Were all sixteen-year-old girls so foolish, then?

Stephen van Dunn had been the boss's son, not to mention wealthy and a feast for the eyes. A charmer, he was forever complimenting Ava's work, hair, or clothing. Stephen's father, Richard, hadn't been around often, leaving managerial duties to his son, and Stephen began asking Ava to work late. That had quickly led to more intimate moments, which became—what she believed to be—a real relationship.

The worst part was that she had *liked him*, had dreamed of the two of them together. Moreover, he'd led her to believe there would be a future for them. *I love you, Ava. You're unlike any woman I've ever known.*

Stephen had frequently mentioned the idea of marriage—right up until the moment she became pregnant. It was then Ava learned the hardest lesson of all: No matter what someone told you, you were on your own in this world.

A weary sigh escaped her lips. No time for those old hurts. She had new hurts to worry about, like the way her feet were aching by the time she arrived home. On top of it all, the evening promised to be an unpleasant one. Dinner would be simple fare tonight—a poached egg and roasted turnips—which would not please her siblings. Unfortunately, Ava hadn't bought anything else so they had little choice in the matter.

A delicious smell filled the building as she climbed the steps. Someone had cooked a wonderful meal. Roasted meat, if she wasn't mistaken. Her stomach growled loudly. One day, that would be her family. Roasted chicken, pork, mutton . . . whatever they could raise on the farm.

The scent grew stronger, causing her mouth to water, and when she put the key in her door she could've sworn the tantalizing odor was from her own lodgings. Must be her imagination.

She entered and stopped short. The hunger in her stomach knotted into confusion. Her three siblings were gathered around the kitchen table, a half-eaten roasted pheasant sitting proudly on the scarred wooden tabletop.

"Ava," Sam said through a mouth full of food. "Look what Tom brought home."

She dropped her carpetbag to the floor with a thud. Her gaze snapped to her oldest sibling, whose expression held a mixture of defiance and pride. *Oh, no. Tell me he didn't.* Disappointment and anger closed her throat.

"Come and sit," Mary said, stabbing more meat on her plate. "It's heavenly."

Eating was the very last thing on her mind. "Tom, I'd like to speak with you in the bedroom."

"Not now. Pheasant's still warm." Tom shoved a large bite past his lips, chewing through a smug smile that had Ava gritting her teeth.

"Yes, now. The pheasant can wait."

They stared at each other, neither speaking, but Ava was determined. She would not back down, would not condone this, and Tom knew her well enough to realize when he was beat. He wiped his hands on a napkin, placed the cloth on the table, and stood. Heels tapping on the wood floor, Ava hurried to the bedroom.

Tom came in behind her and shut the door. He lifted his hands. "Before you start—"

"How did you get the money?"

"Ava, hear me out before you—"

"*Where did you get the money?*"

"Working." He crossed his arms over his bony chest.

"Not at the factory. So what type of employment allowed you to make enough money for that?" She gestured in the direction of the dining area.

"I helped the boys with some of their evening duties."

"Boys meaning b'hoys—the ones in a gang that steal. Did you pick pockets, Tom?" He raised his chin and didn't answer. "Don't lie to me," she told him. "That's the one thing we promised each other when Mama and Papa died. No lying."

A muscle in his jaw clenched. "Yes, stealing. They let me keep what I found, once I learned the trick of it. And you would not believe how much money I found."

"You didn't *find* it," she snarled. "You *stole* it. Don't you see the difference? And that's what these gangs do—they let you keep what you steal at first so it seems impossibly lucrative. Once you join, however, you'll be forced to turn over a percentage of your take to someone else. You're naïve if you believe differently."

"I am not naïve, and I don't mind turning over a percentage. Do you know how much money I had today? I took in over—"

"I don't want to know," she bit out. "And instead of saving that money for a better future for all of us, you went out and bought the most expensive meat you could find."

"Oh, so I shouldn't be stealing, but if I do I should save the money for the family to move to some mythical farm upstate. Which is it, Ava?"

"I don't want you stealing. You'll get arrested, not to mention it's wrong."

"Yeah? Well, what you do ain't exactly on the up and up. I don't see why it's fine for you to swindle people and I can't pick a pocket once in a while. There's no difference, least not to my eye."

"It won't be once in a while after this gang gets you in deeper. It will be a full-time job, Tom. And I don't swindle people."

Their eyes held, a battle of wills Ava sensed slipping out of her control. When had her brother turned so stubborn?

His lips twisted in a cynical, disbelieving smile. "My pheasant is growing cold." He turned and jerked open the door. Nausea churning in her stomach, Ava watched him sit back down and attack the pheasant.

She had to get them all the hell out of here—and soon.

A knock on his office door sounded a second before it opened, and Will glanced up from the contract he was reviewing. John Bennett and his political advisor, Charles Tompkins, walked in, while Will's assistant, Frank, stood just beyond the threshold. Will rose and waved them all in. "Come in, I'm ready."

The two candidates, along with Tompkins, met in Will's office every Wednesday morning. Here, they plotted their campaign to take over Albany. After handshakes were traded all around, they sat down.

Bennett had been elected as a U.S. senator in '81, where he served until '86. Tompkins had been with the former senator a long time, the two of them friends from Yale, and Tompkins had assumed the role of political advisor somewhere along the way. Probably as a way to earn a convenient dollar. Will and Tompkins didn't always agree, but Will was the supporting actor in the troupe so he'd learned to defer when necessary. He knew Bennett and Tompkins only wanted him on the ticket for the prestige of the Sloane name, which Will didn't mind because he had far grander plans. This was merely a stepping-stone.

Nevertheless, he didn't care for Tompkins. Despite Will's repeated protests, Tompkins had done nothing about Madam Zolikoff's presence in Bennett's life. Tompkins held fast to the belief that no disastrous consequences would result from the medium's association with Bennett. Will wholeheartedly disagreed. The other political parties would look for any weakness, any aberration at all, to use as fodder for a smear campaign in the final weeks before the election.

"We have a location for the convention," Tompkins started, and Frank began taking notes in a small book. "It'll be the Saratoga skating rink. So I was thinking we'd hold our own rally there in late July. Get a jump on the crowd. Won't be a problem for you, will it, Sloane?"

They were assuming he'd spend the summer in Newport, as he did every year. However, he'd done that to humor Lizzie, so she would have a summer similar to those of other girls in her circle. But she was Cavanaugh's now, and Will saw no reason to open the cottage just for himself. "No. I'll remain in the city."

"Good," Bennett said, smiling widely as if he'd expected Will to refuse. "Tompkins will get it all set up, and we'll let you know the date."

"That's fine. What do we know about the other conventions?"

"Prohibition is meeting June twenty-sixth in Syracuse, as expected. Dems are gathering in Buffalo on September twelfth, but we don't know where. No doubt Robert Murphy will receive the nomination, with the might of Tammany Hall behind him. Labor will also be in September, but I'm not worried about them."

"I'm not sure you're correct about Murphy," Will said. "He's not as popular, considering he spoke out against the reform bill." The Republicans had tried to pass a bill to stop the rampant election fraud in New York State, and anyone connected with Tammany Hall, the powerful political machine, had vehemently opposed it. What did that say about how politics worked in the Empire State?

"Doubtful," Tompkins responded. "Members of Tammany forced that veto because it would have hurt their own practices, paying the Irish to vote Democrat. Anyway, we can't focus on Murphy yet. We've got to secure the nomination first."

Will wasn't worried about that. Bennett had a gift with crowds, and Will was the well-known businessman bringing cheap, efficient transportation to the masses. Everywhere he went in the state, people shook his hand and thanked him for providing a way for them to visit Aunt Martha or dear, dying Cousin Sally. Railroads had changed the way Americans lived, and Will had played an integral part of that transformation. If this continued, securing the nomination would not be a problem.

The real hurdle was overcoming Robert Murphy and Tammany Hall, considering the iron grip the organization maintained over New York politics. Because to enact any real change for the people of this state, to bring a better way of life to the masses, the corruption and exploitation had to stop.

"Any updates on the Albany rally?" Will asked.

"Should be as we discussed. The Bennett Band will be on hand," he said, referring to the campaign club name the local Republicans had given themselves. "You'll have the parade, followed by a barbecue, then speeches and handshakes."

"That's fine. I'll travel up early that morning."

From there, they talked more political matters, from speculation on opponents to tentative dates for additional rallies. Topics to hit hard in the speeches. Bennett remained quiet, letting Tompkins do most of the talking, as usual. When the conversation drew to its natural conclusion, Tompkins said, "Bennett, will you give Sloane and me a moment alone?"

This was not an altogether unusual request, so Bennett nodded, shook Will's hand, and left. Will tipped his chin at Frank, who quickly collected his things and retreated. When the two men were alone, Tompkins leaned back in his chair. "I heard you arrived at Bennett's home while the medium was there."

"Yes, I did, and you know why."

Tompkins sighed, his heavy mustache quivering. "We've discussed this. She keeps him . . ." He seemed to search for the right word. "Grounded. Bennett is a great speaker and an even better politician. People like him. Before he found Madam Zolikoff, though, he was as skittish as a three-day colt. Convinced everyone was out to get him. Didn't trust anyone or anything. Yet in the year since he found her, he's focused and determined. Do you hear what I am saying?"

"Yes, I do. But I know how these people operate. She is either mining him for secrets she'll use for blackmail, or she works for the opposition and will publicly embarrass him. Either way, all three of us lose."

"You've said as much before, Sloane, and I do not agree. The girl is harmless."

Harmless? Ava was anything but harmless. Will thought of a husky voice that could drive a man mad with lust. A generous bosom that begged for a man's hands and mouth. And lips . . . those goddamn fantasy-inducing lips. The woman was man's destruction wrapped in a petticoat.

He cleared his throat. "My reputation will suffer every bit as much as Bennett's—if not more so—when this woman decides to use him for profit. Therefore, if you will not do anything about it, I will. I plan to convince the girl to back off. Let him find another medium after the election is over."

"He doesn't want another medium. Took him forever to find one he liked. I'm telling you to leave it alone. You'll only make things worse."

Will clenched his fist on the desk. He did not take orders from anyone, least of all this man. It was one thing to follow directions for the campaign, but Will would be damned if Tompkins had sway in any other area of his life.

"I am perfectly aware of why you want me in this race," Will said, leaning forward. "My name lends a certain weight to the ticket, and you're counting on my connections to help secure the governorship—but my name means *nothing* if I become a public laughingstock. Which is precisely what will happen when that swindler gets Bennett to say something he shouldn't."

"You're right. I do want your name on the ticket, but don't forget that Bennett has top billing. He's valuable to me, so let me worry about the people in his life. All you need to do is show up and look handsome."

Will's lip started to curl, and he forced it back in place. Tompkins treated Will as if he were a man about town, a swell incapable of holding a serious thought in his head. The damned idiot. Will had been at the helm of a large company since he was sixteen. Earned a degree from Columbia University while building the Northeast Railroad empire and fighting his way out from underneath his father's shadow. He'd proven himself a formidable leader, just as he would in this case. No more reading the speeches Tompkins prepared for him and following blindly. Will would control his own campaigning from now on.

He rose and slipped his hands in his pockets. "You handle the campaign, Tompkins. Let me worry about my name and those determined to ruin it."

Chapter Five

The carriage pulled up in front of Twelve Washington Square, a large mansion at the corner of Fifth Avenue and Washington Square North. Five stories of red brick and white marble, the eminent structure boasted a columned portico in front and a sturdy black iron fence around the perimeter. It spoke of elegance and social status, a world apart from Ava's existence.

Even in the lamplight, the façade appeared every bit as cold and proper as its owner. "Here you go, miss," the driver called. She quickly pulled coins out of the purse clipped to her waistband and opened the door. "Thank you." After she handed over the fare, she hurried up the walk.

The front door opened before she touched the knocker. A proper butler—wearing a uniform that probably cost more than her yearly rent—regarded her with obvious disapproval. "Good evening, miss. While I am certain you are collecting for a worthy cause, we ask that you pay your call during daylight hours."

"I am not collecting for a cause. I am here to see Mr. Sloane."

The butler's expression turned even more forbidding. "And who shall I say is calling?"

Most social callers would present a card, but Ava was fresh out. As in had never had any printed. "Please tell him Ava is here."

"I shall see if Mr. Sloane is receiving." The door closed firmly in her face and she suffered the indignity of being left on the stoop, though everything in her wanted to flee.

Fleeing was not an option, however. Ava had nowhere else to turn, not if she wanted to help her brother. Tom had been arrested earlier today.

Despite her warnings, all she'd made him promise, her brother had been taken in for picking pockets near Union Market. He was currently sitting in the Thirteenth Precinct, along with two of his gang members, so-called friends who had made an already bad situation worse. The other two boys were well-known thieves, so the police didn't believe Ava that Tom was not a part of this gang. She'd begged and pleaded, but they had refused her request to release her brother. Gangs of thieves were not tolerated, especially not ones with several previous run-ins with the roundsmen.

"These boys are a blight on our city," the sergeant had said. "I'm sorry, miss, but these gangs need to learn their lesson. And sending 'em to the Tombs for a few months oughta do that."

Her stomach roiled anew. Dear God, the Tombs. It was New York City's worst, roughest prison. If Tom went inside, no telling when—or if—he'd be released. She needed to get her brother cleared before he was sentenced.

Which meant someone with enough political and social influence must force the police to listen to reason, to make them understand that Tom was a young, misguided fifteen-year-old—not a hardened criminal. That he hadn't meant to steal. That all of this was really her fault for not getting her family out of the city years ago.

Only two men of her acquaintance possessed the clout

for such an endeavor—and John Bennett had already left for Yonkers.

She swallowed hard, knowing Sloane would never agree to help her, not out of the goodness of his heart. No doubt Ava would need to give him something in exchange, such as the promise to stay away from John Bennett. She hated to be in this position, but she had no choice. She'd gladly give up taking John's money in order to get her brother out of prison.

After all, keeping her from Bennett was what Will had wanted from the start. So if he helped her, she'd agree to anything he asked—and afterward he'd never see or hear from her again.

The heavy wood slid open again. The butler stared down at her, disapproval etched on his haughty face. "You may come in. Mr. Sloane will see you in his office."

Relief propelled her forward, and she nearly tumbled into the entryway. The butler offered to take her coat. Once she shrugged out of it, he led her through one of the most elegant, gorgeous homes she'd ever seen. Black marble, parquet floors, crown molding. Dark, large furniture lined the walls—pristine walls free of marks and handprints. No doubt the staff worked all day to keep the space clean. This was where Will had grown up? An upbringing of this type seemed inconceivable to her.

Deeper into the house, then the butler knocked on a paneled oak door. A clipped voice rang out from the other side, "Enter."

The butler held open the panel and gestured for Ava to step in, so she squared her shoulders and marched forward. She found Will Sloane pacing behind an enormous desk, barking orders. Two men sat in chairs on the other side, both furiously scribbling notes.

Ava waited while Will gave them directives on contract terms, grain prices, transport costs, and a parcel of property in San Francisco he wanted to buy. During this time, she glanced around his study, trying to calm her racing heart. A masculine space, with worn furniture and stacks of papers, the room seemed well used. Rows of books lined the walls while a cheerful fire burned in the grate, the orange light bouncing off the gold accents like topaz. She liked this room far better than anything else she'd seen tonight.

"That's all," Will finally said. "Finish up for the day. After that, go home, and I'll see you both in the morning."

The two men stood and hurried out, but not before casting furtive, curious glances at Ava on the way. She hardly noticed. Intent gray eyes now pierced her and energy crackled in the room. A jolt coursed through her, a heady buzz in her blood that stretched to every part of her body. She recognized that feeling—*attraction*—and instantly resented it. To experience animal lust for a man so far out of her reach was laughable.

Not that she could want such a repressed and arrogant man. She needed to remember as much and put an end to the way her insides reacted to him. If only he were not so damned handsome.

"Ava. This is quite a surprise."

There was no time to lose. "I need your help. My brother is being held at the police precinct, and I need someone with influence to get him out."

One arrogant brow rose as he leaned against his desk. He crossed his arms, the fine wool of his evening coat pulling to show off wide, strong shoulders. "Your brother . . . At the police precinct. What's he been arrested for?"

"Picking pockets," she forced out, her face hot with humiliation.

She expected him to laugh or use the opportunity to draw parallels between the arrest and her own profession, but he surprised her. He strode to the hallway door, opened it, and called for the butler. "Frederic, have my brougham brought around, will you? I have an errand this evening."

Ava nearly sagged to the floor in relief. He was going to help her, thank God.

"This is certainly an interesting turn of events," he said, his attention on her. "Not only will I learn your last name, but I'm to meet your brother as well."

Both of those things were true, unfortunately. "Not by choice. If John hadn't already left for Yonkers, I would have asked him for assistance."

"And how would that have worked? John would have realized your brother is not Russian. Sort of throws the Madam Zolikoff routine in a new light, doesn't it, getting a sibling out of the stir." He grinned, showing a mouth full of teeth.

"I would have figured something out."

"I have no doubt," he said, though his voice suggested otherwise. He rubbed his hands together almost gleefully. "Well, then. My good fortune for remaining in town instead. Let's fetch your coat." He yanked open the door. "You can tell me about this situation in the carriage."

Will assisted Ava into his carriage and followed inside. He could scarcely believe his luck. The mystery of Madam Zolikoff was about to be unraveled, all because her brother had been arrested for picking pockets. What the hell sort of family was this? Were they all engaged in various criminal activities?

Her beautiful face had been shockingly pale when she'd arrived, a small bonnet hanging on for dear life on her head. No doubt the situation distressed her . . . and he found that he *liked* being her knight in shining armor. Stupid, considering their circumstances and how much the woman hated him.

But an unguarded honesty shone in her expression tonight, a naked vulnerability he'd never seen before that tugged at a place deep within him. She'd come to him for help, and Will would be damned if he could tell her no.

Besides, he was used to being needed. He'd raised his sister from the age of eight, including seeing her through the death of their father, the transition into a young lady, her debut . . . But she was now married and expecting her first child. Lizzie had a husband—a coarse, unrefined brute in Will's opinion—whom she miraculously seemed to love, and Will wasn't the most important man in her life any longer. That had taken some getting used to, even though logically he'd known it would happen one day.

So he didn't mind coming to Ava's rescue, especially when it meant she would be in his debt.

"Let's start with the precinct your brother is in."

"The thirteenth."

Good. He knew the captain there, Hogan. Ringing the commissioner would not be necessary. Will gave the direction to the driver and sat back against the plush seat. His shoulder touched Ava's, yet he made no move to pull away. "Now, tell me his name."

"Thomas Jones."

Ava Jones. Excellent. "And he's a pickpocket."

"No," she said, her voice suddenly loud, as if increasing the volume made her statement more credible. "He is not. He works in a cigar factory on Rivington. He's worked there for four years, even though he hates it. He's . . ."

She bit her lip, a gesture Will felt deep in his gut. Predictably, blood pooled in his groin, his body reacting on pure instinct. He'd never met a woman who affected him in such a visceral, earthy way. The urge to taste her, to learn her, had been driving him insane for days. He'd slept with beautiful women of every shape and size, women more stunning than the one sitting next to him, so what was it about Ava Jones that made him want to learn all her secrets? Lose himself inside her?

Whatever the attraction, he needed to ignore it. He could not bed this woman, no matter the stunning bosom she possessed.

"Yes?" he prompted since she remained silent.

"He found a group of boys and wanted to join up with them. I told him absolutely not. But the other night, he came home with a roasted pheasant, one bigger than we'd certainly ever been able to afford before. I was angry. I tried to make him see reason, that stealing is wrong, but he wouldn't listen." Her head swiveled toward him. "And if you say one word about my profession I'll push you under the carriage wheels."

Will held up his hands in surrender. He could sympathize with siblings who wouldn't listen. He'd repeatedly told Lizzie she could not open a brokerage firm, yet she'd gone ahead and done it anyway—thanks to her husband's financial backing. "How many other siblings do you have?"

She sighed, and he knew she hated telling him so much about herself. "Two. A younger brother and a younger sister."

"And do they work?"

"My sister is a finisher in a garment factory. My youngest brother is a newsie."

"Parents?"

"Dead."

So she was responsible for the other three, which is why she'd adopted the Madam Zolikoff persona. No doubt she earned more money off fools like Bennett than all her siblings combined. He almost admired her for it.

"And these friends your brother has been associating with . . . Allow me to guess, the police are quite familiar with them."

"Yes, it appears that's true. When I went to retrieve him,

they told me the other two boys have had several run-ins with the police. They wouldn't believe me that Tom is not a full-time criminal like the rest."

Stood to reason. Street thieves had friends for one purpose only: to help them steal.

"The sergeant said they'd end up in the Tombs." Her voice broke in the middle, and her vulnerability burrowed deep under his skin, gnawing at him. The crack in her confident, brash façade elicited protective feelings in him, feelings bordering on tenderness. Good God, what was happening to him?

He cleared his throat. "Only a judge can decide as much, Ava, and I'll get him out before it comes to that. You'll probably pay a fine, but he'll walk out tonight."

"I am very grateful for whatever you can do."

How grateful? he wanted to ask, but to hint of something lurid in exchange for tonight's help would make him the biggest cad in New York. Still, he did want *something* from her. She wouldn't like it, but that was too damn bad.

The carriage turned down Houston Street. The station sat just up the block, at the corner of Sheriff and Houston. "I want you to wait here," he told her. "I'll go inside and get Tom's situation sorted."

"Shouldn't I come along? I am his sister, after all."

"No. You'll only make it worse. He's undoubtedly feeling guilty, and he won't want you yelling at him in front of the officers or other prisoners. More important, the captain is an acquaintance of mine. It'll be easier to get Tom out if he and I can speak privately."

"Fine." She clasped her hands in her lap with a small huff. "I'll wait here, like the useless woman I am."

"You are not useless. Indeed, your brother will need you. Just don't go too hard on the boy. Being the man of the family at such a young age is not easy." *I should know,* he wanted to say. *I couldn't breathe for the first three years for fear of failure, of losing everything my family had built over four generations. Of proving my father right.*

The carriage stopped and Will threw open the door. "Before I go in, I want to ensure you'll agree to my terms for performing this favor."

Predictably, her eyes narrowed. "And what would those terms be?"

"Are you in a place where you can negotiate?"

Her face hardened, muscles growing taut, but she did not argue. "Quit being so dramatic and just tell me what you want, Sloane."

"You'll find out soon enough, Madam Zolikoff."

Dirty and dark, the police station was unpleasant no matter the side of the bars on which you resided. Even the captain's office, one of the few private areas in the precinct, held an aura of desolation and desperation, a hopelessness that had seeped into the cracked plaster walls.

It took Will twenty minutes to convince the captain to release the lad. Hogan hadn't been keen on letting Jones go—the police had intended to make an example out of all three pickpockets—but finally relented at Will's insistence.

Very few refused Will Sloane, especially when one message from him could cost the captain his position. Moreover, Will had promised that, from now on, the boy would stay out of trouble. That seemed an easy promise, considering Ava would likely keep her brother on a short string beginning tonight.

Hogan departed to retrieve the lad, leaving Will to wait. No sense in sending for Ava yet. He wanted to speak with the boy privately first.

Finally the door opened. Hogan entered, dragging in a young man behind him. Thomas Jones didn't have much substance to him. Thinner than he ought to be, the boy

possessed the gangly limbs of a soon-to-be man who
hadn't yet filled out. His clothes were too small and frayed
at the ankles and cuffs. He bore a strong resemblance to
Ava, with brown eyes and hair as well as that damned
stubborn chin.

"I'd like a moment with Mr. Jones," Will said to the
captain. "Alone, if you don't mind."

"Of course, Mr. Sloane." Hogan left the office, closing
the door behind him.

Ava's brother shifted nervously on his feet, yet set his
jaw and faced Will squarely. Will was impressed; the boy
had spine. "Who are you?" Tom asked warily.

"My name is Mr. Sloane, and I am a friend to your elder
sister." The boy's eyes rounded on that. "Shall we sit?" Will
gestured to a pair of chairs by the desk.

Tom moved to a chair, sitting cautiously. "What's one of
Ava's fancy swells want with me?"

Will settled into the uncomfortable wooden chair. "I
want to talk to you."

"What for? I already told them leatherheads that I—"

"I don't care what excuses you gave the police. I want
the truth. What happened?"

"And just why should I tell you anything?"

Will could understand the boy's suspicion, but this de-
fensiveness bordered on stupidity. "Because I'm the one
who saved you from serving three months in the Tombs.
And if you don't tell me, I shall call Captain Hogan back
in and inform him that I made a mistake."

Tom's face paled, and, as Will suspected, the threat got
him talking. "The other boys, they're just friends. We were
having fun, gettin' a bit of swag. I never thought . . ."

"You never thought you'd get caught," Will finished
when he trailed off. "So were you the stall or the whisk?"

Tom's jaw fell open. "How do you . . . ?"

"Yes, I know how the racket works, Tom. One boy

stalls the mark while the other swipes the goods. So which were you?"

"Neither." He crossed his arms and glanced down. "I was the lookout. Supposed to be watching for the flatty. They said I wasn't ready to do more'n that."

And that had upset him, obviously. Tom was quite eager to join the criminal ranks. "Your sister tells me you work in a cigar factory." The young man didn't answer, and Will immediately knew why. "You quit, didn't you?"

"Don't tell Ava." He sat forward, his eyes pleading with Will. "She'll tear my head off."

"Rightly so, in my opinion. Why are you determined to turn to a life of petty thievery?" The boy opened his mouth to speak, then shut it. Will prompted, "You can tell me, Tom. Whatever you say will be kept in confidence."

"Even from Ava?"

"Even from Ava."

The boy sighed heavily. "Ava's been takin' care of us three—my brother, my sister, and me—for a long time. She works hard. Even moved us out of the tenements and into a decent apartment house on the West Side." He focused on the armrest, digging a groove in the old wood with his fingernail. "I've been working in the cigar factory since I was twelve. Before that, another meaningless job that paid for shit. The four of us, we're barely scraping by. I don't want to barely scrape by no more. I'm tired of being hungry, of sharin' my bathwater. Of cutting my younger sister's food because her hands are sore from sewing all day."

Will had never known poverty such as the boy described, but he'd certainly seen countless grim examples of the struggles some faced in this city. Yet there were opportunities, too. "You don't need to steal and risk arrest to better your circumstances."

Tom snorted and shook his head. "Ain't many other

ways to do it, far as I can see. I'm nearly sixteen. I need to start providing for the family. Besides, it works for Ava."

"What works for Ava?"

"Stealing."

Something tightened in Will's chest, an emotion he was not ready to examine—because he suspected it might be guilt. Hadn't he accused her of that very thing? He heard himself say, "Your sister does not steal. She's a performer."

"A performer? She's no actress."

"You're wrong. She plays a part as Madam Zolikoff, one that people enjoy. She's not robbing anyone or holding a pistol to their heads. They give her money of their own free will."

The bizarre fact that he was defending her was not lost on Will. Yet even though he knew her to be a swindler, there was no reason for her brother to think the same. The family had enough problems.

"I guess that's true," Tom said. "But it ain't all on the up and up, either."

Will couldn't hold back a smile. The boy was bright. "True."

Tom was nearly the same age Will had been when his father died. The Sloanes came from more than a century of wealth and privilege—but what if circumstances had been different? What if Will had been struggling to provide for Lizzie, working jobs that paid pennies and living with two or three other families in a single-room apartment? He might have done exactly what Tom had. What young boy wouldn't at least consider it?

Will arrived at a decision. "I'd like to give you a job."

Tom narrowed his eyes, a reaction far from the relief or jubilation Will half expected. "A job? Me? Doin' what, exactly?"

"Have you heard of Northeast Railroads?"

"Sure. What does that have to do with me?"

"I own Northeast. We have large offices on Vesey Street, not far from City Hall. I can always use another intelligent, hardworking young man in the office."

"What's it pay?"

Will had to swallow a bark of laughter. He liked this boy. "I'll give you ten dollars a week."

That had the desired result. Tom's jaw went slack as he blinked at Will. Then he collected himself, shaking his head. "I don't have any fancy office clothes. I—"

"You allow me to worry on that," Will assured him. "All you need to do is show up at my office on Monday morning. Deal?"

Tom offered a grubby hand. "Deal."

They shook and then Will rose. "Now, let me give you a little advice. Your sister is upset—and justifiably so. All you should do is apologize and not argue with her. Because even if you attempt to explain yourself, you won't win."

Tom came to his feet, smiling broadly. "Yep, you are definitely a friend of Ava's."

Will clapped him on the shoulder. "Yes, which is how I know your ears are going to be ringing all night. Come, let's get it over with."

Chapter Six

Ava tapped her foot, resisting the urge to dash across the street and burst into the police precinct. What was taking so long? According to the watch pinned to her dress, she'd been waiting for nearly thirty minutes.

She never should have involved Will Sloane. God only knew what was happening in there. Why had she listened to him when he told her to remain in the carriage?

Ava was not used to having others tell her what to do, let alone obeying said order. Yet Will Sloane said to stay, and Ava had jumped like a dog to do his bidding. What was wrong with her?

Just as she turned the handle to escape the brougham, the precinct doors opened. Will emerged—and there was Tom. She sagged into the seat. *Thank heavens*. Annoyance quickly replaced the relief, however. Her brother wore a mysterious smile, which struck her as odd considering the boy had been in jail. Did he have no notion of the dangers he would have faced in the Tombs? He should be weeping with gratitude and remorse right now.

She clenched her jaw as the two approached. Will pointed atop the box and said something to Tom. Her brother nodded and, after a brief wave at her, climbed up next to the Sloane driver. Will opened the door and slid inside.

His large frame overwhelmed the small interior of the carriage, his presence seeming to suck up all the abundant air. They were pressed together, shoulder to knee, and she tried very hard to ignore the tingling, rushing sensation sliding over her skin.

He rapped on the carriage wall with the silver knob of his cane. The wheels started moving and silence descended, with Sloane concentrating on the scene beyond the window. His avoidance annoyed her. "Well?"

His head slowly swiveled, one brow lifting. "Yes?"

She wanted to smack his arm. "What happened in there?"

"I retrieved your brother," he said calmly. "As you asked."

"And?"

He shifted toward her, his gray eyes shining. Strong jaw and sensual mouth, he was a striking man. Even when she was annoyed with him, which was often, she could not help but notice him. "What would you like to know, Ava? Merely ask it already."

Why was my brother smiling? What did the two of you talk about? Was he mistreated in there? Why do I want to both kiss and strangle you at the same time?

The questions raced through her mind, the last one in particular causing her to jerk slightly. Where had that come from? She didn't want to kiss Will Sloane. Everything about him was too controlled, too proper. He'd probably never experienced true passion of any kind. She couldn't picture his hair mussed from a woman's fingers, or his clothes rumpled from a partner's impatience.

Dirty and *sweaty* were two words she'd never associate with Will Sloane, even in the bedroom.

"Why are you staring at my mouth?"

He'd whispered the question in a deep rasp that suggested he knew the answer. Embarrassed, Ava tore her gaze away—only to discover him watching her own mouth with the rapt attention of a predator waiting to pounce. Her heart pounded furiously under her corset, the steady beat far too loud in her ears. Unconsciously she licked her lips to moisten them. "Why are you staring at *my* mouth?"

"Because it's the most fascinating thing I've ever seen."

She focused on breathing, desperate to ignore whatever regrettable feelings she'd developed for this man. No good could come of the sudden fullness of her breasts or the rhythmic pulse between her thighs. But there was no escape from it, no respite from the charge building between them. Even if she dashed from the carriage, this thing, this dratted attraction, would follow her.

"I know what I would like in exchange for helping your brother tonight."

She blinked and tried to regain her equilibrium. *Focus, Ava.* "To attend your rally in Albany."

"No, you were going to do that regardless. I've decided I want something else."

The arrogance astounded her. She'd never agreed to travel to Albany and had no intention of going. Better to leave that conversation for another time. As in never. "What, then?"

"I want you to kiss me."

Her breath caught. A rush of longing filled her, spreading through her veins like whiskey and causing her head to spin. It had been forever since she'd felt this way about another person, a blinding desire to pleasure and be pleasured in return. For some insane reason, she was attracted to Will Sloane and part of her longed to act on it.

Yet kissing him would only complicate matters. He already acted as if he had the right to order her around; physical intimacies would only worsen that tendency. No one owned Ava Jones. "Absolutely not."

He cocked his head. "Why? I know you're feeling what I'm feeling. It's too strong to be one-sided, Ava."

Confirmation he was equally attracted to her did not help her resolve. Instead, her belly warmed, the heat moving lower, until she shifted in her seat. *Remember the last time you lost your head over a kiss? Remember the last time you allowed a rich, handsome man to tell you what to do?*

Memories of Stephen van Dunn reminded her to keep her distance from William Sloane. She lifted her chin. "Tell me about my brother. You were in there quite a long time."

His lids fell, shuttering his gaze, and he relaxed. "The captain needed some persuading. Also, I wanted to speak with Thomas alone."

"Why?"

"For a private discussion between men. No need for you to worry over it."

Did he just . . . ? Yes, he had. A sharp throbbing erupted at her temples. "Do not condescend to me. That may work with the other women in your life, but it will not work with me."

His eyes snapped to hers, the steel gray unreadable in the dull lamplight. "Is that what you are? A woman in my life?"

Of course she hadn't meant *that.* "I'm the woman trying to get *out* of your life."

"Yes, I suppose that is why you sought me out this evening. To get out of my life."

She had no response, though she could feel her face growing hot. She'd needed a favor and Will had been the only option. "Well, after tonight, you'll never see me again."

"Wrong. You still owe me payment."

A kiss. Anticipation thrummed in her blood, a reaction she steadfastly tried to ignore. "I won't kiss you."

"Tell me why."

"For many reasons, the biggest of which is that you *ordered* me instead of *asking* me."

Will's mouth hitched as if he were fighting a smile. "Is that so?" He leaned forward, bringing one arm up to rest on the opposite side of the carriage, pinning her in. Instead of fighting, her body grew even warmer, a buzz building under her skin. A horrifying emptiness ached between her legs.

His face now disarmingly near, she could see the hint of evening stubble on his chin. Small lines curved at the edges of his striking eyes—were those from smiling?—and the flush on his unblemished, pale skin suggested he was aroused as well. Sadly, the idea only made him more appealing.

"Intriguing you didn't refuse for a lack of desire." His head dipped, and she froze, unsure what he would do, but his lips merely hovered near her ear. The warm air from his mouth made her shiver—and her resistance began melting like a block of ice on a hot New York street in August.

They stayed there for what felt like an eternity, his face a breath away, the two of them caught on a tightrope above a yawning, dangerous chasm. He was already close, but she craved more, and she had to restrain herself from pressing forward and kissing him. Heavens, she'd never wanted something so badly in her life. She could hear his breathing, fast and harsh, in her ear, the pace matching her own rapid exhalations. *What is happening here?*

"Will you kiss me, Ava? *Please?*"

The last word, whispered over her burning skin, did her in. She hadn't thought Will Sloane even knew the word *please*, let alone was able to utter it in such a deep, rough tone. Without thinking, without *blinking*, she lunged and fit her mouth to his. There were no concerns about the future or worries about the past. Only now existed, only satisfying this unbelievable longing to taste him. To see if she could shake his controlled exterior.

The instant their lips touched, his mouth turned hard and hungry, lips molding to hers, with his hands coming up to cup her jaw and hold her in place. Had she thought him cold? How utterly wrong she'd been. Fire leapt between them, his lips firm and fervent against hers as the kiss turned scorching. She gripped the lapels of his coat to hang on, her head spinning, and then he opened his mouth to slide his tongue along the seam of her lips. She inhaled sharply, then quickly parted to allow him in. He drew her closer as his tongue delved inside, a wicked glide of lush heat that tasted of expensive spirits and spice.

For all his buttoned-up demeanor, Will's kisses were the opposite. Demanding and full of sinful promise. A hint of barely controlled passion lurked under the surface, like steam building inside a kettle. She suddenly wanted to see him unravel, completely undone and unguarded because of her.

No telling how long it went on. Ava lost track of time, her surroundings, her mind . . . There was nothing but lips and tongues, along with the shared breath that could have sustained her all night. The kiss was not gentle or decent; rather, it was messy and harsh—and Ava relished every sigh and grunt that came out of his mouth.

When he broke off, she experienced a pang of disappointment—until his lips began traveling down the column of her throat. *Oh, thank heavens he isn't stopping.* She threw her head back and reveled in the feverish trail of teeth and tongue over her sensitive skin. Her back arched, breasts aching with the need for his attention. She could not get close enough, could not get enough of what he was doing to her.

"You are so beautiful," he murmured into her neck.

The words fell over her like a blanket of icy snow. She'd heard them before, these false compliments, also from an older, wealthy man who hadn't meant them any more than Will did. A cold numbness settled in her chest, and she pushed on his shoulders. "Stop." She inhaled and gathered her resolve. "You need to stop now."

Will stumbled back, his mind confused while lust roared through his blood. Then he noted the vulnerability in Ava's wide brown gaze, a look he hardly recognized. What had happened? He was certain she'd been enjoying their kiss, but something had put her off.

Stupid to have begged for the kiss, but he'd needed one small taste to get her off his mind for good. That plan failed miserably, considering his hunger for her had only intensified. He dragged a hand down his face and collected his breath. "That went further than I intended."

"Further than we both intended, I think."

The knot in Will's stomach tightened somewhat as she continued in a remote, withdrawn voice.

"However, let's not turn this into something it's not. You asked me to kiss you, so I kissed you. Consider it a thank you for helping with Tom."

Helping with Tom? Her indifference rankled, especially when he could still drive spikes with his rock-hard erection. She'd been equally caught up, so why act as if the kiss had meant so little? "Am I to believe that was your only motivation?"

"Were you expecting something more?" she returned.

Anger swept through him, swiftly replacing the desire in his veins. He should let it go, leave her alone. Hell, it was downright necessary to walk away from this woman. She was a spectacle, a swindler one step away from prison.

No matter her noble reasons, she fleeced people for a living. He couldn't respect that—and neither would voters if a whiff of their association were made public.

And yet . . .

There was something about Ava that drew him in, like one of the rubes eager to believe in her "powers." She fascinated him, not something Will could often say of a woman. This city could chew a person up and spit him out . . . yet she had thrived on her own terms. And she certainly wasn't afraid of him, using every opportunity possible to inform him he was wrong. Beyond her tough-as-nails exterior he'd glimpsed a softer, more caring side that intrigued him. What would it take to experience that softer, tender side for himself?

In his world, a woman was entirely predictable and appropriate, with no surprises to worry over when you escorted her to dinner or an event. Such as the debutantes under his consideration for marriage. Each was descended from a proper, old New York family and would conduct herself in a manner entirely befitting a political wife—not run around the city dressed in a costume, performing a two-bit sideshow.

This needed to end, here and now. He had more important things to occupy his time with, like campaigning and finding a wife—not dallying with Madam Zolikoff.

"Fine," he said. "Unlikely we'll have cause to see each other after next Saturday, regardless."

She turned to him, a frown pulling at her full lips. "Next Saturday?"

"Have you forgotten already? The rally in Albany."

A gloved hand waved dismissively. "I am not attending one of your rallies, railroad man, and certainly not all the way up in Albany."

"The journey is merely three hours by train. I'll procure you a ticket. You can take the Northeast Limited departing at eight-oh-five. Even the nine twenty should get you there shortly after noon."

"Do you have all the train tables memorized?" she asked, studying him.

He blinked at the odd question. "For most of my trains out of New York, indeed, I do."

She gave no response and silence descended. A quick look told him the carriage was traveling on the West Side, along Bank Street. Tom would have given the direction to Will's driver, which meant Will would soon learn where she lived. Somehow he was unsurprised to find her living not far from his Washington Square home. Fate had certainly been frowning on him as of late.

She studied the scene out the window, resolutely ignoring him. He wished he could ignore her, but it was impossible. Every cell in his body was aware of her, now imprinted with the memory of how she tasted, the hungry little moans and sighs she gave, the way she made his blood boil. Despite his earlier resolve, he'd very much like to kiss her again.

Get a hold of yourself, man. Have you no dignity?

The carriage slowed and then halted before a sturdy red-brick building. Number fifty-seven. He filed that away. "Nice lodgings." Admirable that she'd moved her family here from the cramped quarters of the Lower East Side.

"Thank you. Again, I am grateful for your efforts in gaining Tom's release."

"My pleasure, and I look forward to seeing you next Saturday."

Her shoulders stiffened, and she pierced him with a frosty glare completely at odds with the woman who'd just kissed him more vigorously than he'd ever anticipated. "A gracious offer, your ultimatum, but I am fairly certain I said no."

"Yes, but I've not told you the reason you will definitely attend."

"Oh? And what might that reason be?" Her mouth curved into a smirk, as if there were nothing he could say that would convince her.

"Because I've given your brother a position in my offices, starting Monday."

Her lips parted on a gasp. "You gave Tom a *job*? Doing what?"

"Not picking pockets, that's for certain. But he won't have a position for long if you don't come to the rally."

"Blackmail again?" she snapped. "Do you have any scruples whatsoever?"

He nearly smiled. Hadn't he asked her that very thing not too long ago? And she should already know the answer. He had no scruples whatsoever when it came to getting what he wanted. In fact, he'd already cabled the Society for Mediumship Research on Tuesday as promised—not that he'd mention that now. Let her find out when the Society arrived and debunked her claims.

"None, in fact, and we are obviously well matched in that regard. Did you honestly believe I'd play fairly?"

Loathing washed over her features, but she seemed to consider his words. "Are you saying you'll fire Tom if I don't come to your ridiculous rally?"

"Without doubt." A lie, but he'd learned Ava's weakness—her siblings—and Will would use that information to his advantage whenever possible. "And you must stay for the afternoon. No skipping out after the parade."

A face appeared in the window. Tom stood on the walk and had obviously grown impatient. "Ava, Mr. Sloane," he called. "Is everything all right?"

Will quirked a brow at her, crossing his arms over his chest and ignoring the boy. "Well, Ava? What's it going to be?"

Her jaw worked, undoubtedly curbing all the curse words she wanted to lodge at him. Just the idea of her ire had his body stirring. *Christ.* He almost believed she *did* possess powers of some kind, based on the way she affected him.

"Why must I be there?"

"To see why I need you to stay away from Bennett. We cannot give the opposition anything to use in a smear campaign against us. The fight will be dirty enough once the conventions are over."

"Fine," she gritted out. "But I won't pay for my own ticket. It's a dratted waste of money."

He conceded that with a dip of his chin. "I'll have a ticket delivered by Thursday."

"If I hear that you've mistreated him . . ."

"You have my word that I will not."

Shoving his hat on his head, he threw open the door and stepped down, then extended his hand to assist her from the brougham. Ava's brow lowered in confusion, yet she placed her fingers in his gloved hand and shifted her skirts to descend. When her heels touched the walk, she jerked her fingers from his grasp. A pretty pink blush had erupted over her cheeks, and Will wondered over the meaning of such a reaction. Embarrassment or—dear God in heaven—*arousal*?

"Mr. Sloane." She dipped her head as if they'd just passed each other during an afternoon stroll on Fifth Avenue—not shared a kiss that would feature in his erotic dreams for weeks to come.

"Miss Jones." He purposely drew out her last name before tipping his hat in farewell.

Her mouth flattened in silent rebuke, but she pivoted to march toward the building entrance. Will's gaze lingered over her form, from the straight shoulders and small waist, to the furious sway of her skirts over her bustle. What he wouldn't give to see—

"Good night, Mr. Sloane." Tom started after his sister, but Will held out a hand.

"Thomas, a word." Ava swung around, and Will gave her a pointed look. "Alone."

She did not care for that, fire crackling in her light brown eyes, yet she disappeared inside without another word. Waiting for her brother just inside the door, no doubt.

"Why did Ava look so damn angry?" Tom asked. The lad's expression was just shy of being perceptive. Another few years and he'd better understand the ways between men and women.

"I couldn't say," Will lied. "But remember my advice. You gave her quite a scare tonight. And if I hadn't been at home, you might have ended up in the Tombs. You owe her an apology."

"Yes, sir."

"Also, a gentleman does not curse, Tom. If you must, use 'dratted' or 'dashed' instead of 'damn.'"

The boy's face, smudged with dirt, screwed up. "I ain't no gentleman, Mr. Sloane."

"As of Monday, when you step inside the Northeast Railroad offices, you are. Start acting like it. Now, do you have any suitable work attire?"

Tom glanced down at his shabby clothing and color lit his cheeks. "I don't . . . That is, I could—"

"Never mind. I shall have some things sent over tomorrow. Consider it a starting advance."

"Thank you, Mr. Sloane."

"You can thank me by being on time and working hard. I have one more request. Your sister is traveling to Albany next weekend to attend a political rally. I want to ensure you will take care of your younger siblings so that she needn't worry."

"Oh, Mary and Sam don't need lookin' after. They do just fine on their own."

Will shook his head. "You're the man of the house. Taking care of them is partly your responsibility. Can I count on you to relieve your sister of this burden? I would consider it a personal favor."

The boy stood a bit taller, importance puffing him up as Will had hoped it would. "Of course, Mr. Sloane. Ava can go to wherever you need her."

"Excellent." Will clapped him on the shoulder. "I think we shall get along just fine."

Chapter Seven

The Knickerbocker Club was only one of the many social clubs Will belonged to in New York. It was, however, the club he frequented most. There were no new undesirables at the Knick; all the members were of the upper set, men Will had known all his life. Men with names like Hamilton, Belmont, and Astor. Strict rules preserved the quality of the club, rules enforced with a heavy hand. Not any man could be admitted, even if he had the money to pay the steep membership fee.

Upholding tradition, more than the exclusivity, mattered to Will. His own grandfather had helped to found the Union Club, and Will had played an active part in moving the Knick to its current location, at Thirty-Second Street and Fifth Avenue.

"Good evening, Mr. Sloane. May I take your hat and cane?"

Will handed over the items to the attendant and smoothed back his hair. "Are the gentlemen upstairs?"

"Yes, sir. All but Mr. Cavanaugh. I am not aware if he has arrived yet."

Will's brother-in-law hated the club, so he preferred to come in through the kitchens and use the staff stairs, like a scullery maid. "Thank you, Colin. I shall be leaving directly after the conclusion of the meeting."

"We'll keep your carriage nearby, then, sir."

Will strode through the quiet halls, well familiar with the wide doorways surrounded by ornate cornices and the tall windows framed by tasteful chintz drapery. From the classic paintings on the plaster walls to the plush Persian carpets adorning the floors, the interior had been designed with a masculine sensibility, where men of a certain standing could enjoy cigars and solitude.

A waiter was stationed outside the usual private room. He opened the door at Will's approach, revealing the small group of wealthy and powerful men with whom Will had aligned himself. The four men met on the first Thursday of every month to assist each other with various business matters. Will preferred to think of it as plotting and scheming to rule the world, but with a dignified air.

"Hello, Sloane." Calvin Cabot unfolded his lanky frame and extended a hand. Cabot was one of the most powerful publishers in New York and Chicago, and his newspapers had helped Will more than once in recent years. "Or should I say, Lieutenant Governor?"

"Not yet. Soon, though. Hello, Harper." Will shook the hand of Theodore Harper, the financial genius behind the New American Bank. "How is your lovely wife?"

Harper's face turned soft, true emotion breaking through his usual stoic demeanor. "She is well, thank you," Harper said, and resumed his seat.

The door bounced open, and the hulking figure of Emmett Cavanaugh strolled in. He relinquished his hat, stick, and coat, then made his way to the table. Will sat, not bothering to greet his brother-in-law. The two of them had never liked each other, and not much had changed despite the fact that Lizzie had gone ahead and fallen in love with the oaf. Will and Cavanaugh tolerated each other for his sister's sake, but barely.

Harper and Cabot made small talk with Cavanaugh while Will gave the waiter a nod to start drink service. A glass of 1868 Chateau Lafite appeared at Will's elbow, a personal stock he kept on hand here at the club. Cabot received a lager, Harper his Kentucky bourbon, and a glass of clear liquid—likely procured from a back alley still—arrived for Cavanaugh.

"You and Bennett had quite a turnout in Yonkers," Cabot said to Will. "The nomination is well in hand from what I hear."

"I certainly hope so. We've another scheduled in Albany on Saturday, complete with a parade. It'll be a relief when I don't have to deal with the elephants and monkeys any longer."

The reminder of Albany brought Ava to mind, specifically the kiss he couldn't stop thinking about. The experience had been every bit as delectable as he'd feared, a small taste to stoke fires he had no business igniting in the first place. Brazen, confident, and determined, she'd kissed him like a dying wish, and Will had enjoyed every damn moment. Too much, perhaps, as the soreness of his right wrist could attest.

Cavanaugh let out a noise. "That's all Albany's got, elephants and monkeys."

"True enough," Harper said with a chuckle. "But Sloane, I don't understand how you're going to continue to run the company if you win. You've never given up control of Northeast before."

"I'll manage."

No one asked for details, but skepticism permeated the room. Will didn't care because he planned to manage the business as well as a political career. He would achieve greater heights than his father, even if he died trying. The idea brought him a sense of smug satisfaction. It would kill his father all over again to learn that Will had been elected lieutenant governor.

The four of them turned to business. Harper and Cabot negotiated a quid pro quo to do with the Chicago Produce Exchange, while Will agreed to drive up transit prices on one of Cavanaugh's competitors in exchange for assistance with a growing labor problem. They all decided, at Harper's urging, to invest in a restaurant with an impressive young French chef at the helm.

This went on for over an hour. Finally, with drinks drained and talk turning to non-business matters, Will stood. "I've got an appointment, gentlemen. If we're finished, I'll bid you good night."

Cavanaugh came to his feet as well. "Wait, Sloane. I need a moment."

"Should one of us stay to serve as a referee?" Cabot asked. The request was a reasonable one; Cavanaugh and Will had thrown punches at each other before.

"Not tonight," Cavanaugh said, shaking his head. "I don't feel like hitting him yet."

"Hilarious," Will drawled. "God knows what my sister sees in you, because it's not your sense of humor."

"Oh, I know exactly what she sees in me," Cavanaugh said, smirking. "Would you like me to enumerate a few of the more interesting reasons?"

"Not if you want to breathe through your nose anytime soon," Will snapped. "Now, what do you want? I have a dinner party to attend." One of his marital prospects would be in attendance, and he was anxious to see how she measured up.

Cavanaugh cleared his throat. "Elizabeth would like you to join us for dinner next week. We're leaving for Newport soon, and I don't want her traveling more than absolutely necessary in her delicate condition."

Will wanted to see his sister, but did he have to go to Cavanaugh's mansion to do it? He clenched his teeth, unable to say the words of acceptance.

"I know how you feel," Cavanaugh allowed. "Sitting with you in my dining room is not my idea of an enjoyable evening either, but I am tolerating it to keep my wife happy. And when my wife is happy, good things occur in my house."

That statement caused nausea to roll in Will's stomach. Jesus, did the man have any sense of decency whatsoever? "Cease discussing my sister in such a disrespectful manner."

Cavanaugh quirked a brow. "I married her, Sloane. I love her, and, by some miracle, she loves me as well. You'd best accustom yourself to the idea."

Before Will could inform his brother-in-law that he'd never accustom himself to the idea, Cavanaugh turned to Harper. "Perhaps you and Mrs. Harper would come as well? At least then I'll have someone to talk with."

"I'm sure Mrs. Harper would like that. She is fond of your wife. Thank you."

"Cabot?" Cavanaugh asked. "Want to join in?"

The publisher shook his head. "I'm traveling to Chicago on Sunday."

"Well?" Cavanaugh crossed his arms over his barrel chest and glared at Will. "What should I tell her?"

Damn. "I'll be there." Then he blurted, "Any night but Monday." He had no plans to attend Ava's performance but preferred to leave the option open just in case.

For some reason, he'd come to look forward to seeing her, a bright scintillating spot in his otherwise dull week.

* * *

She loathed to admit it, but riding the train out of New York was exciting.

Ava sat by the window in a passenger car, avidly watching the green, lush farmland roll by on her first time outside the city. As promised, a ticket had been delivered to her home. No note included, but she hadn't expected one. She'd neither seen nor heard from Will since he helped retrieve Tom from the police, the night they had shared that toe-curling kiss. Or, as the incident had come to be known in Ava's mind, The Mistake.

It had been a mistake to kiss him. Even though it had been wildly improper, the kiss had consumed her every free thought during the last week. Had she imagined his passion, his intensity? The way his fingertips had dug into her skin? The desperate gasps of breath against her mouth?

No, indeed she had not—and the experience had been a revelation. Much more made up the polished and proper Will Sloane than she'd previously believed. The discovery surprised her, and she'd enjoyed kissing him—far more than she should have, in fact. She'd been overcome, like standing in the waves at Coney Island Beach. A rush that swept her away, took her feet out from under her.

Dangerous, that sensation. Ava no longer had the luxury of indulging in such frivolity without knowing the consequences, things like heartbreak, humiliation   or worse. During her affair with Stephen, her one and only lover, Ava had conceived a child. Stupidly, she'd assumed he would be thrilled. After all, he'd often talked about them being together . . . and surely a child meant their future would begin.

How wrong she'd been. How utterly wrong.

The van Dunns were an upper-middle-class family, and Stephen had been full of reasons why he could not see her again. His father would not approve of the eldest son marrying so beneath him. Ava would never fit into his world. Without any money, how would they support themselves? And on and on went the excuses. . . .

She sighed and closed her eyes, fighting the familiar ache in her chest. So much regret. So much sorrow. She had miscarried in the third month, not that Stephen had even inquired. She'd been fired from her position in his father's office as soon as she'd conceived, and that had been that. Stephen had washed his hands of her.

So yes, Will Sloane was dangerous. Ava would not make the same mistake twice.

Just then, Albany was announced. Having never attended a political rally before, she had no idea what awaited her when she left the train. Politics generally baffled Ava. Women were ignored or belittled, while men argued and carried on like children. In the city, the drunken campaign clubs would spill out of saloons to brandish torches in the streets, a march that generally ended in a brawl somewhere.

Why Will would want to join their corrupt ranks, she could not fathom. He had considerable power and wealth already. Was it not enough?

Disembarking, she stepped onto the platform and glanced around, shielding her eyes from the midday sun. Passengers hustled to and fro, jostling her shoulders and arms. So which way was the rally?

"Miss Jones?"

Ava found a stout, older man with a bushy mustache standing there. He seemed perfectly normal, but years in a crowded city had taught her well. "Who wants to know?"

He tipped his hat. "Good afternoon, miss. My name is Charles Tompkins. I serve as the advisor to both Mr. Bennett and Mr. Sloane on the campaign. I've been sent to collect you for the rally."

"Oh. Thank you." Will must have arranged this, and she

was grateful for his consideration. Though she had never met Mr. Tompkins before, John routinely asked Madam Zolikoff questions regarding the advisor. Had Tompkins lied? Did he have John's best interests at heart? Madam Zolikoff encouraged caution because she hadn't firsthand knowledge of the man. Perhaps today would be useful after all.

She waved a hand toward the crowd. "I am ready, Mr. Tompkins. Lead on."

Minutes later, they found his waiting carriage, and he helped her inside. As they bounced and swayed along the street, Ava watched the throngs of people from the window. Astonishing how many men and women had gathered, some standing and talking, some walking in the same direction as the carriage. It was as if everyone within ten miles of Albany had turned out for today's event.

"Have you ever been to a political rally before, Miss Jones?"

"No, I haven't. I don't care for politics."

"Surprising, then, that Mr. Sloane would invite you up from the city."

He obviously wanted Ava to fill in the details, which she would do approximately never. This outing could not conclude fast enough for her liking, and her reasons for being here were no one's business. A mélange of red and blue out the window caught her attention. "Who is that group on the rise wearing the blue coats and the red armbands?"

"Those, my dear, are members of the Bennett Band, our supporters here in Albany. Each town calls the campaign club something different, though we do have more than one Bennett Band. Both Schenectady and Saratoga Springs use that name as well."

She nodded as if interested, though she didn't understand why it needed to be so complicated. Voting should be simple, yet America's electoral procedure seemed more like a drunken circus rife with corruption.

"The agenda for the day is simple," he continued. "First, there'll be a march and parade, then everyone will partake in a public barbecue on the statehouse lawn. Bennett and Sloane will speak briefly and then the revelry will continue well into the night."

Perhaps, but not for her. She planned to be on an afternoon train that would bring her home before dark. Her agenda did not include staying in Albany one minute longer than necessary.

"And you think this will encourage votes in the fall?"

He nodded, his fingers stroking his long mustache. "It's about encouraging growth in our own party, which will translate to votes, yes. Mr. Sloane did not tell me how the two of you are acquainted. Are you a friend of the family?"

"One could say that."

A loaded silence descended until he said, "I feel as though I've seen you before. An event or a party . . . a performance, perhaps?"

No telling if he truly did recognize her, or if he was trying to reveal her as Will's mistress. Both were unsettling ideas, though for altogether different reasons. She doubted, however, he would see a resemblance to Madam Zolikoff, not without a blond wig and heavy stage cosmetics. "I seriously doubt it."

"Fair enough, fair enough—and here we've arrived. I asked the driver to put you near the end of the route. It'll be an easier walk to the statehouse lawn afterward."

The carriage slowed to a stop, and Tompkins descended. He helped her down and then pointed across the street. "The best spot will be there, at that corner. I'll see you at the luncheon. Enjoy the parade, Miss Jones."

"Thank you." She opened her parasol, one of the few remaining items she possessed that had belonged to her mother, and used it to cast shade on her face. Crossing the street took some effort, as the crowds were thicker here. Men in black derby hats and women in bonnets were everywhere, and Ava marveled at the number of people who'd come out to see Will and John. Did every rally attract this many supporters?

Will hoped to impress on her that she was a risk to their campaign. Hard to believe she could cause any significant damage, even if the horde of people gathered here weren't all supporters. How could a campaign with two such well-known figures, backed by the Sloane fortune, lose?

She worked her way into the crowd on the corner, not really concerned with her vantage point. Yes, she agreed to attend the parade, but she'd never promised to enjoy it.

Will propped a shoulder against the window frame and sipped his drink. The parade was well underway, a sea of blue and red marching through the streets with instruments and banners. He and Bennett comfortably watched the revelry from a second-floor room across the street while the Bennett Band entertained the crowd. As usual, the two candidates wouldn't appear until the barbecue.

He tried not to search the crowd for Ava. She should be somewhere in that mob, no doubt miserable and plotting an escape. But she would attend the luncheon; his threat ensured it.

"Another glorious day," Tompkins announced as he entered. "Looks like every voter between here and Schenectady showed up."

"Yes, fine work, Charles," Bennett said. "The brass band of young women at the beginning was inspired."

"I thought so." Tompkins glanced out the window. "Your friend, Miss Jones, arrived safely. I dropped her at the corner, right where the parade turns south toward the statehouse."

Just below his current vantage point. "Thank you. I appreciate your going to the station to welcome her." Will had wanted to go himself, but the desire to see her again was a dangerous one. He should stay away from her, not shuttle her about to and fro.

"Better me than you. Can't have one of our candidates shuffling off to the station like a footman."

They watched the proceedings in silence for a few minutes. Tompkins cleared his throat. "Incidentally, is there any romantic involvement between the two of you?"

Will's fingers tightened on the crystal glass in his hand. "You don't seriously expect me to answer that, do you?"

"No, but the girl looks familiar. I feel as if I've seen her somewhere before."

"I doubt it." Will was sure Tompkins hadn't met Madam Zolikoff in person, but perhaps he was wrong. "And you won't see her again after today."

"Excellent. You can't blame me for being curious, you know. We want you betrothed to one of your debutantes, a girl who will set the papers wagging. Not a woman carrying a dirty parasol that hasn't been fashionable since Lincoln was in office."

Will straightened off the wall. "Yes, which is why *I* thought of the idea in the first place. That aside, whomever I choose to have in my life is none of your concern, Tompkins. And if it becomes your concern, I'll drop out of this race faster than a lame thoroughbred at Jerome Park."

"Now, listen here," Tompkins started, his chest ballooning. "We agreed that you—"

"Oh, no. Those men . . . This could be quite problematic," Bennett broke in to say. "Look there, at that group of white jackets. I think those are Robert Murphy's boys. White Hats, they're called."

Will spun to the window. And there, up on a rise near the conclusion of the route, stood fifty or so young men in white coats and white hats, their attention on the parade. He couldn't tell, but it appeared there were buckets on the ground as well.

"What have they there?" Bennett asked, wiping condensation off the window to get a better look. "In those buckets. Do you see?"

"Are those eggs?" Tompkins peered closer.

No, the shape was wrong. Not perfectly oblong, like an egg. These shapes were all different. Will's stomach clenched, the glass falling uselessly from his hand to the floor. "Rocks. My God, those are rocks!" *Ava.* She would be right in the middle of the melee. One rock could do serious damage, even kill someone. Christ, he had to find her before the White Hats started tossing stones at the crowd.

Spinning on his heel, Will shot out of the room and toward the stairs. Sweat beaded his brow, and he took the stairs two and three at a time, his heart pounding in his chest. Once on the street, he heedlessly dodged pedestrians and horses, shouting an apology when necessary, but kept going.

He anxiously searched the crowd for any sign of her, but she stood shorter than most everyone else, hidden in a sea of unsuspecting people. *Damn. I never should have forced her to come.* An ear-splitting scream erupted to his right, and he saw a volley of rocks arcing across the parade route toward the marchers. Everyone stopped and glanced around, people shouting and pointing to where the White Hats had congregated.

Will covered his head as a wave of confusion and fear rolled over the bystanders. Hundreds began running hither and yon, trying to get out of the path of the rocks, which made traversing the streets impossible. In a few short moments, this could turn deadly. Someone could be trampled.

The noise picked up, more shouting and screaming as rocks rained down, and Will put his shoulders forward to barrel his way through the crowd. He had to find her, had to get her out of here.

A rock smacked his back, a sharp sting through the fine wool of his coat. An older woman fell to the ground not even a foot away from him, so he stopped to help her gain her feet. "Head for the building over there," he yelled, pointing. "Get off the main street." She stumbled away, and he continued on, inspecting every brunette he passed to ensure she wasn't Ava, but there were thousands here today. The chances of finding her were slim.

When he neared the corner, the assembly had denigrated into a brawl. The White Hats were still hurling rocks and Bennett's Band charged after them with brickbats and heavy branches. Everyone else was trying to get out of the way. "Ava!" he shouted, eyes moving swiftly over the faces around him. "Ava Jones!"

His gaze swung wildly, a knot of fear and frustration lodged in his throat. If she were harmed today, he'd never forgive himself. What had he been trying to prove, forcing her to come to this? "Ava!" he bellowed as he stepped onto the sidewalk. He'd scream himself hoarse if necessary. No way he would leave Albany without her. "Ava!"

"Will!"

A small sound, but he'd definitely heard it. *Damn it, where is she?* Craning his neck, he searched for her. "Ava! Where are you?"

"Will! Over here, by the light!"

He pivoted toward the streetlamp and saw the top of her head over the shifting crowd. She clung to the metal pole, her eyes wide and terrified, bonnet askew. Relief poured through him, nearly buckling his knees. "Stay there," he yelled, and, using both arms, fought through the frenzy until he reached her side. Unable to help himself, he threw his arms around her and pulled her into his chest. "Are you hurt?"

She shook her head, her answer muffled by his silk vest.

"Come on. I'm getting you out of here." He tucked her close to his side with one arm, then used the other to shove them through the mass of clustered bodies.

"Wait! My parasol!" She tried to push away from him.

He held tight. "Ava, you'll never find—"

"No! I must find my parasol. It was my mother's." She struggled against him, and he tried not to lose hold of her. Her head swung wildly about, searching the ground for the parasol. "Let me go."

"I'll buy you another," he snapped. The rocks were still coming down, not far from where they stood. Someone could be seriously injured and she was worried about a damn parasol?

Two palms clapped his cheeks, bringing his gaze to meet hers. "Will, I won't leave here without it." The truth of that statement was there in her clenched jaw, and he sighed. *Hell*.

Bending, he shifted to look on the ground near where she'd been standing. After a moment, he spotted it. A crumpled yellow parasol lay in the gutter, a sad casualty of the stampede.

"I see it," he called. With Ava's fists curled into his clothing, he fought the elbows, backs, and shoulders bombarding them from all angles to reach the edge of the curb. He wrapped one arm around her and used the other to retrieve her parasol.

Once he had it, he wasted no time in leading her toward the train station, where the safety of his private car awaited. He would get her out of Albany, no matter what.

Chapter Eight

Ava exhaled and took another sip of the superlative spirits that Will had placed in her hand a few moments ago. French brandy, he'd said, instructing her to drink it directly before he departed to see to their travel arrangements. "*I'm taking you home*" was all he'd said before stepping out of the car.

Her hands were still trembling. Lord above, she'd never been so frightened in all her life. Under normal circumstances, the height difference between herself and most everyone else did not bother her. But in a frenzied crowd settled on violence, that size difference could mean life or death. Hands and feet pushing and shoving from every direction . . . she'd been knocked to the ground twice before finally reaching the lamppost. Once there, her plan had been to wait out the riot until either the police arrived or the men ran out of steam.

In the end, waiting had proven unnecessary. Will had come for her. He'd *found* her, braved that hornet's nest to ensure her safety. She couldn't believe it, especially when the two of them were at odds all the time. Really, who was she to him but a nuisance he wished gone? Why would he bother to rescue her?

She pushed that thought aside. She didn't care about the reason, not now. No doubt she'd wonder over it later, when she wasn't situated in his opulent private car, nestled into velvet furniture while drinking delicious liquor out of a heavy crystal glass. Instead, at this moment, she felt only profound gratitude and relief.

A crumpled yellow heap on the floor caught her eye. He'd saved her mother's parasol, a simple gesture that touched her beyond measure. The item, though not costly, had great sentimental value to her and could never be replaced. Of course, he'd been confused at her insistence to retrieve the shabby thing, but he'd done it anyway.

She took another sip of brandy to wash down the tenderness clogging her throat. It was too dangerous to let herself feel anything for Will. He was high-handed and arrogant, a rigid man used to getting his own way. His world, that of parties and champagne, debutantes and cotillions, was not something Ava could even imagine. She lived in the real New York, the one with dirt and grime, backbreaking work, and never enough time or money to enjoy simple pleasures.

Still, she could enjoy a small taste of his world for a moment. She'd earned that, at least, by coming up here today at his behest.

Relaxing into the soft sofa, she glanced about. The car could easily belong to royalty, though she supposed the Sloanes were as close to royalty as one had in America. By God, this long box was nicer than most houses she'd seen, with its dark mahogany interior and gold fixtures. Stained glass clerestory windows ran the length of the space, allowing mottled light to filter through, which gave the interior a holy reverence. Two separate seating areas contained sturdy furniture covered in lush fabrics, and crystal gasoliers provided additional light. The exotic and beautiful hand-woven rugs beneath her feet had no doubt been imported from a country she hadn't heard of before.

He's the president of the railroad. Did you expect him to travel like the common rabble?

The gulf between them had never felt more acute than at this moment. He'd played the white knight, rescuing her and bringing her back to his fancy castle-car . . . but she was far from a princess.

She hadn't been born of wealth or privilege. Her parents had been hardworking, third-generation New Yorkers who'd struggled to keep the family clothed and fed. When they died of influenza in '85, the lives of the Jones siblings had grown frighteningly grim. Many days Ava had skipped meals in order for the others to have enough to eat. She'd sold every valuable they owned. Mended clothing in dim gaslight until she thought her eyes would cross. Before the Madam Zolikoff idea, there were times when she'd feared that only one profession would ever pay enough to survive.

The door flew open and Will bounded up the steps and into the car. Not a sandy blond hair out of place, his clothes remaining perfectly pressed, one could never tell he'd just braved an unruly mob. What did it take to rattle this man?

"We shall be leaving in ten minutes," he announced on his way to the cabinet where several crystal decanters rested. He snatched the neck of a decanter and poured a healthy amount of amber liquid into a heavy cut-glass tumbler. He downed it in one swallow.

Hmmm. Perhaps more rattled than she thought.

With his glass now refilled, he dropped into a chair opposite the sofa and stretched out his long legs. She hated that she noticed how the muscles of his thighs bunched under his trousers and the broad shoulders that pulled on the fine fabric of his coat. But she was keenly aware of him, her blood overexcited just from being in his presence. Her mother's voice suddenly rang in her head. *I always knew you'd be trouble, girl.* If Ava had a penny for every time she'd heard those words, the Jones family could well afford pheasant every night.

But she could still see Will, charging into the chaos earlier like a general on a battlefield, with nothing and no one able to stop him . . . Her body warmed in a telling place at the memory.

"I hope you understand how much I regret what occurred today," Will said, refocusing her attention. "It was never my intent to put you in harm's way."

"I should hope not. And thank you for finding me. I feared I'd be forced to wait until they all killed one another or it started to rain before I could escape."

The side of his mouth lifted a fraction, the only sign he might be amused. "I assume they would have settled down eventually."

"Not every rally is such a hellabaloo, then?"

"Definitely not. Usually they wait to riot until the food runs out."

She cocked her head and studied him. "I cannot be sure, but I think William Sloane just made a joke."

"You say it as if I lack a sense of humor." Lifting the glass to his lips, he took a drink. "That could not be further from the truth."

Balderdash. Based on their few interactions, the man was as dry as week-old bread. "Indeed? Jolly good fun at the club, are you?" she said in her best upper-crust British voice.

He shook his head. "You are terrible at accents."

"I am not! I can imitate nearly anyone." Several people had remarked favorably on her gift of mimicry over the last two years. And she could throw her voice, a trick she'd already used once on him. "Everyone believes Madam Zolikoff to be Russian."

"If you say so," he replied, toasting her with his glass before taking a drink.

"You're mocking me." Strangely, she didn't mind. They were jabbing at each other, poking, as they usually did, but this exchange lacked the malice found in previous conversations. Perhaps they were both still reeling from earlier, but Ava couldn't work up any anger at the man who'd rescued her from an angry mob. No doubt she'd be fuming at him in a few minutes when he said something infuriating. Right now, however, she was . . . enjoying this.

"I am," he admitted, no trace of apology in his voice. "Why Russian? Madam Zolikoff could easily have been French or Italian. You chose a very difficult accent."

"Fewer people have heard Russian, so I thought it would be easier to get away with mistakes. Also, there were some Russian women in our building at the time." Ava had listened to the older ladies for hours, learning how to pronounce the rough vowels and harsh consonants correctly, until she'd perfected the sounds. "Admit it, William," she said in her best Russian pronunciation, which came out as *Ahd-mit it, Villeum.* "You believed I was Russian when you first heard me."

"Not for one second. Tell me, how many patrons do you see regularly?"

"Including John, eleven. Why?"

"And the rest of your income is from the stage shows?"

"Yes, but I also do a fair number of home séances. Three a month, sometimes more. Those are very lucrative." Strange to discuss her business this way with someone, but Will was also a businessman, and no doubt his practices often bordered on the illegal as well. Perhaps they understood each other better than she'd thought.

"Why so lucrative?" He sounded curious instead of judgmental, as she'd come to expect.

"In addition to the fee for the séance, many of the attendees pay for a private reading after."

"Unbelievable," he scoffed. "Stupidity knows no bounds. Tell me, how did you levitate the table in your show? Someone below the floor?"

Ava took a sip of the brandy, enjoying the warmth as it slid down her throat to her belly, and she debated telling him. She generally did not reveal her secrets, though the trickery in itself took skill. Not everyone could escape from rope bindings or pick a lock behind their back. Being a medium wasn't all trances and hymns; she had studied hard and practiced for months to hone her act. Moving a table required a small, light piece of furniture, her foot under one of the legs, strong leg muscles, and dim lighting. Levitation was a bit more difficult, requiring strings pulled from behind the stage.

But to confide in him would out herself as a fraud, the very thing he'd accused her of all along, and she refused to give him the satisfaction. The second he had confirmation, no doubt he'd run to John Bennett with the proof. "The spirits are very powerful. They lift the table, not me." She hid her smile behind her glass as she took another sip.

He heaved an aggravated sigh. "I wish you would trust me."

I learned a long time ago not to trust men like you. The words burned the tip of her tongue, yet she withheld them. He didn't deserve more information, not when he already knew too much. "Just as you trust me?"

He studied her and drummed his fingers on the armrest. "I do not play a part to fleece people out of money."

"Don't you? Whether you're a politician spouting what the public wants to hear, or you're strong-arming business associates to get what you want, you're playing a part. Everyone performs, if only to show the world what we think they want to see."

"Of course you would believe that's true." He leaned forward in his chair, anger evident in the flattening of his mouth and tightening of his jaw. "I am not—"

The outer door swung open, cutting off Will's tirade, and John Bennett entered the car. Every muscle in Ava's body tensed. She wished the floor would open up and swallow her whole, but no such luck. All she could do was pray John wouldn't recognize her.

Will wanted to curse and snarl at the interruption. When he saw who it was, he could do neither, as keeping the two men from Ava would only increase their curiosity about her.

Bennett strolled into the sitting area, his keen gaze sliding between Will and Ava, with Tompkins following quickly behind. "Good to see you found the young lady unharmed," Bennett said. "Won't you introduce us, Sloane?"

Swallowing his frustration, he said, "Miss Jones, allow me to introduce Mr. John Bennett, the next governor of the great state of New York."

Bennett waved off the words as if they embarrassed him. Will knew better; Bennett loved attention of any kind—which was part of the reason he fancied the visits with his "medium," Madam Zolikoff. "Now, Sloane. You know the voters get to decide the outcome. How lovely to meet you, Miss Jones." He bowed formally, which only seemed to make Ava even more uncomfortable.

The moment stretched, expectation thick in the air. A few words. That was all it would take for Will to ruin her career. He merely needed to open his mouth and tell Bennett the truth. *You've already met her. This is the medium you pay for spiritual advice, Madam Zolikoff.*

Ava's knowing gaze locked with his, a dare sparkling in her round, brown eyes. She assumed he would speak, exposing her. Indeed, why wouldn't he? He'd been trying to ruin her for weeks, to get her out of Bennett's life. But that was before . . . before he met her brother and learned of her hardships. Of the younger sister who toiled in a garment factory. Discovered how this woman had single-handedly provided a better life than either of her parents had managed before her.

Before he'd kissed her and tasted her sweetness on his tongue.

For Christ's sake, get ahold of yourself. He was one of the most sought-after men in New York; developing an affection for someone like Ava would be patently ridiculous. The woman was a complete fraud, and this was Will's chance to end their association now and forever. *Say it. Say it now.* He tried to force the statement past his clenched jaw . . . but the sounds wouldn't leave his throat.

"The pleasure is all mine," Ava said smoothly into the silence, dipping her chin. "Nice to see you again, Mr. Tompkins—though I wish it had been under more pleasant circumstances."

"Yes, today was a disappointment to us all," Tompkins remarked, and lowered into a chair.

Bennett strode to the sideboard and helped himself to a glass of Will's seventy-five-year-old brandy, the action temporarily distracting Will. Bennett's palate was not what Will would call refined; the man couldn't tell the difference between a Bordeaux and a bourbon. As expected, Bennett gulped the expensive brandy as if swigging weak lemonade on a scorching Georgia day.

"Are you interested in politics, Miss Jones?" Bennett dropped onto the other side of the sofa and angled his body toward Ava in an overly familiar way that had Will's shoulders tensing.

"No, I'm afraid not. Mr. Sloane insisted I attend the rally today. Otherwise, I'd be back in Brooklyn, at my father's bakery."

"Brooklyn!" Bennett exclaimed. "Decent hardworking people in Brooklyn. Spent quite a bit of time there myself. So you work for your father?"

"Yes. I knead the bread every morning."

Such a practiced liar, this woman. Will couldn't help but feel impressed. If she held any trepidation over whether Bennett would recognize her, Will could not tell.

A shrill whine erupted from the front of the train, and the wheels jerked forward as the brake was released. Soon, they'd be traveling forty miles an hour back toward the city, putting this godforsaken day behind them.

"Sloane insisted you travel here today, you said? How is it that you know each other?"

"That is hardly any of your business," Will said, his voice hard.

"I am a family friend," Ava answered at the same time.

Tompkins's eyebrow shot up. "A family friend? I didn't think the Sloanes associated with anyone east of Madison Avenue, let alone Brooklyn."

Will tried not to grit his teeth. He preferred no one examine his acquaintance with Ava too carefully. An idea came to mind. "I fear Miss Jones is being considerate. I did not want to tell you, but she works for a newspaper and is writing a feature on the campaign."

Ava took the news in stride, no change on her face whatsoever. "Yes, I work for the *Brooklyn Daily Times*."

The information changed the atmosphere in the room—and not for the better. Tompkins straightened, his expression both calculating and wary as he focused on her. "I haven't heard of that paper—and no one informed me we would have a reporter attending."

"The secrecy was intentional," Ava said. "We want to get a fair perspective on the campaign from the inside, though I planned on speaking with both candidates at length."

Bennett's bewildered gaze bounced between Will and Tompkins. "Well, the additional press will help, won't it, Tompkins?"

Tompkins's shrewd eyes were narrowed on Ava, and Will could see the wheels spinning as the other man examined all the possibilities. "Indeed . . . but I'll accompany you to any further campaign rallies or events. We want to ensure your safety."

"That is unnecessary. I'm certain you have more important duties occupying your time. Furthermore, after today, I am not planning on attending any more rallies."

"Then we hope you will not hold today's fiasco against the campaign."

"Of course not. All is not in your control, no matter how powerful the candidates."

"True, true," Tompkins concurred. "When would you like to speak with Mr. Bennett?"

Will held up a hand. "Calm yourself. Allow Miss Jones to proceed at her own pace."

"Mr. Sloane is correct—unless, of course, Mr. Bennett wishes to speak with me now." Ava shifted and reached for the small ladies' bag attached to her girdle. "I have a pad and pencil in my—"

"No, no. Not now." Bennett rose quickly, his reluctance nearly tangible. "You and Tompkins may work out the details. I feel a headache coming on, so I'd best lie down in my car for now. A pleasure to meet you, Miss Jones."

Will recognized the satisfied twist of Ava's lips. How had she known Bennett would refuse? She was very good at reading people and highly intelligent. His admiration for her grew.

"Oh, certainly, Mr. Bennett. I will be in touch regarding a date."

Bennett said his good-byes and strode to the door that led to the next car. Tompkins stood slowly, reached into his breast pocket, and removed a vellum card, which he offered to Ava. "I look forward to hearing from you, Miss Jones. We do appreciate all the efforts of our fine newspapermen and women to bring the truth to the good people of New York State. Anything I can do, you only need ask."

"Thank you, Mr. Tompkins. You are too kind." The tone suggested the opposite, but Will said nothing as the other man left.

When they were alone, her mouth flattened into a furious line. "A reporter? What were you thinking?"

"I was thinking to clear the car so they would leave us alone . . . which worked, by the way."

"You idiot, what will I do when I need to interview John for a paper that doesn't exist?"

"Well, why did you invent a fictitious newspaper?"

She heaved a sigh, one that suggested the answer grotesquely obvious. "Because I can't have Tompkins checking up on me, asking around at established papers for an Ava Jones."

Will smoothed the fine wool of his trousers. "I wouldn't worry. I can get the story printed somewhere." Indeed, Calvin Cabot owned two newspapers in the New York area alone.

"There is no story!" she snapped. "Are you *listening* to yourself? Mercy, this entire day has been a disaster."

Color washed over her cheeks and throat, turning her skin a dull rose, and a pang of remorse echoed in his chest. He'd forced her into this, and she was right—the entire endeavor had been a disaster.

Still, she'd been brilliant, and he couldn't help but wonder if the blush she sported had spread to other more interesting parts of her body. His gaze dropped to her bosom, which was now heaving in outrage. Hellfire, that was one luscious sight.

His eyes came back up to her face, where he found her watching him, a strange light in her brown depths. He cleared his throat. "At least Bennett did not recognize you as Madam Zolikoff."

"I wasn't overly concerned he would. The wig tends to distract people. What will you tell them when no story appears?"

He finished the last of his brandy then set the crystal glass on a small Louis XVI side table near his chair. "I'll think of something. Bennett will likely be relieved, though Tompkins may be persistent. How did you know Bennett would refuse to talk right now?"

"Because I know him. He consults Madam Zolikoff before most interviews, to ensure the spirits believe it a good idea."

"Is that so? What about other decisions?" *Just how much influence does Madam Zolikoff have over the campaign?*

"Yes, he asks about those, too." She paused, her smile showing more teeth than usual. "In fact, I'm the one who told him bringing you on the ticket was a good idea."

"I beg your pardon. You told him . . ." Will couldn't spit the rest out. His participation in this campaign had been conditional on Madam Zolikoff's blessing? How could something so important have been decided in such a cavalier way?

"There were a handful of names under consideration as a potential partner on the ticket. Any fool could've seen your society connections would most benefit the campaign, so I told them the spirits favored you as the best choice."

Favored me? "Dear God." He shot out of his chair and went to the side of the car. Bracing an arm on the window casing, he watched the landscape roll past, anger burning in his stomach like a lump of coal. Damned stomach pain. He absently rubbed the area and wondered if Bennett planned to consult Madam Zolikoff for the rest of his life. That sort of dependency would be crippling to their administration when elected.

"If it soothes your wounded pride," she said, "you were the favorite. Bennett merely needed spiritual confirmation."

He said nothing, uncertain he could speak without shouting. The rustle of clothing and the soft tread of her boots distracted him, causing a rush of awareness to prickle over his skin. He thought of her clinging to him as they escaped the riot, the small-yet-powerful hands wrapped around his waist, her face pressed into his chest. Now that the danger had passed, he could dwell on what it had felt like to hold her, to feel her lush curves intimately. The memory only caused him to want her more.

If he were less than a gentleman, he'd drag her over to the sofa and perform at least one hundred wicked things to her body.

"Even if Madam Zolikoff had chosen another," she was saying, "I cannot see how you would have suffered. You're certainly not in danger of losing your wealth or prestige. Why do you even care about winning this election?"

Because his father had wanted it, badly. Will would never forget the day he'd escaped his tutors to play with a puppy in the park. He'd been eight years old and much more interested in being outside than learning math tables. When he was found out, his father had shouted at him for an hour. *"You're a Sloane, for Christ's sake. You're not a street urchin, with no responsibilities and no future. With this complete lack of discipline, you'll never accomplish half of what I've achieved."*

Every single thing Will had done since his father died had been based on those words. Raising Lizzie. Building the business. Growing the holdings. Gaining political office.

But he couldn't explain any of that to her, so he told a half truth instead. "Because Bennett and I have the ability to guide the political landscape in the correct direction. If we'd given our speeches today, I would have proven how we can truly help people."

"Well, win or lose, you'll never suffer for a lack of arrogance, that's for certain."

"We'll win. And when we do, Bennett will move to Albany. So unless you're planning to move there too, you might as well stop seeing him now."

"Bennett will understand that I cannot move, at least not to Albany."

"Meaning you want to move elsewhere?"

She shifted to stare out the train window, her expression pensive, almost sad. He knew so little about her, and he felt hungry for any scrap, any hint she'd share. The woman was a mystery—an annoying, beautiful, ravishing mystery.

"Ava, tell me."

"You'll laugh, but there are farms upstate and I hope to purchase one before the year's out. Then I'll be able to remove my brothers and sister from the city."

Though he couldn't imagine her farming, neither could he imagine her leaving in a few months. His mind rebelled against the idea with a vehemence that shocked him. He swallowed hard. "Farming is not an easy life. Long hours and hard work . . . and you're dependent on the land and weather."

"That is what Tom said. He isn't keen on leaving New York."

"So why do it?"

She pressed her lips together with a small shake of her head. Still, he could not let it go. "Come on, Ava. There has to be a reason."

She exhaled heavily. "My youngest brother is not in good health."

"The newsie?"

"Yes. He's always been small and prone to illness, but there are times when he has trouble catching his breath, as if he can't pull in enough air. And Mary's hands . . ." She dropped her head to study her own fingers. "They hurt from sewing all day long. I want to give them a better life, one with open space and fresh air."

"And you think farming will be easier? You're deluding yourself. Tom is settling in nicely at the office, and I have high hopes for the boy. Moving your family may prove a rash decision."

"Spoken by a man who has been given everything. How long should I let them both struggle when I can do something about it?"

He didn't care to argue with her, not when the decision was her own. Who was he to say she shouldn't move to the moon, if that's what she wanted? "I know the desire to protect one's younger siblings. My sister was my responsibility from the time I turned sixteen."

"Was?"

"She recently married."

"I'm guessing from your pinched expression that you don't care for her husband."

Will shoved his hands in his trouser pockets and thought about how to best describe his feelings for Emmett Cavanaugh. "He's . . . unworthy of her."

"Because he mistreats her?"

"No! God, no. I'd beat him black-and-blue if he laid a hand on her in anger."

"So, he's poor. Is that it?"

"No. Wealthier than most anyone in New York, including me."

"I must be missing something. Does he smoke opium? Drink excessively? Restrict her independence in some way?"

Will let out a short, wry chuckle. "Definitely not, and he's indulged her constantly. He even funded her investment firm."

Ava's brows rose as she crossed her arms. "Sounds fairly perfect to me. If you tell me he's handsome, I just might jump off the Brooklyn Bridge."

"He's an oaf."

Light dawned in her irises, a bloom of comprehension that had him avoiding her eyes. "I think I understand. You said he's unworthy, which means he's not of the social elite. Not one of your blue bloods. Am I right?"

Will clenched his jaw. He didn't want to say it, not to her. That Emmett Cavanaugh was not of his world, people who understood and upheld the right values of this city. Rules. Tradition. Not the overstated vulgarity of the new money or the recklessness of the middle class—

"Oh, dear," she said, interrupting his thoughts. "How does it feel up there in your tall tower, your highness? Bet you're lonely with all that expectation and disappointment weighing you down."

He stiffened and shot her an icy look, the one that normally caused employees to scurry. Ava merely smirked, however, those delectable, full lips challenging him and redirecting his anger into something else entirely.

His pulse began to race, every part of his body igniting with a staggering intensity. Infuriating, maddening woman.

He wished he hadn't a clue how well she kissed, or how eagerly she responded to him . . . but he *did* know. Quite unlikely he'd ever forget, the kiss had been *that* spectacular.

He caught her stare and held it, unable to look away or hide the need stealing his breath or the dark yearning flooding his veins. The only saving grace was the dark, hooded gaze reflected back at him, a sign she felt this as well.

"Are you offering to keep me company in my lonely tower?" he asked quietly.

"Is that a proposition?"

His body grew heavy, blood pumping to his groin, her boldness affecting him like a plate of oysters at Sherry's. "Perhaps—or perhaps I'm merely flirting with you."

"You don't strike me as the type of man to flirt. You take yourself much too seriously to have fun."

The words were like the strike of a match to his blood. Two steps brought him close enough to catch the scent of roses surrounding her. "The other night in my carriage was certainly *fun*. From what I recall, you thought so as well."

Rapid, short breaths fell from her parted lips, her chest expanding and contracting above her corset. "You are more skilled at kissing than I had imagined. I was caught by surprise, is all."

Equally offended and flattered, he leaned in, his mouth hovering over her ear. "What had you imagined, exactly?"

"Cold," she breathed, a husky, rough sound of pure sin. "I had thought you would be cold."

He dipped his head and slid the tip of his nose along the softness of her cheek. Would she be this soft and sweet everywhere? He was suddenly desperate to discover the answer. "I am anything but cold around you." He brought a hand to her waist, holding her steady as the train suddenly rocked. "You make me burn, Ava."

She was panting now, and both of their bodies nearly

vibrated with restraint. Will could feel his control slipping as the desire to pounce grew. He was painfully hard, pulse pounding along his length, an animallike instinct roaring through his veins. He didn't want to make love to her. Didn't want to gently bed her or leisurely pleasure them both for hours. What he wanted—what he needed— was to take her, hard. Possess her. To lose himself in her lush, velvety warmth and brash attitude for days and days, where he could relieve this inexplicable craving for her.

But this was madness. She could be a virgin for all he knew, and he had no right to seduce her. He kept his affairs tidy, always with women experienced enough to agree to an arrangement at the start. No complicated emotions or entanglements, the encounters were clean and easy. Ava was messy, complicated. A constant thorn in his side. He should walk away and stop pursuing her. So why couldn't he leave her alone?

Because he was a fool, that's why.

Gathering every bit of strength he possessed, he drew back. "I apologize. I should not say such things to you."

Glazed eyes, dark with passion, searched his face. "Why?"

He pressed his lips together, trying to keep more insanity from falling out of his mouth, and started to step away. She clutched his arm, stopping him. "Do you never allow yourself to lose control? Just stop and *feel*, instead of always moving forward at high speed?"

No, he absolutely did not. Sloanes were supposed to set examples of proper, rational behavior.

"Do you allow your clothes to wrinkle?" she continued, her voice like smoke. "Or a woman to run her fingers through your hair? What does it take to shake your very foundation?"

You, he wanted to say. *You scare me down to my soul. Because once I have you, I'll never want to stop.*

Perspiration broke out on the nape of his neck, under his shirt collar. "You are asking dangerous questions, Ava. A woman, alone in a private car with a man, should not encourage him to lose control."

"Why, because you'll ravish me?" She laughed, the husky sound like a stroke over his stiff cock. "My dear man, I'm having the hardest time preventing myself from ravishing *you*."

Chapter Nine

He lunged.

Ava found herself pressed against the side of the car, her bustle riding up as Will covered her with his tall frame. His mouth descended, taking hers with an uncivilized force that electrified her. She clutched at him, equally desperate, and he ran the tip of his tongue over the seam of her lips, seeking entrance. When she opened her mouth, he delved inside, emitting a growl from deep in his chest that sent a thrill through her limbs. His tongue skillfully stroked and licked, stealing her breath. *God above, what is happening?* He surrounded her, his chest crushing her breasts and his woodsy, clean scent winding through her like a drug.

She'd been bold, pushing him a few moments ago, but a fierce curiosity to see what could happen had urged her on. Might he lose some of his precious control? As he ravaged her mouth, she was thrilled to discover the answer was unequivocally *yes*.

Her fingers threaded his hair, holding tight to the silky strands, as the kiss dragged on. Had she ever thought kissing him a mistake? Raw and wild, Will's kisses felt necessary to her very survival. If he pulled away now, begging might not be out of the question.

Please, don't stop.

"I won't," he said against her mouth, and she realized she'd spoken aloud. "I can't. I need to kiss you, Ava."

She whimpered and he groaned, their mouths meeting once more to devour each other. Her skin felt too tight, all the need and hunger threatening to break through at any moment. Strong hands gripped her waist, fingers digging into her corset, and her breasts ached with a delicious, sweet torture. Though it had been years, she remembered the excitement of being touched there. Her nipples puckered, frantic for attention, and she arched her back, shameless for more.

Will's palms traveled higher, along her ribs. He took her lower lip between his teeth and bit down gently. Ava inhaled sharply, the bite of pain echoing between her legs, slicking her cleft.

"Your mouth, my God. The things I want your lips to do. . . ."

Shifting to press open, wet kisses on her throat, he placed his palms over her corseted breasts. She'd never wished for less clothing in her life. "*Will.*"

"Shall I stop?"

"Do not dare."

He chuckled, a rare laugh from such a usually somber man. She liked this rough, unrestrained side of his personality. He kneaded her breasts over the layers of fabric and whalebone. "I wish I could see all of you. Undress every creamy inch of your pink skin."

Her hands glided over his sturdy shoulders, muscles shifting beneath the fine fabric. "I'd much rather see all of you."

He kissed her once more, his tongue finding hers as she wrapped her arms around his neck and dragged him closer. His arms banded about her torso, the heat pouring off him to make her limbs weak and heavy. Then he bent his knees and rolled his hips, pressing his heavy erection to the juncture of her thighs, and she moaned into his mouth. She was drowning, reeling, unable to reach the surface, the heady desire muddling her mind.

She swayed, rubbing her aching breasts across his silk vest, the nipples taut against the rough fabric of her chemise. He slipped his hands below her bustle to cup her buttocks, then lifted her to her toes, rocking their groins together. Hardness against softness. Pure wickedness, a devil in the flesh. She sank her teeth into his bottom lip and was gratified to hear him growl in the back of his throat.

"May I touch you?" he broke off to ask. "I need to feel you, to stroke you. Please, Ava . . . I am delirious with it."

"Yes," she rushed out, beyond the point of caring. "God, yes."

His fingers left her backside, and air rushed over her calves. Fabric rustled as her skirts rose, and Will dropped scorching kisses on the side of her throat above the neckline of her shirtwaist. Higher went her skirts until clever fingers reached between her thighs, into her drawers. He wasted no time, dragging one finger through her folds, causing her to shiver.

A deep rumble of masculine satisfaction gusted across her jaw. "You are so wet. You want me, don't you?"

She nodded, incapable of much else, and his fingers began exploring. She clung to his shoulders as he found her mouth, his lips sucking and working to drive her mad. He traced the folds of her sex, teasing—so close—but not where she ached most. He rimmed the entrance to her body, moisture easing the way, and dipped a fingertip inside. It wasn't enough. She craved the fullness, the stretch of tissues deep within her.

He continued the shallow thrusts of one finger, never going in far enough. All her concentration, all her eagerness focused on that one motion, and the restlessness of his denial caused her to rock her hips, chasing him. His palm swept over the tight bundle of nerves at the top of her cleft, leaving her panting.

"Is this fun enough for you?" his deep voice whispered over her cheek, bringing back her earlier words. "Do I seem *fun* now?"

Everything in her began to wind tighter, the pleasure climbing. "Will!"

"Beg me, Ava."

Desire had shredded her pride, and she did not think twice about complying. "Please, Will. Please, give me more."

Without warning, he sunk the digit to the hilt, sliding all the way in, perfectly filling her. She threw her head back, loving the slight burn that accompanied his invasion.

"Oh, my darling woman. I've died and gone to heaven."

Ava thought perhaps she was the one experiencing eternal bliss, especially when he withdrew and pushed forward again. After a few more thrusts, he added another finger and increased the pace. She bit down on her bottom lip, squeezed her eyes shut, muscles drawing taut. He seemed to know precisely how to touch her, the best angle, the most delicious pressure, and she could only hold on and try not to melt into a puddle at his feet. Then his thumb flicked the swollen bud, and she feared her eyes might roll back in her head.

Within seconds, the sensation crested, orgasm rushing through her, while her vision sparkled and her limbs trembled. "Ah, God, yes!" She clung to him, riding out the exquisite sensation until her limbs stopped twitching.

As she floated down, she realized he was supporting her with one arm, keeping her upright, and kissing the exposed skin of her neck. His labored breathing rushed over her skin, proof that he desired her but had restrained himself.

Part of her longed to unbutton his trousers, free him

from his underclothing, and draw him into her primed body—but a bigger part recognized that as a terrible idea. She had let desire ruin her life once; it would not happen again. No matter how enticing or attractive, Will Sloane was no good for her.

He withdrew his fingers, his forehead dropping to her shoulder as they both recovered. "I may very well go to hell for that, but it was damn well worth it." She heard him suck his fingers, the ones he'd used on her, into his mouth. His resulting groan set off a quiver deep inside her.

Stepping back, he cupped her elbow and led her to the small sofa. Once she sat, he strode to the crystal decanters and poured two healthy glasses of a dark liquid, giving her ample opportunity to study him. With his clothing out of place, hair askew from her fingers, eyes dark and wild, he looked like a man on the razor's edge of sanity. His bespoke trousers could not hide a sizable erection. *I'm responsible for that*, she thought with none too little satisfaction.

The man beneath the polished veneer was entirely unexpected. Raw, earthy, demanding. No doubt used to getting what he wanted since birth, he was appallingly highhanded. But this Will Sloane, the one who took care with her, who repeatedly asked her permission, who made her body sing and demanded nothing in return . . . this man was dangerous.

She could actually grow fond of him.

"What is wrong with you tonight?" Lizzie asked as she lowered onto the sofa.

It was Tuesday evening, and Will was stuck in his brother-in-law's garish mansion for dinner. The upside was spending time with his sister, whom he saw infrequently now that she'd married.

Lizzie poked his shoulder. "You are more ill-tempered than usual. Are you not feeling well?"

Will smoothed the fine wool of his evening trousers, trying to gain some time before answering. Truthfully, he did not know the cause for his dark mood. He'd been feeling off ever since Saturday. Edgy. Restless. His stomach ached more than usual, and he'd been distracted at work.

"Come on, Will. Tell me what's going on with you. Are you upset over the riot at the rally on Saturday?"

He winced at the mention of the rally, but not for the reasons she would assume. The day hadn't turned out anything like he'd expected. He could still taste the sweet tang of Ava's arousal, hear her breathy cries when she'd reached orgasm. Feel the way her walls had milked his fingers. His blood simmered at the mere memory.

Touching her had been unbelievably inappropriate, yet he burned to do it again.

Exhaling, he shifted to meet Lizzie's concerned gaze. "The rally was disappointing, but we cannot expect them all to run smoothly. And I'm not ill-tempered."

"Aren't you? Some days, I think you are a doddering old man."

"Thank you, dear sister." He threw back a healthy portion of Cavanaugh's Armagnac. An unpleasant burn in his stomach resulted, a sharp twinge of the near-constant pain he was experiencing. He set the crystal goblet on a side table.

Her astute gray gaze, so like his own, remained trained on his face. "Are you all right? Should I be worried?"

He waved his hand, unwilling to cause her concern. She was due to give birth to his niece or nephew in December. Furthermore, he'd tried to protect her so often it was second nature by now. "I'm fine. Far better than you, I hear."

She grimaced. "My stomach cannot seem to settle, no

matter what I do. I have yet to throw up, but the urge occurs all day long."

"Delightful," he murmured. Proof of the pregnancy continued to unnerve him. He did not want to imagine Cavanaugh in bed with his petite younger sister. If he did, he might very well throw up first.

"Stop." She shoved his shoulder once more. "I know what you're thinking, and I love him."

"I know, and I'm trying. I'm here, aren't I?"

"Yes, though you've spent more time talking to Mr. Harper than my husband."

"True, yet so has your husband, I might add." If Harper weren't here, silence would have been the theme of the evening. "How did you like the tea set I sent over yesterday?" Handcrafted Haviland china, the tiny porcelain set was perfect for a child's tea party.

"It is too precious. I burst into tears when I unwrapped it." She clasped his arm. "Thank you. I cannot express what your excitement over your niece or nephew means to me."

He shifted, taking a moment to straighten his cuffs. Sounded silly to be so overly excited about his sister's child, but he'd nearly raised Lizzie. He felt close to her . . . proud of her in ways he couldn't articulate. "Someday, perhaps you'll return the favor."

"Yes, your search for the perfect bride. How goes the hunt?"

He waved a hand. "Miss Rives is due to become engaged to the younger Bryce boy, so I've eliminated her. Other than that, no progress."

She took a moment to sip her tea. "The papers mentioned you escorting a woman from the parade route in Albany to your railroad car. Anyone I know?"

Will took pains never to read articles about himself.

They were generally false, the facts lost somewhere between gaining readership and plain incompetence. The only person he trusted was Calvin Cabot, and that's because Calvin printed exactly what Will told him, verbatim.

"You shouldn't believe everything you read," he said by way of answer.

"I generally don't, but this was quite a specific report."

"Lizzie," he sighed.

"Fine, but if you're serious about this marriage business, you should not be running higgledy-piggledy with a mysterious woman."

"I have never, ever run higgledy-piggledy in my life—and I thought you were against my marrying."

"I want you to marry, but not any of the girls from your list. I prefer you to have something real, a marriage that will make you happy. Like what our parents had. And what Emmett and I have."

Ignoring the guilt over the comment regarding their parents, he shot a glance at Cavanaugh. The steel magnate was across the room, speaking with Harper and Harper's wife, but his gaze was locked on Lizzie. "Please," Will drawled. "My dinner is still settling."

She laughed and Will's mouth hitched in amusement. He'd missed her. She had been a constant presence in his life for twenty-one years, and to not see her every day still struck him as odd. Lizzie and Northeast had been his only focus for more than a decade.

"My darling brother, you would be unbearable if I didn't love you so much."

"May I have a word?" a deep voice broke in.

Will glanced up to find his sister's husband hovering by Lizzie's side. Cavanaugh lifted his wife's hand and kissed her fingertips. Feeling like an interloper, Will rose. "I'll leave you two alone, then. Excuse me."

"Wait, Sloane. It's you I need to speak with."

That was unexpected. The only two things they had in common were Lizzie and business. Will didn't particularly care to discuss either at this moment. "Can't it wait?"

"No. Follow me to my office." He leaned over and kissed Lizzie's cheek, then straightened. Will trailed the other man into the hall, where Cavanaugh led him deeper into the gaudy house. Christ, how did his sister stand it? The amount of gold leaf was embarrassing. At least the artwork was tasteful, with a few Dutch masters sprinkled in with popular American painters, like Flagg and Whittredge.

Cavanaugh's office, which Will had visited before, was a tomb, the modern equipment silently waiting for business hours to begin. Cavanaugh threw the switch, lighting the space, and gestured to a chair. "Have a seat. Cigar?"

Will selected a cigar from the enamel box Cavanaugh presented, and his sister's husband followed suit. When they both were settled, lit cigars in hand, Cavanaugh spoke. "I want to buy Northeast Railroad."

A mouthful of smoke descended into Will's lungs, causing him to sputter, and his eyes filled with water. He struggled to compose himself. "Jesus," he wheezed. "Are you insane?"

Cavanaugh grinned. "As much as I enjoy catching you off guard, I'm entirely serious."

"No. The answer is *no*."

"Wait, hear me out first."

Will folded his arms across his chest. Cavanaugh had been after Northeast ever since that business with the fraudulent investment firm late last year. Yes, Will had suffered a financial setback, one that had sent Lizzie to seek out Cavanaugh in the first place, but the company had recovered. Handsomely so. Northeast was no longer in danger of collapsing—and Will had no intention of selling.

When it was clear Will would not argue or walk out, Cavanaugh said, "I know you've recovered from the embezzlement disaster. The company is in excellent health—"

"Thank you," Will said sarcastically.

"But I'm uncertain how you plan to give Northeast the attention it needs if you're in Albany. Let me buy you out. You'll remain on the board, keep your stock. But I think I can do better, especially when I join it with East Coast Steel."

"Join it!" Shooting to his feet, Will pushed his evening coat open and placed his hands on his hips. "You arrogant bastard. You think I'd allow the company I've built to be absorbed into your holdings, allow it to disappear? If so, you're out of your goddamned mind."

"Be reasonable. You know how business operates. For every successful company, there are fifty failures. Do you want to let Northeast falter when you can't devote enough time and energy to it—or would you rather see your legacy built upon? I promise you, together we can put Carnegie out of business."

"I have no intention of allowing Northeast to falter," he ground out.

"Then you are deluding yourself. I don't understand your desire to hold political office, but the idea must have some significance for you. If you win, that will take up most of your time. What happens to Northeast, then?"

"There are plenty of competent members of my staff who can oversee it in my absence."

"Who, Pryor and Helmstead? Come, Sloane. You know those men cannot grow the business like I can. You'd be lucky to survive six months with either one. Don't be a fool."

Unsurprising that Cavanaugh had pegged the two Northeast vice presidents as Will's choices for the temporary president position. Cavanaugh traded in information, never afraid to use muscle or money to learn what he wanted to know. Still, Will seethed, his stomach roiling. "I am not a fool, and I do not plan on selling. Even if I did, it certainly would not be to you."

Cavanaugh shook his head, a muscle twitching in his jaw. "I know you and I share a rocky past, but our association works for a reason. We've made each other very wealthy in the last four years. Not to mention I'm married to your sister, for fuck's sake. If I cheated you on this, Elizabeth would never speak to me again."

Will opened his mouth to say that result would suit him fine—but Cavanaugh held up a hand. "Don't say it. She's mine and I'm keeping her." He stood, shoved his hands in his pockets. "Think about letting me buy you out, that's all I ask."

"Is this fun enough for you? Do I seem fun now?"

A hot flush blossomed over Ava's body as she remembered Will's words. She hadn't expected him to be so . . . seductive. Wild. Tempting. Yes, she had pushed, recklessly taunting him into a reaction. God only knew what had come over her on the train, but she'd needed to affect him. Needed to discover what lurked under that polished veneer.

The result had knocked her sideways.

He had appeared equally off-kilter after their devastating kiss. The rest of the ride to Grand Central Depot had been spent in silence, then he'd insisted on driving her home. At her door, he'd kissed her cheek, whispering, "I don't regret one minute of it. Good night, you maddening woman."

Maddening, how? Because she had provoked him?

"Madam Zolikoff, what are the spirits saying?"

Damn. Ava shook herself. She was in the middle of a reading, deep in a trance to communicate with spirits from the other side. Every Wednesday, she rented a cheap hotel

room in order to see clients. There was no time to waste
with daydreams of a railroad tycoon.

The slate tablets in her hands were heavy, yet familiar.
She slipped a finger underneath the bottom one and
scratched on the surface with her fingernail. With her free
hand, she grasped Mr. Holiday's arm. "Do you hear that?
The spirits are writing to us!"

"What is it?" the man asked eagerly.

"They have a special message for you." She continued
with the scratching, a movement her client would never
detect in the dimly lit room. The trick was a relatively easy
one: Before she started, she showed Mr. Holiday four
blank slate faces in quick succession—but one empty face
was shown twice. The one face she didn't show already
contained a pre-written chalk message, one she'd crafted
this morning.

After a sufficient amount of "writing" time for the
spirits, she slid her toe under the slight gap between the
table leg and the floor, jerking upward to bump the table.
Mr. Holiday gasped, and Ava announced, "The spirits have
completed your message."

Turning over the slate containing the writing, she presented him the message. "*I forgive you. Please forgive
yourself.*"

Mr. Holiday's hand shot up to cover his mouth.

A medium's success hinged on knowing as much as
she could about her clients, then using that information to
improve the accuracy of the readings. Mr. Holiday, a
long-standing client, had lost his wife three months ago.
Unfortunately, he and his wife had argued the day she'd
died, leaving their last words as angry ones, compounding
his grief. Since then he'd been unable to return to work and
had recently lost his banking job. Ava hoped to set him free
from the guilt.

By the time Mr. Holiday left, he was pumping her hand effusively and expressing his gratitude. He promised to see her in two weeks' time for another reading.

Ava closed the door behind him and heaved a sigh. Some days it was hard to take money, knowing she was performing parlor tricks—even if it was to give them what they wanted. But she tried to do right by her clients, to give them positive messages that would help improve their lives, like to stop having affairs, spend more time with their children, or donate to worthy charities. This underhanded altruism was the only way she could sleep at night.

Though lately, sleep had been elusive for an altogether different reason. *Yet another ill to lay at railroad man's feet*.

And the problem was only growing worse. The more she was around Will, the more likable she found him—not that she'd see him again. He had wanted her to attend the rally, and she'd upheld her end of the bargain. She did not need Will Sloane in her life, disrupting it with his disapproval and disarming kisses. Bad enough she had to listen to Tom champion the man's genius every night around the dinner table.

Apparently, Will was well regarded in the Northeast Railroad office as something of a prodigy. He'd taken over the family business at a young age and built it up into one of the most successful in the country. He was a fair and kind boss—Tom's words—and never too busy to speak with even the lowliest employee. According to Tom, Will worked continually, at his desk before everyone else arrived and remaining well after the rest went home. The drive made no sense to Ava; the man was flush. What in God's name was he trying to prove?

Thank heavens Tom had immediately taken to the job.

Ava would always be grateful to Will for saving her brother from a dark and dangerous future.

A knock sounded on the door. Odd, since her clients had finished for the day. Peeking out, she found two well-dressed strangers standing on the threshold. One had a long beard, and the other had a scar running down his cheek. She did not want to know the circumstances behind that injury.

"Madam Zolikoff, may we have a moment of your time?" the bearded man said, peering down at her.

Instantly wary, she said in her Russian accent, "What is this about?"

The man with the scar held up his hands. "We mean you no harm, miss. We would like to discuss a business proposition."

She made no move to let them in, her hand gripping the door tightly. The location placed her in a precarious position, and there would be nothing stopping these two from hurting her once inside.

The bearded man seemed to understand her dilemma. "You may leave the door open, if you wish. We only want to speak with you."

Swallowing, she nodded and stepped back, keeping the door ajar. She had a pistol in her carpetbag, not that she'd be able to reach it in time should the men do her harm. Still, the presence of the firearm offered her some comfort.

"My name is Mr. Grey and this is my associate Mr. Harris. We have been watching you for quite some time. You're impressive."

"Yes," Harris said. "Your Monday night performances gain a wider audience each week."

"Thank you," she said cautiously.

"The reason we are here is because we work with several other mediums in New York. Have you heard of Mr. Harold Glade?"

"Of course." One of the most popular mediums in the city, Glade regularly performed at Madison Square Garden in front of thousands of people.

"And what about Mrs. Kitzinger? And Mrs. Paulson?"

Again, Ava nodded. "What do they have to do with me?"

"We work with them on a little creative . . . project. You see, you have clients who trust your opinion. They come to you looking for advice, such as what to do with dear old Agatha's estate or which stocks to purchase. That's where we come in. We own a company—nothing more than a front, really—that you can direct your clients to invest in. We then take that money and give you a percentage."

"And what do my clients receive?"

Grey lifted a shoulder. "We give them modest returns on their investment at first. Then, after a spell, the company goes under and we start another one. It's foolproof."

"The company goes under, yet you keep all the profits."

"Which we share with you, of course."

"Of course." Nausea rolled through her stomach, bile rising in her throat. They were confidence men, out to bilk money from any source they could find. The irony was not lost on her—that she performed a less obvious version of this—but at least she gave her clients something in exchange. These two men were outright thieves.

"You stand to earn a lot of money from us, Miss Jones."

Ice shot through her veins and she stiffened. No use maintaining the accent, then. "How . . ."

Their smiles shifted from pleasant to something more sinister. "We've been watching you, taking note of your career. You should be flattered. You are quickly becoming one of the premier mediums in the city."

Flattered? No, that was not close to what she felt at the moment. More like panic, fear, resentment, anger . . . "I cannot help you, gentlemen. I appreciate the offer, but you'll need to look elsewhere."

They exchanged an unreadable glance, then Harris said, "You misunderstand, Miss Jones. When we say we're offering you this opportunity, it's not one you can turn down."

"I'm afraid I don't follow."

Harris slipped his hands in his pockets and strolled about the room. Ava tried to keep one eye on him while Grey spoke. "The mediums who turn us down quickly find themselves out of business. We'd hate to bring attention to your performances and expose you of fraudulent activity."

"You're threatening me." Might as well put the truth in plain words.

"Yes, though there's no reason to refuse us. The scheme is tried and true, with none the wiser except those directly involved."

"And now that we've told you our little secret," Harris said from directly behind her, "it would be a shame if we had to reveal yours."

She dug her fingernails into her palms. She had no leverage. They could expose her at any time if she didn't agree. Of course, her clients might not take up her recommendations, especially if given vaguely and halfheartedly.

"I need time to think it over," she told them.

"Of course," Grey said smoothly. "But not too much time. We wouldn't want you going to any of your prominent friends for help."

Did he mean Bennett—or worse, Will? Heart pounding, she tried to control her breathing and retain her wits. "You'll have my answer next week."

Chapter Ten

Early summer nights, with their lazy, crisp air, were Ava's favorite. The city had yet to turn into the furnace of July and August, where the heat suffocated one's lungs from the inside out. Now the evening temperature remained cool enough to require only a light wrap, the perfect weather for an aimless stroll after dinner where she could clear her mind.

The streets were quiet tonight, with most of the families abed at this hour. Her current neighborhood was a far cry from the constant rowdiness and squalor of the Lower East Side tenements. The West Side had more working families who were up early to get to their clerical and service jobs. While it may not be their ultimate destination, the Jones family was much better off here.

A simple life, that was what she wanted. A better existence for her and her family. One without heartache and struggle. One with space and green things. One without trickery and costumes.

One without blackmail.

Never thought she'd be blackmailed—exposed as a fraud, possibly, but not blackmailed. Would those two men truly follow through with their threats if she didn't agree?

If it were merely her, if they hadn't discovered her real name, Ava would tell them to go to hell. But how could she put her siblings in jeopardy by refusing?

A noise from close behind caught her attention—a boot heel on the walk. Spinning, she tensed, prepared to defend herself against any manner of riffraff out in the darkened city. Except no one was there. She peered hard, squinting into the gloom. "Hello?"

Silence. She resumed her walk, the pace now a bit brisker. She rarely felt unsafe in New York, even when alone, but the back of her neck was tingling tonight. The visit from Grey and Harris, perhaps?

Turning the corner at her block, she noticed a large black brougham in front of her house. A beautiful chestnut bay was tethered to the front, a smartly dressed coachman on the seat. That was strange. One generally did not see this sort of opulence in her neighborhood. Several heads hung from windows in the surrounding town houses, curious neighbors wondering over the fancy swell who owned such a fine carriage.

A fancy swell. Her stomach tightened with both anticipation and dread. Could it be . . . ? While she wanted to see him again—in truth, she wanted to *kiss* him again—she needed to stay as far away from Will Sloane as possible.

Her feet slowed, and she debated turning around—

The carriage door swung open and long legs wrapped in black worsted wool emerged. Sure enough, a familiar blond-haired man unfolded from the carriage, straightened to his full, impressive height, and flicked a cigar into the gutter. *Oh, my.* She nearly stumbled, he was so dashing. He'd changed from his day suit into impeccably tailored evening clothes, the snowy starched shirtfront and necktie a beacon in the lamplight. He was . . . breathtaking. Commanding and arrogant. A man whose wealth and privilege went bone deep, the expensive clothes fitting him perfectly, as if he were born to wear them. Which, she supposed, he had been.

No doubt he had a fancy event to attend, one where men would court his favor and women would seek his bed, while she had hours of mending ahead of her. Their circumstances could not be more contrasting.

Still, she wasn't ashamed of her life. She'd fought hard for what little they had. Other women may be intimidated by Will, but she would not be one of them—and he could jump into the North River if he didn't like it.

She lifted her chin. "Mr. Sloane. What brings you to Bank Street tonight?"

He slipped his hands in his trouser pockets. "Good evening, Miss Jones. I needed to speak with you. Will you join me in a short drive?"

That stopped her cold. The idea of being in a closed carriage with him terrified her. She'd thrown herself at him in the train car—which had led to his hands beneath her skirts. No telling what might happen next. "We should talk here." She glanced about at the near-empty sidewalk. "There's not a soul about."

"Not quite true." He tipped his chin toward the buildings. "There are eyes and ears all around us. Shall we?"

Was the drive about privacy for their conversation—or hiding the existence of his visit? God forbid his cronies learned of his slumming with the common folk. He'd probably be kicked out of his fancy clubs. Disinvited to Mrs. Astor's annual costume ball. Or chased down Fifth Avenue by a mob wielding cocktail forks.

She rubbed her temples. Her thoughts regarding this man were a jumbled mess. "Will, I cannot see how this is a good idea."

"Please, Ava," he said quietly. "A few moments. I'd walk with you, but I'm not exactly dressed for a stroll about the city."

"Is there any chance you'll give up and drive on to wherever it is you're expected tonight?"

His mouth hitched, amusement glowing in his gray eyes. "None."

"Get in the carriage with him, miss," called a female voice from somewhere above, one of the older neighborhood residents enjoying the performance. "If you don't, Lord knows I will." Several chuckles rained down around them.

"Oh, for heaven's sake," Ava muttered, and stomped toward the brougham. Seconds later, she settled into the cushions. Will soon followed after a quick exchange with his driver.

There was little room in the interior. Their shoulders and hips lined up, pressed tight, the contact burning through her clothing and heating her skin like the flat of an iron. She wriggled, trying to put space between them, but it was no use. The wheels began to roll, and she resigned herself to the distraction of his nearness.

"There, was that so difficult?" he asked.

She didn't dare glance at him. He was much too close. She could kiss him if she leaned forward slightly, send him off to his event with the taste of her on his lips. Such wicked, wicked thoughts. Honestly, the devil grabbed hold of her every time Will Sloane came near.

She kept her gaze on the small window and folded her hands in her lap. "What is it you wanted, Will?"

He smoothed the fabric of his elegant trousers. "How have you been since I last saw you?"

The truth nearly tumbled from her lips, the whole sordid mess. There was no more capable man than Will Sloane, proven the night he rescued her brother and the day he saved her from the riot.

"We wouldn't want you going to any of your prominent friends for help."

Even despite the implicit threat, the urge to tell Will was tempting. Yet, if he helped her out of this trouble, where would that leave her? Dependent on a rich, powerful man to solve her problems, that's where. She swore she'd never allow that, no matter what predicaments she landed in. No, best if she handled this herself.

"Fine," she lied.

"You are a terrible liar. Which must mean something is wrong. What is it?"

She hated that he possessed the ability to read her so well. No one ever challenged her word except for Will. "Leave it be, railroad man. It's nothing you can help with."

"Ava," he sighed. "You will tell me before this ride is over."

Oh! The nerve. Her head swung toward him. "Do not presume because of what happened on the train that you can control me. You haven't a right to a thing."

"Wrong." His lip curled slightly, and the air inside the carriage grew charged, like an engine gathering steam. "It is precisely because of what happened on the train that I deserve to know. Are you in trouble of some kind? Is Thomas in trouble, or one of your other siblings?"

"You are insufferable. You don't see me asking you personal questions about your day."

"My day was boring, filled with business deals and meetings. I sense yours was a bit more exciting."

The silence stretched, wheels clattering over the cobblestones. Trusting him was out of the question. So where did that leave them? With nothing, nothing at all, except this strange pull in the pit of her stomach every time she thought of him.

And therein lay madness.

"Will, I cannot understand what you want from me."

"I . . ." A muscle jumped in his jaw, the lamplight highlighting the bold angles of his face. "I want you, Ava. I keep telling myself it's a terrible idea, but I cannot seem to stay away. I use every excuse I can think of to see you, and I'm not certain there's anywhere you could go that I won't chase after you. So it's you—that is what I want."

The words were so much more than she anticipated. Honest and raw, they devastated her resistance, laying waste to all the reservations she'd harbored. Not a declaration of everlasting love, of course, but she wouldn't have believed one. This unwilling admission of the torment between them, the strange attraction that neither person expected nor understood, melted her insides.

Then he leaned in and sealed his mouth over hers, cutting off any further thought with a kiss she'd been craving since Saturday.

Will could not control himself around this woman. Her plump lips, her sharp tongue and quick mind. A body that would tempt a bishop . . . It was like she had unlocked something in him that could not be shut away once more. He was a madman in her presence and, against his better judgment, he'd finally put all his cards on the table. But Ava was like no other campaign he'd waged; she held all the power over him. He would do nearly anything she asked for another taste of her.

She kissed him back eagerly, as if her craving matched his in intensity. The wet heat of her tongue melded with his as he stroked inside her mouth. Her fingers wound into his hair, holding on, and he deepened the kiss, cupping her jaw to perfect the angle. She tasted of mint and determination, her boldness affecting him more than any liquor or cigar. His head swam, need clawing at his skin, pushing him past reason. If he could lift her skirts here in the small carriage and impale her onto his erection, he would.

God in heaven, she was turning him into a barbarian.

He glided his mouth over her jaw, nipping her, and she whimpered. His heart hammered in his chest, blood pounding along his length, the demand for friction obliterating all else. He wanted to feel every creamy, lush inch of her, for as long as it took to sate this unmanageable desire. Hours . . . days. *Years*.

"I cannot stop thinking about the train," he said against the skin behind her ear. "How you felt on my fingers. The sounds you made when you found your pleasure. I need to hear those sounds again."

A shiver racked her body. "Will . . ."

"Tell me, Ava. Tell me you need me." *Tell me I'm not alone.*

"Yes, I need you." Her fingers clutched at his arms as she tried to drag him closer. "Just once more."

He shifted and took her mouth in a frantic kiss. Lips and teeth clashed in desperation as they breathed in each other. His hands roamed over her arms, shoulders, down over her corseted breasts. She arched her back, pressing into him for more, and he was ready to crawl out of his skin. "I'll tell Palmer to take us to a hotel. I want to undress you. See you. Taste you. Bury myself between your thighs. Repeatedly."

"A hotel?" she panted.

He reached for her skirts with one hand, gathering the fabric above her knees. *Just one quick touch of bare skin. One swipe of her cleft to feel how wet and hot.* "Well, we cannot go to your apartments, and my house is out of the question."

She gripped his arm, preventing her skirts from going any higher. "Why is your house out of the question?"

The tone of her voice had shifted, from molten metal to cold, hard steel. Her palm pushed against his shoulder in order to see his face, and he felt himself frown. "Ava, I don't bring women to my home."

"Women?"

Her lips compressed into thin, white lines, so he tried to explain, to get them back on track. "I've always kept my affairs discreet, mostly as a way to protect Lizzie. And there's the staff to consider." Not to mention the campaign. He did not want to jeopardize the race, not when he and Bennett were so close.

She swallowed and briefly closed her eyes. "You want to keep this a secret."

"Yes, it's how I've always conducted my private life. I expect discretion in my affairs and prefer long-term partners who are amenable to an up-front arrangement."

"An up-front arrangement? So, you want me as your mistress."

He lifted a shoulder. "Yes, I do, though I don't care what name we give it, and you can set the—"

Pain exploded across his cheek, a sharp crack echoing as his head snapped to the side. "Go to hell, Will."

Damnation, that hurt. He'd never had a woman slap him before. His jaw clenched while humiliation and anger burned in his stomach. Slowly he looked over at her, trying to get a grip on his fury, when he noticed her eyes were glistening. Were those . . . tears?

She banged on the roof. "Let me out here!" she shouted to Palmer.

"Keep driving!" he yelled over her. Then he pointed a finger at her. "You are not leaving this carriage until you tell me why you are upset."

"You stupid man, I don't owe you any explanations. I don't owe you a damn thing. Let me out!"

She tried to lunge for the door handle, and he grabbed her shoulders. "Ava, calm down. I want to know what happened. Why are you nearly crying?"

"I am not crying!" she said. "I am so angry I could strangle you with my bare hands. How dare you attempt to make me your mistress. The entire offer is insulting."

"It is practical. We want each other, you've admitted as much," he heard himself snarl as he released her shoulders. A thought popped into his head, one he'd briefly considered before but stupidly hadn't bothered to investigate. He nearly winced as he asked, "Are you an innocent?"

"No, I am not. Which I'm certain doesn't surprise you in the least. Who'd expect anything else of a woman like me, correct?"

"I never expect anything of you—other than I will never receive a straight answer. You lie and evade my questions at every turn."

"Because I learned a long time ago never to trust men like you. Men who think women are here for their pleasure, and then use them and throw them away. But I will not allow you to treat me disrespectfully, no matter who you are and where you live."

"Who?" His hands curled into fists on his thighs. "Give me a name."

"Absolutely not. You have no right to that information. Besides, it doesn't matter any longer."

"It matters to me, very much. Because you are holding another man's sins over my head."

"No, Will. I'm holding *your* sins over *your* head. You treat everyone as if they're beneath you, that anyone not born with blood as blue as yours is unworthy. I will not become your mistress, some secret you are too ashamed to admit."

"So what are you asking for, Ava? That I court you? Be serious."

She took a deep, shaky breath, one that told him more about her turmoil than the practiced bland expression she wore. "I am most definitely serious—and I want nothing from you. Absolutely *nothing*."

No response came to mind. He stared at her blankly, his brain attempting to untangle the mess of this conversation. They'd been locked in a passionate embrace one minute, snarling at each other the next. He wanted her. Badly. But he had no clue what she was after. For him to court her publicly? The idea was ludicrous. He would not sacrifice everything he'd built just to bed her.

Her hand shot up to pound on the roof. "Here, please," she shouted, her gaze locked with his, holding, as the wheels slowed. He did not speak—and neither did she.

Cursing himself a fool ten times over, he threw open the door and helped her down. They were just up the street from her building. God knew how many times Palmer had circled the block.

She shook out her skirts and carefully smoothed the cloth before tilting her head back. "Good-bye, Will Sloane."

"Gentlemen, I believe we've covered enough ground for one afternoon." Will stood from the head of the long oak table and gathered his papers. The men around the room, Northeast's highest-ranking employees, began to rise as well, their faces all trained toward Will. "We'll approach Frick with a proposal for coke production next month, once we settle on the details."

"He'll never agree," Henry Young grumbled. Young had been one of Archibald Sloane's cronies and the biggest thorn in Will's side. "Frick's on Carnegie's payroll."

True, but loyalty only went so far in business—especially between those two men. Perhaps Will would speak to Cavanaugh about a partnership. With Northeast Railroad and East Coast Steel in bed together, Frick would be a fool not to choose them.

Will held up a hand. "Let me see what I can do. We'll pick this up next week."

Murmurs followed him out of the room. Ignoring them, he found Frank, his assistant, waiting in the hall.

"Mr. Sloane," Frank started as they continued along the corridor to Will's office. "A few cables have arrived, and Mr. Pearson telephoned. He asked that you ring him back as soon as you are able." He held out a stack of telegrams, which Will accepted and quickly read.

"Get Pearson on the line as soon as we return," he said, still concentrating on the telegrams. His step faltered when a name at the bottom of one jumped out at him: Ava. Had she changed her mind? He peered closer and saw, no, that was Abe, not Ava. His shoulders slumped.

He'd tried not to think about her over the last few days. Refusal was unusual, a bitter tonic he'd rather not swallow. Between his bank balance and his social standing, he'd never had a woman turn him down before. But Ava had said no, and he . . . he had to find a way to accept it.

Stomach suddenly burning, Will yanked on the outer office door and hurried through, with Frank following behind. Over his shoulder, Will gave his assistant answers to some of the cables as they walked to his office. "Bring me the morning's trades," he told Frank when they reached his desk. "I want to see where the stock finishes."

"Yes, sir," the young man answered. "Anything else?"

"Find me some bicarbonate of soda." He rubbed his abdomen as he sat. "That'll be all."

A tentative knock on Will's door caught his attention. Tom, Ava's brother, stood on the threshold, looking nervous. The sight of him brought forth unwelcome thoughts of Ava once more, though Will could hardly take out her stupidity on the boy. "Yes, Tom?"

"May I have a moment, sir?"

Frank's eyes widened at this request, since he preferred

to handle requests to meet with the boss. No doubt Tom would be getting a stern lecture about office propriety from Frank in a few moments. "Frank, find me the bicarbonate and I'll speak with Tom."

"Of course, sir." Frank hurried from the room, shooting Tom a disapproving glance on the way.

When the door closed, Will said, "Don't mind Frank. He's quite protective of my time, though sometimes he overdoes it a bit."

"I apologize," Tom said. "I'm doing my best to learn the way things work around here."

"From what I've heard, you're doing a stellar job. Frank said he's moved you to the ledgers because you're proficient with numbers."

"Proficient?"

"Very good at," Will supplied.

"Oh, yeah, proficient. I like numbers. Always have, ever since I had a dice game going off Canal Street."

Will suppressed a smile. "I'm assuming your sister is unaware of said dice game."

Tom's face paled a little, an answer all to itself. "No, she'd have my head if she knew. You won't tell her, will you?"

"You have my word I will not." No use mentioning he'd never see Ava again. Now there was a depressing thought. "What did you wish to speak with me about?"

"Well, I was going through the ledgers and thought maybe I should compare them to last year's numbers—"

"Why would you want to do that?" Will interrupted sharply. Last year's ledgers were . . . an embarrassment. Will had missed his investment firm stealing money from Northeast Railroad, and he'd removed the evidence of his stupidity from the office. No one would see those ledgers but himself.

"To give you an idea of how the company is performing

year to year. I thought if we compared this week to the same week last year, you'd be able to see how much growth has happened. But I can't find last year's ledgers."

The boy was smart, no doubt about it. Will liked Tom's initiative, performing a task that hadn't been assigned in order to improve Will's understanding of the company. "Those ledgers are private for a reason, Tom, but I appreciate your diligence. Perhaps you could compare to the previous year instead?"

Tom nodded. "I was worried someone took off with your ledgers, Mr. Sloane. I'm glad to hear you know where they are."

"Indeed, I do." He rocked back in his chair. "Was that all?"

"Yes, sir. I'll leave you to it, then."

Spinning, Tom started for the door, but Will called after him. "Wait, Tom. Tell me . . ." He wanted to ask the question so badly, find out any scrap of information about her, but pride thankfully stepped in. "How are you enjoying your position here?"

A grin split Tom's face. "I love it, Mr. Sloane. Thank you for the opportunity."

Will waved that away. "It's my pleasure. I have a keen eye for talent, and you've been a great addition to the staff. What about your friends, the ones you were arrested with? Any word from either of them?"

"No, sir." Tom threw his shoulders back. "And I want nothing to do with either of 'em. You know, when we were in the jail, they wouldn't tell the coppers that it was my first time working with them. They made it sound as if I was a regular dip. What kind of friends do that?"

"Not very good ones," Will said. "I am glad you've distanced yourself from that life. You have a bright future ahead of you, Tom. Never forget that."

"I won't, sir. And thank you again for taking me on."

"Of course." Nodding, Will dismissed the boy. But just

as Tom turned the knob, Will heard himself ask, "And how is your sister?" He nearly winced. So much for pride.

"Mary?"

"No, the other one."

"Ava?" Tom rubbed the back of his neck. "Don't know, really. She's been quiet these past few days. Keepin' to herself. She's happy about my job, though. Said we'll be able to move upstate quicker, thanks to my wages."

Will's stomach clenched, the burn firing up once more. Where the hell was Frank with that bicarbonate? "Is that what you want, then? To move upstate?"

"Hell—I mean heck, no. That's Ava who wants to move. Not me. I never want to leave the city."

"Good. Maybe you can talk some sense into her."

The side of Tom's mouth hitched, amused. "Ava's as stubborn as they come, Mr. Sloane. Suspect I'd have better luck convincing a pig to sprout wings and fly."

"Madam Zolikoff, thank you for coming this evening!"

Phillip Price came toward the front door, his hand outstretched. A handsome, wealthy widower in his early forties, Mr. Price owned a prosperous textile factory. His carefully oiled brown hair had a shot of silver at the temples and he wore a neatly trimmed beard. He'd been one of Ava's regular clients for the last seven months.

Slipping on her gracious smile, she transferred her heavy carpetbag to her left hand and used her right to shake. "Of course, Mr. Price," she said in her Russian accent. "I look forward to assisting your guests tonight."

"Excellent! I'll show you the parlor we can use for the proceedings." He took her elbow and led her down the main hall to a set of wooden doors, which he promptly threw open. "Here we are. I think this has everything you require."

The heavy curtains had been pulled shut, darkening the room, so Mr. Price flicked the switch of the gasolier and illuminated the space. The furniture she'd requested—the lightweight round table, the screen in the corner, the coat rack—all seemed to be in place. "This is exactly what I needed. Thank you. What time shall they arrive, then?"

"The guests should start arriving in fifteen minutes or so. I'll take them into the front parlor, and you may join us when you are ready."

Ava nodded, and then Mr. Price left the room, quietly closing the doors behind him. She told her hosts that she needed to "sense the energy in the room" ahead of time, but, in truth, there were several pieces to arrange first. Placing her carpetbag on the ground, she opened the clasp and pulled apart the sides to reveal the necessary items for this evening. A tambourine. A long, retractable rod. A small strip of cheesecloth. Deck of playing cards. She moved the chairs closer to one another. Last, she turned off the light to ensure the room would be sufficiently dark. When she had everything arranged the way she wanted, she left the room and headed to the parlor.

Mediums in New York and London were in high demand, and she knew Mr. Price's friends would all wish to speak to her beforehand. Ava didn't mind because she could often pick up one or two personal tidbits to use during the séance from these chats. When making conversation with a polite stranger, people often revealed information they assumed didn't matter, information she would store in her brain for later use. Because the more real facts Ava included in the séance, the more authentic her powers would seem to the others.

In the parlor, there were six well-dressed guests. Mr. Price was not exactly high society but, thanks to his hefty bank account, he rubbed elbows with many of the prominent families. That caused her to think of Will, an occurrence guaranteed to sour her mood. She hadn't seen him in five days, since the night he offered up his offensive proposition. *"I prefer long-term partners who are amenable to an up-front arrangement."*

No doubt there were a string of long-term partners in his past, all bored society women who fell over themselves for the opportunity to share his bed. Not Ava. She had no interest in becoming some rich swell's bird. Her life was complicated enough.

It's because you've developed feelings for him, and you want him to like you in return.

Wincing, she screwed the lid—tight—on her inner voice. That inner voice of hers was nothing but trouble.

Mr. Price noticed her standing by the door, so he came over and took her elbow. "Here's our star this evening. Everyone, this is the great Madam Zolikoff. She will be performing our séance."

Heads swung her way, and she was soon enclosed in a tight circle of guests as they peppered her with questions. Did she think the spirits would cooperate this evening? Did she have a spirit guide, as many of the popular mediums claimed? Was she ever scared, talking to the spirits as she did? Had she reached out to Abraham Lincoln's ghost?

Ava tried to answer them patiently and carefully, her accent never slipping. She asked them questions in return, learning all she could in a short amount of time. One woman had just lost her sister, one of the male guests his uncle. One couple was contemplating a trip to the Orient. Mr. Price said nothing, merely remained at her side, until he finally glanced at his pocket watch. "We are waiting on two more guests. Then we'll begin."

Since he was paying an absurd amount for the evening, Ava did not complain. The fee from tonight's séance would pay one quarter of their rent and food bill this month. "Of course," she told him. "We should wait for everyone to arrive. The more people, the more energy to summon the spirits."

"Have you always been able to commune with spirits, Madam Zolikoff?" one of the male guests asked, his eyes firmly on her bosom.

Ava tried to remain calm. It certainly wasn't the first time a male guest had stepped over the line of propriety with her, yet it still bothered her. She made a mental note to watch this man closely. "Ever since I can remember," she answered.

The doors behind her opened, and Mr. Price's head snapped toward the sound. "Excellent, you're here. We can start."

Ava casually glanced over—and her heart froze. Everything inside her careened to a hard stop.

A familiar, tall blond man in stark black evening clothes stood framed in the doorway. Will Sloane. He was as handsome and commanding as ever, while a dazzling, young blond woman clung to his arm. An older woman, probably the girl's mother considering the similar features, hovered nearby. Ava watched as Will smiled and reached out to shake Mr. Price's hand. "I apologize for our tardiness. Miss Baldwin was keen on seeing the lights along Madison Square so we took the long way over."

Will was . . . here. And he was with a woman.

Chapter Eleven

Will glanced about the room, taking a quick measure of the others attending the dinner party, when his gaze landed on a familiar set of lips. His body jerked, the shock of seeing her here like a physical impact. What in the hell was Ava doing at Price's home? Then he noticed the blond wig and the dark clothing. *Goddamn it*.

Madam Zolikoff, in the flesh.

His jaw clenched. Miss Baldwin had not mentioned that a séance would be taking place this evening. If he'd known, Will certainly would not have offered to escort her and her mother. Now he was stuck here, unable to leave, because he hadn't arrived alone.

Ava turned away to speak with another guest. He could tell by the set of her shoulders that she was unhappy to see him, though he didn't know why. She wasn't the one who had been rejected. Will had made a perfectly reasonable offer, one many women would have been amenable to, and she'd thrown it back in his face.

That had stung, yet it hadn't stopped him from wanting her.

"Good evening, Mrs. Baldwin, Miss Baldwin, Mr. Sloane.

May I offer you all a drink before we get started?" Price asked.

"Yes, thank you," Mrs. Baldwin answered.

"The strongest you've got," Will muttered.

Price lifted a brow but said nothing before walking away. Mrs. Baldwin excused herself to see a friend in the crowd, leaving Miss Baldwin alone with Will. The girl's hand tightened on Will's forearm as she leaned into his side. "I hope you don't mind there's a séance tonight. It should be good fun."

A debutante from one of the very best families, Miss Baldwin was the current favorite in the Mrs. William Sloane derby. The eighteen-year-old had impeccable manners and a cool blond beauty that appealed to Will. Right now, her pale blue eyes were glowing with excitement. "And I'm told that we can ask for a private reading afterward."

Dear God, this night would never end. He tried to keep his annoyance from showing. "Are you certain you wouldn't rather go to dinner, just the three of us?"

"Oh." Her smile dimmed significantly. "We could leave, I suppose."

Will suddenly felt like an ass, the stuffy bore that Lizzie always teased him about. But how could he expect to stay in the same room as Ava and not lose his mind?

The back of his neck prickled, awareness sliding through his body, and he looked up to find knowing brown eyes appraising him. Daring him. Ava obviously expected him to turn tail and run. Did she think him afraid of her?

He threw Miss Baldwin an affable grin. "No, I apologize. It was rude of me to suggest, especially when you are so keen on staying. I'll gladly suffer, if only to see you happy, Miss Baldwin."

Her face lit up once more. "Please, when we're alone, you may call me Charlotte."

He nodded. "Then you must call me Will."

"Here you are," Price said, returning. First he presented Charlotte with a glass of champagne, then he handed Will a heavy crystal glass with a splash of amber liquid on the bottom. "That's the finest whiskey imported from—"

Will threw it back in one swallow, the rich, woodsy liquor burning all the way down to his troubled stomach. He handed the empty glass back to Price. "Thank you. Shall we get started?"

Price blinked but turned to the rest of the room. "Everyone, let's adjourn to the back parlor."

Will glanced at the other guests as they filed into the hall. Eager faces surrounded him, like fatted calves being led to the sacrifice, these fools who believed in Madam Zolikoff's powers. How much would she profit from these ridiculous proceedings?

Head high, she breezed by him, and he caught a whiff of lavender and spice. His muscles tightened, the memory of her orgasm on his fingers resurfacing and setting fire to his blood.

He should keep away from her, find another warm and willing bed partner instead. Of course none of those women would have Ava's wit or bravery, or her sharp tongue that could flay a man like a bullwhip. She had so much fire. Scorching heat. The two of them would be explosive together, if she'd allow it. Perhaps he could request a "private reading" and try to convince her once more.

Why cannot you accept her refusal? It wasn't his nature to beg or plead. He'd discussed what he wanted, and she declined. Pride demanded he forget her. And yet . . .

"Ladies and gentlemen," he heard her say as he entered the dark performance room. "If everyone would have a seat." Madam Zolikoff gestured to the round, wooden table. The chairs were close, putting the guests shoulder to shoulder with one another. He quickly led Charlotte to the seats directly opposite from where Ava had positioned herself. *Stay far, far away from her.*

"Please, everyone sit. Then we will begin."

Once Charlotte had arranged herself, Will squeezed into a seat. There must be a reason why Ava needed the guests so cramped together, but damned if he could figure it out.

Price slid the wooden doors shut, which left only a dim standing lamp behind Ava's chair. She sat and held up her hands. "You have all come here this evening," she started in her Russian accent, "to commune with the spirit world. If you do what I say and clear your mind, we might succeed. But if there is negative energy in this room, we will not be able to reach the spirits."

Will swore he felt her staring at him though her eyes were on the others. Negative energy, indeed.

"Now, everyone please, remove your gloves and clasp hands with one another. Once you are ready, we will begin by chanting."

Charlotte stripped off her gloves and eagerly grasped his hand. Everyone at the table did the same until they were all touching, including Madam Zolikoff. "Chant with me. 'Spirits of the past, come forth and visit with us.'" She repeated the phrase a second time, and the guests began echoing the words—all except Will, of course.

Again and again, the words were repeated, faster and faster. He could hear Charlotte struggling to breathe properly in her corset and keep up with the chant, and Will assumed most of the women in the room were on the verge of passing out. How could this be healthy?

The lamp suddenly went off, plunging the room into total darkness. The guests, including Charlotte, all gasped. "I sense we are close!" Madam Zolikoff declared. "Do not drop your hands, the chain must remain intact! Everyone keep chanting!"

Will could not see a thing. The heavy curtains prevented

even the glow from a streetlamp to enter the room. He could only feel the small hands of the ladies on either side of him. A few seconds later, a tambourine rattled—and all the guests quieted. "I sense a spirit is with us!" Madam Zolikoff said, and Will rolled his eyes in the pitch black. "Are you from the other side?"

The instrument rang again, and the guests tittered with excitement.

"Excellent. Are you a relative of someone in the room?"

No sound, so she asked, "Then can you help us speak with those on the other side who wish to reach a loved one?"

Riiiiiiing.

"Please, everyone, think of the loved one you wish to contact."

The guests were quiet, and Will tapped his foot impatiently. Was everyone buying this drivel?

"I'm seeing a spirit. It's a woman. Older. She's had heart trouble. A heart episode—"

"My mother!" one of the other guests breathed. "Is it my mother?"

"I think so," Madam Zolikoff said. "Her name begins with an M or an N . . ."

"P!" the same guest shouted. "Her name was Pauline."

"Yes! Pauline!" A short silence. "She says you have been taking her death extremely hard. She wishes for you to move on with your life, to take the trip you've always wanted."

"Out West. My mother knew I've always wanted to go out to California." The woman's voice trembled as if on the verge of tears. "Tell her thank you and I will!"

Will let out a heavy sigh. This whole exercise was ridiculous.

"Oof," he grunted as a sharp, sudden pain exploded

behind his head, rocking him forward in his seat. A damned forceful smack, as if someone had walloped the back of his head. He spun around, but his eyes had yet to adjust to the complete darkness. His ears remained keen, however; yet he'd heard no rustling and presumably the group still locked hands.

"Is everyone still holding hands?" he asked. "Did anyone break away?" Everyone murmured their assent, confirming that hands remained clasped around the table, but Will knew the person responsible.

Ava. Somehow, she'd managed to get out of her seat and strike him. He would bet his life on it.

Madam Zolikoff relayed the woman's message. Nothing was amiss in the placement of her voice, leaving Will baffled. How had she done it? *Damn her.*

The séance continued with all the same tricks. More ringing of the tambourine. More messages from the great beyond. At one point, Will felt a strange touch on his shoulder, almost like a metal rod. None of the spirits wanted to commune with him, thank God. Probably because Ava knew he would not play along with this farce.

Just wait until he got her alone.

The séance lasted little more than an hour. After that time, Madam Zolikoff requested a few minutes to collect herself. Price obligingly cleared the room, and Ava was able to take her first deep breath since seeing Will walk in tonight.

The man did curious things to her insides—tangible, earthly things that were not figments of anyone's imagination. No, these were altogether real, as real as they were unwelcome. Butterflies had filled her stomach while she sat across from him. At one point she could've sworn his foot had rubbed against hers, causing her to nearly jump out of her skin.

She lifted a glass of water and brought it to her lips, trying to cool herself off. As much as she hated him, her body still remembered. Late at night, when reason fled and exhaustion crept in, she debated saying yes to his offer. After all, as she'd admitted, she was no virgin, and they clearly had some sort of physical connection unlike anything she'd experienced to date. Why not indulge it? Did she not deserve a bit of harmless fun, after the years of hard work she'd endured?

Furthermore, it wouldn't be like what happened with Stephen van Dunn. With Stephen, she'd believed the two of them had a future, that they would build a life on love and laughter. Will was not deceiving her. Quite the opposite, in fact. He'd been brutally honest about the entire business, putting it plainly that the two of them had no future together.

Was she crazy for reconsidering? Not to being his mistress, but to enjoying the pleasures two people could discover in a hotel room now and then?

Price stuck his head in the door. "Are you ready for a reading, or would you like a few more moments?"

"I am ready. Thank you, Mr. Price."

"Please," he smiled, "I would appreciate it if you called me Phillip."

Mr. Price had been quite kind, but the unnecessary touches and glances tonight made her wonder over his motives. He would not be the first man to assume Madam Zolikoff amenable to earning money in another manner.

She inclined her head politely. "Thank you, Phillip."

One after another, she saw three guests privately for readings. Thankfully, their faces gave away most everything she needed to know. When people desperately wanted to believe, they were eager to provide clues to help her along. Rolling her shoulders to relieve the tension, she wondered if Will would be foolish enough to ask for a reading.

The door opened, and a blond head appeared. Not Will, thank God, but this was the woman Will had escorted this evening. Miss Baldwin, as Phillip had pointed out earlier.

This was Will Sloane's future, a woman such as this. Beautiful, refined, perfect manners, with a willowy figure. The consummate political wife. No doubt the girl would obey his every command.

"Madam Zolikoff," the young woman said. "I hope you don't mind performing another reading for me."

"No, of course. Come, my dear. Sit. Let's see what the future holds for you."

Miss Baldwin, dressed in a sleek mauve-and-cream silk dress, arranged herself in the chair and placed her money on the table. As Ava collected the fee, she studied the other woman closely. Miss Baldwin was stunning, with classic features and milky white skin that had never seen sweat or sun, and young, likely eighteen or nineteen. Ava felt like a grizzled old crone in comparison, though she was only a few years older.

That Will and Miss Baldwin were an excellent match was obvious, even to someone like Ava. So why had a lump-sized ball formed behind her ribs? It couldn't be jealousy. Definitely not. That would mean she had feelings for the stiff railroad man, which was ludicrous.

Focus, Ava.

"Before we start," she said, "are there any specific questions you want to ask? Anything in particular you are curious about?"

The girl's lips twisted in a self-satisfied smile Ava did not care for. "I want to know about my future husband."

Of course she did. Swallowing her reluctance, Ava pushed her sleeves up and reached for Miss Baldwin's hands. "I should have known. It's what any young woman wishes to know, eh? When will you find the man of your dreams . . ."

"No, I've already found him. I want to learn specifics about our life together."

Already found him? Dear Lord, had Will *proposed*? That piece of information spun around in Ava's brain like a Coney Island carousel. "Are you . . . ?" She could not even spit the rest out.

"No," Miss Baldwin said with a flick of her dainty wrist. "But everyone knows he is considering only me and Miss Iselin for a bride. She is lovely, but . . ."

She drifted off, the implication clear. *But not as lovely as me.* Bile rose in Ava's throat, a sour-tasting dislike of both this woman and the competition Will had initiated. It would serve him right to end up married to this self-centered girl.

The hollow feeling in the pit of Ava's stomach returned. She gave herself a strong mental shake, then took Miss Baldwin's hands and placed them palms up on the wooden table.

"Excellent, let us see. This is your Head line." She traced the line in the middle of the girl's palm. "It is long and straight, meaning you overthink things. This can also be a tendency to talk yourself into a course of action, where you lead with your brain instead of your heart." The girl nodded, eager for Ava to continue.

"This here, this is your Heart line." Without questioning the reasons why, she said, "See how it starts under your middle finger? That means you have not yet found love." Miss Baldwin did not appear too concerned, so Ava pointed to a spot on the girl's hand. "And the break in the line? That means your true love is out there waiting for you, waiting to join you and complete the line on your hand."

Miss Baldwin started chewing her bottom lip. "Are you certain? Perhaps I've met him, and the line will complete once he's kissed me."

So they haven't kissed yet. Ava didn't know why that knowledge gave her a tiny thrill, but it did. "No, that is not what the lines mean. If that were the case, you would have a short, curvy Heart line starting at your index finger."

"Will my true love at least be rich?"

Oh, indeed, Will was well rid of this woman. Ava studied both palms, as if searching for an answer. "Your Fate line, here, is very faint. And it crosses the Life line, starting at the base of the thumb. This generally means you will need the support of those in your life, such as your family."

"Or my husband."

"Not without the Love line connected," Ava said patiently. "You have not met your future husband as of yet."

Miss Baldwin left moments later, her porcelain brow marred by tiny wrinkles. Ava felt a bit like one of the witches in *Macbeth*, causing mischief with her other-worldly powers and playing upon the weakness of others—not that she was experiencing any guilt, however. Will should thank her for saving him from such a shallow, conceited harpy.

A knock sounded before the latch turned. Ava expected to see Mr. Price—and found Will instead.

"Madam Zolikoff," he said with exaggerated effect, a sharp bite to the words. "I would like a private reading."

He closed the door and stepped into the room. Gray eyes burned from his great height, causing her insides to dance under her skin, an avalanche of longing and desire. Could he tell? Could he see the effect he had on her?

She let out the breath she'd been holding since he appeared. "I do not perform private readings on nonbelievers."

He crossed his arms over his chest. "Even paying non-believers?"

"Especially paying nonbelievers. They are doubly disappointed, seeing it as a waste of both time and money."

"I've already wasted my entire night. Where's the harm in five more minutes?"

Everywhere, considering she was struggling to contain herself around him. "I am certain your Miss Baldwin is eager to return home."

"She is not *my* Miss Baldwin and she may wait. I wish to speak with you."

"Two hundred dollars."

Will let out a choked sound in the back of his throat. "Pardon?"

"A reading. Right now, it will cost you two hundred dollars." A small smile escaped her lips. No way he would pay it. He'd storm off in a "waste of money" huff, and she'd never see him again.

He paused for a moment, his gaze locked on hers, then one hand slid into his jacket. He withdrew a long leather billfold, flipped it open, reached inside, and pulled out a stack of paper. Carefully he counted out two crisp bills and placed them on the wooden table in front of her. Two hundred dollars.

His mouth curved in a predatory smile of white, even teeth. "Sold."

"That buys you just a reading," Ava snapped in her normal voice. Will was glad to know the Madam Zolikoff act had now been dropped, at least between them.

"Of course," he said, and inclined his head. Taking the

chair opposite her, he stretched his legs out. "What else would it possibly buy?"

He knew what he wanted, of course. *Her*. But this stubborn woman could not be bought, cajoled, threatened, or forced into doing anything—a trait that angered him as much as he respected her for it.

"What do you want, Will?"

Drumming his fingers on the table, he debated where to start. So very many things he wished to discuss with this woman . . . "You hit me." Her brows rose, so he clarified. "During the séance. You hit me on the back of the head."

"I did no such thing. You must have angered the spirits— most likely with your arrogance."

He chuckled at the tart response. One could always count on Ava for the unexpected. "Ava, what are you doing here tonight?"

"If you haven't figured that out by now, I certainly cannot help you."

"Do not be flippant. I never would have attended if I'd known you would be here. I would not wish to cause you any discomfort while you were working."

She gave him a patronizing look, one he'd seen from her on numerous occasions. "You do not cause me discomfort. Did your Miss Baldwin not inform you of tonight's agenda?"

"Again, she is not *my* Miss Baldwin, and furthermore, no. She did not tell me anything other than we were attending a dinner party. I saw you gave her a reading."

"Yes, I did."

The blasted woman did not elaborate, though she knew damn well what he was dancing around. "I am curious about the contents of said reading."

She folded her hands on the scarred wooden table. "I believe it's none of your business."

So it had to do with him. "Please tell me you didn't say anything to her about—"

Her shoulders flew back, horror washing over her features, and Will felt himself relax. Ava hadn't revealed anything personal. "Absolutely not. She asked silly things, really. About her love life and future husband."

"And what does the future hold for her in those areas?"

Ava's generous lips twisted into a smirk, one that heated his blood. He longed to kiss that devious expression right off her face.

"Oh, William. Worried I ruined your chances with her?"

Charlotte couldn't possibly know that Will was considering her for a wife, so the questions must have been generic, the frivolous musings of an unmarried debutante. Which meant Madam Zolikoff had no influence over the outcome either way, thank God. Still, he didn't like not knowing what had been discussed. "No, of course not. She's a debutante and therefore expects to marry soon. Stands to reason she'd be curious about her fate."

"And money," Ava muttered. "Of which you seem to have plenty, so you're perfectly matched."

Something about her tone of voice . . . *Holy Christ.* "I cannot believe it—you're jealous."

"That is ridiculous. I'm certainly not jealous over any woman you choose to spend time with. They can all have you, as far as I'm concerned."

Lies on top of lies. Could he ever get a straight answer out of this woman? "Is that so?" She nodded emphatically, and he suddenly needed for her to admit the lie. No woman kissed like Ava did, with her whole body and soul, unless she felt something for the other party involved, at least not in Will's experience.

"I'd like my reading now," he said, and slid his bare palms onto the table. She swallowed and glanced down, leaving him to wait. He'd been craving her touch, the slide of her bare skin against his, for more than an hour now. If this was the only way to get her to touch him, so be it. "Come now, I've paid handsomely for it."

"Fine." She exhaled sharply and then reached for his wrists. At the first touch of her fingers, his body jolted. His pulse began to race, every nerve ending suddenly attuned to that precise area.

She pursed her lips and pretended to study his palms. "I see that you are stubborn and arrogant. You've been indulged since childhood and are convinced you're always right. You'll die a miserable, lonely old man with only your money and servants to keep you company." She released him and sat back. He'd believe her unaffected if it weren't for the furious flutter at the base of her neck. She was attracted to him and fighting it damn hard.

He tried not to smile. "A bit on the light side for two hundred dollars."

"Take it up with the union," she snapped, not meeting his eyes as she smoothed her sleeves down over her wrists.

"I'd like to read your palm."

Head shooting up, her startled gaze locked with his. "What?"

"Your palm." He crooked his finger at her. "Come, let me read it."

"No. You're hardly qualified to understand—"

He reached forward and snagged her right hand in both of his palms. His breath caught. The same electric current jumped between them, the simmering desire on the verge of boiling over, a sensation that raced along every nerve ending.

Thankfully, Ava seemed too stunned to fight, so before he lost his chance, he stroked his thumbs over the smooth surface of her palm. A nearly imperceptible shiver went through her arm. *Excellent*.

With the tip of his finger he traced the longest line on her palm. "You have a sturdy, long Life line, which means you're clever and hardworking. You have many responsibilities but handle them admirably. You're resourceful."

"That's . . . that is not what a long Life line means. You're making all of this up."

He looked into her bewildered brown eyes. "This is my reading. Stop interrupting." Shifting in his chair, he continued. "This is your Love line." He dragged his finger slowly across her delicate, creamy skin, tracing the slight indentation as if memorizing it.

Perhaps he was. He wanted to learn everything possible about her body, feast on her until he was sated. Satisfy this obsession for her and then return to the way things were before Madam Zolikoff. The calm predictability where no one challenged him.

But first . . . first he would have her.

He cleared his throat. "You do not trust easily because you've been hurt in the past. You are suspicious of your passion, of your feelings. But there's so much passion inside you, Ava. It's as plain as the lines crisscrossing your skin." He slid his fingertip down the length of each of her fingers, one by one, mapping her digits with his touch. Her lips parted, and he heard a small sigh escape. "So much passion it makes you ache."

Lifting her hand to his lips, he placed a tiny kiss on the pad of every calloused finger, until he'd given attention to all five, then he pressed his mouth to the middle of her palm. Her small hand trembled beneath his lips, and he gently nipped the heel of her hand with his teeth. She gasped but did not pull away, and the sound caused his cock to swell behind his trousers.

"Do you ache, Ava?"

"Yes," she breathed, her chest now rising and falling rapidly.

Sensing victory, Will drew another line on her palm. "This is your Fate line," he said, holding her stare. Her brown depths were dark and glassy, and his erection throbbed in response. Soon. He would have her very, very soon. "Would you like to know what your fate holds?"

She nodded, and the words tumbled out of his mouth. "There is a man you know, one very close to you. He wants to bring you pleasure, more pleasure than you can possibly stand. Worship you with his hands . . . with his mouth. Take you to bed and love you until you beg for mercy. He will take very good care of you, Ava. So good, you'll never doubt again."

A becoming flush crept up her neck, her mouth going slack with arousal. The air turned thick, like breathing in humid air on a hot summer day, and Will had to remind himself of the reasons he could not pounce on her now. "Will you meet me tomorrow?"

He held his breath, waiting for any sign from her. Finally, just when he thought she wouldn't answer, she nodded. Satisfaction roared through him, lust tightening his belly. "Meet me tomorrow at the café inside the Washington Street Hotel at one o'clock sharp." Another nod of acknowledgment.

Standing, he crossed to her side of the table and leaned down to quickly brush his lips across hers. "Until tomorrow."

Chapter Twelve

Ava could not stop trembling. She sat at a small iron table in the hotel's crowded café, thankfully an establishment where women were permitted to dine alone or with other women. Otherwise, an unescorted woman would have presented a problem.

But Will had known, obviously. The careful consideration of this location should not surprise her, undoubtedly a result of his many illicit trysts over the years. He was clearly experienced in seducing a woman, evidenced by his ability to turn her into a puddle of desire last night at Mr. Price's house. How could she have possibly refused him?

Something about seeing him there with another woman had caused her to act rashly. Ridiculous, when she had no right to be jealous. Logically, she'd known as much, yet a small part of her needed Will to want *her*—not some girl only interested in his money. And whatever the reasons behind this line of thinking could be unearthed precisely never.

The urge to flee welled up for the thousandth time since accepting his proposal. The man was pompous and privileged, the complete opposite of her in nearly every way. *It's not too late. You can still leave.* But she wouldn't, not now.

Because you deserve one afternoon of selfishness. One afternoon to merely enjoy herself. How long had it been since she'd done that? Years, most likely. There were countless things to do every day, responsibilities she could not shirk. And every penny had been saved or spent on the family—never on her.

One afternoon. That was all she wanted. All she needed. After today, no more selfishness. This day would sustain her for years, the memory of an afternoon where a handsome, enthralling man had been desperate for her. Then she would walk away with her heart intact.

A tall figure across the room caught her eye. *Will.* Heart pounding in her throat, she watched the shift of his broad shoulders, the length of his long, confident stride. Thigh muscles bunched under his navy trousers with each step. Heavens, he was beautiful. Men should not be this appealing; it was unfair to the women of New York.

His mouth hitched when he saw her, something akin to relief shining in his gray gaze as he sat at her table. "Miss Jones," he murmured in his cultured, deep voice. "I had my doubts you would actually show."

She swallowed. "I'm a woman of my word, Mr. Sloane."

He reached into his coat pocket and placed a handkerchief on the table. Then he leaned in and said quietly, "Inside is a key to room four-oh-four. Take the stairs there now, and I'll follow in a few minutes. Did you settle your bill here?" He indicated her half-empty china cup.

"Yes, I did." She stared at the white linen handkerchief. Was she truly going to do this? How could she *not* do this? No one had ever caused her to feel this dizzy or desperate. When would a chance like this, with a man she craved to the bottom of her toes, arise again?

"I cannot risk conception."

He jerked slightly at her quietly blurted words. "Of course. We'll take precautions to prevent a child. I would never want to add to your burdens, Ava. And you should know that, should a child accidentally result, I promise I will accept responsibility."

She believed him. He was different from Stephen van Dunn, so much more open and forthright. Will did not mince words or spout platitudes; he said what he meant and damn the consequences. Stephen had been weak, too afraid to stand up to his family for her. Will Sloane was the strongest man she'd ever met, with a drive and force of will unlike any other.

Decision made, she slid her hand across the metal table and fisted the cloth. The outline of the large key bit into her gloved palm as she rose. "Good afternoon, sir."

He stood and tipped his derby. "And you as well, miss."

The stairs loomed inside the lobby, and she took them carefully, slowly, thanks to wobbly knees. Up she went until she reached the fourth floor. Brass placards on each door proclaimed the room number. Breathing hard, she unearthed the key from the cloth in her hand and fit the end into the lock. Turned. Pushed the wooden door open.

A large room came into view—along with an equally large bed. Against the wall stood a wooden dresser with a porcelain pitcher and washbasin on top, but her focus remained on the bed. Would she truly be taking off her clothes and lying with Will Sloane? The skin of her face burned just considering it. Yet Ava was not particularly shy or timid, and she did trust Will to take care with her. He'd already demonstrated that ability on the train from Albany.

She exhaled and removed her gloves. Then she unpinned her hat, placed it on the dresser. Before she could worry over what else to take off, a knock sounded at the door. Opening it, she found Will on the other side, his lids heavy as he swept down her frame. "I appear to have the right room," he said softly, then came inside.

When the door shut behind him, he stepped in closer and cupped her jaw in his large palms. "I hardly know where to start, you exquisite woman. I want to do quite a number of dirty things to you."

Her heart raced inside her chest. "Someone as proper as you, dirty? I'll believe it when I see it."

"Always challenging me," he murmured. His head dipped, mouth drawing closer. "Brace yourself, then, because there is no limit to the amount of pleasure I plan to bestow on you this afternoon."

He kissed her, a swift sealing of their lips that stole her breath. He did not tease or hesitate; instead, he was impatient and demanding. His tongue wasted no time in sliding past her lips to invade her mouth. Slick heat assaulted her, and a wave of need unfurled low in her belly. The unexpected wildness went a long way in reassuring her, the idea that he might crave her enough to forget his well-bred manners.

One of his large hands settled against the side of her neck, and the other burned through the clothing on her hip. Her own hands crept along his lapels and then twined around his neck, leaving her fingers to tangle in his silky hair. He clutched her tighter, her breasts now crushed to the flat plane of his chest, and he let out a frustrated grunt.

"Too many blasted clothes. May I undress you?"

The portentous question hung between them as they both struggled for air. There would be no going back after this moment. Will's intense gaze, so full of hunger, burned down at her, almost as if he wanted to devour her on the spot, and all doubt fled. She brought her fingers to her throat to unfasten the small pearl buttons at the top of her collar.

Will stepped back, his mouth curving in a half grin as

he shrugged out of his frock coat. By the time the top of her throat lay exposed, he'd already shed his necktie and vest. "Here, allow me."

Just when she thought he would assist with her clothing, he scooped her up and carried her to the bed. With one knee on the mattress, he placed her near the center of the bed and then stretched out beside her.

He leaned over to capture her mouth, his body pressing her into the mattress. She would never tire of his kisses, the skilled assault on her senses. So unlike any of the others she'd shared with a scant number of men over the years, Will's kisses held wicked promise, the lure of something momentous ahead. If she hadn't told herself this was a onetime occurrence, she might be worried of becoming addicted to him.

Breaking away from her mouth, his lips trailed along her jaw. His fingers clasped her hand and brought it to her chest. "You work on the top half, and I'll work on the bottom."

Before she could garner any embarrassment, he was moving down the bed. He began lifting fistfuls of her skirts, raising them to her waist, exposing her drawers. His eyes, hot and intense, raked her from hip to toe. "You are impossibly lovely. I cannot think of a more beautiful sight than you, right at this moment."

He found the tie to her bustle and, rolling her, removed the padded piece. Then she was on her back, and he slid between her thighs. His shoulders held her legs wide open, his face right above her mound. His hot breath gusted over the thin cotton of her drawers. What was he doing down there?

She'd expected for them both to remove their clothing, after which they would join their bodies. Quickly. Feverishly. A lovemaking that would satisfy this insane burning. Then she could put her clothes back on and leave, resume her daily routine. In all her musings, never had Will remained mostly clothed and placed his face between her legs.

"I do not see you unbuttoning," he reminded her.

"I am waiting for these dirty things you promised."

"Oh, indeed?" He reached forward and parted her drawers, revealing the most intimate part of her. His head dipped, and she wondered what he—

The wet slide of his tongue swept through her cleft, and Ava's hips jerked off the bed. Mother Mary, what had he just done? The tingles reverberated down her legs and caused her toes to curl.

"Hmm," his deep voice rumbled. "I think you're going to like the first dirty thing as much as I will."

Will had died and his tongue had gone to heaven. It was the only explanation for the exquisite taste of her, this maddening woman who had been driving him crazy for weeks. But he had her now, and he had no plans to let her go until they were both exhausted.

Settling deeper into the mattress, he devoted his attention to Ava's sex, nibbling and licking, sucking and biting. He hadn't been able to wait—certainly not the eternity it would take to undress her—before tasting her. And the experience thus far substantially outweighed his imaginings.

Her heavy breaths soon turned into moans, and those quickly transformed into cries. He relished each one, using his mouth to drive her higher and his fingers to increase her pleasure. His erection throbbed between his abdomen and the mattress, and he briefly worried he'd spill in his trousers. But he would not stop, not when her thighs began to shake and her muscles drew taut.

She tasted sweet and spicy, a flavor all her own, and he lapped the wetness like the most delicious delicacy. Caviar, oysters, champagne . . . all of them paled in comparison to

the arousal on Ava's skin. A few minutes later, she let loose
a string of husky, incoherent words and the thin hold on his
control began to unravel.

His cock screamed for friction, and Will tried to resist,
he truly did. But when the walls of her cleft tightened, her
fingers knotting in his hair to hold him in place, he lost the
battle. Instinct took over—that and the fear he'd finish in
his clothing.

He shot up to his knees and began struggling with the
fastenings at his waistband. "*Damn it.*" His dashed fingers
would not work properly.

"Hurry, Will."

A button flew off and landed on the coverlet. The buttons
to his combination were next, and he'd never cursed the
modern fashion sensibilities before now.

Finally he reached in and withdrew himself, positioned
the blunt head of his erection at the slick entrance to her
body, and pushed. Tight, wet heat gripped him, and he slid
in only about a quarter of the way before he felt her flinch.
He gritted his teeth and froze. "I beg your pardon. I should
have been more careful."

"Give me a moment. I . . . It has been a while." Discomfort had replaced desire in her expression, her lids now
screwed tight.

An uncomfortable feeling settled throughout him, one
he did not experience often. Yet, he recognized the slight
nausea in his stomach from his childhood. *Shame*. He'd
assumed . . . well, she hadn't been a virgin . . . so he'd
thought . . .

Goddamn it. He fought the urge to thrust, to bury himself inside her. Instead, he withdrew, perspiration breaking
out on his brow.

"Wait, I'm all right." Ava tried to grab at him, but Will
held up a hand.

"I'm rushing. I want you to enjoy this, not endure it. Now, let me undress you."

Instead of listening, she propped up on an elbow and reached toward him with the other. He didn't guess her intent until her fist wrapped around his erection. He hissed through his teeth. "Stop, Ava. I cannot—" She stroked him firmly, base to tip, and Will's hips flew forward. "No, please. I want to prepare you."

"So prepare me," she breathed. "And I'll prepare you."

A dry chuckle escaped his throat—which turned into a groan as she tugged on his cock once more. "I'm quite prepared, thank you."

"Still so polite," she murmured. "That must mean you can stand for a bit more preparation, I believe."

He should have known she would argue with him. The two of them were born to be at odds. Strangely, he did not mind it at the moment.

She dragged her thumb over the sensitive spot on the underside of his penis, and his eyes nearly crossed. "*Oh, Christ.*"

"I think you mean, 'Oh, Ava.'"

"Yes, that too." He trailed a finger around the entrance to her body. Her skin glistened with arousal. Gently he pushed one digit inside her. Jesus, so tight. Her hips rose up a bit to meet him, her breath hitching. He pumped a few times, then added a second finger. She bit her lip, her grip on his erection constricting. Then a third.

"Oh, God," she said, her back arching.

"I think you mean, 'Oh, Will.'"

Lids heavy, she glanced at him, a wide smile overtaking her beautiful face. Something in Will's chest expanded, lightened, like he'd been filled with steam. A buoyancy of emotion, one he didn't quite understand. One he wasn't sure he liked.

She distracted him by working his erection once more.

"You are already unbearably arrogant. I'll give my praise to a deity instead."

A challenge. Now this was familiar territory.

He withdrew his fingers, momentarily bemoaning the loss of that lush, narrow passage, and quickly yanked his suspenders down. Without bothering to remove any more clothing, he fitted himself to her opening and angled his hips.

She threw her head back, arms splayed uselessly on the mattress, and he continued to press forward. She was snug, but not impenetrable, so with shallow, steady thrusts, he sank until fully seated. He paused for a long moment, enjoying the first superlative feel of her slick walls surrounding him. *Absolute heaven.*

He folded over her, rested his weight on his elbows, and put his mouth near her ear. "I'll have you calling my name before the afternoon is over, Ava. Even if I kill myself trying." He pulled his hips back and then snapped forward.

She sucked in a breath. Her hands found his shoulders and held on. "I suppose we'll see who wins out, then."

He started to laugh, but she rocked her hips, pulling him deeper, and pleasure surged along his shaft and up his spine. He smothered a growl. He'd never felt so out of control in his life.

He dropped his head and kissed her hard. She met his tongue with her own, not holding back, and he began to move in earnest. Reaching down, he lifted one of her legs and wrapped it around his waist. She followed with the other leg, her body now cradling him, the angle allowing him to fill her completely. Her hand slid under his shirt, over the fabric of his underclothes, and he suddenly craved her touch on his bare skin. He broke off from her mouth and lifted his shirt over his head. Then he unbuttoned his combination, pulled his arms free, and pushed the garment down to his hips. She rewarded him by running her fingers over every inch of his torso.

"I wish you were naked," he murmured into her throat as he pumped into her. "I want to see every inch of you." Especially her breasts. They were full and round, and he knew they would be soft in his hands with pink, hard nipples. . . . The image caused him to surge forward, his cock driving into her channel with deliberate force. White-hot charges erupted along his spine, the back of his knees, and nothing mattered more than being inside her right now.

His entire world was Ava. The sounds she was making in the back of her throat, the nails digging into the skin of his shoulders. The hot breath that fanned across his cheek. The warm clasp of her body and the tightening of her legs around his waist. Her responses propelled him higher, until he was fighting off his release.

Just when he thought he'd finish first, her thighs began trembling. He adjusted slightly, hitting higher inside, then grinding against her on the downstroke, until he found the right combination. Once, twice—and she tensed under-neath him. Her face went slack, and she cried out.

"Say my name," he growled, riding through her release and trying to hold off his own. Ava didn't answer, merely shuddered, her limbs pulling taut as she came. *Stubborn woman.*

Such was the last coherent thought he had before his own orgasm overtook him. It started all the way down at his toes and raced up the back of his legs and through his balls. He jerked out of her, the cold air a shock to his over-heated erection, and used his hand to quickly bring him-self to completion, finishing on the bedclothes. Tiny shocks went through his limbs, the orgasm drawing out until he turned sensitive.

Panting, he dropped next to her on the mattress. "You are amazing."

"You did all the work, railroad man," she said through heaving breaths. "But if you'd like to give me credit, I'll accept it."

The side of his mouth hitched. "Fine. You may shower me with gratitude, then."

"I'd rather run naked through the lobby downstairs."

Had he thought bedding her would turn her sweet and pliable? If so, he should damn well have known better. When was the last time he'd found himself laughing in bed with a woman? Yet he laughed now as he rolled to face her. She appeared deliciously disheveled, a well-sated woman— well sated and, unfortunately, still clothed. "I would pay money to see that."

Ava turned on her side as well, their faces close on the pillow. "I'm afraid you'll have to settle for the private version."

Gray eyes flashed in appreciation of that suggestion. This side of him—the relaxed, playful, *normal* side— appealed to Ava. A lot. His laugh . . . his smile . . . the serene set of his lips . . . He appeared more his age, like a young, carefree, handsome man.

She openly admired his trim, bare torso, with its valleys of bone and ridges of muscle. Strong arms and wide shoulders. Dark blond hair dusted his sternum, down his flat stomach to the opening in his trousers. He'd already tucked his shaft back into his combination.

"When?" he asked.

She had already forgotten what they were discussing. She glanced up. "When, what?"

"The private version. When may I see it?" He lifted a hand and swept the hair off her forehead. "Now?"

Now? "I assumed . . . That is, aren't we finished for the day?"

He chuckled as his fingers found the tiny buttons at the top of her shirtwaist. Flicked one open. Then another. "I told you there would be no limit to the pleasure I would give you this afternoon. Or did you forget?"

"You did give me pleasure." He continued working the buttons with one hand, a feat that impressed her. Were most men this adept at women's clothing? Before she could let that question ruin her mood, she continued. "Quite a lot of it, actually."

"If you thought I would race out the door as soon as we finished, I'm sorry to disappoint you. I've been fantasizing about you for days and now that I finally have you here, I shall not waste the opportunity."

He had fantasized about her? Ava didn't know what to make of that, or the idea they were not nearly done. Her mind raced with possibilities. "Are you going to undress me?"

Buttons undone, he slid her shirtwaist over one shoulder. "Yes, and then I will finish undressing myself. Once that's accomplished, I'll return to your pleasure." He helped slip her arm out of the sleeve, then turned his attention to her corset cover.

Stephen, her one and only lover, had been more of the one-and-done variety. There hadn't been a concerted effort for Ava to enjoy their coupling. Now that she'd experienced otherwise, she could see Stephen had been a selfish man—and not only in the bedroom.

"You are not what I expected."

His fingers kept at their task though his gaze found hers. "And what is it you expected?"

She bit her lip, debating how to best put it. "Less," she finally settled on.

Her corset cover came off next. "Less," he repeated with a frown. "You do not have a high opinion of me, but I do hope to change that today. On your stomach."

Ava turned to lie face down on the bed. Her boots were removed, then Will unfastened her outer skirt and petticoat, pulled the pieces down her legs. When he plucked at the strings of her corset, loosening it, she was able to draw in deeper breaths and think a bit more clearly. "I expected you to be, I don't know, more reserved."

He leaned over and put his lips near her ear. "Perhaps you bring out the worst in me."

She didn't have time to wonder over such a statement before he shifted her to her back and deftly unhooked her corset. Before she could blink the heavy edges fell to her sides, leaving her only in a thin chemise, drawers, and stockings.

He paused, his hands cupping her breasts through her chemise. The fleshy mounds more than filled his big palms, and he stared at her chest in avid fascination as he caressed her. "And if we are being honest with each other, you are much more than I expected."

"You mean my bosom?"

His gaze locked with hers, his expression serious. "No. More beautiful. More responsive. More bold. More passionate than I imagined—and I spent quite a lot of time imagining you."

She swallowed, the compliments disconcerting her. It was much easier to be at odds with this man. "Thank you," she said softly, not wanting him to think she did not appreciate his candor.

"Yet you're squirming. Have I discomforted you?"

Yes. Less talking was preferable. No risk of tender

emotions that way. Reaching, she pulled him down as she rose up to kiss him. She tasted the surprise on his lips, but only for a second, until he moved his mouth over hers. He settled on his elbows and angled his head, slipping his tongue past her lips, and she sighed into his mouth.

After a moment, he broke off and bent to kiss the skin above the edge of her chemise. At the same time, he lifted the hem and began sliding it over her hips, stomach and head, until she was bare from the waist up.

"My God, you are lovely." His hand palmed her right breast while his tongue swirled around her left nipple, teasing. She writhed as the ache built, her back bowing in a silent plea. He took his time, nibbling, his teeth sinking playfully into the soft skin and avoiding giving her what she craved. With her fingers in his hair, she tried to urge his mouth to her nipple. "*Will.*"

She felt him smile before his mouth closed over the tip and he drew deep, sucking hard. A sharp sizzle raced down her spine and settled between her legs. *Oh, heaven above.* His mouth was magical. She'd suspected his extraordinary talents when he'd licked between her legs, and this confirmed it.

Fingers toyed with the nipple not currently being worshipped with his mouth, and slickness built between her legs once more, a tingling in her sex as if she hadn't just climaxed minutes earlier. What was happening to her? Will Sloane—the proper, reserved, snobbish man she'd bickered with for the last few weeks—was turning her into a pile of sensual mush.

She dragged her hands over his shoulders, enjoying the lean muscle and solid bones, then explored his chest. Firm pectoral muscles and crisp hair. Her nail grazed his nipple—and he gasped, his mouth releasing her.

He slid his nose over her cheekbone while grinding his

obvious erection against her hip. "I want you again," he growled.

Yes, please. She did not voice the words, however. Her body was primed to take him once more, but she longed to see him undone. There had been glimpses earlier, but she needed to torment this man. To give and take more in one afternoon than either of them had experienced in a life-time. Perhaps then she could walk away without regrets.

Pushing on his shoulder, she forced him to his back. He went easily, bringing her atop to straddle his hips. The position exposed the full, pale globes of her breasts to his heavy-lidded, hungry gaze. "I've died and gone to heaven," he murmured, before cupping both mounds, using thumbs and forefingers on her nipples to drive her crazy.

She rolled her hips down the long ridge in his clothing— and he groaned. His answer was to pinch the sensitive tips between his fingers—and she groaned in response. Equally matched, neither one of them backing down . . . How could she have expected anything less?

Scooting down his thighs, she edged out of his reach. His arms dropped to the mattress as she unfastened the rest of his trousers buttons and tugged the garment off his legs. This left him in just a tight combination, which clung to his sharp hipbones, thick erection, and the long muscles in his thighs. The undergarment made him appear unbelievably virile. Rugged, like the frontiersmen they talked about.

As appealing the view, however, she was dying to see underneath.

She removed the last of his clothing, taking his socks along with the undergarment, and then Will was completely bare. Sand-colored hair covered his legs and groin. His heavy erection and balls rested between muscular thighs. Her fingers itched to touch him, to map his body and learn everything that comprised this complicated man.

"Do I meet with your approval?" he asked when the silence stretched.

A wave of self-consciousness went through her. She'd been caught admiring him. Lusting after him, even. The man's sense of self-worth would never deflate at this rate.

"Actually, I was expecting more flash underneath it all. Diamonds—or at least emeralds. Decorative gold leaf, perhaps." She grasped his erection and gave him a swift stroke. "Turns out, though, that you're just a man."

Chapter Thirteen

Yes, Will was a man like any other . . . and he reacted to her ministrations as any man in his right mind would. He panted and trembled as Ava worked him with an eagerness that made up for any lack of skill. And when she touched her tongue to the tip of his cock, he thought he'd lose his ever-loving mind.

Encouraged, she slipped the head into the lush heat of her mouth. "Christ, Ava. You don't need to do that." Not every woman liked a man's arousal in her mouth, though Will had long dreamed of seeing Ava's plump lips wrapped around his shaft. Happily, the reality far exceeded his expectations, and if she ceased he very well might cry.

She released him with a wet pop. "Do you want me to stop? I thought most men . . ."

"Yes, we do," he finished quickly. "But you don't need to do anything today that you're uncomfort—"

Her mouth engulfed his penis once more, cutting off whatever he'd been saying, and his eyes rolled back in his head. The tight suction . . . the flutters of her tongue. Dear God, he'd come in minutes if she didn't let up.

Yet he didn't halt her. His gaze bounced between her mouth and the gently swaying, naked breasts on full, tantalizing display. He'd never seen a more erotically charged sight than the one of Ava, naked on her knees, pleasuring him. His balls ached, a familiar tightening that signaled an impending orgasm. *No, no, no. Not yet.*

Levering up, he lifted her off his cock. Confusion wrinkled her brow, so he told her, "I want to be inside you again. Not finish in your mouth." He rapidly untied her drawers and worked them down her hips. She helped, pushing the garments and her stockings down her legs. Finally he had her completely naked.

"Come here, beautiful creature." He fell back on the bed and swung her legs over his hips. His erection nestled against her cleft. Rolling his hips, he dragged his cock along the lips of her sex.

"Oh," she breathed. "That feels wonderful."

He couldn't wait any longer. Raising her slightly, he lined up and let her fall, her channel swallowing him up. When their groins met, she ground down and bit her lip. "You feel much deeper this way."

"Yes, it's the angle." He could hardly wait to take her from behind. If she thought he was deep now . . . "Ride me, Ava."

She began to move, slowly at first, but Will didn't care. Her slick walls dragged over his length as her heavy breasts bounced. Her nails dug into his stomach, her thighs straining at the effort, and he had to close his eyes or risk finishing too soon.

It was no less intense this time around. He hadn't been this greedy for a woman . . . ever. Will could not get enough. Every sigh, every sweep of her delicate hands, every taste only caused him to want her more.

When he felt her begin to tighten around his shaft, he grabbed her hips and took over, pumping up into her with a primal force that surprised him. Ava didn't seem to mind, however, her cries growing louder as Will found the one sensitive spot deep inside her. She clutched at his arms as her head dropped, long brown hair escaping from her coiffure to cover her breast. "God, yes, please," she said in his favorite low rasp, and he bucked wildly, the pleasure building under his skin, behind his thighs.

He rolled the swollen bud between her thighs with his thumb and her walls immediately clamped down. She let out a shout, limbs trembling, as the orgasm engulfed her, and he'd never seen a more erotic sight. When she ceased shivering, he let go, unable to hold out a moment longer. He jerked her off his hips and then moved his hand furiously over his cock until he came with a roar. The orgasm sped through him, his muscles shuddering with the force of it, spend flinging onto his stomach. When he finished, he closed his eyes and tried to recover his wits. "That was better than the first time."

She didn't respond, just flopped down on the bed beside him. He raised up to clean himself off with a corner of the bedclothes, then he wound his arms around her and pulled her close. A thin sheen of sweat covered them both, but he could not let her go. Exhaustion overcame him, a result of the two fantastic orgasms and the soft, warm body in his arms. He closed his eyes and kissed the top of her head. "So much more than I expected. Thank you, Ava."

Ava knew the second he fell asleep. Will's arms went lax, falling to the mattress, and his breathing grew even and deep. This was her chance to leave.

Gently she disentangled herself from his enticing limbs and stood. Her clothes were strewn about, so she quickly gathered them and went to the small water closet to dress. Living with her siblings in a small apartment, she was used to dressing herself quietly in a small space. After fifteen minutes, she had seen to her needs and put herself back to rights as best she could. Too bad she hadn't a brush handy for her unruly hair. She repinned it and affixed her bonnet.

Careful not to make any noise, she crept from the water closet through the hotel room. Most women would likely regret what had occurred here . . . but Ava did not. Not when Will had been so unexpectedly passionate. He hadn't made her feel tawdry or sinful. Instead, she'd been worshipped. Adored. Pleasured to within an inch of her life. He'd taken more care with her in one afternoon than Stephen van Dunn had in five months.

Nevertheless, that was all it could be, one afternoon. Today's interlude would not be repeated. She'd already begun to feel too much for him, thanks to his tender words. *"You are so much more than I expected . . . More beautiful. More responsive. More bold. More passionate."* The remaining ice surrounding her heart had melted clean away after that, leaving a warm, full sensation in her chest that scared her.

He had no plans to marry her. Hell, he didn't even want to court her. He'd admitted as much when they'd first discussed meeting in a hotel. There was no future for Will Sloane of Northeast Railroad and Ava Jones of Bank Street. This wasn't a fairy tale, and she certainly wasn't a princess. She would not be a rich man's mistress.

Grasping the door handle, she turned back for one more glimpse. Sprawled on the bed, naked, Will was a sight to behold. A lock of sandy blond hair had fallen over his forehead, and her fingers itched to touch him. He appeared young. Disheveled. Relaxed and well sated. She could stare at him like this for hours, marveling over the contradictions in him. Ruthless one minute, tender the next. Selfish and demanding, yet he had been a giving and generous lover. Some Fifth Avenue debutante would be one lucky woman someday.

That woman would not be Ava. She had allowed herself

one afternoon of hedonism. One afternoon to experience pleasure at his hands. And though it had been spectacular, this could not be a habit. She had too much to lose.

Ignoring the weight in her chest, she left the room and continued down the hall toward the stairs. The walk home would do her good, help to clear her head. No other guests were about, a fact she was quite grateful for as she made her way down the flights of stairs and into the lobby.

As she passed the door of the café, she paid no attention to the diners, the wealthy women and well-dressed men enjoying their lazy afternoon. This was an entirely unknown crowd for the likes of Ava Jones.

So she nearly tripped when she heard a man's voice call out her name. Panic welled in her throat, and she hastened out the door and onto the walk. The fading June sunshine momentarily blinded her, and she wondered how long she and Will had been upstairs. Two hours? Three? She needed to get home and start supper for her family.

She had taken only four or five steps before a hand fell on her shoulder. "Miss Jones."

With no choice but to stop, she turned around. Mr. Charles Tompkins stared down at her, his bushy mustache twitching. "Mr. Tompkins. Hello."

"I was surprised to see you in the lobby. Were you dining in the café?"

"Yes," she lied. "I met a friend here for a late afternoon tea. You?"

"I had a business meeting in the restaurant. I am glad to bump into you. Would you be interested in having a quick drink? I wish to speak with you."

"I'm sorry but I must get home—"

"I insist," he said, and took her elbow. "I promise I won't keep you long." He began leading her back toward the last place she wanted to be. However, short of digging her heels in, there was nothing to do to prevent it.

Still, she tried to reason with him one more time. "No, really. I must be getting home. Perhaps we could meet tomorrow?"

"I don't believe so. You're a hard woman to find."

Dread settled in her stomach like a stale blintz from a hawker's cart. He'd been looking for her? Damn Will and his lie about her working for a newspaper. Her mind began to race with what Tompkins might wish to speak with her about. The interview with Bennett? She straightened her shoulders as they entered the café. Indeed, she'd lied her way out of stickier situations. She could handle Tompkins.

They settled at a table. A waiter appeared and Ava ordered tea, Tompkins a cup of coffee. When they finished, Tompkins relaxed his large frame into the small metal chair. "Let's start with the truth. You don't work for the *Brooklyn Daily Times* because there is no such paper."

"Yes, that's true. However, it's best if you remain unaware which paper employs me. We prefer to keep that information from the candidates until after the story is finished."

He cocked his head. "That is certainly unusual. No paper I've dealt with in New York, New Jersey, or Philadelphia operates in that fashion."

She lifted one shoulder, not caring whether he believed her or not. Rule number one of telling a convincing lie was to stick to the lie no matter what. "Nevertheless, my editor prefers it this way."

The waiter promptly returned and set up their drinks. When he departed, Tompkins asked, "So when may we expect this story to appear?"

"I'm not certain." She stirred sugar into her tea. "Before the election, obviously."

"Well, I should hope so. Still, it would be helpful to know if the story will be favorable or not. Since nearly all of the papers are controlled by one of the predominant political parties, it's advantageous for me to have a positive story at the ready, one that may counteract any negative story that appears."

"I hadn't realized political strategy was so complicated," she demurred. "You must be very good at your job."

His intense expression changed not a whit at her compliment. "I am very good at my job. Which is why I won't allow Bennett or Sloane to make a mistake that could jeopardize the campaign. For example, it's one thing to have a quiet, discreet affair with a rich society widow, but another altogether to carry on with a young, unmarried newspaper reporter." He lifted his coffee cup to his mouth and sipped, while Ava tried to find her tongue. "Do you see what I mean, Miss Jones?"

Her skin became a tight, fiery layer of embarrassment. Though she was not truly a reporter, the comparison struck home regardless. She was aware of how damaging it would be to Will's campaign should his association with her and/or Madam Zolikoff be discovered. Nevertheless, this overbearing man had absolutely no right to order her about.

Anger sizzled in her blood, wiping out the embarrassment. She leaned in closer. "You are under the misguided impression that you have any say over when and with whom I decide to 'carry on.' I do not answer to you, Mr. Sloane, or any other man, for that matter." She came to her feet. "Thank you for the tea."

She left the café, not glancing back even once.

Political support in New York didn't merely mean large rallies and parades; campaigning also included small, intimate dinner parties with a select group of supporters, ones who donated large amounts of money. Since those supporters usually included men Will had known from years of parties and clubs, they were generally enjoyable evenings. On this night, however, Will was having trouble mustering up any enthusiasm whatsoever.

He gave his hat and stick to the butler and then shook hands with Mr. Updike, an elderly gentleman and a big supporter of the Bennett/Sloane campaign. Updike also happened to sit on the board of Northeast Railroad. "Thank you for hosting us tonight."

"My pleasure, William. Anything to help the Sloanes, you know that. Your father would be so proud of you."

Will tried not to grimace. Pride was not an emotion Will's father had ever experienced in relation to his only son. The stick by which the Sloanes measured success had always been set ridiculously high, and Will had certainly never come close during his father's lifetime. No matter his marks, no matter the praise heaped on by his instructors, Will had been considered a "disappointment." The memory shouldn't bother him, considering everything in Archibald Sloane's life had disappointed him. His wife, his company, his children . . . A more miserable man had never been born to such privilege.

Will hoped the old man was roasting over a spit in hell, green with envy over what his "lazy" son had accomplished.

Nevertheless, one did not disparage one's parents, even if they were long dead. "That is kind of you to say," Will answered. "He certainly respected you."

Updike's chest puffed up. "Damn shame he didn't live longer. Well, come in." He waved Will through the threshold. "Most of the other guests have already arrived."

Within the Updike drawing room was the usual crowd: Bennett and Tompkins, of course, as well as the chairman of the New York Republican Party. Other members of high society were here as well; faces Will had known his entire life.

A footman stopped and presented him with a crystal

glass of champagne. Will accepted it just as a familiar voice called out, "There you are, Sloane!"

He turned and found Tompkins waving him over. Next to the campaign advisor stood John Bennett, Mr. Robert Iselin, and a young brunette who was not Mrs. Iselin. The daughter, perhaps? Will had never met her in person, but she was one of the debutantes on his list of candidates for a wife.

He waited for the usual rush of eagerness when the completion of a goal was in sight . . . but it strangely did not come. More than anything, Will wanted to walk out of Updike's house, take his carriage to Bank Street, and demand Ava tell him why she'd snuck out of their hotel room two days ago without a damn word.

But he could not. Responsibilities called, so Will threw back his champagne and strolled to the small group situated near the empty fireplace. "Good evening."

"Good to see you, Sloane." Tompkins slapped him on the back, an overly familiar gesture that set Will's teeth on edge. Perhaps because he did not care all that much for Tompkins. "I trust you know Mr. Iselin."

"Indeed, I do. How are you this evening, Robert?" The men shook hands.

"I am quite well, Sloane. I don't believe you've met my daughter." He smiled fondly at the petite girl. "My dear, this is Mr. Sloane, the candidate running with Mr. Bennett."

"Miss Iselin," Will said with a bow over the girl's gloved hand. "It is an honor to meet you."

"The honor is mine, Mr. Sloane." She had a nice, clear voice. Confident. No giggles. He liked that she held his gaze, too. "I've been closely following your campaign."

"Better watch out, Sloane," Bennett said. "She knows more about politics than you and I put together!"

Everyone laughed, including Miss Iselin, and Will said, "Then I certainly look forward to hearing more."

"I believe dinner's about to start. Why don't you escort Kathleen, Sloane? I'm certain she's tired of hearing her father talk already tonight," Iselin suggested, and Will silently chastised himself for not coming up with that idea. Wasn't he supposed to be hunting a bride?

"Of course, it would be my pleasure. Miss Iselin, would you do me the honor?" He held out his arm, and she dutifully placed her hand on his sleeve.

The crowd began to filter out of the room and into the hall. "I apologize for that," Miss Iselin said under her breath.

He glanced down at her and found her clear blue eyes studying him. "For what?"

"For being foisted on you. I'm afraid my father isn't very subtle."

"I never mind when a beautiful girl is foisted on me. And, as a debutante, it cannot be the first time for you."

"No, but it is uncomfortable all the same, so I beg your pardon on both of our accounts."

The girl had impeccable manners and a forthright approach that Will appreciated. He should be giddy with possibility right now . . . but he felt nothing. None of the expected excitement over the idea that he may have found the perfect political wife with ties to society.

Stop thinking about Ava. Stop wondering over why she left without a word.

He needed to focus. He and Bennett were nearly assured of receiving the Republican nomination, and the support of the men here could go a long way to securing Albany this fall. Wringing his hands over a woman he could no more control than the wind would not help the campaign.

"There is no need to ask for forgiveness, Miss Iselin. I am grateful you attended this evening. These dinners are usually as boring as a rainy day."

The dining room sparkled with cut crystal and sterling silver. He found them seats and assisted Miss Iselin into her chair. He took the seat next to her, with Tompkins settled directly across. Bennett was at the end of the table, near Updike.

Dinner service began, and Will's mind drifted to a familiar topic: the hotel with Ava. The afternoon had been astounding. Passionate. Wild. Even having her twice hadn't begun to sate his longing. When he awoke to discover her gone, he'd felt disappointed . . . and confused. Unusual for a woman to slink away from his bed when his back was turned. It worried him that she might regret what had happened between them.

Not that it mattered. He had plans to convince her of a command performance.

"What do you think of the movement to give workers fairer conditions and benefits, Mr. Sloane?"

Will glanced at Miss Iselin, who was watching him curiously. "I am for it. Owners who do not treat workers fairly can hardly expect to retain them. Wouldn't you agree?"

"Yes, though many owners, such as Carnegie, certainly do not. How are Northeast employees treated?"

"Quite well, though likely there's always room for improvement. Perhaps you could visit sometime and illuminate me."

"I'd like that," she said quietly.

Tompkins beamed in approval, as if Will had already proposed marriage. Irrationally, Will was irritated at the advisor's admiration. Yes, Miss Iselin had shown promise this evening, but one simple exchange did not a wife make.

He had to know more about her, test their compatibility. There were probably dozens of issues they would disagree on. After all, he and Ava barely agreed on the time of day, let alone anything else.

"You probably support the strikes on the part of workers," he told Miss Iselin.

"Oh, no." She wiped her mouth with her napkin. "Only when they are conducted peaceably. I do not condone violence."

He peppered her with questions in an attempt to find a subject the two of them would lock horns on. But every answer she gave matched his own thoughts. Kathleen Iselin was smart, articulate, had a sense of humor, and came from the same background as he. So why did he feel numb?

"Are you traveling to Newport for the summer, Mr. Sloane?" she asked as the dinner plates were cleared.

"No, I hadn't planned to open the cottage this year. When do you leave?"

"Tomorrow, as a matter of fact. Father is anxious to sail."

"Sloane has a beautiful yacht in Newport, don't you, Sloane?" Tompkins gave Will a pointed stare. "Perhaps you could take Miss Iselin sailing."

Will was too well bred to let his vexation show, but he did not appreciate Tompkins's lack of subtlety. "Yes, I would be delighted if you would accompany me one day on the water, Miss Iselin. I should be able to get away in the next few weeks."

A very becoming blush stole over her pale skin. "I should like that very much, Mr. Sloane."

"Excellent," he said with far greater enthusiasm than he felt. "I'll cable you with a date."

Ava finished with her last client and glanced around the hotel room to check she had all her belongings. She'd been on edge all day, certain that Grey and Harris would walk in at any moment. However, the two blackmailers had been noticeably absent. She was relieved, hopeful they'd forgotten about her. She did not want to participate in any fraudulent scheme those two had cooked up.

She didn't even bother to remove her costume. The wig, heavy cosmetics, and black clothing could be dealt with at home. The sooner she left, the better.

More than ready to leave, she opened the door and took a step into the hall. She stopped short. Grey and Harris waited there, casually leaning against the opposite wall and staring right at her. *Damn.*

"Madam Zolikoff," Grey said, tipping his derby. "How nice to see you."

She swallowed a sigh. "Mr. Grey. Mr. Harris. Is there something I can do for you?"

"Shall we talk inside?" Harris pointed to the hotel room behind her. "I think we've a few things to discuss, don't we?"

With little choice but to allow them in, Ava stepped back inside the room. The two men followed, the slam of the door behind them like a harbinger of doom.

"Nice group today," Harris said. "You must've pocketed quite a bit of coin."

She said nothing as the men prowled the space. They went in opposite directions, obviously hoping to keep her off balance. It worked. She could only see one of them at a time, which increased her nervousness over what the other man was doing.

"Have you thought about our offer?" Grey slipped his hands in his trouser pockets. "We think you'd be a nice asset to our group."

"An offer? More like a threat."

"You act as if there is risk involved. Our plan is fool-proof. No one gets caught and everyone makes money."

"But people get hurt."

Harris and Grey exchanged a surprised look. "Hurt? These are sheep, Miss Jones. Fools lining up to get advice from performers such as yourself. Throwing money about as if it were water. They can hardly be trusted to think for themselves."

"So we're doing them a favor by stealing from them?"

"I don't care for your tone," Grey said. "Or the word 'stealing.' We are opportunists, Miss Jones, as are you. Please do not pretend your motives are pure."

She could hardly argue with that, though she liked to think she provided a service in exchange for the money she received. What Grey and Harris were proposing was out and out fraud. Could she steal from people who put their trust in her? She had enough trouble sleeping at night with all the worries weighting her down. Could she add one more and still remain sane?

While she was mulling over a way out of this mess, Harris said, "Let us be clear. You will be exposed if you say no. Exposed and humiliated."

"Exposed and humiliated, yet not imprisoned."

Grey laughed, his long side whiskers shifting. "Imprisoned? My dear woman, no one is going to jail—at least not for this."

"What if I agree not to tell anyone of your plan and we part ways amicably?"

"I'm afraid that is no longer an option," Harris said, the steely menace in his voice as terrifying as the long scar on his cheek.

"I'm curious, what does Mr. Sloane think of your career?" Grey asked behind her.

Her face must've given away her shock because Harris said, "Yes, we know all about your special *friendship* with Mr. Sloane. How do you think it would affect his campaign if your relationship were made public?"

She froze, unable to breathe. They had been watching her closely—more closely than she'd assumed. "No one expects politicians to be free from scandal," she muttered.

"True, but those who are have a much better chance at being elected. Will he forgive you, I wonder?"

The walls began closing in, the tangled web of her own deceit strangling her. One thing for certain, she would not bring shame to Will or his campaign. He desperately wanted to be elected to office, and she would not allow their association to be used against him.

If it were only her, she might risk saying no. But her family needed her, needed her income, and Will did not deserve to be humiliated. Her only hope was that she could hedge, stall in producing any clients willing to pay money to a fictional company, which should give her a bit of time to figure something else out. In a few weeks, she could think of a way out of this mess, couldn't she?

"Fine. Tell me what you need me to do."

Chapter Fourteen

"Ava, come look at this," Tom's voice called from the fire escape. All three of her siblings had retreated outside after dinner, hoping to cool off a bit.

Their apartment contained two tiny windows, one in each bedroom, much too small to allow for a cross breeze between their three rooms. Which meant the entire space remained sweltering all summer long. Sleep proved difficult starting in June until late September. In fact, Sam, her youngest brother, slept on the fire escape most summer nights.

Though it was mid-June, the temperature today had soared to the low nineties, dropping only a few degrees now that the sun had set. Neighbors could be heard shouting and arguing through the open windows, a nightly serenade in the misery of a hot New York summer.

Ava wiped sweat off her brow as she rinsed the last of the dinner dishes in the sink. She hadn't been sleeping well either, but the heat had little to do with her anxiety. She still hadn't figured a way out of Harris and Grey's scheme. Perhaps she could make a few fake payments for "clients" until Will's election concluded.

The idea depressed her. Paying off Grey and Harris from her own savings meant her goal of getting out of the city would take that much longer. Yes, Tom's increased wages at Northeast helped, but it wouldn't be enough to replenish blackmail money. And Lord knew, once one started paying blackmailers, there was no respite. They would only expect more money as time went on. She sighed as a trickle of sweat rolled down between her shoulder blades. What was she going to do?

"Ava!" Tom called again.

"In a minute," she replied. She needed to clean the kitchen before bedtime, because once she sat she might not have the energy to get up.

"Hello, Mr. Sloane," she heard her brother say, and her body jolted. Had he said . . . 'Sloane'? Her ears must be playing tricks on her. No way would Will Sloane be visiting. She hadn't heard from him in two days, and there was no reason for them to see each other again.

"Yes, she's here. Come on up. Third floor."

God, what was Tom saying? Ava glanced down at herself, horrified to discover she was covered in flour, soapsuds, and sweat. Her hair must appear a total fright. Was it truly Will?

Stop being a fool. Why do you care what you look like?

She tried to calm her racing heart. *He's just a man underneath.* Yes, a man who'd never been touched by flour or soapsuds, and had likely never broken a sweat.

Wrong. You felt his sweaty, naked body only two days ago.

That memory caused her body temperature to soar even higher. Dragging in a breath, she reached for a hand towel and did her best to clean her hands and dress.

"Ava, did you hear?" Mary asked as she stepped through the window. "A man is here to see you."

Sam followed, a wide grin on his small face. "And you should see his carriage. He must be *rich*."

Tom smacked the back of Sam's head as he entered the room. "He is rich and he's my boss, so be on your best behavior."

"That's your boss? The one who asks after Ava all the time?"

Ava blinked. Will had spoken to Tom about her? Why hadn't her brother ever mentioned as much?

A knock sounded at the door and a knot formed in Ava's throat. Before she could force her legs to move, Sam darted for the knob. "Sam, wait—" she started.

Too late. Her youngest brother had opened the door. Ava braced herself.

"Hello, Tom's boss. Won't you come inside?" He bowed with a flourish, which caused Mary to giggle.

"Hello, Tom's brother. Thank you." Will Sloane stepped into the tiny room and removed his top hat. He was dressed in a stark black tailcoat with a white vest and shirtfront, so absurdly handsome that Ava's stomach dropped.

His sharp gray gaze bounced around the room until it landed on her. One side of his mouth hitched ever so slightly. "I beg your pardon for interrupting your evening."

"We don't mind, do we, Ava?" Tom came forward a few steps. "Please, step in and make yourself at home, sir."

"Thank you, Tom." He set his top hat down on their dining table and followed the three Jones siblings to the shabby couch and chair. Sam dropped into the chair, so everyone else had no choice but to sit on the couch. Unbelievable . . . Will Sloane, here in her apartment. He looked entirely out of place here in his evening finery. No doubt he'd just attended some fancy dinner party or event. So why come to her apartment?

Her siblings must not learn she'd slept with Will. She didn't like the idea of them knowing about any of her relationships, not that there had been any, but in particular this one. The younger two would get the wrong idea, romanticizing it into something it wasn't, and Tom would be upset. Not only was Will his boss, Tom was old enough to realize what a rich man like Will wanted with a woman like Ava.

The sooner she got rid of him, the better. Snapping out of her stupor, she stepped across the narrow space to the seating area. Thank goodness she'd cleaned earlier today. At her approach, Will shot to his feet—and Tom quickly followed suit. Will moved aside, as if to give her his seat, but Tom said, "Ava, please. Sit here."

Her brother . . . being chivalrous? Ava tried to keep her shock from showing. "Thank you," she murmured, and assumed Tom's seat.

Will lowered once more and an awkward silence descended. Finally he cleared his throat. "Tom, perhaps you'd like to introduce your brother and sister."

"Oh! Of course. I don't know where my damn—dashed head went. This is Mary, my sister. And over there is my brother, Sam. Meet Mr. Sloane, head of Northeast Railroads."

"A pleasure," Mary said quietly.

"The pleasure is mine, Miss Mary," Will said with a charming smile, causing the young girl to blush.

Sam's eyes narrowed suspiciously. "Do you really build railroads?"

"Yes, I do. Quite a lot of them, actually."

"Sakes alive! I'd love to ride a train. I took the elevated once."

"I helped to build those, too."

Sam's eyes bugged out. "You did? Gosh, you must be rich."

Ava closed her eyes and snapped, "Sam!"

Will only chuckled. "Yes, I am that as well. Perhaps you could go and ride a train one day. Your brother could arrange it."

"I could?" Tom asked, his brows lowered in confusion.

"Of course. Northeast employees get discounts on train fares. Ask Mrs. Pritchard to give you the information tomorrow."

"Thank you, sir! I'll do that." One would have thought Will had just handed Tom the keys to the kingdom by the way her brother's chest puffed up. The hero worship she saw on Tom's face worried her, not to mention the fascination worn by the other two.

Will's gaze traveled to the window. "Is it always this warm in here?"

"This is cool compared to what it was an hour ago," Sam said. "All of us'll be sleeping on the fire escape tonight."

"You sleep . . . on the fire escape?" Will frowned. "Isn't that dangerous?"

"Only if you roll off and fall!" Tom joked.

That only caused Will's frown lines to deepen. "Is that a possibility?" He cast Ava a glance, and the pity she saw there caused her spine to straighten. She needed to find out why Will was here and then get rid of him.

"Boys, Mr. Sloane does not want to hear about our problems." She rose. "Mr. Sloane, may I speak with you in the hall?"

"Ava, don't be rude," Tom said under his breath.

"No, that's quite all right." Will came to his feet. "I do not want to intrude. Perhaps it's better if I speak with your sister and let you continue your evening."

"You are welcome to visit anytime," Tom said, standing. "We'd be honored, sir."

"Thank you, Tom. I appreciate your hospitality."

"What does 'hospitality' mean?" Sam stage-whispered to Mary.

"The kind treatment of guests or strangers," Ava answered. "All of you should get ready for bed. I'll return in a few moments. Follow me, Mr. Sloane."

* * *

As Will followed Ava into the hall, he cursed himself a fool. He hadn't planned on driving to her apartment, yet heard himself give the direction to his driver. When they had pulled up, he had every intention of staying in the carriage and waiting to see if Ava went out strolling as before. Only then he'd spotted Tom on the fire escape, and Will found himself getting out of the carriage and asking if Ava was home.

He could not control himself around this woman, apparently.

Unfortunately, she looked anything but happy to see him. She hadn't smiled once, her mouth pinched, as if she'd just sucked on a lemon. He, on the other hand, could hardly concentrate on anything *other* than her. The wisps of damp brown hair clinging to her slim neck. The rise and fall of her luscious bosom. The smudge of flour below her ear. He wanted to lick her, taste her . . . drag her off to a dark corner and have his wicked way with her.

She closed the door behind them and moved toward the end of the hallway. The empty corridor was gloomy, the lone gas lamp throwing off a faint yellow glow to reveal peeling paper and threadbare carpet. "What are you doing here?" she hissed in a furious whisper.

He propped a shoulder against the wall and crossed his arms. "I wanted to see you."

"Why?"

"Tell me why you left the other day when I fell asleep."

"Shh." Her head swiveled as if to ensure no one was listening. "I don't want anyone finding out about that."

"Why not?" He knew why he needed to keep their relationship a secret, but what was she embarrassed about? She wasn't one step away from a scandal that might ruin her chances for a political career.

Her expression said he'd lost his mind. "Because people will get the wrong idea. They'll believe this"—she motioned between them—"is something it is not."

"So what is this, then? Perhaps you could enlighten me. Did you not enjoy yourself?" A flush stole over her cheeks, a sight so rare he couldn't help but reach out and stroke her soft skin with his fingertips. "Does that blush mean yes?"

"You know very well that I did. But we had that one time together and that is enough."

His hand dropped to his side. "Enough for whom? Not me, certainly. I would very much like to know when we can have another afternoon together."

"Keep your voice down," she snapped. "And we cannot have any more afternoons together. The hotel was a one-time occurrence, Will."

He stared down at her, trying to see a chink in the walls she'd erected around herself since the hotel room. He didn't like what he saw. She wasn't sniping at him or driving him mad; instead, she was . . . resigned. As if it had been decided and he did not get a vote.

But Will had not built a fortune—along with railroads crisscrossing the United States—without learning how to get his way. He would have Ava again. Soon.

"If you wish, Ava," he agreed with a nod, and then changed tactics. "I like your siblings."

She blinked but said, "Thank you. I fear you've made quite the impression. No doubt they'll pepper me with questions the instant I return."

"And what will you tell them?" He dragged a fingertip through a smudge of flour on the side of her neck.

She slapped his hand away. "That we are friends. Only Tom would suspect otherwise, and I hope to be able to convince him this is innocent."

He leaned in and heard her breath hitch. Satisfaction caused his heart to pound. "If he believes that, then he is a fool. You are far too beautiful for innocent friendships with men."

Her eyes warmed considerably, her skin flushing once more at his compliment. "I cannot be your mistress. I just . . . cannot."

"If it's the word you object to, then we need not use one. I don't want to own you, Ava. I don't need to have you languishing on silken sheets at my beck and call. But for God's sake, don't tell me I cannot bed you a second time. I cannot stop thinking about you."

"Will . . ."

"Tell me you haven't thought of me—not once in two days—and I'll walk away. You'll never see me again. Otherwise, we will repeat what happened the other day. You have my word."

She bristled, her shoulders straightening as her jaw tightened. "Your word is not law here, railroad man, not with me. Everyone else may jump to do your bidding, but I won't."

"You did not answer my question. Have you thought of me? Of what happened in that hotel room?"

"Of course I have—but that doesn't mean I want to meet you again."

Images floated through his mind . . . her lying on her back. Legs spread, her naked folds glistening with desire. Head thrown back in ecstasy as he licked her cleft. The hard, puckered nipples as she rode his cock. He stepped closer, bringing his chest nearly flush with hers. "Liar."

She swayed toward him, the front of her breasts touching his starched shirtfront. His heart raced, desire flooding his veins. Rapid exhalations fell from her parted lips—lips that he longed to nibble and suck. He reached to clasp her hips, jerking her against the erection building in his trousers. Her hands clutched the lapels of his jacket as her lids fluttered shut. "Feel that, Ava? Feel what you do to me. I know you feel the same."

With a growl, she pushed him back. "Go away, Will. I don't have time for this. I need to get Sam and Mary settled for the night."

She stepped around him, but he snatched out and caught her wrist. "On the fire escape? That hardly seems wise."

"We don't have a choice, not when the rooms are stifling. They'll be fine. Don't worry. It's no different than any other summer in New York." She pulled free and started to walk away.

"Let me take you all to a hotel tonight."

She froze then spun toward him. "A hotel? Have you lost your mind?"

He had no idea where the offer had come from, but now that he'd said it, he would not back down. Their rooms had been sweltering, which could not be healthy for the children. "It makes sense, Ava. Let me treat all of you to one night of relief. They say it will rain tomorrow and break the heat. So for tonight, allow me to make all of you comfortable."

"You are crazy." She rolled her eyes to the ceiling. "You cannot take us all to a hotel. That would be—Wait, where are you going?"

He'd already passed her on his way to the apartment door. He rapped on the wood sharply. As Will suspected, Tom immediately answered the door. The young man had likely been standing with his ear pressed to the wood. "Yes, sir?"

"Tom, get back inside," Ava ordered, but Will paid her no attention.

"Would you and your siblings like to spend the night at my home? I have plenty of ice, and I'm certain I can scare up an electric fan or two."

Tom's shock was nearly comical. "Your home?"

Ava roughly pushed Will out of the way. "He's delusional from the heat," she told her brother. "Do not pay him any mind."

Will stood his ground. "You told me no hotels. You never said anything about my home."

"Stop splitting hairs. Go away, Will."

Tom's eyes nearly popped from their sockets—whether from the arguing or Ava's use of his first name, Will didn't know. "Why?" Tom asked him.

"Because I don't like the idea of all of you sleeping on the fire escape. I also have the space, which I would happily extend to your family for one evening. Wouldn't you care to cool off, if only for one night?"

He could see the longing on the young man's face, but Tom turned to his sister. "May we, Ava?"

"Please, Ava?" two more voices called from inside the apartment.

Ava frowned and studied the floor. Will could almost hear the arguments building steam in her brain, yet he knew she would not refuse. Not when all three siblings were on his side.

"Fine," she gritted out. "Everyone put some things in my satchel."

"You have to speak to me at some point."

Ava lifted her chin and kept her gaze trained on the street as the carriage traveled to Washington Square. Yes, she'd speak to him precisely never.

He'd played that quite nicely. A powerful man used to getting his way by whatever means necessary. She'd underestimated him, obviously. And now they would all be spending the night at his *home*. Had he lost his ever-loving mind?

Her three siblings followed in the hack Will had procured on Bank Street. How was she to explain this to them? As a gesture of good will on the part of Tom's boss? The younger two might believe that, but Tom would be suspicious. No doubt all three would be disappointed when they went back to their tiny rooms tomorrow.

More disturbing was how she'd felt upon first seeing him tonight, her heart leaping as if this were some grand romance in a novel. *He hadn't forgotten about me.* The relief that had coursed through her was terrifying. Until that precise moment, she hadn't realized how much she wanted to see him again. He'd burrowed under her skin somehow, brought about yearnings she could not indulge.

So instead, she nursed her anger, used it as a cloak against all the other emotions brewing inside.

"Ava, how was I supposed to leave the three of you there, in that heat, sleeping outside on a minuscule fire escape?"

"It would have been no different than any other hot summer night. You showing them how the rich high-step it in the heat won't help when we must return home tomorrow."

"Then stay with me for the summer."

Her gaze snapped to his. "You're insane."

He shrugged one arrogant shoulder. "Why not? I have the room. And it's not as if you can claim any impropriety, not when all four of you are staying. I'm merely offering an employee and his family a place to stay for the summer."

"And to how many employees have you made such an offer?"

"Well, none," he admitted. "But no one would know that—except my staff, of course."

"It doesn't matter because we're not staying longer than one night. And if you dare mention the offer of the summer to one of my siblings, I will smother you in your sleep."

He chuckled, the bastard. "I would not put it past you. In fact, I'll be sleeping with one eye open tonight."

"Wise of you."

"It should be said that I don't expect anything from you in exchange. I did not do this to get another night with you."

"I should hope not," she said. "Because I'll be sleeping with Mary—not you."

That caused him to fall silent, and she wondered if he already regretted his proposal. A small part of her was grateful for his generosity—most men of his status wouldn't even step foot inside their crowded rooms, let alone have opened their homes to a lower-class family— but she still resented the high-handed way he'd arranged it.

They turned along Washington Square, past the stately Greek revival mansions of the city's bluest bloods. These were families who clung to tradition and status, like the Sloanes.

"What will the neighbors think?" she asked him.

"I hardly care. Let them think what they want."

Her jaw fell open in exaggerated surprise. "Who are you, and what have you done with William Sloane?"

"Hilarious," he drawled.

The carriage wheels slowed as they reached the corner of Fifth Avenue and Washington Square North. When the driver pulled to a stop, Will flung open the door and gracefully stepped down. He waited to assist Ava and then strode to the hack to deal with the driver. The front door parted, and Ava recognized the Sloane butler, who was now wearing a familiar look of disapproval.

She ignored the servant and went to help her siblings.

Sam appeared first, his expression filled with wonder and excitement. "This is where he lives?" Sam whispered to Ava. "Damn me."

"None of that," Ava told him. "Best manners, Sam."

The boy nodded, straightened, and swaggered up the walk. She half expected him to swing an imaginary walking stick. Shaking her head, Ava helped Mary down. The girl said little, but the happiness and curiosity in her eyes told Ava enough. "Go and join your brother," she said quietly.

Tom unfolded from the hack next. "Are you sure this is all right?" he asked Ava. "You didn't look nonc too happy when you got into Mr. Sloane's carriage."

"It's fine," she assured her brother. After all, what could she do now? Forcing them to leave would only confuse and hurt the younger two siblings. If Sloane was willing to suffer the slings and arrows of social recriminations from associating with the riffraff, who was she to say otherwise? "It's only for one night, though."

Tom nodded. "Right. That's what I told the other two. Is he doing this because—" His gaze bounced over her shoulder, and she knew why he hadn't finished the question.

Will plucked the satchel out of Ava's grip and handed it to her oldest brother. "Tom, let's get everyone inside, and my staff will see you settled."

"Yes, sir." With a tip of his cap, Tom set off for the front door.

Will took Ava's elbow. "Stop frowning. This will be an adventure for the younger two. Let them enjoy it."

Undoubtedly, he was right, and she was being churlish. Nevertheless, how did he know? "I'm certain they will. The question is not how this benefits us, but why you suddenly developed an altruistic streak."

He said nothing as they approached the front door. Mary and the butler waited just inside the threshold, lines of disapproval multiplying by the second on the servant's face. If Will noticed, he gave no indication as he said, "Frederic, the Joneses are to be our overnight guests this evening. Have Paul carry their bag up—"

"Ava! Wait until you see this place!" Sam tore down the main staircase, jumping the last few carpeted steps to the bottom.

Tom followed more slowly, a sheepish expression on his face. "Sorry. I tried to catch him."

Will reached out to ruffle Sam's hair. "No problem. Feel free to explore. Just stay out of the east wing."

"Why?" Sam asked. "What's in the east wing?"

Bending at the waist, Will put his face on the level with Sam's. "Monsters."

Ava bit back a laugh because Sam's expression showed a mixture of horror and fascination. "Truly? What kind of monsters?"

"Big ones. *With giant fangs dripping blood.*"

"Can I see one?"

"No," Will answered seriously. "They eat little boys. In fact, I used to have four brothers."

Sam swallowed hard. "I won't go there, then. I promise."

"Smart boy. Now, Frederic, it's late, let's get them all settled, shall we? And I want them to have as much ice as they need to keep cool."

"Very good, sir," the butler replied. "The fourth-floor rooms?"

Will frowned and put his hands in his pockets. Ava wasn't certain, but she sensed he was uncomfortable. "No, the front rooms on the second floor. One for the gents and one for the ladies."

"Did you hear?" Sam elbowed his brother. "He called us 'gents'!"

"Sam, please, that's enough. Mr. Sloane, the fourth floor is perfectly—"

Gray eyes pinned her to the spot. "No, absolutely not." He spun to the rest of her family. "I have work yet to accomplish this evening, so I will bid you all good night."

Tom whipped off his hat and gave a bow. "Good night, sir. And thank you."

"Yes, thank you very much, Mr. Sloane." Mary dipped an awkward curtsy.

"You're a decent swell," Sam quipped, "even if your house does have monsters."

Will grinned and something tightened in Ava's chest. He was good with her siblings. She didn't know why that surprised her, but it seemed she had a lot to learn about Will Sloane.

"Thank you, Sam. That's quite a compliment from the likes of you. Please ring the bell if you need anything from the staff, and I'll see you all at breakfast."

With a nod in Ava's direction, Will set off through an arched doorway, striding deeper into the house. She tried not to watch his broad, capable shoulders disappear, but Tom's frown told her she'd failed miserably.

"Follow me," Frederic announced in a brittle tone, then marched to the elegant staircase. With no choice but to obey, the four Jones siblings climbed the stairs to experience an evening of unexpected splendor.

Chapter Fifteen

Will pored over the reports that had arrived from his surveyor in San Francisco. There was a piece of property outside the city he wanted to buy, one that might contain a vein of silver. He didn't imagine spending any serious amount of time out West, however. His home was, and always would be, New York. But if his man's estimates were correct and silver was discovered, Will would profit handsomely.

When will it be enough? he could almost hear Lizzie ask him. *Never,* was always his answer. Because he still felt restless, as if there were more to do. When he stopped experiencing the itch to buy, build, and acquire, when he felt *satisfied*, that was when he'd relax. Not before.

Tonight, however, he was restless for an entirely different reason. Ava was here, under his roof. A floor above his head. Uncorseted. Likely wearing some piece of thin, transparent sleepwear that revealed the dark pink tips of her full breasts. He groaned and adjusted himself in his trousers. This had to stop; otherwise, he'd go mad by morning.

Truthfully, he hadn't invited them here in order to bed her. He'd merely been concerned about the four of them in that shabby apartment, sweltering in the stale air, and sleeping outside on a metal fire escape. Of course his body wished otherwise, but Will wasn't about to give his staff reason to talk by taking advantage of a woman's presence in his home. No lover had ever spent the night here, in fact. He would absolutely have Ava again, but not here . . . and not with her family sleeping a few rooms away.

With the brandy glass by his elbow now empty, Will stood and refilled it. Perhaps he could drink himself into a stupor. Then he wouldn't be tempted to tap on Ava's door in the middle of the night.

"I'll be sleeping with Mary—not with you." She had truly been angry on the drive over. Unfortunately for both of them, her fire and sass only made him want her more.

The clock on the marble mantel chimed once. Will stretched his shoulders, rolling them to alleviate the tension in his back. Thanks to the heat, he'd removed his coat earlier and folded up his shirtsleeves. The office windows stood open, and a cool breeze now blew in from the park. Sitting, he resumed his work, determined to make the most of this sleepless night.

Not long after, a respectful tap on the door gained his attention. Hadn't he sent the butler to bed? "Yes, Frederic?"

The panel cracked and Ava's lovely face appeared, followed by her even lovelier body. *Oh, Christ.* She wore a white cotton wrapper over what appeared to be a long, matching nightdress, her hair damp from a bath. Will's heart stuttered behind his ribs. When she started toward him, her luscious unbound bosom bouncing with every step, blood pooled in his groin, hardening his cock.

Not tonight. But soon.

He cleared his throat and put down his pen. "Why are you still awake?"

Soft steps brought her to his desk, where she leaned a hip against the rosewood. Her gaze swept his shoulders and forearms, causing his skin to prickle. "I couldn't sleep. I see you're still working."

"I only need a few hours' sleep. I'm usually awake at this time." He saw the flush on her pretty skin. "Is the heat keeping you up? If so, I can have the staff locate a fan for you."

She shook her head, her teeth clamping down on her bottom lip. "No, it's comfortable up there. Sam and Mary were too excited to settle, but finally fell asleep about midnight." Her fingers trailed the edge of his desk as she drew closer to his chair.

"But?"

"But now I'm the one who can't settle."

"Why?"

She slid behind his chair, and her gentle touch ghosted over the top of his shoulder. His breath caught. "Because you're here in the house somewhere and I keep waiting for you to come for me." Her hand slipped down over his chest to his sternum. "Your heart is beating so fast," she murmured.

"I told you I wouldn't come for you." He tried to turn around, but her hands held him in place. Letting his head fall back, he closed his eyes and tried to keep from springing up and ripping that flimsy nightdress from her body.

"I know, and I'm not sure I believed you until about fifteen minutes ago." Pressure on his throat as she undid the knot of his bowtie.

"Did you want me to come for you?"

"Yes and no." The silk slipped free, and she dropped the edges. She plucked at the studs of his shirt collar, removing them, and finally the collar. Will's erection pushed against his underclothes, a willing partner to whatever Ava had in mind . . . but they shouldn't be doing this, not here.

"Ava, let's not start this now."

Hot breath tickled his ear. "Too late, railroad man. It's

already started. In case you hadn't noticed, I'm seducing you."

"I noticed," he chuckled, dryly. "It's been driving me crazy that you're here, under my roof."

She unfastened his vest, her fingers brushing his abdomen through his clothing as she dealt with the buttons one by one. He felt ready to crawl out of his skin by the time she finished four. "And yet you did nothing about it. Do you want to bed me?"

"Hell, yes." He grabbed her wrist and brought her hand between his legs to cup his heavy erection. "That is what I've been fighting for the last two hours."

Instead of shying away, as he'd half expected, she curled her grip around him as best she could through his trousers and underclothes. "What a waste of two hours," she purred, and his cock jumped in her hand.

He clutched the sides of his chair as she gave him a tentative stroke. His chest heaved with his labored breathing, lust tearing through his insides. He could smell her, vanilla and roses, along with the faint hint of her arousal. "Damn it, Ava. Not here."

"Yes, here."

He shot to his feet and spun around. Her gaze widened, as if she hadn't expected him to argue. "I can't undress you here and take my time with you. I want to taste every inch of your skin. Not lift your nightclothes and fuck you on my desk."

"You said . . ." Her lips curved in a playful smile. "Why, I didn't think you even knew such a coarse word."

He bent and swooped her off her feet, his arms cradling her bottom. She squeaked and clung to his shoulders as his feet started for the door. "Not only do I know that word, I'm about to show you what it means."

* * *

His bedroom was everything she expected: large, simple, and dripping with understated luxury. Thick Eastern carpets, tasteful landscape paintings, patterned wallpaper . . . Not much furniture, but the few sturdy pieces were crafted from dark, thick wood. Probably antiques. The enormous bed included a wide wooden headboard with intricate carvings. A six-light gasolier hung from the ceiling, casting a yellowish glow on the cream coverlet.

She hardly cared about any of that. Her body was on fire, burning with a fierce need only this man could assuage. For the last two hours, she had imagined seducing him until the reality became necessary to her very survival. Her feet had carried her through the darkened house, to his office, where she hadn't held back from voicing her desire. He'd already asked for another afternoon in a hotel room. What difference did location mean?

Will brought her to the bed and placed her on the satin coverlet. She immediately reached for him, trying to pull him on top of her, but he backed up a few steps. His heavy-lidded gaze burned bright as it raked her body. "You are so beautiful," he murmured.

Anticipation tightened her muscles as he shrugged off his vest then lowered his suspenders. He removed his shirt, tossing the studs carelessly to the ground, and went to work on his trousers. When he peeled them off and straightened, the outline of his erection pushed through the fabric of his combination as he began to struggle with the tiny buttons.

Feeling overdressed, she untied her wrapper and let it fall open, revealing her thin, summer nightdress to his hungry stare. Plain white cotton, the garment was low-cut on her breasts and stopped just above her knees. "Jesus," he whispered, and yanked at his combination, sending buttons flying to the floor as the fabric parted.

A second later, he was naked and climbing over her. His

mouth dropped to her breast, sucking a cotton-covered nipple into his mouth, causing her back to bow from the intense pleasure. He teased her, sucking and laving, his hands cupping the plump flesh, until she squirmed. "I thought you wanted me naked," she breathed, her fingers threading his golden hair.

He released her nipple and kissed his way along her neck. "I want you in every way I can possibly have you."

With undue haste, he shed her of both the wrapper and her nightdress. He loosened her drawers and slid them down her legs, then tossed the garment to the floor. "I'll go slower our second time. But right now, I need to be inside you."

He pushed her thighs apart and ran his hands up her legs, all the way to the apex. His thumbs stroked the lips of her cleft, gentle sweeps over the slick flesh that had her writhing. He seemed content to touch her and watch, but she was about to come out of her skin. "Will," she pleaded.

One wide finger nudged inside her, and he pumped his hand a few times, preparing her. That soon became two, stretching in the most spectacular way, before he lowered himself on top of her. His delicious weight pressed down on her, surrounded her, and she wrapped her legs around his hips. Clutched at his strong shoulders. "Hurry," she told him.

The blunt tip swept through her wetness and lined up at her entrance. Will's hips began to drive forward, his hardness filling her, and the muscles in his arms bunched as he levered up to see where their bodies were joining. "Look at that. I love to watch you taking me. Damn, you feel like heaven."

He sank until their hips met. She reveled in the fullness, the space he took up both in and around her. The whole world was this bed and this man's skin sliding over hers. The way her heart raced. The pulsing between her legs that demanded he move. She rocked her hips, desperate for friction.

The motion spurred him into action. He bent and captured her mouth, kissing her feverishly as his hips began churning. The pleasure became relentless, the drag and glide of his shaft over her sensitive tissues . . . the way his body caressed the tiny bud at the top of her cleft with every thrust. He drove her higher until she clawed at his skin, clinging as her muscles drew taut. "OhGodohGodohGod," she chanted into his throat. "More, Will. Harder."

"Jesus, Ava," he gritted out above her, slamming into her with such force that she traveled up the bed.

Reaching between them, his fingers found her bud and pressed. That was all she needed before the streaks of electricity raced up her legs, down her back, and threw her over the cliff. She jerked as her body began to spasm, and Will covered her mouth with his, drinking in her cries. Her orgasm seemed to set off his own, because just as her mind reassembled itself, he withdrew and spilled on her stomach and thighs.

There were no words. For a long moment, she tried to catch her breath as Will sat back on his heels and did the same. He appeared disheveled and undone, a man who'd lost his precious control for a few moments. A satisfied grin pulled across her face.

He smoothed his palm over her knee. "I like to see you smile, especially in bed."

"You've only seen me in bed twice," she reminded him.

"I know, but you've smiled on both occasions. I like to think I had a bit to do with your conviviality."

"Arrogant man." The words lacked heat, sounding almost affectionate.

He pinched the inside of her thigh playfully, which caused her to squeak. Laughing, he slid off the bed and went to the washstand. He returned with a wet cloth and proceeded to wipe his spend from her skin. Then he rinsed the cloth and washed himself. Ava could watch him for hours. He moved with such elegance and grace, a man completely comfortable with himself.

After turning down the gas on the overhead light, he dropped onto the mattress next to her. The room darkened considerably, yet she could still see him clearly. "Why did you come to Bank Street tonight?"

He slid one hand behind his head and reached for her with the other, pulling her into his side. The heat of his body warmed her sweat-soaked skin as she draped her arm over his chest. Her head settled on his bare shoulder.

"I wanted to see you. I didn't like how you snuck out of the hotel room the other day while I was sleeping. There was a chance you regretted what had happened, and I thought I might need to convince you of all the reasons you shouldn't."

"I didn't regret it, but leaving seemed a wise course of action at the time."

"Why?"

Because it had been too good. Too real. Too tempting to never leave. "Were you disappointed when you awoke?"

"Yes, of course. Did you think I would be relieved?" She didn't answer, and he swept his hand down her back, lingering just above the curve of her buttock. He leaned in and pressed a soft kiss to her forehead. "If you're waiting for me to lose interest in you, I fear you have a considerable amount of disappointment ahead."

Her chest swelled, elation wrapping around her heart. Dangerous. This man was altogether too dangerous. And yet, she knew almost nothing about him, about his life outside of what little she'd seen. She stroked the fine blond hair on his chest. "You were very kind to Sam and Mary."

"You sound surprised."

"I didn't expect you to like children, I suppose. Busy railroad barons aren't exactly known for being family men."

"Do you know a number of railroad barons, then?"

She traced the outline of his nipple and felt a shiver go through him. "Only one."

"I like children quite a bit. I practically raised my sister." He took a deep breath and held it for a long moment. When he finally exhaled, he said, "My mother died when I was twelve. She was . . . I've never told anyone this." A dry laugh escaped his lips, and Ava said nothing, remaining perfectly still atop him.

"The servants know, of course, but she was unhappy. Miserable, really. My father was a cruel man—not to anyone outside the family, mind you. No, everyone loved Archibald Sloane because he reserved his tyranny for behind closed doors, for my mother and me. She received the worst of it. The biting comments and constant disapproval. I watched her wither before my eyes."

"That must have been hard," Ava said quietly. She didn't know which she was more surprised over: that he'd experienced a less than idyllic childhood or that he was sharing the truth of it with her.

"I didn't know any different until I started to read. Through books I began to learn that not all families were like mine, that we were not normal. That not every mother cried all the time, hiding in her suite because she dreaded receiving her husband's attention. I shudder to think of the circumstances under which Lizzie and I were conceived."

"How old was your sister when your mother died?"

"Four. I don't think Lizzie has any real memories of her."

"What do you mean 'real'?"

He tensed underneath her. "Most of her memories are from stories I told her, ones I based on Clara Peggotty from *David Copperfield.*"

"The housekeeper?"

"Yes."

"And your father? Did he treat Lizzie in the same manner?"

"He mostly ignored her, though he did occasionally read the stock tables to her at breakfast. I told him she had a head for numbers—a fine one, at that—and he said, 'At least one of my children does.'"

"Will, that's terrible!"

He shrugged. "I'm sure you're thinking, 'Poor little rich railroad man.' Can't say I blame you. It's silly to complain when I've been given so much."

Everything except the one thing that mattered. "And he died when you were in your teens?"

"Yes, sixteen. Pneumonia took him fast, otherwise I've no doubt he would have made provisions to sell the company rather than let me have it."

"Well, you've proven a hundred times over how capable you are. Most men of your status don't work nearly as hard as you."

A warm palm closed over her breast, fingers toying with her nipple, setting her blood aflame. "And I'm about to work even harder," he murmured as he rolled them over and covered her.

Will woke up alone the next morning. Ava must've slipped out once again after he'd fallen asleep. Damn. This was beginning to be a habit with her, one Will didn't care for.

Probably for the best, however, as her presence in his bed would've shocked the staff. He did not ever bring women here, even after Lizzie had moved out. This was his home, not some bacchanal boardinghouse in the Tenderloin.

The scent of her still clung to his skin, his sheets. He

inhaled, thinking back to the second and third times he'd had her last night. Each round had been better than the last, his lust for her not abating one bit. In fact, he couldn't wait to have her again.

Ignoring his diamond-hard shaft, he rose and rang for his valet. He could likely get in a few hours' work before the Jones siblings descended for breakfast. They had no reason to be up this early, at least he didn't think so. Were the youngest two working today, on a Sunday? Ava had mentioned the sister was a finisher in a garment factory and Sam was a newsie. Wasn't everyone allowed at least one day of rest a week?

He glanced at the clock and nearly choked. Dear God, it was after ten. He hadn't slept this late in . . . ever. So much for working this morning. He just prayed Ava hadn't departed already.

As quick as he could, he bathed and dressed, then hurried to the breakfast room. Voices greeted him, causing him to frown. More voices than he expected. He stepped inside—and his heart stopped. Lizzie and her husband were seated at the breakfast table, as were Ava and her three siblings. Ava appeared as shocked as Will felt.

He stood there, reeling, his limbs refusing to move. "Lizzie," he croaked. "I thought you were in Newport."

His sister's smile was all-too knowing as she rose and moved toward him. "I returned because of a meeting to-morrow, so I'd hoped to catch you at home today." Coming up on her tiptoes, she pressed a kiss to his cheek. "And catch you, I did," she murmured for his ears alone.

She patted his lapel and then took his hand, dragging him to the table. "Sit, Will. Please join us. Emmett and I were just getting to know your houseguests."

Cavanaugh's face was positively gleeful. "Yes, do sit, Sloane."

Will clenched his teeth as he took his rightful place at

the head of the table. Figured Cavanaugh would be here to witness Will's humiliation. A sharp burn suddenly flared in his stomach, and he gingerly rubbed the area. Food no longer held any appeal. He tried to catch Ava's eye to offer a silent apology, but she resolutely avoided looking in his direction.

Lizzie poured him a cup of coffee. "So I understand Tom works for you."

"Yes, that's true. He's turning into one of our most promising new employees." Not a lie. Tom was a hard worker, intelligent. Will had high hopes for the young man and encouraged him every chance he got.

"And Sam here is a newsie, while Mary works for one of the garment makers." Lizzie picked up her own cup and took a sip of coffee. "What is it that you do, Ava?"

Ava raised her head and flicked a glance at Will, and he could see the uncertainty swimming in her hazel depths. Will held his breath and willed her not to speak the truth. Hell, he'd never hear the end of it from Cavanaugh, let alone his sister.

She cleared her throat. "I'm a newspaper reporter."

Will nearly sagged in relief until Sam snorted from down the table. "A *what*? Ava, you—"

Tom quickly leaned to whisper in his younger brother's ear. Sam flushed, nodded, and shoved a jam-coated biscuit in his mouth.

"Oh," Lizzie said, her smile slipping only slightly. "That must be exciting. Which paper do you write for?"

"The *Brooklyn Daily Times*."

"I've never heard of that paper," Cavanaugh quipped, then grunted as Lizzie's foot obviously connected with his shin.

"It's fairly new," Ava lied. "When they found out my brother worked for Mr. Sloane, my editor assigned me to the gubernatorial race. I'm covering the campaign."

"I think that's wonderful," Lizzie said. "I hope you portray my brother fairly. He can be a bit rigid at times, but his heart is in the right place."

"Lizzie," Will warned. "We shouldn't tell Miss Jones how to do her job."

"No, that's fine," Ava said. "She's concerned for you, as any sister would be. I have no intention of hurting your brother's chances for election, Mrs. Cavanaugh."

Something about the statement caught his attention, as if she were speaking about their personal relationship and not the fictional one.

"Call me Lizzie, please. And if you need more information or insight on my brother, you are welcome to come visit me."

Ava blinked a few times. "Thank you." She exchanged a pointed glance with Tom and then pushed her chair away from the table. "We really must be getting home."

"Aw, really? But I thought—" Sam started before Tom's hand squeezed the little boy's shoulder.

"Yes, we must go." Tom pulled Mary's chair out for her and helped the girl to her feet. "Thank you, sir, for your hospitality last evening. My family appreciates it."

A chorus of gratitude reached Will's ears as he stood. "It was my pleasure. I'll see you out."

They said their good-byes to Lizzie and Emmett, and then Will walked the Jones family to the front door. Palmer had a hansom waiting at the curb. Will tried not to let his disappointment show. He'd wanted a few more minutes with her—preferably alone—but he'd been willing to take what he could. Everyone was conspiring against him today.

Will reached in his pocket and pulled out a few bills, then gave them to Tom. "For the fare."

"Thank you, Mr. Sloane." They shook hands. "See you in the morning, sir."

Ava gave him a pitiful attempt at a smile. "Yes, thank you, Mr. Sloane. I'll be in touch if I need anything further for the article."

He caught her hand and brought it to his lips. "Yes, Miss Jones. Do be in touch."

Chapter Sixteen

Ava pulled her hand away and hurried the siblings down the steps, toward the hansom. Will watched them a moment, until the carriage pulled away from the curb, and then he shut the heavy wooden door.

As he made his way back to the breakfast room, Cavanaugh came sauntering out, chuckling at the scowl on Will's face. "I'm off to a meeting. I'll retrieve her later, after she's through with you."

"Wonderful," Will murmured, and brushed by the other man.

"Ho!" Cavanaugh called, and Will turned. "Have you thought about my offer?"

Will glared at his brother-in-law, who merely smirked. "So stubborn. Just like your sister. Think about it, Sloane. It's a smart business decision."

"For you, perhaps."

"And for you, you pompous ball-bag. Also, for what it's worth, it was nice to see this morning that you're human just like the rest of us."

"You mean stupid."

Cavanaugh lifted his giant arms, palms out. "Your words,

not mine. And you could do worse, Sloane. She's beautiful and obviously loves her siblings."

"There's nothing between—"

"Save it. You might convince Elizabeth of that shit, but not me. I've seen that particular look a time or two."

"What look?"

"The one that says you're scared witless over a woman." Shoving his hands in his pockets, Cavanaugh strolled through the entryway, whistling.

Will's mood deteriorated significantly, thanks to that exchange, so by the time he reentered the breakfast room he felt on a razor's edge. He poured a fresh cup of coffee and tried to avoid his sister's keen gaze. When the silence stretched, he snapped, "Well?"

"I hardly know where to start. I'm still trying to wrap my head around it."

He certainly wasn't going to fill her in. Sipping his coffee, he waited while her too-logical brain put the pieces together.

"Is she your mistress?"

Will choked, hot liquid spewing from his mouth and onto his vest. He quickly grabbed his napkin and tried to clean himself up. "My God, Lizzie."

"I'm sorry. I just couldn't think of any other way to ask it."

"I do not have a mistress." He wiped his vest and sleeves, then placed the soiled napkin on the table.

"Fine. Are you sleeping with her?"

He sighed. "No, I'm not sleeping with her."

"You're lying. Your forehead is doing that thing"—she pointed to her brow—"that happens each time you lie. So, she's . . . what?"

"Nothing. She is the sister of one of my employees. And this is an inappropriate conversation."

"Will, I'm married. I think I am allowed inappropriate conversations, even with you. Do you like her?"

He slumped a little in his seat. Did he truly need to have this chat, especially when he could practically still taste Ava on his tongue? "Leave my private life alone. I'd rather not discuss this with you."

"Why? You've never left my private life alone. Why can't I discuss yours?" When he didn't answer, she huffed. "You know, for years I didn't think you *had* a private life. You worked all the time and never even escorted a woman to dinner or the theater. Then, after I debuted, I overheard two women discussing you at a cotillion, saying you had a long-term mistress and weren't interested in marriage."

Will closed his eyes and pinched the bridge of his nose. "I'm sorry—"

"Sorry? You have nothing to apologize about. When I heard those women talking, I was relieved. I'd been so worried about you, thinking you were lonely and that you'd have no one in your life after I left." She reached over and gripped his forearm. "I don't want you to be alone, growing old in this big house by yourself. You deserve love and laughter—and you know what I heard this morning? Something I haven't heard within these walls for a long time. Love and laughter, Will. I cannot imagine the last time I saw you smile so often."

Lies upon lies. He did not intend for Lizzie to get the wrong idea about Ava. "She's a medium, not a newspaper reporter." He heaved a breath, the weight of the one lie off his chest.

Lizzie sat back, her eyes blinking rapidly. "A medium? I don't understand. She tells fortunes?"

"Have you heard of Madam Zolikoff?"

"Yes, as has most everyone in New York. Edith hired her for a séance recently, though I wasn't able to attend. Are you . . . Ava is Madam Zolikoff?"

He gave a curt nod. "So you should not accustom yourself
to the idea of a future between Ava and myself."

"Why not?"

His eyes went wide. Was she serious? "Because the
woman fleeces people for a living. She's a confidence
man—or woman, in this case."

"Oh, I see." Lizzie picked up a spoon, dropped more
sugar in her coffee, and stirred, the clink of the spoon
against the china the only sound in the room. She placed
the spoon in the saucer with a snap. "You think she's not
good enough for you."

"I didn't say that," he said, angrily. "But I cannot marry
her."

"I don't see why not. People change. Look at my husband. He was once a thief and probably many other things
I'd rather not know about. But that is his past and I'll not
think less of him for it. He did what was necessary in order
to survive and meet me, which is what matters. Every step
we take in life brings us along on a path to someone. Do
not judge her for the choices she made before reaching
you."

"I might not judge her harshly, but everyone else certainly will. Can you even imagine the gossip? I would not
put her through it."

"Her—or you?"

"Does it matter?"

Lizzie cocked her head and studied him. "Does she
make you happy, Will?"

"Will you watch my forehead to see if I lie?"

"Yes, so do not even attempt it." Her expression soft-
ened considerably. "And I saw your face when you looked
at her this morning. It's how I knew."

"Knew what?"

"That you care for her. It's the reason you invited her
family here last evening, wasn't it?"

"Their apartments were sweltering," he found himself mumbling. "They sleep on the fire escape to keep cool. It seemed unsafe."

"Oh, that's terrible."

"Then why in God's name are you grinning?"

"Because it's finally happened. My big brother has fallen in love."

I'm so weak, Ava thought as she attempted to catch her breath. Her sweaty, naked limbs were currently tangled with Will's atop rumpled hotel sheets. Since the night in his home two weeks ago, she'd met him at the Washington Square Hotel each Thursday afternoon. He'd pounced on her both times, their lovemaking greedy and desperate, as if this was their last encounter. And perhaps it was. She kept telling herself she wouldn't meet him again . . . yet here she lay, sated and blissful from his attentions once more.

"You ruined six of my meetings this week. My concentration is pitiful, when all I can think about is what you taste like." Will nibbled her neck so she tilted her head to encourage him. The scrape of his teeth over her skin caused her to shiver. "What you smell like." He took a deep inhale through his nose. "You're destroying me, Ava."

She sighed. *This* was why she kept returning. For such a proper, rigid man outside the bedroom, Will turned out to be tender and affectionate inside it. The contrast intoxicated her . . . as did his kisses. "Is that why I've noticed you rubbing your stomach here and there?"

"I do?"

"Yes. I've been wondering if you have a stomach ailment or merely a poor diet."

He drew her earlobe into the lush heat of his mouth,

his large hand sweeping over her rib cage. "Meet me on Monday afternoon. I cannot wait an entire week to see you."

"I cannot. And why are you avoiding my question?"

"It's a stomach ailment," he sighed into her throat. "My doctor believes it's from working too much."

"Which I would believe, since I've never met a man more driven. What does he suggest you do?"

"Take time away from the office, which is why I desperately need you to meet me on Monday." He stroked her stomach with his fingertips. "To get me out of the office."

"Indeed, a smoothly voiced effort, but my answer is still no." Meeting him once a week pushed the limit of her pride. Twice a week would weigh her down until she went under.

Because she knew something Will would never discover: She'd fallen in love with him. Yes, the cynical, hardened, world-weary Ava Jones had made a monumental mistake, one she had promised to never, ever do again. She'd developed feelings for a man above her station, a man who could never marry her. A man who only wished to bed her.

The situation depressed her. Humiliated her. Yet she couldn't stop meeting him on Thursday afternoons. This one day was a little pocket of heaven in her bleak existence, a temporary sanctuary that would not last forever. Should she not enjoy them while she could?

"I can persuade you," he whispered, the deep timbre of his voice melting her insides. His fingers dipped between her thighs, performed lazy circles around her entrance.

She felt her resolve slipping, so she pushed his arm away. "You just don't like to hear the word 'no.'"

"True." He flopped on his back and folded his hands beneath his head. "And yet, you keep saying it."

"Poor railroad man," she drawled. "He has to rely on all his other women for company."

Narrowed gray eyes pinned her to the mattress. "There are no other women, Ava. Only you."

Her heart gave a tiny leap at that news, even though she had no hold over him. There were no illusions about what this was between them. "What about Miss Baldwin?"

"I haven't seen her since the night of the séance. Are there other men?" He actually sounded worried.

"No."

"So why won't you meet me on Mondays as well?"

"Because I am busy, Will, as are you." *And the more I see you, the harder it is to walk away each time.* "This arrangement suits me perfectly."

"What about Tuesdays, then? Or Sundays? Or tomorrow, for God's sake."

A smile pulled at her lips. She traced his belly button with her fingertip, stroked the thin trail of light hair leading down to his groin. "You'd tire of me if I saw you so often."

"Not a chance. I could never tire of you. I could bed you every day for a year and still discover new ways to make you sigh. Are you worried you'll tire of me?"

"No," she replied honestly. He was complicated and demanding, sweet and insecure . . . she loved every facet of this perplexing man. Under no circumstances could she see herself tiring of him. "But I have responsibilities to my clients as well as my family. I cannot flit about the city and then drop everything when you are able to fit me into your life."

The room fell silent. Noise from the street—the clatter of a nearby omnibus, the shouts of peddlers, even the distant sounds of an organ grinder—floated through the open window. Ava hated that she'd answered harshly, yet it was the truth. She would not become his mistress. His occasional lover was one thing; she could live with that status. But to surrender herself to him, make herself available whenever he had time for her, would crush her soul a little at a time.

"The offer stands should you change your mind. And if there is anything I can do, anything I have to bargain with, just name it."

"I thought the first rule of negotiation was to never give your opponent any advantage. What sort of railroad tycoon are you?"

He rolled, coming up on an elbow to loom over her. His free hand cupped her jaw. "One who is willing to beg for whatever scraps his beautiful, enchanting opponent throws at him." Bending, he pressed his lips to hers, gently at first, but when she responded, the kiss turned heated. When he finally released her, they were both panting. "You have turned me inside out, Ava."

Unable to come up with an appropriate response, she brushed her lips over his. Then she changed the subject. "Is there another rally this weekend?"

"No. I'm spending the weekend in Newport."

"Oh. Seeing your sister?"

"Yes, and a few other obligations."

She could imagine such obligations. Parties, champagne, oysters, yachting . . . Actually, no. She couldn't begin to imagine them. Those activities were completely foreign to her, a level of wealth she never even bothered dreaming of. Why dream of something she'd never have?

"Any séances this weekend?" he asked, dipping his head and kissing her collarbone. It was as if he couldn't stop touching or kissing her, and Ava loved every minute.

"Yes, as a matter of fact. I have one every weekend into July."

"Do you like it, portraying Madam Zolikoff?"

"I do, yes. It allows me greater freedom than if I were an actress onstage. Not to mention more money."

He nuzzled the outside of her breast, licking and gently

nipping. Her nipple puckered and, without thinking, she arched toward him. "Your brothers and sisters are lucky to have you," he murmured. "Almost as lucky as I am to have you."

She chuckled. "Right now, you aren't having me. You're teasing me."

"Indeed, I am." He swirled his tongue around her nipple, not giving her what she wanted. She squirmed underneath him, but he ignored her. "You have fantastic breasts, in case I haven't said."

"You have said—many times, in fact—but I never tire of hearing it."

He gave a satisfied grunt and switched to the other breast. "Tell me about the man. The one from before who hurt you. Was he your first?"

"I don't want to talk right—"

"Talk or I shall stop what I'm doing," he threatened, his mouth hovering over her nipple. She tried to grab his erection to distract him, but Will was faster. He clasped both her hands, brought them over her head, and held them tight with one of his. "Tell me, Ava."

"Why? It was a long time ago."

"Because I want to know—and I always get my way." He blew on the hardened tip of her breast, the air only adding to her frustration. Her cleft throbbed, and she would soon be begging. Damn him.

"Please, Ava."

The *please* never failed to convince her. Heaven help her if he ever figured that out. "Several years ago, I worked in an office where the boss's son began to pay attention to me. Woo me, really. After a fashion, he told me we'd be married, that we would spend our lives together, and I believed him. In truth, he never had any intention of a future between us. I was . . . convenient."

Will's head snapped up, a frown on his handsome face. "What happened?"

She pressed her lips together, unwilling to discuss the pregnancy—especially with this man. "One day he stopped speaking to me. He acted as if I no longer existed. Then I was fired."

"He fired you?" He drew up on his elbow, a muscle clenching in his jaw. "That bastard. Tell me his name."

"No, Will. It's long over and you cannot stir it up again." If Will didn't know the van Dunns, Ava would eat her tambourine. Even still, she did not want him performing acts of retribution on her part. The past should stay there. "Truthfully, losing my job was for the best because I discovered Madam Zolikoff shortly after."

"He should be punished."

"Last I heard, he'd lost his trust fund betting on the horses. He was forced to marry a truly awful woman for her dowry."

"Is this a man with whom I'm familiar?"

"Perhaps. They were not of your social caliber, though. More like upper middle class."

The lines around his mouth deepened. He suddenly appeared gravely serious. "You know I've never lied to you. I've tried to be straightforward with you from the start, to ensure there would be no expectations—"

"Indeed, I haven't forgotten. I do not expect more from you, Will." Her head knew there was no future for them, but her heart . . . Her stupid heart had ideas of its own. Deep down, she yearned for *everything* with this man. His love. His life. His future. There was no point in admitting it to him, however. He'd either find it amusing or pathetic, and both reactions would break her. "This is merely a way to pass the time."

A flash of something unrecognizable twisted his features

for a brief second. What had that been, regret? Anger? Or
gratitude that she'd agreed with him?

"Then, by all means"—he dropped his voice—"let us
pass the time once more. Where would you like me to start,
with my mouth on your breasts or between your legs?"

She raised a brow as if to say, *Need you ask?* With a
smirk, Will slid down the bed and parted her thighs.
"Excellent choice," he murmured, and she forgot all about
unpleasant conversations regarding circumstances she
could not change.

The deck of the *Athena* rolled beneath Will's feet, the
salty ocean spray coating his face. Under normal circumstances, the situation would find him relaxed and happy.
The yacht had always been his favorite place. An excursion
that offered freedom from his desk, the paperwork, and the
responsibilities that dogged him every day. Here, he could
enjoy the fresh air and ocean breezes. Today, however, he
wished to be someplace else. With someone else.

And the realization did not sit well.

"The water is beautiful, isn't it?"

Will glanced down at Miss Iselin—Kathleen, she'd
insisted he call her in private. She and her mother were two
of fifteen guests on the boat today, all members of the
Newport elite, along with Tompkins and Bennett from the
campaign. The ribbons of Kathleen's sun bonnet flapped in
the wind, the dress molding to what appeared to be a mod-
estly curvaceous figure. He waited to feel something . . .
anything. Disappointed, he tore his glance away. "Yes, it is.
Do you like sailing?"

"I do." She leaned against the rail and closed her eyes.
"Something so freeing and humbling about being on the

ocean. A reminder of how little control we have in the universe."

"That's very astute." He'd often thought the exact same when on the boat. Yet another reminder that Kathleen was deeper than most girls her age. "And yes, it can be humbling, especially in poor weather."

"My father's boat isn't nearly this size," she remarked. "You must love sailing."

"Yes, though I do not indulge in it nearly enough. I used to go out more, when Lizzie was younger."

"Your sister is quite charming. I can imagine it was hard for you when she married, with the two of you so close."

Sensitive, too. Not many people would assume that— and if they did, they wouldn't mention it to him. He liked that Kathleen had. "She is happy in her new life, which is gratifying. It's all I've ever wanted for her."

"But?"

He chuckled and leaned over, resting his elbows on the wooden railing. "There is no 'but.' You must have been happy for your older sister when she married a few years ago."

She shrugged. "I was happy for the wedding to be over. It seemed like a tiresome process to me."

"Isn't a big, fancy society wedding every woman's dream?"

"Not mine." Her expression turned wistful, almost shy. "I find the bigger the wedding, the less attention is paid to what the words mean."

A weight settled between his shoulder blades, a tightness that contrasted what his head was telling him, that this girl seemed utterly perfect. She said all the right things, intrigued him, was intelligent, beautiful, and came from the same social background. Will should be filled with satisfaction, the knowledge that everything he wanted was now within reach. Instead, his skin pulled uncomfortably, as if he were trying on a coat two sizes too small.

"Ah, here you both are," Tompkins said, arriving at Will's side. "Beautiful day for a sail, isn't it?"

Will grunted noncommittally while Kathleen politely responded, "Yes, it is."

"Miss Iselin was telling me earlier of her interest in charitable works," Tompkins said to Will. "She even donates her time to a small orphanage in Battery Park."

"It's only a few hours each week." She waved her hand. "My good deeds are not nearly on the grand scale of what Mr. Bennett and Mr. Sloane hope to accomplish when they win."

"Perhaps the two candidates could stop by the orphanage, give some attention to a worthy cause. That is, assuming the orphanage could benefit from the publicity."

Miss Iselin flushed, her porcelain skin turning a becoming pink. "I am certain they would appreciate it. Why don't I check with them and let you know?"

"That would be wonderful," Tompkins said into the silence when Will did not respond. "Please, inform Mr. Sloane the moment you speak with them."

"I will. If you gentlemen will excuse me." Gracefully Kathleen floated along the deck to rejoin the others. Will exhaled in relief, grateful he could focus on something else for a few moments.

"She is absolutely perfect for you. I hope you realize that," Tompkins murmured. "Yet I detect a distinct lack of enthusiasm on your part."

Tompkins's barb, while true, irritated Will. "My enthusiasm, healthy or otherwise, is hardly your concern."

"Isn't it?" Tompkins moved closer, lowering his voice. "I believe I know the reason you are not pursuing Miss Iselin more ardently. Need I say it?"

Will locked eyes with Tompkins, and the truth was waiting there in the man's gaze. No idea how Tompkins knew of Will's affair with Ava, but he did. At least, the advisor was aware that another woman held Will's attention, not of Ava specifically. "Again, my concern, not yours. You need to back off. If I decide to marry, it will be on my timetable, not yours."

"Are you hearing what you are saying? The campaign needs your betrothal. That will put your photo all over the papers, and voters will adore Miss Iselin. She's innocent, smart, dedicated to do-gooder causes. Moreover, she is of your same social caliber. Anyone else would be a liability, one we cannot afford. One *you* cannot afford. Do you have any idea how they are snickering over the Sloanes since your sister married Cavanaugh and went into business?"

Will did not like Ava referred to as a "liability," though he'd certainly had the same thought a time or two. He was starting to care less and less about what the voters wanted, however. "Anyone who snickers over my sister will answer to me. And allow me to worry about my liabilities."

"I would, if I thought you could handle them. It's becoming apparent to me that you cannot, that you are allowing a two-bit whore to ruin—"

Anger, swift and fierce, rushed over Will, and he acted on pure instinct. Striking out, he snatched the front of Tompkins's shirt. "Do not refer to her in such a manner ever again. If you do, I'll cut you down where you stand, Charles."

Tompkins sneered at him, disrespect so obvious that Will wanted to pummel him. "You goddamned idiot. And here you were worried about that medium embarrassing the campaign through Bennett. If the opposition catches wind of you sleeping with the sister of one your employees . . ."

He let the comment hang, so Will snapped, "My private life is no one's concern but my own. If the opposition breathes one word about her, I'll bury them."

Tompkins pulled free then smoothed his necktie and vest. "You won't be able to shove the information back into a sack once it's out, Sloane. And how will Miss Iselin feel, reading about your weekly trysts in the paper?" Will had no answer for that, so Tompkins continued, "You're playing with fire. See that we don't all get burned."

Chapter Seventeen

The afternoon had been a profitable one.

She'd performed six private readings, with two of them for new clients. This meant a higher initial "consultation" rate and good news for her monthly income. Perhaps she could throw a little bit of money at Grey and Harris's fictional corporation, ease their anxiety a bit. The blackmailers expected Ava's clients to start investing more and more each week, and the absence of such investments would only make the two men suspicious.

Opening her satchel, she tossed the blond wig inside. Blasted thing had been itching her for the last hour. A knock on the door gave her pause. Could it be Grey and Harris again? Her stomach sank. Should she ignore them? Perhaps they would go away if she didn't answer the door.

"Madam Zolikoff, I know you are there."

She couldn't place the familiar male voice. A client mistaken regarding the time of his appointment? Reaching back into her bag, she drew out the wig and pulled it on as best she could. When she opened the door, she found Charles Tompkins, Will and John's campaign manager, waiting in the hall.

He wore a dark blue checked suit, with a matching vest

stretched tight across his large belly. A derby in his hand, he smiled at her through bushy whiskers. "Good afternoon. I hope I'm not interrupting."

"No," she said carefully in her Russian accent. "Though I am curious what Mr. Bennett's campaign manager wants with me. Is everything well with John?"

Tompkins waved. "Oh, John is fine. Right as rain. May I come in?" Without waiting on an answer, the man barreled into the room, brushing by her on the way.

She quietly closed the door. Though trepidation bubbled in her veins, she tried to appear calm and collected. "Was there something you wanted to see me about?"

"You may drop the Russian accent, Miss Jones. We are well acquainted with each other, I think."

"I . . . You know who I am?"

He gave a curt nod. "Yes, I have known for some time. Quite . . . enterprising of you. Not many women would have the courage to do as you've done."

She said nothing. He was here for a reason, and she wished he would get to his purpose.

"John doesn't know, of course," he continued. "I haven't had the heart to tell him."

A threat hung in the air, one that caused the hair on the back of her neck to rise. "But . . . ?"

He strolled deeper into the room, swiped a gloved finger over the smooth surface of the wooden dresser as if inspecting it. She wasn't fooled. Ava was a performer; she knew how to build tension with an audience. And though they were not on a stage, he was putting on a show as sure as the sun rose over the East River.

"William Sloane was a careful choice for John's running mate, Miss Jones. He has impeccable breeding, impressive connections, wealth, and charisma. The fact that he's smart and attractive certainly does not hurt either." He stopped moving and leaned against the dresser, his hands finding his pockets. "These two men are absolute certainties for the Republican nomination. The honorable party of Lincoln, a force against the tyranny of Tammany Hall. And once I have the full weight of the party behind them, the Democrats will be hard-pressed to beat us."

Her back straightened. One of the qualities necessary for her line of work was the ability to read people. Currently she was reading Tompkins so well, he may as well've been typeset. Therefore, she knew what was to come—knew and resented it.

"You must realize how your association with Mr. Sloane jeopardizes our campaign hopes. How one word in the wrong ear could bring down everything we hope to accomplish."

"I'm not certain why you're laying this on my doorstep. Mr. Sloane is your candidate, after all."

His gaze traveled the length of her form, slowly, almost as if peeling off her clothing with his eyes. Revulsion pebbled her skin. Thank goodness she was covered from neck to toe.

"Men are notoriously stupid when it comes to pussy." She jerked in response to the crude word—one she'd never heard spoken aloud before   and his resulting smile was cruel and cold. "You don't mind if I speak plainly, do you? I assume you've heard all manner of words in your charmed life downtown."

How dare he . . . Hatred burned in her chest, rising up to clog her throat. "Actually, that is one I have not heard spoken before."

The side of his mouth hitched, as if he were amused. "You should familiarize yourself with it, Miss Jones, because that is what you are to someone like William Sloane. A quick fuck. Meaningless. Convenient. A warm body to spread her legs and relieve his tension. Men can be blinded by it, when it's exceptionally good."

She could not speak. Her tongue felt thick and useless, full of anger and outrage. The words hurt, as he had known they would. She held no illusions about her relationship with Will, but to hear it put so plainly wounded her as surely as a swift blow.

"Good Christ, I can't believe it. I can see it on your face. You were under the impression that he actually cared for you." He threw his head back and gave a few deep laughs that shook his prodigious middle. "What did you think, he would marry you? That society would look past your illustrious career and accept you? That Mrs. Astor would invite you for tea? Come now, Miss Jones. I thought you were smarter than that."

In the dark parts of her heart, the ones no one saw, the ones she barely acknowledged, Ava had hoped for a portion of that dream. One where Will wanted a respectable forever with her, where society and Mrs. Astor didn't matter, only their love for each other.

But she'd been raised in the slums, where one rapidly learned that dreams were for fools and children. Her heart may have wanted a forever with Will, yet her head had never lost sight of the fact that it would not happen. Their circumstances prevented a happily ever after—not the one she wanted, anyhow.

"What is your point?" she asked, surprised that her voice sounded steady despite the rioting emotions inside her.

"My point, dear lady, is that you'd best break things off with William—quickly. If you do not, I will be forced to reveal your little scheme to the newspapers. Madam Zolikoff will be run out of town on the very next train."

"You wouldn't, because exposing me also exposes Bennett as a fool. Not to mention all the sensitive matters he told me in confidence. You aren't the only one with stories for the newspapers." Not that she would ever break Bennett's trust. But Tompkins didn't know that.

And yes, you are what he first accused you of being: a blackmailer.

Tompkins nodded as if he'd expected this. "Will New York believe a decorated war hero and former United States senator, or a charlatan out to make a quick buck? And that would bring Stephen van Dunn into it. Quite an interesting man, our Mr. van Dunn. By the way, he has a shockingly good memory, especially when I promised to keep his name out of any of the stories." She pressed a hand to her stomach, the room swaying under her feet. "I am not a fool. When I realized what was happening between you and Sloane, I quickly learned all I could about Miss Ava Jones. You'll be lucky to make it out in one piece when I'm through."

Humiliation burned her skin, the horrors of her past washing over her like a bucket of cinders. Stephen, the affair, the pregnancy . . . *Dear God*. The idea of it all becoming public knowledge, used in some sordid attempt to discredit her, sent shivers along her spine.

Yet everything inside her rebelled against backing down. She hated bullies, hated the idea that her life was no longer hers to control. Mind spinning, she tried to think it through. Perhaps the truth wouldn't ruin her. After all, she'd suffered far worse and had recovered. Thrived, even, in a city where only the strongest and smartest survived. And besides, the newspapers would hardly print something so salacious, not with Comstock's laws in effect, would they?

Arrived at her decision, she set her jaw. "I do not appreciate threats. If Mr. Sloane wishes to stop seeing me, he may tell me so. Not you."

"I hated to do this, but you leave me no choice." He heaved a dramatic sigh, withdrew a piece of newsprint from his inner jacket pocket. "Do you know where Mr. Sloane spent his weekend?"

"In Newport."

He unfolded the paper carefully. "Yes, that's true. But do you know why?" She hesitated, and his lips twisted cruelly. "Of course you don't. Mr. Sloane is wooing a woman, Miss Jones. A young woman of his social standing, one he intends to ask to marry him before the summer is out."

Mouth gone suddenly dry, she attempted to swallow. Yes, he'd escorted Miss Baldwin earlier in the summer to the séance but, according to Will, the two hadn't seen each other again. "Miss Baldwin?"

Eyes glittering with malice, Tompkins held the piece of newsprint out. "No, not Miss Baldwin. He had four candidates for marriage this spring, and all have been eliminated except one. Here, read it for yourself."

She stared at the paper, knowing she should refuse. Whatever that article contained would not be welcome news. Yet she could not stop herself. Knowing was always better than not knowing, wasn't it?

Hand shaking, she took the paper and began to read.

RAILROAD SCION WOOS ISELIN HEIRESS!
SLOANE HOSTS PRIVATE SAIL FOR BEAUTY!
SOURCE CLOSE TO PERFECT PAIR SAYS,
"BETROTHAL IMMINENT"

Obligations, he'd told Ava. Was the Iselin heiress that obligation, or had Will just preferred to keep this from Ava? She drew in a reedy breath. The truth stared up at her in stark black-and-white. *If you continue, that makes you the other woman. The mistress.*

The back of her lids stung, a case of oncoming tears to further her humiliation. She beat them back through sheer force of will. Tompkins would not see her cry.

"Fine." She handed the newsprint over. "But let me tell him myself. Otherwise, he'll never believe it."

Tompkins nodded, satisfaction blazing in his dark eyes. He tucked the paper into his pocket once more. "Of course, Miss Jones. But it had better be within the week."

Will arrived late on Thursday afternoon, thanks to a board member who had been incapable of brevity. He took the stairs, anticipation hopping through his veins, a tripping of lust and hunger that only one woman could sate. As was their habit, she'd left the door unlocked, so he threw it open and stepped into the hotel room, hopeful of finding Ava on the bed. Naked.

Instead, she sat primly in a chair, her back ramrod straight. In all the weeks he'd met her here, she'd never appeared so . . . serious. Was this a game? Were they to role-play this afternoon? His lust spiked once more.

Unable to hide a wolfish grin, he shut the door and strolled toward her. "Hello, darling. Are we to play parts today? What is this, disapproving schoolteacher and recalcitrant student?"

"Will, we need to talk—"

"Oh, I have no doubt." He shrugged out of his frock coat and threw it toward the dresser. "About my poor marks? Or have I been causing trouble in class?"

Ava shot to her feet and wrapped her arms around her waist. "No. You misunderstand—"

"Ah, is it the grieving widow and overattentive iceman?" His fingers went to his throat to loosen his necktie. "Or an ill soldier requiring nursing from a blushing innocent?"

She pinched the bridge of her nose, a reluctant smile breaking out over her face. "My God, how many of these can you think up?"

"Oh, I'm just getting started. Woman seducing her husband's older, more handsome brother. Doctor examining his beautiful patient. Busty milkmaid and farmhand. Sultan and his favorite harem girl—"

"Stop," she laughed. "Just stop talking, you infuriating man."

Hands on his hips, he cocked his head. She was serious, he realized. "What is it, Ava?"

She heaved a sigh, one that signaled unhappiness, and Will's trepidation grew. He wanted to take her into his arms, kiss her until she smiled, but there was a distance in her posture, so he shoved his hands in his pockets instead. "Is something wrong? Did something happen?"

"I know about Newport. About Miss Iselin."

"Newport?" He tried to think why she would be concerned about the sailing party with Kathleen. "I'm sorry, I don't understand."

"The newspaper had a full report of the sail, said you are planning to marry her."

He frowned. How had the papers learned of the events on Saturday? Tompkins? Will meant to have a conversation with his campaign manager at first opportunity. He did not want the details of his private life in the paper.

But wasn't that the reason for courting Kathleen in the first place? The publicity to help the campaign?

Mind swirling, he dragged a hand through his hair. "Ava, you shouldn't believe everything you read about me in the paper. I never even bother to glance at the gossip pages any longer."

"So you're not planning on asking her to marry you? You didn't have four candidates for marriage this spring?"

"I did, but . . ." He didn't even know what to say. That his enthusiasm for marriage had waned significantly since the two of them started sleeping with each other? That he couldn't stop thinking about her? That he craved her every single second, down to the marrow of his bones?

"Will, I can't be the other woman. I cannot be the one

getting the scraps of your time and attention. It would—"
She snapped her jaw shut.

"It would, what?" he croaked.

She licked her lips and took a deep breath. "It would
destroy me."

A heavy weight settled on his chest, the heft of the circumstances that separated the two of them. He felt her
slipping away, and it scared him. "What are you saying?
What do you want from me, Ava?"

"I can't see you again. We knew—"

Will's palm cracked against the top of the wooden
dresser. Impotent fury surged through his limbs, unabated
by his small outburst. He wanted to keep hitting something, just keep striking, until he could deal with the
emotion tangling up inside him.

"We knew this was temporary," Ava continued, her voice
louder and stronger. "I will not be your mistress and circumstances being what they are . . ."

"Fuck circumstances," he snapped. He hated the sad
resolution he saw in her gaze. Was she so ready to give him
up, then?

"You do not mean that. Our lives could not be more different, Will. Our backgrounds, our responsibilities. You
would resent me if I forced you to change any of that. I
won't cause you any regret."

He folded his arms and tucked his clenched fists under
his armpits. "Is it really so easy for you to walk away?"

A flash of hurt flitted across her face before she masked
it. That brief crack in her icy resolve gave him hope. Perhaps he could convince her to change her mind.

Striding toward her, he cupped her jaw in his palm. Her
skin was soft and supple, and he knew how perfect it
tasted. Drawing her face up, he forced her to look at him.
"Is it?"

"It hardly matters whether it's easy or difficult," she

whispered. "Life doesn't always give us painless, simple choices, but the choices must still be made, regardless."

"Yes, but why must those choices be made *now*?"

"Because it hurts, Will. And it will hurt worse tomorrow, even worse the day after. Every day that I fool myself into thinking you're mine—and only mine—merely causes it to hurt worse."

A sharp stab of pain flared behind his rib cage. How had this day gone so terribly wrong? He longed to go back to bed and start all over, to come here and find her smiling and eager for him. "Give me more time, Ava." The pad of his thumb stroked her jaw. "I'm not ready to let you go."

"I'm sorry, but I can't." Moisture gathered in the corner of her eyes, a sight that nearly sent him to his knees. Christ, no tears—anything but tears. He'd rather have her shouting at him, throwing a paperweight at his head.

Leaning down, he pressed his mouth to hers, a simple melding of lips that tasted like home. Like everything he'd ever wanted, love and happiness. Laughter and liveliness. She paused but soon began kissing him back, her mouth meeting his in a delicate exchange tinged by unhappiness. When her fingers trailed over his shoulders and tangled in his hair, he deepened the kiss, giving her his tongue and taking hers in exchange. They stayed there for a long minute, tasting, savoring, until she finally pulled away.

"Will, please. Don't make this harder than it needs to be."

"So I should make it easier for you to walk away?" He grabbed her hips and pulled her flush to his body. Let her feel how much he desired her. "I can't do that, lovely woman. I want you too desperately to allow you to go without a fight."

Her forehead dropped to his chest, her shoulders sagging. "*Will* . . . ," she whined.

He pressed a kiss to the top of her head. "*Ava* . . . ," he said in a matching tone.

She said nothing, but her hands found their way to his hips, up his rib cage, over his stomach. He craved her touch everywhere. "Please, Ava. Don't leave me. Stay."

Without waiting for an answer, he knelt and began sliding her skirts higher. His fingers skimmed her stocking-covered calves and knees, then along her drawers to the part between her legs. "Hold these," he ordered, shoving the mounds of fabric up at her. Chest rising and falling rapidly, she gathered her skirts in her hands, leaving Will free to find the slit in her drawers.

He could smell her, the enticing aroma of her arousal, and his pulse pounded along the length of his erection. "Do you want this?" he asked before leaning in to breathe her in. "Tell me, Ava. May I have you this afternoon?" Everything hinged on her answer. If he could convince her today, chances were good he could continue to convince her in the future. And he was willing to play unfairly to get what he wanted.

Trembling, she stood there, her cleft bared before his avid stare. "You are the devil, Will Sloane."

"That is not an answer." He slid his nose over the velvety skin of her inner thigh, and she gasped. "I want to hear you say it."

"It would be a shame to waste the hotel room, I suppose."

A sweet rush of victory filled him, a grin twisting his lips. He rewarded her with a swift flick of his tongue over the taut bud of her sex. She jerked, her fingers knotting in his hair, but he held still. "Tell me you need me, Ava. That you need *this*."

"Yes, Will. God, yes."

He lunged, ready to devour her. To prove to her that no one else could ever compare. To bind her to him and prevent her from ever leaving. To gain more time. He couldn't allow this to be over just yet.

She suddenly grabbed his head to prevent him from

moving, so he glanced up, curious. "I won't meet you again. This is the last time, Will. Please understand that I cannot continue, not the way things are."

Disappointment crashed through him, and he surged to his feet. "Goddamn it, Ava. You're being unreasonable. I'm not even betrothed!"

Skirts fell to cover her enticing legs and ankles. "And you're using the attraction between us to manipulate me. To get what you want. Stop thinking only of yourself!"

The need to shout and scream, to argue until he won, burned his tongue. But he knew she was right; he was being selfish. So he stalked to the window and glanced down at the street traffic. He'd always loved New York, but right now his beloved city felt like a noose around his neck.

Why did she have to be so stubborn? He could not marry anyone he pleased, that was not how society worked, not for a man in his position. And wouldn't his father have loved Will thumbing his nose at over two hundred years of breeding and status to marry a medium? *"You'll run it all into the ground,"* his father had often said. Will would be damned before he'd prove the old man right.

After a moment, small arms wrapped around his waist, and the heavy weight of her breasts pressed against his back. He held onto her wrists, searching for the right words. But there were no words, at least none that would soon ease the ache in his chest. "You know you can change your mind at any time," he finally said, watching the afternoon sun bathe the buildings in stripes of orange and red. "A part of me will always be waiting for you."

He heard her drag in a shaky breath. "Oh, Will. A part of me will always be with you."

Street noises whirled around them, while they clung to each other like moss on a rock. Was this love, this all-consuming need to breathe the same air as this woman?

How in hell had she come to mean so much in a short period? He'd never had difficulty separating from a paramour in the past. However, right now, the city could crumble and Will would be hard-pressed to care.

Her hand found his shoulder, and she turned him slowly. Sadness lurked in her irises, but there was mischief there too. "One last time, railroad man. Better make it count."

The early evening drizzle matched Ava's mood as she hurried along Hudson Street. Her feet hurt, her back throbbed, and her heart . . . well, her heart felt as if a team of horses had dragged it the length of Manhattan. Twice.

Six days since she'd last seen him, since they'd shared a bed. Seemed more like six minutes. She kept waiting for the ache to recede, for the pain to lesson. No such luck. Even a glimpse of the elevated caused her to tear up. Heaven help her if she stepped a foot inside Grand Central Depot.

Knowing she'd done the right thing was little solace, especially when she still yearned for him.

Yet she'd faced worse, hadn't she? When she'd lost her baby. When Stephen had turned his back on her, abandoning and firing her. Or when her parents had died, leaving her to support three siblings. All of those events far outweighed the loss of one upper-crust millionaire—and she had survived.

You'll survive, Ava. You always do.

She had insisted on leaving the hotel room first. *Better to walk away than be left behind.* If she'd stayed, she might never have found the courage to go. The temptation of sleeping on sheets that smelled of him would've been too great to resist.

She had taken one of his shirt studs, however. It hadn't

been hard to distract him and slip the tiny solid-gold and pearl stud into her pocket. Foolishly she'd fancied a piece of him, one small token to carry with her. Eventually she would send the stud back to him—after she'd worn it in her collar for a few months.

Removing a key from the small purse on her waist, she aligned the metal with the hole in her front door.

"Miss Jones."

The deep voice behind her caused her to drop the key, where it clattered to the stoop. Spinning, she found Mr. Grey and Mr. Harris looming there. *Damn.* She did not like these men outside her home, near her siblings. Mary and Sam would already be home, possibly Tom as well. The last thing she needed was for one of them to overhear this conversation.

"Good evening, gentlemen." She bent and picked up the key, wrapping her fingers around it tightly. "How may I help you?"

"We missed you today at the hotel." Grey cocked his head. "No clients today?"

She tried not to react, her face a stoic mask. "None. I took a week off." A lie. She had changed hotels to avoid these two.

Harris chuckled, the scar on his cheek twisting. "A week off? You? Traveling to your summer cottage, then?"

"Something like that. I trust you received the money I sent last week."

"Oh, we did," Grey said, moving forward to lean one foot on the first step. "But we were a bit confused about that. Why, exactly, did the money come through you and not one of your clients?"

She cleared her throat. "Because they are uncomfortable dealing with outsiders. They trust me to place the investment for them." Another lie, may God forgive her.

She hadn't pressured any of her clients to invest in Grey and Harris's venture. Instead, she'd sent money out of her own pocket, hoping to appease the two for a bit.

"That is not how this works," Harris added, climbing the stairs until he stood in front of her. Grey followed, saying, "See, we want to know you're doing your part. That you're not just sending us money when you feel like it."

"I should hardly think that matters, as long as you get paid." She inched back toward the door.

"It matters. We can bring them in, get them to invest in other ventures, once you send them to us. Only, you're not sending anyone to us."

"I did not realize that was what you preferred." She attempted to put more distance between them. "I will make a concerted effort starting tomorrow." *Like hell.*

Harris crowded her against the door. He stood less than a foot away, using his bulk to intimidate her. "See that you do, Miss Jones. If we don't have someone by Friday, everything you've built, all that you've worked for, will be gone. You'll be the laughingstock of New York."

Grey appeared next, his sneer terrifying—even in the low light. "Not only will you be ruined, several others will be going down with you, once you're exposed."

"Ava?"

Grey and Harris stepped back, and Ava saw Tom down on the walk, his brow furrowed in concern. "Are you all right?" her brother asked.

Harris lifted his palms as both men descended the steps. "No worries, son. We're just having a friendly chat with your sister."

Grey grinned at Ava as if they'd just been catching up over tea. "So we'll see you Friday, ain't that right, Miss Jones?"

"Yes," she said weakly. "Friday."

The two men sauntered down Bank Street toward Hudson, but Ava turned her attention to Tom. She couldn't say anything, horrified to even ask how much he'd overheard.

He came up the steps and shot a worried glance to where Grey and Harris were disappearing. "What was that all about?"

"Nothing. How was your day?" She turned and started to open the door with her key—only her damn hand wouldn't stop trembling.

"Ava." Tom's palm landed on her hand. "Stop and tell me what is going on. Who were those two men? What did they want with you?"

"Readings, of course."

"Bull. You forget who you're talking to. I'm not one of your clients that you can bamboozle. I want the truth."

"Those two are a problem I'm working on. You needn't worry over it."

Hands on his slim hips, he stared at her disapprovingly. Though not even sixteen, he was growing, rapidly evolving from a young boy into a man. "I am not a kid any longer. I have a job and I am the man of the family. You cannot treat me like the other two. I deserve to know what's going on."

She pressed her lips together. On one hand, it would be nice to have help in carrying the burden every now and again. But her brother should not be involved in this mess. The less he knew, the better.

"I know you want to help, but there's nothing you can do this time. I'm in a bit of a pickle, but I'll figure it out."

"Does this have anything to do with why you ain't been eating or sleeping this week?"

No, she wanted to say. *That had to do with Will Sloane.* "I didn't realize you were taking note of my habits."

"Kind of hard to miss when we eat and sleep in such a small space, Ava. Besides, your clothes are hangin' on you like flour sacks."

She glanced down at herself. Perhaps her shirtwaists were a bit looser. "Tom, let it go. I'll figure out what to do." She had no idea how, but there was little choice. They didn't yet have enough savings to leave New York. Though perhaps they could go to New Jersey for a bit . . .

"If you don't tell me the truth, I will go up there and tell Sam there is no Santa Claus."

"You wouldn't dare! He's the only one who still believes."

Tom quirked a brow in challenge, and Ava's shoulders fell. Fine, he wanted to know, then she'd tell him. It wouldn't change anything. But perhaps Tom could help her come up with a way to get money to Harris and Grey without knowing it came from her.

"A little more than a month ago, those two men came to see me. . . ."

Chapter Eighteen

The Park Row offices of the *New York Mercury* bustled with activity. Reporters, assistants, and typesetters were focused on the next day's issue, their anxiety nearly palpable in the space as they raced the clock. Will paid no attention to any of it. He walked quickly toward his quarry in the back, Tom Jones right on his heels.

A secretary rose from a desk at his approach. "May I help you, sir?"

Will did not even break stride or slow down. "He's expecting me."

"Yes, but I still need—"

He went past her, through the door, and into the publisher's private domain. A large space with floor-to-ceiling windows, the fourteenth-floor office overlooked City Hall. Two men stood in front of a desk, their gazes tipping up at the interruption.

Calvin Cabot, publisher of the *Mercury*, straightened to his full, lanky height, a smirk breaking out on his face. He wore no frock coat, just a vest and shirtsleeves, his face unshaven. "Sloane, this is an unexpected treat. Jim"—he turned to the other man—"give me a few minutes and then we'll get back to this."

"You got it, Cabot." Gathering some papers, the employee left the room, shutting the door behind him.

"Cabot, this is Tom, one of my employees."

Cabot came around the desk, shook Tom's hand, and then slapped Will's shoulder. "You look like shit, Sloane. Late night?"

Will gritted his teeth. He hadn't slept well in a week. His concentration was shot, his mood black. The Northeast employees were giving him a wide berth these days, all except Tom, who had been lodging frequent suspicious, assessing looks in Will's direction.

"Some of us work for a living, Cabot. Not everyone visits beer halls and boxing matches every night." Cabot's raucous lifestyle was the stuff of legend. How he managed to oversee three newspapers never failed to perplex Will. Yet, Cabot could be counted on to spin a story in precisely the right manner to cause magical things to happen.

And Will desperately needed that magical touch today.

"Tom, I'm sorry you are trapped working for this fuddy-duddy," Calvin said, gesturing to the two chairs in front of the desk. "Anytime you want to have a little fun, you come see me about a position."

Will unbuttoned his frock coat and sat, Tom doing the same. "Thank you, sir," Tom said politely.

"Sir?" Calvin shook his head. "This ain't a regiment, son. Call me Cabot. Everyone else does."

"Are you done?" Will snapped at Cabot. "I am on a schedule today—and don't you have a paper to print?"

Cabot dropped into his chair and leaned back. "And here I thought you were coming to see me about a favor."

Will huffed in annoyance. Cabot was right; Will was being a bastard. Still, this was timely. "I apologize. I do need a favor. I need you to run a story for me in tomorrow's paper."

"Tomorrow's paper?" Cabot's eyes went wide. "Jesus,

Sloane. That's been set already and they'll start the presses in"—he glanced at his pocket watch—"fifteen minutes."

"Tell them to wait."

Cabot stared at Will, his expression not giving anything away as he stroked his jaw. After a moment, he stood, went to the telephone box on the wall, and turned the crank. Once someone picked up, he said into the mouthpiece, "Charles, tell them to wait. I may need to make a few changes."

He resumed his seat and beckoned with his hand. "Let's hear it."

"I need a pair of blackmailers exposed." Cabot's brows rose, a speculative gleam in his eye, so Will addressed Tom. "Tell him everything you told me."

Tom cleared his throat and inched forward in his seat. "My sister is Madam Zolikoff."

"The medium?" Cabot asked, brows shooting high. "Saw her last year. She's good."

Tom nodded, his chin lifting. "Yes, she is. A month ago, two men approached her and demanded she tell her clients to invest in their company—"

"Which doesn't exist, of course," Cabot finished. "Then the 'company' goes under, taking all the money with it, which these men pocket and move on. Not very original, but effective, unfortunately. So what did your sister say?"

"She didn't want to do it. Tried to tell them no, but they threatened to expose her as a fraud. Reveal her identity and run her out of town."

"That's what I'd expect. It's their only leverage. So what, they're getting impatient 'cause she's stalling?"

Will marveled at Cabot's quick mind. A reporter at heart, Cabot could sniff a trail faster than any man or woman Will knew.

"Yes," Tom answered. "She tried sending her own money, claiming it was from investors, but they didn't buy it.

Pushed back. They've given her until tomorrow to have someone show up at the fake offices, ready to invest."

"She could send someone there with some dough. A friend or relative."

"You don't know Ava," Tom said with a slight chuckle. "She's not one to ask for help."

A gross understatement, Will thought. In fact, if Ava knew what Tom and Will were doing at this very moment, she would be furious. But Will didn't care. He had the power to help her, so he would see this problem resolved—whether she wanted him to or not. It was the least he could do for her.

"Who are these two charming gentlemen? Do you have names?"

"She told me their names are Harris and Grey. Gave me a pretty good description, too."

"Harris and Grey? One's got a long beard, the other a scar down his cheek?"

Tom nodded and Cabot threw his head back and laughed. "Christ, those two are from Tammany. Have they no shame?"

Will didn't bother to answer, since the question was clearly rhetorical. "So can you expose them? I want it in tomorrow's edition, before they come back to threaten her again."

Cabot's mouth hitched, his lips twitching as if he were fighting a smile. "Tom, I need to speak to Sloane in private. Do me a favor and wait in the outer room, will you? Feel free to help yourself to some coffee."

"Sure thing. Thank you, sir. Mr. Cabot, I mean."

Tom fled the room, and Will braced himself. Cabot was no fool.

"I do love this story. Cigar?" Cabot reached into the box on his desk and withdrew a perfectly rolled cigar. Will selected one as well, grateful to have something to do with his hands for the moment. Once both cigars were snipped and lit, Cabot leaned back in his chair, and placed his booted feet up on the desk. "So, it's the sister."

Will slowly exhaled a mouthful of smoke. "I don't know what you mean."

"The reason for your shitty mood. The bags under your eyes. The way your suit hangs off your shoulders. And it's not like you to get involved in something like this without a dashed good reason."

Christ, did Cabot have to be so perceptive? "Any chance we could avoid having this conversation?"

"None." Cabot grinned and pointed at Will with his cigar. "Not if you want your story printed, big boy."

"Sometimes I truly hate you."

"Nah, you love me—just like everyone else in this fine city. But I'm not going to hold the presses for much longer, so you'd best tell me your story."

"Do you promise to keep her name out of it?"

Cabot scratched his whiskered face. "Gonna be a challenge to write a story about a woman being blackmailed when I can't use the woman's name. Do you have feelings for said woman?"

"Yes," Will admitted, shocking even himself. "We were . . . intimate. But no longer."

"Will Sloane and Madam Zolikoff," Cabot said with a delighted sigh. "I think my reporter's heart has died and gone to heaven. What I wouldn't give to print *that* story."

"Well, you can't—not if you want to keep your balls intact."

Cabot barked a laugh. "I can't believe it! Will Sloane just threatened my second favorite body part. I'd expect that of Cavanaugh, not you. This woman must've done a number on you."

She had, but Will wasn't about to discuss that now. Rubbing the ache in his stomach, he clamped the cigar between his teeth and puffed.

"I hear you are courting Miss Kathleen Iselin," Cabot said slyly, stirring the pot in his usual style. "At least that's what the *Sun* is reporting."

"Merely a rumor, thanks to Tompkins. I invited her and her mother for a sail in Newport."

Cabot stared out the tall windows for a moment. "You should watch out for Tompkins. He's . . . dangerously ambitious. Enough to not care how he gets to the top."

Will thought about that for a moment. He'd never liked Tompkins, but the man had served his purpose thus far. Still, Cabot was usually right about people. "So will you run the story?"

"Of course." Cabot came to his feet. "Two reasons, the first being that I love to poke at Tammany every chance I get."

"And the second?"

"You're going to owe me a damn large favor in return."

Hunched over her kitchen table, Ava picked at her buttered roll. If she took to her bed for the day, would anyone care?

Grey and Harris would notice, of course. No doubt the two thugs would track her down later today. She had no idea what to do. Time had run out, and no amount of stalling would pacify them. Tom had told her not to worry before leaving for work a few minutes ago, but his optimism had not caught fire. Nothing had gone right in Ava's life lately. Why should this be any different?

She unfolded the faded piece of newsprint. An advertisement for an idyllic farmhouse in upstate New York stared up at her. Picket fence and two floors. A porch perfect for a swing and a decent yard where the kids could play. The ad had appeared several years ago, but she'd kept it as a reminder of possibilities. The goal of a better future.

A lump formed in her throat. She needed to leave New York—now more than ever. Memories lingered in every corner, along each street. Every time a fancy carriage went by, her eyes strained, hoping for a glimpse of sandy blond hair . . . God, she was pathetic. But she didn't yet have enough saved to buy this house, or one like it. Tom's wages at Northeast had helped tremendously and their savings had grown, but Tom maintained he had no interest in leaving the city.

How could she split the four of them up? The idea of leaving her eldest brother behind and starting a new life somewhere else without him was painful. But there was Sam and Mary to consider. Tom would be fine, working for Will and building a future here, but the two younger siblings still needed a way out. Looking after them was Ava's responsibility.

Without warning, the door opened, startling Ava. Tom burst in, a newspaper under his arm. "I thought you left for work," she said, alarmed. "What's wrong?" Had Will fired him?

"Here." Tom tossed the *Mercury* on the table. "Read that."

She'd purposely avoided newspapers since learning of Will and Miss Iselin. The last thing she could handle right now was to see a betrothal announcement or some other tidbit about the perfect society couple. "Why?"

"Ava, just look."

She allowed herself a peek at the headline—and gasped.

TAMMANY BLACKMAIL PLOT UNCOVERED!
GREY AND HARRIS DEFRAUD HUNDREDS!
FAKE COMPANY USED TO LURE INVESTORS!

"How . . ." And then she knew. Will had done this. Somehow, Will had learned of what was happening, and he'd convinced the *Mercury* to run this story. She dragged her fingertips across the black type, fighting tears as the ink smudged her skin.

He loved her.

She did not doubt it. Will would never write her an ode or a letter of devotion, but this . . . this was her railroad man's way of expressing his feelings.

"You told him."

"Yes." Tom said. "I knew he'd help. I saw the way he stared at you when you weren't looking. And it's obvious why he invited us to his house on that sweltering evening. I don't know why you're both walking around like someone killed your dog, but I had to ask him for help."

She began to read the article, ignoring the small thrill that Will was suffering as well. *"A part of me will always be waiting for you."* Perhaps he hadn't finalized his betrothal yet—not that it mattered. He could never marry her, and Ava could never be his mistress. The newsprint blurred before her eyes, and she took a deep breath, struggling for composure.

"He kept your name out of it," Tom added.

"That's a relief."

"I thought you'd be happier. Mr. Sloane said those two men will be arrested today."

She forced a smile. "I am happy. Very. This is a relief, especially since I hadn't yet figured out what to do about them. Thank you, Tom."

"You're welcome. I keep telling you that I can help. You shouldn't have to do this alone anymore, Ava."

She nodded, fighting fresh tears and unable to speak. Tom seemed to understand. He placed his derby on his head. "I should go, or I'll be late for work."

"Do you like working there? What if we . . ."

His expression hardened, determination causing him to appear much older than fifteen. "I love working there.

I don't miss my old life one bit. And don't ask me to leave, Ava, because I won't."

She nodded. His answer hadn't surprised her, and she had no right to force him to give up something he was fond of. "Run along before you land yourself in trouble."

Tom turned and reached for the knob. "Any message you'd like me to pass on?"

Her gaze fell to the newspaper once more. "No," she answered quietly. "I'll take care of that myself."

The opera droned on, one aria blurring into another as the night dragged. Will paid little attention, unable to feel the stirring voices and rousing music as he usually did. In fact, he hadn't felt much of all in the past nine days.

She made you feel. She made you feel more than you ever thought possible.

Yes, and she was gone. Christ, when would these depressing thoughts cease? And even these thoughts were a stroll through the park compared to the dreams plaguing him at night. Those were charged with sexual tension, so hot he woke up sweating. *Hell.* He'd never consumed so much alcohol in his life.

The crowd began to clap, so Will joined in. When the din died down, Mrs. Iselin leaned over. "I see a dear friend I'd like to visit with."

Will stood, ready to escort her to a neighboring box, but the woman placed her hand on his arm. "Thank you, Mr. Sloane, but I will see myself over. It's not a great distance. You and Kathleen enjoy yourselves."

He waited until she disappeared before retaking his seat. Kathleen peered over at him. "You seem distracted."

"I apologize. I've had a long week, which is a poor excuse but also happens to be the truth."

She waited a beat before saying, "It was very kind of you to escort us tonight."

"My pleasure. I was happy to receive your mother's note, requesting an escort. Will you be in the city a long time?"

"Only the weekend. My father had to return, and so I convinced Mother to come as well."

"And why was that?"

She tucked her chin, avoiding his eyes, and he suddenly understood. *He* was the reason she'd returned this weekend.

The knowledge should thrill him, considering his plans for a wife. And Miss Iselin was a perfect choice. Politically minded, intelligent, beautiful, innocent, with a social pedigree to rival the Sloanes . . . So why wasn't he elated?

Because you desire someone else.

That hardly mattered. Ava had made her mind up. She wanted nothing to do with him.

"I see," he said, unsure of how else to respond.

"You sound unhappy over my return. Should I have stayed in Newport? I thought . . ."

She drifted off, though he understood her plainly. *I thought you would be pleased to see me.* Christ, he was a cad. This girl was off thinking of him, hoping he returned her interest, yet he was focused on someone else—a woman he'd never have.

What else did you expect Kathleen to think, since you invited her sailing and escorted her to the opera?

Suddenly the weight of the room—the expectations and audaciousness of their precise little world—pressed down on his chest. His bowtie constricted his airflow, and he could not breathe. He shot to his feet. "I think I'll fetch a drink from the salon. Something for you?"

"Champagne, please."

Will hurried to the outer portion of the box and poured

himself a tumbler of scotch. He'd just tossed it back when Kathleen appeared in the doorway. Swallowing, he grimaced at the unholy burn that erupted in his stomach. *At least I can feel that.*

Without commenting, he removed a bottle from the silver ice bucket and poured her a glass of cold champagne. She accepted the flute, her small fingers wrapping around the stem. He started to turn away, but a hand on his arm stopped him. "Will, wait."

He paused, staring down at her. "Yes?"

Color stained her cheeks, but she lifted her chin, as if she'd come to an important decision. "One of the reasons I haven't been courted much this year is because I'm too perceptive. I have a fortune, yes, and I'm pleasing enough to the eye. But men—well, men *my* age—don't want to hear my opinions and thoughts. They want to impress me with their knowledge of horse racing or yachting. But you're different. You not only talk to me as an equal, you listen to what I have to say."

God, he had to stop this. It was too much, her regard. He didn't deserve it. "Kathleen—"

"No, wait. Let me finish." She took a quick sip from the crystal flute. "I should like us to be honest with each other. I'm not some empty-headed debutante out to trap a husband, regardless of his feelings on the subject. I want a good man, an honest man. More importantly, one who wants to be with me. Do not feel as if you must pretend."

He sighed. "I . . . I don't know what to say. It was not my intention to cause you discomfort."

"I'm enjoying myself; I always do at the opera. However, I can sense your unhappiness. Your wish to be somewhere else. And I am deeply sorry for forcing you to escort us this evening. If I had known, I never would have asked my mother to write to you."

"Do not apologize. I am the one who is sorry. When I agreed to escort you, I'd forgotten how perceptive you are."

She smiled, and her loveliness struck him once more. But he still didn't feel anything except admiration and friendship for her. Which meant he had to do the honorable thing.

"While you will make a wonderful wife for one fortunate man someday, I'm afraid that man will not be me." Once he said the words, his entire body relaxed . . . and he knew it had been the right thing to do. He could not make this woman happy, and she deserved better.

"I understand," she said quietly. She absorbed the news and then drew herself up. Her lips twisted into a small smile. "Honestly, I'd rather find out now than several months down the road. I hope we may remain friends, however."

"Indeed, I should like that. You're an intelligent, beautiful woman, Kathleen."

"Thank you, Will. Our acquaintance has filled me with hope. Even if you are not my future husband, this proved there was at least one man out there willing to listen."

He chuckled. "No doubt there is another, and I am certain you'll find him."

"The great Madam Zolikoff!" Mr. Ashgate, the evening's host and the man who'd hired her, had to shout to be heard above the noise. "Welcome!"

Guests crowded the space behind him, a larger group than she'd anticipated. Would all these people join the séance?

The evening had been arranged only a few days ago. Though she'd given a séance just the night before, Ava had been desperate to work, to keep her mind off one particular person, and so she'd jumped at the opportunity without doing any of her usual research. Normally she asked questions, such as whether she knew the host or not. Who would be attending? How was the room set up? Would she have complete control over the environment?

This time, she'd asked zero questions, and unease slithered down her spine. She fought it and smiled pleasantly. "Good evening, Mr. Ashgate."

He pumped her hand, jerking on her shoulder. "We are honored to have you here tonight. This is indeed a treat. A night we'll all remember, to be certain." He led her forward. "Come, let's introduce you."

"If you don't mind, Mr. Ashgate, I should like to see the room where the séance is to take place."

"There's time enough for that. Come."

She soon found herself mingling and meeting the guests, an act she did not mind under regular circumstances. But Ashgate's enthusiasm held a touch of something other than excitement. She couldn't put her finger on it, but an underlying current pulsed through the room, one she did not care for.

Breathe, Ava. You're being ridiculous.

The guests contained prominent members of society, the wealthy and privileged elite who reminded her too much of Will. Undoubtedly, he would know each one, whereas she had only seen their names in the newspapers.

An older man approached her. "Madam Zolikoff, I am Robert Murphy." He bowed over her hand. "It is a pleasure to meet you."

She smiled and made all the appropriate responses, but her mind began swirling. She knew him . . . but how? Robert Murphy. Why was that name familiar? Ridiculous when both were common enough names. Still, she couldn't shake the feeling that she'd met him before.

"A pleasure to meet you, Mr. Murphy."

"You have quite the reputation. I am prepared to be vastly entertained tonight."

"I certainly hope so." Speaking of that, where was Ashgate? He'd disappeared ten minutes ago, saying he would return. She smiled at Mr. Murphy. "Is this your first séance?"

"Yes. I hear you are well connected to the spirit world. In fact, Mr. Bennett sings your praises."

"You know John Bennett?"

"Indeed, for many years. I'll be running against him for governor."

More unease wormed through her. So this was the Democratic favorite, the one backed by Tammany. "Is that so?"

"It is, though one never knows. Bennett and Sloane may not get the nomination. Politics in New York are a tricky business."

Eager to escape, she nodded politely and excused herself to hunt for Ashgate. Perhaps she could withdraw her entertainment for the evening. Claim the spirits were not receptive. Fake an illness. Anything to get out of here.

"There you are!" Ashgate appeared at her side. "Would you care to see the parlor?"

You can do this. A quick one-hour performance and then you can leave.

Ashgate led her to the room where the séance was to take place. Anxious to see the space and set up, she followed him. There were more guests tonight than she anticipated, and she wanted to see how big of a table Ashgate had provided. Any more than six or seven guests made a performance impossible.

He slid back a pocket door and led her inside. "I certainly hope to *see* a spirit tonight."

"Not all spirits like to be seen," she said, dropping her

carpetbag to the floor. "If we can coax them, they might oblige us. But they are a slippery group, Mr. Ashgate."

"I understand, I do. It's just that the other séances we've had here, none have been able to produce an actual spirit. But I told Mrs. Ashgate that if one woman could perform such mystical feats, it would be Madam Zolikoff."

"Thank you," she murmured. Summoning apparitions was tricky, especially without a reliable partner in the room. Ava would need to pretend to be the spirit herself, while throwing her voice to her seat at the table. Thank goodness she'd packed cheesecloth.

After she'd assured him the room was sufficient, he withdrew, giving her privacy, and Ava went to work. In no time, she had her props ready, chairs positioned, and lights sufficiently darkened.

Not long after, the door reopened. Ashgate, along with several other guests, including Murphy, strolled in and took seats around the table. There would be seven in total, five men and two women—unusual for a séance, as more women normally attended than men. But she didn't mind; as long as they paid her, the family dog could participate.

Once they were comfortable, she dimmed the lights further and led the group in a series of chants. The air in the room turned stifling, stale, as the chanting progressed. When she sensed the guests were ready, she began calling to the spirit world, summoning forth a spirit guide.

"Our spirit guide is here!" she announced, and several guests gasped. "I can sense her. A young woman wants to help us tonight, help us to commune with the other side. Are you here, miss? Can you show yourself?"

Ava moved the table with the tip of her boot and one guest squeaked in surprise. "I felt it!" the woman whispered to her neighbor.

The spirit guide answered questions for those attending,

everything from inquiries about dead relatives, to the future, to solving dilemmas with neighbors. As the hour wore on, Ava grew tired. She decided to end the night with something memorable.

"May we see you, spirit guide?" When the spirit guide hesitated, Ava instructed the group to chant forcibly, in hopes of changing the ghost's mind. While the guests recited, Ava removed herself from the table. Since she'd never been holding hands, her neighbors would never know she'd left. Her skirts didn't rustle and the darkness cloaked her movement as she stepped behind a tall screen in the corner, withdrawing a piece of cheesecloth from her bag. Slipping on gloves, she grabbed the jar containing oil of phosphorous—

A quick tug on her skirts startled her, and she spun to see what had caused the sensation . . . but found nothing. Perhaps she'd caught her petticoat under her heel.

Once the oil soaked the fabric, the cloth turned an eerie white color. She clipped the piece to the end of the retractable rod in her pocket so that the ghostly layers draped like an apparition. Then, after removing her gloves and shoving them in her pockets, she thrust the rod into the room.

The guests expressed their shock and dismay, and Ava began asking the spirit guide more questions. After a suitable amount of time, she asked for more chanting and whisked the cloth quickly back into her bag. Sufficiently hidden, she took her seat once more.

The lights came up unexpectedly, causing her to squint, and she found a man at the switch, a smirk on his lips. Two other men rose from the table.

"What is this?" she asked in her haughtiest Russian tone. "The séance is not yet over."

The man by the switch threw open the pocket doors to

the parlor. The other guests, the ones from the drawing room, began filtering in, their gazes filled with avid anticipation. A cold ball of dread settled in her stomach.

"Madam Zolikoff, I am Neville Sedgwick," one of the men said in a clipped British accent. "These gentlemen are my associates from the Society for Mediumship Research. We should like to have a word with you."

Her throat tightened, the pieces falling into place. Tonight's entertainment would not be centered around her performance.

It would be centered around her downfall.

Chapter Nineteen

Will wound his way through the tables of well-dressed diners enjoying the evening at Sherry's. Black and white spread across the room, with ostrich feathers standing at attention to break up the monotony. He nodded to acquaintances along the way and finally stopped as two men rose to greet him.

"Good evening, Bennett. Tompkins."

Handshakes were traded before all three men took seats. Political strategy was not high on Will's list of items to accomplish on a Sunday evening, but Bennett and Tompkins had been insistent. Truth be told, the diversion probably did Will some good. Other than the opera, he'd been working round the clock for ten days.

"Thank you for meeting us," Tompkins said. His prodigious whiskers were subdued tonight, but there was a calculated gleam in his eye. "We have a few things to discuss and dinner seemed like the best way to do it."

Never mind that they met in Will's office every week. Tompkins did like the candidates to be seen about town, however. He said it landed them in the paper more often, which kept them top of mind with voters. Will failed to see how a mention of his eating timbale of lobster at a restaurant equated to votes, but he didn't have the heart to argue today.

"Not a problem. I hadn't made plans this evening."

They ordered drinks from the waiter and relaxed for a few moments. Will watched the couples dining together, the tentative smiles from the ladies. The hungry stares from the men. He regretted that he'd never taken Ava to dine. Or to the opera. And why hadn't he, because he'd been afraid of the gossip if he openly consorted with a woman not of his class? It seemed ridiculous now, considering the opportunity was now lost to him forever.

Grimacing, he rubbed his stomach and willed the guilt away. The aperitifs arrived at that moment, and they engaged in casual conversation as they sipped. Bennett was unusually quiet, while Tompkins chattered incessantly. In fact, Will had never heard the man so loquacious.

The waiter soon returned, and a dinner order was placed. Will wasn't particularly hungry, but he needed to eat. His valet had threatened to quit if Will's suits needed to be taken in any further.

"Do we know the location of the next rally?" he asked.

"Buffalo in three weeks," Tompkins answered. "Then Rochester."

Good. The trips would give him something to focus on other than Northeast business—and Ava.

"How are things progressing with Miss Iselin?" Bennett asked.

Will set his glass down. "They are not progressing. I won't be courting her."

Tompkins leaned forward. "I thought we discussed this. We all agreed, Sloane."

Unwilling to be intimidated, Will angled in as well. "We agreed on nothing. I won't continue down a distasteful path because you believe it's best for the campaign."

"Distasteful? Is that what you're calling it now?" His

jaw tensed as he reclined in his seat. "She must have her hooks in you pretty deep."

"I don't know what you're talking about," he fired back, steel in his voice.

"Don't you?"

"Sloane, a word."

Will's head shot up to find Calvin Cabot standing by their table. "Cabot. Good evening."

Cabot jerked his head to the side. "Need a word. Quickly."

Alarm shot through Will's veins. Cabot was easygoing by nature, so the concern haunting the publisher's blue eyes had Will rising hastily.

They took a few steps away from the tables, where they could be private. "Heard something about a friend of yours tonight. There's a group just in from England, Society for Mediumship Research. Know anything about it?"

Will's breath hitched, every muscle tensing. *Oh, hell.* He hadn't ever cabled the society to take back his request to expose Ava. "Are they here to . . ."

"Yes. Ashgate's arranged a séance at his house and they're going to expose her."

"Ashgate?" Ashgate was a close friend of the other party's nominee, Murphy, both being long-time Tammany men. Why was Tammany getting involved in Ava's—

His eyes closed as the truth fell like an executioner's blade. *Because of you.*

Somehow, Tammany had learned of his association with Ava, and they were using her to drag him—and Bennett by association—through the mud. He had to get over there and stop the whole thing.

"When?"

"Seven. I came to get you right after I heard."

Will muttered a curse word he didn't say aloud very often. It was already seven forty-five. "I have to go. I have to get to Ashgate's and try to help her." Spinning, he started for the exit. "Tell Bennett and Tompkins I had to leave."

"I'm coming with you. You might need a friend."

The last word caught Will's attention, and he glanced over his shoulder. "Thank you, Cabot."

"Sloane!" Tompkins caught Will's elbow, pulling him to a halt. "Where are you going?"

"I am needed elsewhere." Annoyed, Will stepped free. "My apologies for the abrupt departure."

Instead of nodding and moving away, Tompkins closed in. His voice pitched low, he said, "Ashgate doesn't know about the two of you. All Tammany wants is for the case against Harris and Grey to be dropped."

Will's body stiffened as if electrified. "*You?* You did this?" He could hardly wrap his head around it. Tompkins had set up Ava in exchange for Harris and Grey? Jesus Christ.

He snatched Tompkins's lapel and snarled, "You idiot. What the hell is the matter with you? Do you know what you've done?"

"She's ruining our plans. Do not go over there and let her take you down too. Not after all I've done to protect you."

"Sloane," Cabot said gently. "This is neither the time nor the place."

Will's head snapped up and took in the curious eyes around the room. Cabot was right; they did not need a public scene. Releasing Tompkins, he withdrew. "I will deal with you tomorrow," he promised before striding out the front door.

A hum of excitement hung in the air, a feeling Ava did not share. The rest of the crowd had filtered in around the walls of the room to encircle her. To partake in her humiliation. She felt a bit like Mary Shelley's monster; all that was missing were the pitchforks.

"The Society for Mediumship Research," Mr. Sedgwick continued, "has investigated mediums all over England and even some in Chicago and Boston. We've been summoned here, to New York, in order to verify the existence or nonexistence of your powers, Madam Zolikoff. And I must say, tonight's performance has gone quite a ways in illuminating an answer."

The Society for Mediumship Research. A memory resurfaced, one of Will threatening her with this very thing. This was Will's doing? He'd gone ahead and requested their presence in debunking Ava's talents. *Damn you, railroad man.*

She took a deep breath and tried to remain calm. Proving the lack of psychic phenomenon was nearly as difficult as proving the existence of it. As long as they did not search her things, there could be no proof.

"I welcome your scrutiny, Mr. Sedgwick. Where should we begin?"

He blinked, as if her willingness surprised him. No doubt most of the mediums either broke down in tears or tried to make a break for it. Ava would do neither.

He gestured to his colleague. "Mr. Evans, if you please."

Another man came forward. "The first trick was the moving of the table. Madam Zolikoff accomplished this by sliding the tip of her boot, which has a convenient lip on the end, I noticed, under the closest leg. She then used her leg muscles to adjust the position of the table."

Ava threw herself into a chair, tried to slide the toe of her boot under the table leg, and sighed. "I'm afraid I'm not strong enough to do what you're suggesting." With a heave, she gave an ineffectual jerk of her leg. "See, I am not able to move furniture with just my foot."

The edges of Mr. Evans's lips twitched. "I suspect, with

the proper motivation, we might observe a different result. Nevertheless, I shall move on. There were questions about my aunt Katie, who passed from a stomach ailment, which Madam confirmed with her spirit guide." He shook his head with mock regret. "I do not have an aunt Katie, nor has she passed from a stomach ailment."

"The spirits can get confused," Ava said smoothly. "Perhaps someone else in the room had an aunt or cousin who died from a stomach ailment."

"I think you've just described nearly everyone present," Sedgwick said dryly. "What have you, Mr. Blackburn?"

Another member of the SMR stepped forward. "When the spirit guide arrived, I detected movement in the room. I suspected that movement was Madam Zolikoff, readying her spirit."

"I never left the table. You can ask the guests on either side of me. We were clasping hands and I never broke hold." Never mind the two guests had been holding hands with each other, not her. No one knew that but her, however.

"Is that so?" Blackburn asked. "Then it's indeed fortunate that I cut a small piece of fabric off the person's skirts."

"Ghostly skirts," Sedgwick interrupted with a smirk.

"Yes, ghostly skirts." Blackburn produced a swatch of fabric from his pocket. It was black. Exactly like Ava's skirts.

Damn.

She couldn't help herself; she shifted to fold her skirts over on themselves. "There's no proof that bit came from my skirts. There are three women in the room right now wearing black."

"Yes, but perhaps you'd be so kind as to stand and let us examine your clothing."

Before she could say anything, Sedgwick added, "And

once your clothing has been thoroughly examined, we shall turn our attention to your belongings."

Her stomach plummeted, a free fall worthy of Steve Brodie. *This* was what she'd dreaded. All those years of hard work, building a reputation, perfecting her craft . . . and one moment would ruin it all. Everything she'd hoped for, gone. Sam and Mary out of their miserable jobs. The small farmhouse with a picket fence. Fresh air and wide-open space. Gone.

There would be no lying to escape this, no performance to distract them. She'd been caught.

The faces around the room were nearly salivating at the spectacle before them. She understood; not many could say they'd attended a performance where the medium was proven a fraud. Still, her spine straightened. They would not humiliate her. No matter what they found, no matter what they said, Ava Jones would walk out of here with her head high.

Slowly she rose to her feet. "Go ahead, sir. Do as you—"

"What is going on here?" a familiar voice asked from the threshold.

Ava's gaze snapped to the door, and she found Will standing there, his jaw hard and angry. He wasn't focused on her, however. No, his intense gray stare had locked on Sedgwick and Blackburn.

Had he come to witness his handiwork?

Pain lanced through her chest, the betrayal deep. He'd never approved of Madam Zolikoff, but she'd believed he made peace with her career choice in the last few weeks. Obviously not. Not only had he summoned the SMR, he'd dragged himself to Ashgate's to observe the bloodbath.

"Sloane, what a surprise," Murphy said. "We hadn't expected you this evening."

"Yes, so I was told." Will moved farther into the room,

his movements jerky and stiff. "What is this, some kind of a witch hunt?"

Sedgwick blinked. "Sir, this is the society's function, to ferret out fraud where we must. I thought you were the one who—"

"No," Will snapped, his tone offering no argument. "I most definitely did not organize tonight's gathering."

Ava felt herself frown. Was he telling the truth? If not him, then who had orchestrated this farce?

"Do you know this woman?" Sedgwick gestured to Ava. "She's . . ."

"A liar," someone in the crowd muttered.

"A cheat," another voice called, louder.

"She is neither of those things," Will replied sharply, outraged on her behalf, as he turned toward the door. "Cabot?"

Another man, one Ava hadn't noticed, came forward. Lanky and handsome, he threw Ava a wink and then grinned wide. A true showman, he spread his arms and addressed the room.

"For those of you who don't know me, I am Calvin Cabot, publisher of the *Mercury,* the *Bugle,* and the *Chicago Morning Star.* This woman is Ava Jones. She is a reporter who has been working for me, undercover, in order to ferret out corruption in the psychic community."

"I . . . I'm afraid I don't understand," Sedgwick murmured. "Isn't that what we do?"

"No, not like my girl here. You've all heard of Nellie Bly?" This was asked of the crowd. Everyone nodded; not a soul in New York didn't know Nellie Bly. Joseph Pulitzer had hired the female reporter to expose the terrible conditions in the asylum on Blackwell's Island. "Jones here is my Nellie Bly. I send her into the belly of the beast, so to speak, to write about the experiences firsthand."

"So she is . . . pretending to be a medium in order to

write about how the tricks are perpetrated? She plans to explain how she fooled audiences into believing her?" Blackburn scratched his face. "But she's been performing for years."

"All at the paper's behest, I assure you. We had hoped to prove how eager audiences were to believe these frauds—no offense," he said to the crowd, "in hopes of helping the true mediums, the ones with legitimate gifts. Her story was nearly completed, too. A darn shame, Miss Jones."

He looked at her expectantly, his eyes ordering her to agree. "Oh, yes," she said. "A darn shame, Mr. Cabot."

"And what is your involvement in all this, Sloane?" Murphy asked. "Don't tell me you were part of the investigation, because we all know you and Miss Jones shared a *special* personal relationship."

Ava's skin flamed, heat covering her scalp and neck. The meaning of "special personal relationship" would not be lost on anyone in the room. And just when she'd thought the worst was over . . .

She swallowed and found her voice. "Mr. Sloane is merely a friend."

"A friend who spends every Thursday afternoon with you in a room at the Washington Square Hotel."

Two ladies gasped, and Ava longed for the floor to open up and swallow her whole. She snuck a glance at Will's face, expecting to see mortification or disbelief. Instead, his body vibrated, muscles tense with fury, angrier than she'd ever seen him. In fact, she wouldn't be surprised if he reached out and strangled Mr. Murphy.

"Are you calling this woman's honor into question?"

Murphy didn't back down. "Yes, along with your judgment, apparently."

"Miss Jones is my fiancée, Murphy. You are insulting my future wife."

Ava's shoulders stiffened, her mind stumbling over those tersely said words. Fiancée? Had he lost his ever-loving mind? Were the social repercussions of an affair with her so abhorrent that he needed to tell such a gross lie about their association? "Mr. Sloane," she said, weakly. "You—"

"No, Ava. I know you preferred to keep the news between us a little longer, but I need for them to hear it."

Murphy chuckled, his tone laced with disbelief. "Wait, you're *marrying* her? You cannot be serious. Whether she's a medium or a reporter, she's a *nobody*. Your father would roll over in his grave, not to mention what society will say."

"Still, I believe the decision is mine."

Will stood tall and proud, a dynamic force of nature that drew every eye in the room. Ava's heart hurt just looking at him. It was clear he'd summoned Cabot to concoct the story about an investigation, preventing her professional reputation from being shredded, and she'd always be grateful for his intervention. But the lie about the betrothal bothered her. She was tired of the lies, tired of feeling inferior because of where she lived and her background.

Her career as a medium may now be over, but that did not mean she and Will had a chance at a future together. They both knew otherwise—as did everyone else in the room, apparently.

Regardless, she was done. They could discuss whatever they wanted, but Ava would not stick around and listen to them snicker. Heartsick and exhausted, she rose and slipped off her blond wig. A few guests tittered, but she ignored them and crossed the room to collect her carpetbag.

"If you will all excuse me," she said, and walked straight out the door.

* * *

The next morning, Ava shoved her blond wigs into a bag. Strange to put the Madam Zolikoff persona away, when it had been such a staple of her daily life for two years, but perhaps another medium could put the things to use. A knock sounded on the door, interrupting.

She stretched her back and debated not answering. Her three siblings had left for work already, all of them blissfully unaware of what had transpired at the Ashgate house last night. She had no idea how she would supplement their income after Madam Zolikoff's demise, but she'd figure something out. Better not to worry the siblings until she'd lined up another position.

Another knock rang out. Sighing, she went to the door and pulled it open. A large man in a tweed morning suit faced her, one she had met before. He appeared more disheveled than she recalled, a strange light shining in his eyes.

"Mr. Tompkins."

"Miss Jones. May I come in?"

Ava stepped back and pulled the door wide. Once he was inside, she shut the door, leaving it cracked a tiny bit. "How may I help you?"

"Do you have any idea," he started, strolling around the room as if he owned it, "of what you've done?"

Her head jerked. She hadn't seen the accusation coming. "Of what I've done?"

"Yes, you ridiculous charlatan." He faced her squarely, his arms crossing his chest. "Of what you've done. You have ruined *everything*."

"I have no idea what you're talking about, but I'd like

you to leave." She started for the door, but he snatched her arm, gripping tight.

"No, I won't be leaving, Ava," he snarled, leaning in. "Not until we understand each other."

She recoiled from breath that smelled of spirits and onion. "Let me go and get out of my rooms."

He thrust her away from him and she stumbled. "They'll never win the election now. Hell, they won't even win the nomination. They're *done*. Finished in politics. All thanks to you."

"I didn't ask him to attend last night. I have no idea how he even learned—"

"Cabot learned of it. I had the entire thing so carefully orchestrated and Cabot intervened, goddamn it." He weaved in place, unsteady. "And it all went to hell."

"Wait . . . you orchestrated it? You brought the SMR to New York?"

"No, that was your *betrothed*," he said, spitting the last word out, and Ava's spirits sank at the confirmation that Will had contacted the SMR to investigate her. He'd threatened it and had obviously followed through without telling her. Good thing she'd never see him again, or she'd have a few choice words for that man.

"And because you two couldn't keep your drawers on," Tompkins continued, "I now have two candidates who couldn't get elected if they were the only two running. I'm *ruined*."

"Well, you're not ruined. Perhaps Sloane and Bennett might have a difficult—"

His hand curled into a fist, which he promptly pounded on her old wooden dining table. "Of course I'm ruined. Who do you think has been pulling the strings on this campaign? Bennett? He's not capable of foresight, of planning past his next meeting. And Sloane had other things on his mind, his business, his mistress . . ."

She clenched her teeth, desperate to keep the denial from bursting forth. *I was never his mistress.* Little good the distinction did her, however, when all of New York society now knew the truth. Mercy, she'd been such a fool.

"People like them," she said, remembering the crowds in Albany. They had carried signs and marched in support of the Bennett/Sloane ticket. "This could boost their popularity. You know how the public adores a good scandal."

"You haven't seen today's paper, have you?" Rocking back on his heels, he reached into his jacket and withdrew a page of newsprint. "Read your handiwork, Madam Zolikoff."

Unable to prevent it, she leaned in to see the headline.

SLOANE'S MEDIUM MISTRESS!
CANDIDATE'S PARTNER, BENNETT, ALSO A CLIENT!
REPUBLICAN PARTY DISOWNS BOTH CANDIDATES!

Oh, no. Poor Will, he'd fancied that nomination so desperately. She swallowed. "I didn't want this," she whispered. "Not for either of them."

Beefy fingers wrapped around her upper arm and shook her. Hard. "You stupid cunt. How could you not know this would happen?"

He shoved her away from him and Ava lost her balance. Teetering on her heeled boots, she tried to right herself—only she tripped over a dining chair. With a thump, she crashed to the floor, her skirts astray and her bustle crushed.

Damn. That hurt.

Excitement lit Tompkins's eyes, and fear tore through her veins. They were alone, and, though the door was slightly ajar, Ava couldn't believe that any of her neighbors would respond to her cries for help.

"You look good on the ground, like the bitch you are." He unbuttoned his frock coat and started to shrug it off.

Her breath coming fast and shallow, she tried to get to her feet, scramble away—anything to put distance between the two of them. "Get out of my house!" she shouted.

"*What the hell?*"

Will Sloane had one hand on the now-open door, his lips white with fury. Ava breathed a sigh of relief. At least she wouldn't need to worry over Tompkins raping her this morning.

Tompkins spun toward the sound. "Figured you'd come sniffing around her house," Tompkins sneered. "Just can't get enough of this low-class whore—"

In a blink, Will reached Tompkins, cocked his arm, and plowed his fist right into the man's nose. Tompkins staggered back, arms flailing, until he fell to the ground with a crash. Will shook out his hand, cursing, and then turned to Ava. "Are you all right?" He extended his other hand, the one that hadn't flattened Tompkins.

She gripped his wrist, and he pulled her upright. "I'm fine," she said quietly, and let go of him.

Tompkins's nose gushed blood, soaking the front of his vest. "You bastard! You broke my nose!"

Will left Ava's side to stalk over to Tompkins. He leaned down and growled, "If you don't get the hell out of here, I'm going to break a lot more than just your fucking nose!"

Instead of waiting for Tompkins's answer, Will grabbed the large man's lapel, jerked him to his feet, and dragged him to the open door. "If you ever, *ever,* speak to Miss Jones again, I will see you destroyed, Charles. Your money, your standing, your *family* . . . I will take it all away. I have the means to do it—and you know it. So think very, very carefully before you consider talking to her ever again."

Tompkins wrenched free of Will's grasp and stumbled into the hall. He glanced over his shoulder derisively. "Is this what you've given it all up for? Is she really worth it?"

The next words out of Will's mouth caught Ava entirely off guard.

Will grasped the door and said, "Without a doubt," just before slamming it in Tompkins's face.

Chapter Twenty

Will stood there a moment, trying to catch his breath and regain his control. Goddamn Tompkins. Figured the man would blame Ava for everything. Will should have come to see her first thing, instead of prowling about his house until a reasonable hour.

He felt no small amount of guilt over what had transpired with Ava, from the business with Miss Iselin to the Society for Mediumship Research. Now Tompkins had assaulted her. Would there be no end to this madness?

Yes, there would, he told himself, drawing in a deep breath. This all stopped today because Will meant to make amends.

"Are you all right?" he asked her, turning.

Big brown eyes blinked at him. Disheveled, red-cheeked, and angry, she'd never appeared more beautiful. "Yes. You arrived before things . . . turned ugly. Well, uglier, anyway."

"I apologize for that. I didn't think he'd seek you out."

"Hardly surprising after last night. Indeed, any moment now, I expect a long line of society matrons at my door, their claws sharpened for the woman who dared to steal one of their men. After which I'll have to tell them the betrothal story was naught but a lie."

"It doesn't have to be."

Her brows dipped together. "I beg your pardon?"

"A lie. The betrothal story. No reason it has to be a lie."

"You're joking."

"No, I'm not." He'd blurted the fib at Ashgate's to protect her reputation, but he'd had all night to think on it. And the more he pondered the idea, the more a marriage made sense. The campaign was no longer a factor, and any other argument no longer deterred him. He wanted her, every day. Every night. Society be damned. "I want to marry you, Ava."

"You want to . . . marry me?"

"Yes, I do."

Her face gave nothing away as she stared at him. He wished he knew what she was thinking. Did the idea of marrying him appeal to her? No reason it shouldn't, not after the passionate way she'd responded to him. The two of them were perfectly suited; surely she could see that.

"I'm sorry, but I cannot."

His brain tripped over the words, and it took a few seconds for him to put them together. *She said no.* "You . . . cannot marry me. Why not?"

"Will," she sighed, and smoothed the front of her shirtwaist. "Be reasonable. A marriage is not what you want."

"Of course it is. Why wouldn't I want to marry you?"

"Because you're . . ." She gestured to him, as if that were her answer.

He glanced down at himself, holding out his arms. "I'm, what? I don't understand, Ava. How are you so clear on my feelings, when I've only just figured them out for myself?"

Her lips formed a flat, tight line. "It's lust, Will. You

merely want to bed me once more. I'm certain the feeling will soon pass."

"Doubtful, and you're telling me how I feel again, Ava. I want to hear how *you* feel about it."

"Fine," she snapped. "Then I'll tell you how *I* feel. Last night, you found yourself humiliated in a room full of your friends and peers, caught in an affair with a woman unworthy of your blue-blooded kisses. So you made up the betrothal story to—"

"Wait, you think the betrothal was for *my* benefit?" A reluctant laugh escaped his throat. "Ava, nearly every man I know has a mistress on the side, most actresses or shopgirls. Dancers. I'd be lauded for having Madam Zolikoff as a side piece. The lie was for your benefit. To protect your reputation from scandal."

She rolled her eyes to the ceiling. "Indeed, when scandal is such a large concern for a woman like me. Oh, no!" She put her hands to her cheeks. "Shall I stop receiving invitations to the balls and cotillions?"

"Hilarious," Will drawled. "You'd best worry about a scandal, especially when it could appear in the papers. What would your siblings say when their sister is raked through the mud on the front page?"

"It's already happened. Haven't you seen today's paper?" She gestured to the newsprint on the dining table, and Will cringed at the headline. He'd purposely avoided the rags this morning.

"And it doesn't matter," Ava continued. "That is your world, not mine. My siblings would understand."

"Wrong. That may be my world, but it's also yours by default. If you're involved with me, you must learn to deal with it."

"I'm not involved with you any longer!" she nearly shouted. "Are you listening to yourself? You are arguing in circles."

Shoving back the sides of his frock coat, he put his hands on his hips. "If you believe that, then you are not listening to me. We are far from over, Ava."

"You don't get to decide that! You cannot decree we are to be married and expect that I'll bow down to your wishes. That I'll be grateful you are bestowing this honor on me, the important honor of becoming your wife. Me, the poor little struggling waif, just waiting for a strong, rich man to make all my problems go away. Go to hell, Will!" She spun away to face the window, presenting him with her back.

He blinked. Her anger surprised him. Not that he'd expected gratitude, but he'd expected . . . something favorable. Excitement? Relief? Affection? Ava never failed to confuse and bedevil him. Would he ever understand her?

"You're wrong," he said gently. "I do not see you that way, Ava. You're strong, possibly the strongest woman I've ever met. The honor would be mine."

"Is that so?" Her gaze found his, and he did not like the pain reflected there. "Is this how you would have proposed to Miss Iselin, Miss Baldwin, or any of the other debutantes you were considering? Where is the ring? Where are the tender words?" She swallowed and folded her hands. "You don't have them, do you? Because it never occurred to you that you would need them. You expected me to fall over myself in agreeing to marry you—which proves you don't really know me at all."

His chest tightened, regret and self-recrimination weighting him down. "Ava, give me some latitude. The idea only occurred to me last night. I'll buy you a ring—"

"I don't want you to buy me a ring. And I don't want a marriage in which I'm forever made to feel inferior. I need equal footing, Will. I need a partner, not an overlord."

"I want to be a partner to you. I want you by my side, sleeping with me and giving me children. You, no one else."

She was shaking her head before he even finished. "No, you don't. You want a woman such as yourself, a woman from one of the very best families who can move about in your world with ease. One you can show off at the opera or take sailing in Newport. One who can act as a politician's wife."

"This is ridiculous! You act as if you're a leper. You can be all those things, Ava. You pretended to be a Russian medium, for God's sake."

"I won't pretend to be someone I'm not, not even to be your wife. It would kill me, a little bit at a time, every day, until there was nothing left. Whoever marries me will need to take me as I am, for better or worse."

"Christ," he exhaled, dragging a hand through his hair. "You are the most difficult woman I've ever met."

"Because you're unaccustomed to being refused. Another reason we would not suit." She turned away from him to stare out the window, the outline of her form an unmoving silhouette in the sparse morning light.

Grasping the back of an old wooden chair, he leaned over and bowed his head. The morning's headline glared up at him. SLOANE'S MEDIUM MISTRESS! Will could only hope Cabot's papers had a more favorable retelling of last night's events.

How had this gone so terribly wrong? All he wanted was this woman. The end. The last two weeks had been miserable. He could give her tender words, of course, but would it help? She was stubborn, his Ava, but he was not ready to give her up. Not by a mile.

"I care about you," he said quietly. "I want this to work. You and me. Married."

"When did you summon the Society for Mediumship Research to New York?"

He blinked at the change in topic. They were discussing this now, after he'd begged her to marry him? Still, he owed her an honest answer. "When you first refused to attend the rally in Albany. And then I forgot . . . With everything that happened, I never contacted them again to revoke the invitation. I apologize, Ava."

She nodded and kept her gaze trained on the window, not saying a word.

"I didn't mean for any of this to happen," he told her.

"I don't doubt it, but this was inevitable. There are times we must accept whatever obstacles life throws in our way."

"No, I don't believe that—and neither do you. Both of our lives have been full of obstacles and they haven't stopped us yet. Don't give up on me, Ava."

"I'm done fighting, Will." She sounded tired, and he hated the defeat he heard in her voice.

"Well, I'm not finished fighting yet. So brace yourself— I've only just begun."

Standing up from his desk, Mr. Cabot extended his hand, which Ava readily shook. "I am glad you've taken me up on my offer, Miss Jones."

A newspaper reporter. Ava could hardly believe it, but the idea thrilled her. Exposing corruption, righting wrongs, and giving a voice to those who went unheard—Cabot had promised her all of those things. Her career as Madam Zolikoff had ended almost a week ago, and she couldn't wait to get started in this next phase of her life.

"Thank you again, Mr. Cabot. I'm grateful for the opportunity."

"Nonsense. The *Mercury* is proud to welcome you aboard. Before you get settled, I have your first assignment." He grabbed his frock coat from the back of a chair. "Come along with me. We've a news conference to attend."

"A news conference?" she asked, trailing after him, her feet moving twice as fast as his to keep up.

"You know, when a bunch of newsmen—and women—gather to hear an announcement of some kind. Then we all run back to our desks and try to get the story out first."

"Sounds intense."

"Oh, it is, Miss Jones. The newspaper business is a nasty one, full of cutthroat tactics and underhanded deals." He grinned as he started down the stairs. "Which is why I love it."

"Please, call me Ava."

"Well, then I'd be honored if you'd call me Cabot. Nearly everyone at the paper does."

"All right. Thank you."

A brougham was waiting at the street, and Cabot helped her inside. He followed, and soon they were headed west. "So where are we going?"

"To a company on Vesey Street. Apparently a big merger is taking place."

She nodded and fixed her gaze on the street traffic and St. Paul's just ahead. Of course they were traveling to Vesey Street. Yet another reminder of Will, as the Northeast offices were located there. She hated that so much in the city brought forth memories of him. Would she ever stop thinking of his steel gray eyes or his broad, flat chest? The arrogant twist of his lips or the kisses that had made her dizzy?

Swallowing, she pushed all that from her mind and firmly back into the past, where it belonged.

They finally pulled up to a large Federal-style building, crafted in red brick with limestone trim, framed with block windows on seven floors. Cabot assisted her down, and then the two of them climbed the stairs to the main entrance. Other men were milling about, some standing and smoking cigars, others writing in small notepads. "Should I have something to write with?" she asked Cabot once they were in the lobby.

"Not today. You're here to observe. We need to go to the fourth floor."

More stairs and then Cabot led her down several corridors. Two doors were propped open, the room beyond filled with chairs aligned theater-style toward a dais in the front. Reporters filled most of the chairs, brown and black derby hats every which way Ava turned. Cabot's name was shouted by numerous voices, and he spent a few moments shaking hands and slapping backs. Her new boss was quite the legendary figure in publishing, especially impressive for one so young.

By the time they sat, the only open chairs were near the rear of the room. "Bet you've got the inside scoop," a man whispered from behind her.

She glanced over her shoulder to ask what the man meant, but Cabot said, "Shut your flytrap, Jenkins."

The man sat back and closed his mouth, careful not to meet Ava's eyes.

"What did he mean?" she whispered to Cabot.

"Never mind him. We're starting." He pointed to the front where a door had opened behind the dais. "Get ready."

The reporters leaned in, a hum of excitement buzzing in every row. This must be a considerable announcement, to garner this sort of reaction. Ava had no idea what was about to happen, but she found herself on the edge of her seat as well.

A young man holding a stack of papers placed them on a high pedestal at the front of the platform. She craned her neck, trying to see around the large figures and hats surrounding her. A tall blond man stepped through the door and every reporter stood, shouting questions in a frenzy for attention—every reporter save one. Ava couldn't move because she knew that tall blond man. *Will.* Why was he here, at the news conference? Was he speaking? And why had Cabot brought her?

Her chest squeezing painfully, she turned to Cabot, who was staring at her intently. "Is this a joke?"

"No, Ava. I wouldn't do that to you. Give him a chance, please?"

Without answering, she glanced at the sea of dark suits boxing her in. Fighting her way out seemed ridiculous— and impossible. Damn it. She pinched the bridge of her nose and dug deep for patience.

"Everyone take a seat, please. I won't begin until you're all seated." Will's voice rang out over the din, his tone authoritative and decisive. "Sit, all of you. Then I'll start."

It took several minutes, but the reporters finally calmed down, giving Ava her first full look at Will in almost a week. He appeared tired, though still handsome. Predictably, her insides fluttered, breath quickening, as she took him in. His blond hair was perfectly oiled, his face clean-shaven. Dressed to perfection in a morning suit of navy wool that offset his gray eyes. Shoulders relaxed and chin high, he was the commander of all he surveyed. Wealthy and privileged and so untouchable, he brought tears to her eyes.

"I must go," she said to Cabot, and started to rise out of her chair.

"Ava, wait. Don't leave just yet. I promise, you'll want to hear this."

Swallowing, she held her breath and settled. Will's sharp gaze searched the crowd until he landed on her. She couldn't read what he was thinking, but he visibly exhaled, as if relieved to find her there.

"Gentlemen—and lady," he started. "As all of you know, I inherited Northeast Railroad from my father. I took the company and expanded it many times over, tripling and quadrupling profits year after year. We've not only crisscrossed the United States with rail lines, we've helped to build the elevated lines here in New York. But it's now time for me to step down as the head of Northeast Railroad—"

A collective gasp went up around the room. The reporters recovered quickly and began shouting questions. Will held up his hands once more. "I promise I will answer all of your questions, but I want to say a few things first."

The noise level tapered off, and Will said, "Someone I respect once told me there are times we should accept the obstacles life throws in our way. That some things are inevitable." He paused, and Ava felt her face flame. Why would he bring her words up now, of all times?

"But I have always believed people have the ability to change. That we, as a collective, are stronger, fairer, smarter, and better than all of us separately. I had hoped to bring real change to the state of New York, along with John Bennett, after the election this fall. Better the lives of many through honest politicking, not graft, and give a voice to those left unheard. But life threw an obstacle in my way, and I must now decide to change course or give up."

He chuckled softly. "For those familiar with me, you know I don't give up easily. And I realized, I have the ability to change my own course. Granted, it's on a smaller scale than Albany, but no less important to me and those whom I love." His eyes focused on Ava, and nearly every head in the room swiveled to stare at her. She ignored them, captivated by the man at the front of the room.

"You see, there's a woman I want to marry, and she won't have me until we're on more equal footing, as she calls it. So I'm handing Northeast over to someone, a man who will take excellent care of the company. Which is good because I'll be unemployed and I'll need my stock dividends." Laughter broke out in the room. "This should leave my time free for convincing this particular woman to marry me. Because I love her and I'll never stop trying to convince her."

Ava put a hand to her mouth, shocked and overcome at the same time. He *loved* her? Her throat closed, and she wished she could touch him right now, ensure this was not a dream.

"Now," Will continued, his voice a bit gruff. "I'd like you to meet the new owner of Northeast, my brother-in-law and owner of East Coast Steel, Emmett Cavanaugh."

The reporters flew to their feet once more, expressing their surprise and excitement over the news. Ava's head reeled from it all. Giving up his company? He loved her? Didn't he loathe his brother-in-law?

The giant form of Emmett Cavanaugh strode out to the dais and stood next to Will. "Calm down, you jackals," Cavanaugh growled. "I'll answer all of your questions about Northeast, my company, and what the future holds for both—but only if we do this in a civilized manner, not like a Bowery saloon brawl. Now, who's first?"

Heart pounding, Will pushed open the door to the empty office not far from where reporters were still peppering Cavanaugh with questions. He found Ava standing at the window, and the sight of her calmed him. Whatever transpired after today, he didn't care because this, this woman right here, was worth risking everything for. Now he just had to convince her.

She glanced over her shoulder as he started forward. "Will," she breathed, her eyes shining.

"Hello, Ava." He came close, but remained far enough apart that they weren't touching. His fingers itched to trace her skin, but he held back, shoving his hands in his pockets instead.

"I can't believe you gave it away."

"To be fair, I sold it. Cavanaugh has been after Northeast for some time and I finally let him have it."

"Why?"

He'd been asked this many times in the last few days, and this was his first honest answer. "Because of you."

"*Me?* I don't understand. When I said equal footing, I hardly meant for you to give up your company."

"I know. I didn't take those words literally, Ava, but I understood what you meant. I haven't enjoyed running Northeast in a number of years, yet I was driven to keep going forward. To achieve more, no matter the cost to myself or anyone else."

"The stomach pain?"

"Yes, that's part of it, certainly. The hours, the worry, the headaches . . . I kept at it, though, because I wanted to prove I was better than my father. That he was wrong to doubt my abilities." A joyless laugh escaped. "Ridiculous to worry over what a dead man thought, but I did. There were certain things I needed to achieve, and no less than the best would do. Until I met you."

"Because I'm not the best?"

"No, my dear, because you are not what I had planned. You were not on the list of what I wanted for myself, but sometimes life . . ."

"Throws obstacles in your way?" she finished when he trailed off.

"Exactly. You shook up my carefully constructed world, Ava. You are unlike any woman I've ever met, with more heart, integrity, and grit than anyone on earth. You weren't what I wanted, but . . . you're better than what I wanted. You are what I *need*."

She swallowed and closed her eyes briefly before asking,

"How can you be sure? You might change your mind and come to regret me. Because I won't change, Will."

"I don't want you to change," he said definitively. "I fell in love with a confidence woman, for God's sake—and I don't care whether she's accepted in society, or whether she cares for yachting. None of that matters, as long as that wife is *you.*"

He dropped down to one knee and reached inside his jacket pocket. With his other hand, he clasped her fingers tightly. Her eyes grew huge, her mouth forming a tiny O as she stared down at him. He said, "Ava Jones, I love you with everything I am. Everything I have, everything I will have. I sold Northeast in exchange for love and laughter together with you, to raise our children and your siblings, to be present every day. Because with you by my side, I won't want to miss a single moment."

Ava's lip wobbled, her gaze glassy, but Will didn't wait for her reaction. Taking his grandmother's four-carat diamond platinum ring in his fingers, he slipped it on Ava's ring finger. "Will you do me the honor of becoming my wife? I know you never wanted a blue-blooded millionaire for a husband, but I swear I'll make you happy."

Her jaw dropped and nothing came out. He waited, his stomach in knots, mouth gone dry, while her lips worked. Jesus, if she said no, he might not survive it. Then it happened, a small motion that soon grew into a nod. "Yes," she whispered. "I will marry you."

Rising, he wrapped his arms around her and pulled her tight, holding her close to his chest. "Thank God. You had me worried."

She buried her face in his necktie. "You are insane, Will Sloane."

"But?" he prompted.

Her lips found his jaw. "But I love you all the same."

Leaning down, he captured her mouth with his, kissing her gently, sweetly, for a long moment. "Please tell me you agree to a short engagement and a long honeymoon."

"Yes to both. Though I'll have to see if Cabot will give me time off for a honeymoon."

"I think he'll agree. We've just made him very happy."

"We have?"

Will withdrew a piece of newsprint from his jacket pocket. "This is from tomorrow's *Mercury*, which is being printed as we speak. I asked for an advance copy of the front page to show you." He unfolded and handed it to her. "The *Mercury* will be the only paper to have this story in tomorrow's edition."

She took the paper and read it. He knew precisely what the headlines said:

SLOANE SELLS NORTHEAST TO EAST COAST STEEL!
"I DID IT FOR LOVE" SAYS THE RAILROAD BARON!
SLOANE TO MARRY MERCURY REPORTER AVA JONES!

Ava's lips quirked. "A bit sure of yourself, aren't you? What if I'd said no?"

"Then I would have kissed you until you said yes. And possibly kidnapped you."

She chuckled. "You never did fight fairly. How was I ever to resist you?"

Smiling, he leaned down to kiss her. "Heaven knows why you even bothered to try."

Chapter Twenty-One

Oceancrest
Newport, Rhode Island
September 1888

"I believe we have trouble on our hands."

Ava turned at the sound of her new sister-in-law's voice. The Cavanaughs were hosting an end-of-season lawn party at their Newport estate on the ocean, and a huge crowd had gathered. Kids, including the Jones siblings, ran together on the grass, while the adults drank, mingled, and played croquet.

"We do?" she asked Lizzie.

"Yes, over there." Lizzie slipped her arm though Ava's and pointed her free hand toward the edge of the tent.

Tom stood close to Emmett Cavanaugh's fourteen-year-old sister, Katie. Ava and Lizzie watched as Tom produced a single flower from behind his back and held it out to her. Katie's cheeks flushed as she shyly accepted the bloom.

"Oh, no."

"Indeed. Your brother is a decent young man, but Emmett

is . . . well, protective doesn't really begin to describe how he feels about his sisters."

Ava had been around the man enough to notice that. "I'll talk to Tom."

"No, don't scare him off. I think we should let it play out. They're only kids, after all, and it's sort of sweet. But Tom should make a concerted effort to keep any romantic gestures private, where Emmett won't observe them."

"Yes, excellent idea. I definitely do not want to anger your husband."

Ava liked her new sister-in-law. The two women surprisingly had a lot in common, more than merely a shared love of Will.

"Who is that Will is talking to?" Ava asked Lizzie. Her husband had spent the last half hour intently listening to a man Ava hadn't yet met.

Lizzie craned her neck to see where Ava was looking. "Oh, that's Teddy. He's a longtime friend of the family. Come, I'll introduce you."

"No, that's—"

"Nonsense. He used to live out West, you know. Teddy has a thousand interesting stories." Lizzie practically dragged Ava to where Will and the other man stood.

"Teddy!" Lizzie called, and the man turned, a grin breaking out below his mustache.

"Hello, Lizzie." He kissed her cheek. "The ocean air certainly agrees with you."

Will wrapped an arm around Ava's waist and pulled her close. "Ava, I'd like you to meet Mr. Theodore Roosevelt. Teddy, this is my wife, Ava Sloane."

"The newspaper reporter who went undercover as a medium." Teddy bowed over her hand. "That takes guts, Mrs. Sloane."

"Coming from a man who is currently campaigning

for Benjamin Harrison," Will drawled, "that is quite a compliment."

"Ah, but he's going to win the presidency, Will. And then I'll be moving to Washington."

That's where she knew his name, Ava thought. Theodore Roosevelt had been a state assemblyman and had also run for mayor.

"And"—Teddy turned to Ava—"I'm trying to convince your husband to join me."

"In Washington?" She glanced at Will. "Whatever for?"

"Teddy thinks I should run for the House of Representatives in two years."

"Congress?" Lizzie asked. "Is that something you're interested in?"

Will shrugged. "I'm not certain. I would need to discuss it with my wife first." He squeezed Ava's waist.

"Of course," Teddy agreed. "Wouldn't dream of doing anything without my Edith's approval. But the party leaders were impressed with your campaigning, Will. Said you were twice the draw Bennett was. And I suspect, with your recent marriage, you and Mrs. Sloane would be very popular, indeed."

"Me?" Ava blurted.

"Yes, you, my dear. You've become quite the celebrity since Cabot revealed you, the beautiful reporter who has reeled in the city's most sought-after bachelor."

"Well, I keep trying to throw him back," she said, and Teddy threw his head back and let out a booming laugh.

"I like her," Teddy told Will. "You've got a live wire on your hands."

"Don't I know it." Will squeezed her waist again in a private sign of affection Ava had grown to love. "And I'm grateful for it every single day."

Teddy waved at someone across the lawn and then said,

"I must go, but think about it, Will. I'd love to have you in Washington with me."

Teddy said his good-byes and Lizzie soon departed to locate her husband, leaving Will and Ava alone in the well-dressed crowd.

"I wasn't aware you wanted to move to Washington," she said, looking up at her handsome husband's profile. Her chest pulled tight, a giddiness bubbling under the surface of her skin. Every time she was in his presence, the same reaction occurred. Would she ever grow immune to the sight of him?

"Would that be so bad?" He slid his fingers under her jaw, a swift, simple touch that caused her to shiver. His lips twisted into a small smile and he did it again.

"Stop distracting me," she said, and slapped his hand away. "This is serious, Will. I am not certain you want me as a political wife."

"Darling, who charmed Mrs. Astor at our wedding? Who sweet-talked Cavanaugh's tough-as-nails thug, Kelly, into waltzing with her at the reception? And who saved a stuffy railroad man from a lifetime of loneliness?"

She rolled her eyes. "Now who is sweet-talking? You know politics is an entirely different thing."

"Teddy wasn't lying. I've been keeping the papers from you during our honeymoon, but the new Mrs. Sloane is garnering quite a bit of attention. In fact, Cabot wants an exclusive feature when we return to New York."

"On us?"

"No, on you."

Her jaw fell open, and her husband closed it with his finger. "Ava, you'd best accustom yourself to the notoriety. Soon everyone will know why I fell in love with you."

The sincerity in his voice and the tenderness on his face caused her heart to swell. She loved this man.

"No matter what I do," he was saying, "I want you by my side. I'm not leaving you alone in New York for those other reporters to ogle." Will was convinced most of the male reporters at the *Mercury* were half in love with her. A ridiculous notion, but she liked to see him a little jealous on occasion.

But her, a political wife? "Will——"

"Ava, you can do whatever you set your mind to. You may not have a spiritual gift, but you have remarkable powers all the same."

"Are you certain you wouldn't rather keep Northeast? It's not too late to change your mind, and your stomach pain has improved."

They'd had this conversation a hundred times, and his answer never wavered. "No. Selling to Cavanaugh was the best decision. The two companies together will give Carnegie a run for his money. Literally. That's why I'm staying on the board of the new company, so I'll have a hand in. Besides, I thought you liked having me around."

"Which I won't, if you run for political office."

"Then I'll say no."

"You would do that?"

He put his hands on her cheeks, holding her stare with serious gray eyes. "There is nothing I would not do for you, wife. Nothing. You mean more than any position, office, nomination, or company."

She knew he meant it, and her heart swelled with emotion. This man was everything to her, and preventing him from doing more was pure selfishness on her part. Will had the charisma, drive, and intelligence to enact real change in this country. Why would she deny him that opportunity?

"I think I need convincing," she said in the low husky rasp he adored.

His mouth curved into a wicked smile. "Do you?"

She bit her lip and nodded. Will took her elbow and began leading them through the crowd. "You look tired. Perhaps I should show you to a bedchamber where you can rest for a spell."

"Don't you mean where *we* can rest for a spell?"

"Oh, my dear. I might be lying down but I will definitely not be resting."

Keep reading for a special preview of *Mogul*,
the next book in the Knickerbocker Club series,
coming in February 2017!

As owner of a well-respected national newspaper,
Calvin Cabot has the means to indulge his capricious
taste for excess—and the power to bring the upper crust
of society to its knees. So when a desperate heiress begs
for his help, Calvin agrees . . . as long as she promises
to stay out of his way. Except, like the newsman,
this willful beauty always gets what she wants. . . .

Infamous Lillian Davies lives a life brimming with
boundless parties, impressive yachts, and exotic
getaways. But when her equally notable brother
disappears, Lily knows that blood runs thicker than
champagne, and she'll spare nothing to bring him back
alive. Unfortunately, the only man who can help her
is the one she never wanted to see again. Can Lily keep
Calvin at arm's length long enough to save her brother
and protect her name . . . even when the tenacious
powerbroker turns out to be absolutely irresistible?

Don't miss *Magnate*, out now,
and *Tycoon*, available as an eBook novella!
And look for Joanna Shupe's Wicked Deceptions series
wherever books are sold . . .

Chinatown
New York City
April 1889

She never expected to find her former husband in an opium den.

Lily inwardly cursed her terrible luck and turned to the man standing next to her, the one who'd found her quarry. "How long has he been here?"

"Two days, ma'am."

Good heavens. Dark and depressing, the place reeked of a nutty, sweet scent, one that forced her to cover her nose and breathe through her mouth. Males and females of all ages and skin colors reclined, glassy-eyed, on small cots, long pipes remaining within reach. Several scantily clad women hovered nearby, as did the owner, who no doubt wanted her gone.

Which made two of them. She would rather be sailing on the Chesapeake or lounging in her family's Newport cottage. Riding her horse in Palm Beach. Shopping in Paris. Anywhere but standing right here, looking at the one man she'd hoped never to see again.

Calvin Cabot. She peered at him while he slept and tried to assess the changes, if any, that had occurred over the last four years. Still long-limbed and well proportioned. Impossibly handsome, despite the shaggy light brown hair and the whiskers covering his face. He also stank, if the odor reaching her nose was any indication.

He'd ignored her letters for almost two weeks, each one returned, unopened. Furthermore, every time she arrived at his office or his home, he'd disappeared. No matter the hour, no matter which day she chose, he remained one step ahead of her. There had been no choice but to hire investigators and kidnap him.

They had a delicate problem, one he needed to help solve before someone else discovered it.

Yet she'd never expected to find him *here*. Was he addicted to the pipe? The man ran two of the city's most popular newspapers as well as another in Chicago. How did he manage a hop habit and his empire? Not that she'd ever understood him. They had been oil and water—or, as Calvin had been fond of saying, oil and champagne. Though he hadn't always hated the wealth and privilege her family represented. . . .

"What would you like to do, ma'am?" the man at her side asked. Mr. Jessup, he'd said. She'd hired twelve men to find Calvin, and Jessup had been the one to earn her two thousand dollar reward.

Lily turned to the owner. "How much does this man owe?"

Avarice lit the owner's dark eyes, far from the first time Lily observed that emotion when someone noticed her clothing and jewels. But she was her father's daughter, not some silly, easily intimidated female. For goodness' sake, she'd served as the president of the Davies Mining Company since her father's death. No one got the best of Lillian Davies.

"Three hundred."

She laughed at the outrageous sum. "Now the real amount."

The owner glanced at Mr. Jessup, obviously weighing his chances of flimflamming her out of more money without getting pummeled. Not that Lily would ask the Pinkerton to step in. She did not need a man to solve her problems.

"One hundred and twenty dollars," the owner said.

Lily nodded, though she'd have paid more. She desperately needed Calvin. "Fine."

The transaction was completed quickly, and she turned to Mr. Jessup, who hadn't left her side since they arrived. Pointing at the unconscious man on the cot, she said, "Throw him in the carriage, if you would."

Hotel Fauchère
Pocono Mountains, Pennsylvania
Four years ago

"Lily, darling, the skin on the side of my cock is beginning to chafe— "

"Poor man." Lily bent and used her tongue to soothe the abused area. Calvin, her husband of less than three weeks, fell back on the bed and let out a moan comprised of equal parts pain and bliss. "Let me help you."

"You're not actually helping," he wheezed as she dropped kisses along the sensitive skin. His body responded immediately, with his erection growing, expanding beneath her lips. Instead of pushing her away, strong fingers threaded her blond hair, pulling the strands away from her face, exposing her ministrations to his hungry blue gaze. "This is what caused the trouble in the first place. A man needs recovery time, woman."

Lily ignored him, fully focused on her task. She loved the way he tasted, how the smooth velvet length felt on her tongue. Soft skin stretched tight over hardness. Most of all, she loved how he responded to each and every thing she did, like he couldn't get enough of her. She understood the feeling well; she didn't ever want to stop touching or kissing him. Didn't want to stop breathing his same air. In fact, since the honeymoon began twenty days ago, they had barely even left the bed.

The courtship had happened quickly, with the two of them introduced a mere two months before they decided to elope. While many would call her foolish, Lily hadn't been more certain of anything in her entire life. Calvin was everything she wanted. Intelligent and adventurous, he worked tirelessly as a reporter for the *New York Bugle,* where he championed the causes of those less fortunate. Exposed corruption. Revealed the hypocrisy in New York politics. He was handsome as well, with brown hair and bright blue eyes, and a tall, slim build that vibrated with energy and confidence. He had ambition and strong convictions, a man who would achieve wondrous heights in his lifetime. Lily looked forward to assisting him every step of the way.

No doubt her father would require convincing to accept the marriage, but Lily had her arguments ready. Calvin maintained that Warren Davies would be furious his only daughter had married a mere reporter, a man without money or prestige, but Lily had faith in her father. After all, he'd gone off to the Dakotas in his teens to earn his fortune and emerged with a prosperous silver mine. He respected hard work and determination, any man who relied on his wits and guts to make his way in the world. Undoubtedly he would come to like Calvin once the two became acquainted.

She released Calvin with a wet pop, and her husband's erection dropped to his stomach. "Do you want me to stop?" she purred, dragging her fingernails up the insides of his thighs.

Calvin shivered. "God, please no. I know I don't have much, but I'll sign it all over to you if you'll just let me in deeper—*Yes, like that,*" he groaned when she reapplied hot, slick suction. "Oh, if this kills me, it'll be worth it."

He rarely stopped talking, even during intimate moments.

Words were not only his livelihood, they were both a source of comfort and a weapon. Intent on shutting him up, she reached below to roll his balls in her palm, squeezing gently, and he stiffened. "Faster," he said. "Tighter. Jesus, Lily, I'm burning alive."

She doubled her efforts, bobbing up and down, lips pulling, tongue fluttering, until his muscles began shaking. The rougher she was with him, the more she scratched and squeezed, the more he loved it. Soon he cursed, his hips rocking as he thrust into her mouth. With a shout, he spent down her throat, his body atremble.

When the pulses finally ceased, she shifted to press kisses to the red scratch marks she'd left on the taut plane of his abdomen. Her own core was wet with desire, arousal throbbing in time with her heart. How long would he need to recover?

"Come here, you witch." Large hands slipped under her arms and lifted her over his body. His expression achingly tender, he pressed a kiss to her lips. She relished the taste of him, the way their lips fit together so perfectly, the rasp of his tongue as he invaded her mouth. Love burst in her chest, every pore filled with a sense of rightness that settled in her bones. "I love you madly," she whispered when they broke apart.

The backs of his knuckles found her cheek, and he rubbed the skin gently. His blue eyes were dark, drunk with pleasure, his smile crooked. "I love you utterly and completely, Lily my love. Forever and always."

Her heart swelled behind her ribs. "How lucky I am to have met you."

"The fortune is entirely on my side. You're Lillian Davies, you could have your choice of men—"

She placed a finger over his lips. "If that is true then I choose *you*, Calvin—and you're being modest. I know there is a string of women in your past." Though he may not have been wealthy, Calvin was the type of man that women watched. Striking looks and lanky build, he exuded power and grace, with a swagger to his gait that stopped just shy of bravado. His sharp eyes missed nothing, while a twinkle in the blue depths hinted at a secret joke. This was a man who caused a woman's mind to turn to wickedness. To wonder what the devil might be capable of inside a bedroom . . .

How fortunate that she no longer needed to stare and wonder. No, she knew precisely what talents he possessed in this area—and she had no intention of ever giving him up.

"In my past, perhaps, and that is where they shall stay." He cupped her breast, clever fingers teasing the nipple until it peaked under his touch.

"They had better. I have no intention of sharing you, not with anyone."

He squeezed the tender, plump mound, causing her to gasp. "Nor I you. All those beaux you were stringing along better be cut when we return to New York."

"*Stringing along?*" She tweaked his nipple, and he gave a gasp this time. "Take that back. I do not string men along."

"Are you growing angry? You know what it does to me when you're peeved." Removing her hand from his chest, he brought her fingers to his mouth and kissed the tips. "And I count no fewer than four of Manhattan's most eligible bachelors who hope to ensnare you, my lovely. Shall I name them?"

"They merely want my father's fortune, not plain Lily, the stubborn, bossy daughter of a miner."

"You are wrong. I see how they stare at you, with adoration in their eyes, not greed. It's the exact same manner in which I stare at you."

Her belly warmed and dipped, and she held the compliment close, never wanting to forget the sweetness this man had brought to her life. She tangled her legs with his, rubbing his rough skin with the soft pads of her feet. "The night we met, you asked me to dance. I had no idea who you were."

"I didn't know your name, only that you were the most beautiful, captivating woman in the room. I couldn't stay away. I had to learn all I could about you, touch you, even if just to dance."

"And you, the mysterious reporter in the room, watching the party with observant, clever eyes. No one quite had a clue what to make of you."

"I think most of the crowd mistook me for a footman," he said wryly.

"Not a chance. Your bearing is about as subservient as . . ."

"Yours?" he offered.

She laughed, and his lips found her throat. He nipped and licked, teased her skin, until she squirmed against him. Desperate. Wanting. "How much recovery time did you say you needed?"

He rolled her onto her back and settled between her thighs. "My lovely Lily, my mouth never needs any recovery time." Sliding down her body, he kissed a trail to the very heart of her and proceeded to steal her breath.

A knock on the hotel room door penetrated Calvin's brain. He stirred, fighting the effects of both sleep and an insatiable wife, stretching out the soreness in his lower back. Only one person would dare to disturb them, and Calvin knew he would not knock unless it was urgent.

Hoping not to wake his wife, Calvin shifted to the edge of the mattress and reached for his trousers. *Wife.* He liked saying that. He liked it quite a lot. His childhood had been spent traveling the globe with parents devoted to spreading their religion, never staying in one place for very long. Temporary lodgings, temporary friends. Never anything permanent or real—not until Lily. She now belonged to him.

He glanced over his shoulder to glimpse her sleeping form. Blond hair streamed over the cream sheets like a streak of sunshine. She lay on her side, both hands under her cheek, prayer-like. Emotion welled up in his chest, a feeling he'd never allowed himself to even contemplate before. They were from two different worlds; Lily's comprised of parties and champagne, while his was one of sheer determination and grit. Yet somehow it worked.

Another knock brought Calvin to the door. Hugo, his best friend and sometime valet, stood in the hall, eyes full of worry. "Her father's here."

Calvin froze. "Her father? Lily's father? *Here?*" At Hugo's nod, Calvin's stomach plummeted to the ground. "Shit. He's supposed to be in Dakota."

Hugo shrugged. "All I know is he's downstairs, right now, asking for you."

Calvin's mind spun. He hadn't met Warren Davies, but he knew the man's reputation. A hard-hearted businessman who crushed rebellion and dissension by any means possible, even bloodshed. The last attempt to organize a union at Davies's silver mine had resulted in the death of over fifty men. Davies was known for getting what he wanted . . . and Calvin suspected this would not be a pleasant visit.

"Give me two minutes and I'll be down."

He shut the door and hurried to collect his clothes off the floor. Though he'd bathed regularly, he hadn't worn clothing in at least a week, not since he'd left the room to buy Lily ice cream from a parlor down the street—a treat he'd licked off her delectable, naked body, he recalled with a smile. He found his shirt, clean but wrinkled, and his necktie was a crumpled mess. Not exactly the way he'd wanted to meet his father-in-law.

After he dressed, he checked his face in the mirror. A two-day growth of unkempt whiskers covered his jaw. He winced. No help for it now, he thought as he ran a comb through his unruly hair.

"Calvin? Where are you going?"

He spun at the sound of his wife's husky, sleep-roughened voice. She levered up on an elbow and pushed her hair to one side. "Your father is here."

"Daddy's here?" She sat up, the sheet dropping from her body and revealing the most luscious breasts he'd ever set eyes on. His fingers itched to touch them, to pluck her nipples and feel them harden. *No, no time for that now.*

"He's downstairs." Calvin reached for his frock coat and tugged it on. It was his best coat, a dark blue wool one he'd purchased only last year. He brushed dirt off the sleeves and fixed his cuffs.

"How did he find out where we were?" On her feet now, Lily scrambled for her clothing. He noticed her hands were shaking as she fumbled with her chemise. "He's supposed to be visiting the mine."

"I haven't a clue. I figure we'll soon find out." He strode over and grasped her shoulders, stopping her frantic movements. "Darling, wait." She straightened and stared at him, eyes wide with panic. He kissed her nose. "We'll be fine. He will understand, I promise."

She swallowed but nodded. "Of course. You're right. I should come down with you, though."

"No, that's not necessary. I'll head down first. Take your time getting yourself ready. There's no rush."

"I will." Her fingers gripped his lapels. "Calvin, I love you."

He smiled at her, sliding his hands down to palm both her breasts. "And I you. Hurry, before he decides to storm the room."

He left Lily to dress and went into the hall. As he headed downstairs, he reminded himself of all the reasons Warren Davies should approve of him as Lily's husband. Like

Davies, Calvin had grown up in poverty but was making his own way in the world. He was gainfully employed, had all his limbs. Even had all his teeth. He would never mistreat or harm Lily. Most of all, he loved her with all his heart. What father wouldn't want his daughter to be happy and well loved?

Hugo waited at the bottom of the stairs, a scowl on his dark face. "He's in the front parlor," Hugo said. "And he does not appear pleased. Two men are sittin' outside in his carriage, one's at the parlor door."

That information did not bode well. Why had Davies brought an army with him? "Thank you. Lily will be down in a few moments. Will you see her shown in?"

"Yes, sir. And good luck."

A large man guarded the parlor. At Calvin's approach, the man opened the door and quickly shut it after Calvin passed through. Once his eyes adjusted to the afternoon light, Calvin found a stocky, well-dressed man at the front window. Warren Davies.

Davies came forward, and Calvin saw the resemblance to his daughter right away. The same whiskey-colored eyes, light brown with flecks of gold, and a similar stubborn jaw. Davies had short gray hair and a long mustache, one you might see on a cowboy out in the Dakotas. His expression held no warmth, however, and foreboding settled into Calvin's bones.

"You are Calvin Cabot?"

"Indeed, I am, Mr. Davies." He extended a hand in greeting, which Davies made no effort to accept. After a beat, Calvin dropped his arm and said, "I know this may come as a surprise, sir—"

"A surprise?" Davies sneered. "Boy, a *surprise* is coming home to find your cook's baked your favorite dessert. A *surprise* is when you run into an acquaintance on the street. A *surprise* is having a good day on the exchange. This is

no surprise. Finding out this"—he gestured at Calvin—
"piece of shit has gone and married your only daughter is
a goddamned catastrophe."

Calvin's skin went up in flames, anger rising in his veins
like a flood. *Stay calm*, he told himself. Nothing good
would happen if he lost his temper. He had to appease the
older man, explain how he felt about Lily. "I know I seem
an unlikely choice, but I love her. I will—"

"I don't care how you feel about her. Christ, marriage is
not built on *feelings*, boy. It's about legacy and position.
She's just had her come-out, and I had plans for her. Not
one of those plans included a two-bit muckraker from a
newspaper no one's ever heard of."

The jab drove deep, and Calvin crossed his arms over
his chest to keep from punching Davies in the jaw. Yes, he
worked as a reporter for the *Bugle*, but he had ambition.
He wouldn't always be a two-bit muckraker. Davies, it
seemed, didn't care about any of that. He only cared about
Calvin's suitability as Lily's husband *now*.

"Why are you here?" he asked bluntly.

Davies's mouth hitched. "Now we get to the point. I
have annulment papers for you to sign."

"I'm not signing any fucking annulment papers," he
snapped, civility swiftly evaporating. If Davies wanted a
fight, Calvin would more than gladly provide him one.
"No matter what you say, I won't give her up."

"How much?" Pushing the sides of his coat back, Davies
thrust his hands in his pockets. "How much do you want?"

"I don't want your money. You don't have enough to
force me to leave her."

Davies threw his head back and laughed. "You know
precisely what I'm worth. I've no doubt you researched me
long and hard before approaching Lily. Before filling her
head with your lies."

Calvin clenched his teeth so hard he feared his jaw

might snap. "I have never lied to your daughter. And I did not approach her because she's your daughter. I had no idea who she was when—"

"Save your breath, son. I don't have the time or the patience for bullshit. When I tell you what I've learned about you, I think you'll change your mind about those annulment papers."

Mind racing, Calvin tried to think on what secrets from his past Davies could have unearthed . . . but nothing leapt out at him. He hadn't led the life of a monk, yet he hadn't committed any serious crimes. "Is that so?"

Davies lowered into an armchair and placed his elbows on the rests. "I have two pieces of information you need to hear. The first is, though I love my daughter, I will cut her off without a penny if she stays married to you. The two of you won't get one dollar from me or my estate. I'll write her completely out of my will."

Calvin frowned, his heart sinking. When they eloped, he hadn't thought far enough ahead to worry about finances. Hell, he'd been raised with nothing and survived, but Lily loved the life of a rich society girl with their wild parties, lavish dinners, and expensive toys. And while he absolutely had not married her because of her family's money, he also hadn't considered that such a lifestyle would be taken away from her. She'd be reduced to . . . lean cuts of meat instead of foie gras. Lager instead of champagne. Mending her dresses instead of buying new ones. Forget fancy balls and social engagements; she might need to find work as a secretary or a shopgirl.

But how could he possibly walk away from her? Perhaps her father was bluffing. After all, Lily claimed Davies doted on her. Surely her father wouldn't—

"I can see you don't quite believe me," Davies said. "So let me tell you the second item. It's about your wife, the one back in China."